Maid of SECRETS

JENNIFER McGOWAN

SIMON & SCHUSTER BFYR

New York London Toronto Sydney New Delhi

SIMON & SCHUSTER BFYR

An imprint of Simon & Schuster Children's Publishing Division

1230 Avenue of the Americas, New York, New York 10020

For information about special discounts for bulk purchases, please contact Simon & Schuster Special Sales at 1-866-506-1949 or business@simonandschuster.com.

The Simon & Schuster Speakers Bureau can bring authors to your live event. For more information or to book an event, contact the Simon & Schuster Speakers Bureau at 1-866-248-3049 or visit our website at www.simonspeakers.com.

Cover design by Lucy Ruth Cummins

Interior design by Laurent Linn

The text for this book is set in ArrusBT Std.

Manufactured in the United States of America

First SIMON & SCHUSTER BFYR paperback edition June 2014

2 4 6 8 10 9 7 5 3 1

The Library of Congress has cataloged the hardcover edition as follows:

McGowan, Jennifer.

Maid of secrets / Jennifer McGowan.

p. cm. — (Maids of honor)

Summary: In 1559 England, Meg, an orphaned thief, is pressed into service and trained as a member of the Maids of Honor, Queen Elizabeth I's secret all-female guard, but her loyalty is tested when she falls in love with a Spanish courtier who may be a threat.

ISBN 978-1-4424-4138-5 (hardcover) — ISBN 978-1-4424-4140-8 (eBook)

[1. Courts and courtiers—Fiction. 2. Spies—Fiction. 3. Elizabeth I, Queen of England, 1533-1603—Fiction. 4. Sex role—Fiction. 5. Love—Fiction. 6. Orphans—Fiction. 7. Great Britain—History—Elizabeth, 1558-1603—Fiction.] I. Title.

PZ7.M4784867Mai 2013

[Fic]—dc23

2012033573

ISBN 978-1-4424-4139-2 (pbk)

For my mother,
who always believed I could

ACKNOWLEDGMENTS

My sincere thanks to:

My agent, Alexandra Machinist, whose remarkable expertise, insights, and energy have already proven to be life-changing. Thank you for this—and all that is to come.

My editor, Alexandra Cooper, for saying exactly the right thing when we talked about my book—and then spectacularly delivering on that promise. It's been a great adventure, and I look forward to continuing it with you.

My dear friends Kay, Kristine, Liz, Misti, and Mona, who have shared different parts of this journey with me, a journey which, for some of you, began over a decade ago. Thank you for always being there.

The groups of fellow writers who have taught me so much over the years, both in craft and in friendship: The women of OVRWA, the Five Corners, the 007s, the Fire Breathing Unicorn Starcatchers, the Success Sisterhood, and perhaps most especially the Phenomicons. Thank you for sharing so much of yourselves, and for welcoming me so completely.

And to Geoffrey, who not only has made me a better writer, but who one day suggested I put all of that interest in Elizabethan history to use, and try writing about teens, for teens. You see? Eventually I listen.

CHAPTER ONE

APRIL 1559
LONDON, ENGLAND

Mule-brained Tommy Farrow would ruin everything.

To my credit I didn't even flinch as I caught sight of the boy's white-blond hair bouncing through the crowd. I'd been trained better than that. But the fat purse I'd just lifted from an unsuspecting lord now felt too heavy in my hand. I shoved it deep into the folds of my overskirt with perhaps a bit more force than necessary.

Stepping away from my mark, I smiled easily and strolled forward a few lazy paces along the crowd's edge; just another young English lady, out enjoying the day's spectacle.

No one so much as glanced at me.

I ducked under a faded coronation banner that still whipped proudly above a milliner's storefront, and paused to scan the knot of Londoners clumped together in the inn's courtyard. Tommy wasn't hard to spot.

Where is the silly little bit going?

The youngest—and by far the most hopeless—thief in the Golden Rose acting troupe could barely pick the pocket of the simplest of villagers, but this was *Londontown*. With his mutton hands and clumsy feet and a mouth that galloped well ahead of his brain, Tommy would be branded a thief before he'd bobbed his first lord. And then he'd be branded in fire, a white-hot poker pressed into the soft skin of his hand, forever announcing him a criminal.

My mouth tightened into a grim line. No child deserved that. No matter how straw-headed.

I threaded my way through the gawkers, steadying my nerves by snipping off another loose bauble from a velvet sleeve as I passed. Then the tuft of blond hair abruptly changed course in the crowd, and panic squeezed my heart.

For Tommy, who couldn't tie his own breeches without getting his fingers trapped, crowds were a disaster. The boy somehow always went after the one mark in the mob who'd never be taken in by his sweet-faced charm and big blue eyes.

Show Tommy a hundred people to fleece, and he'd always choose the worst. It was almost a gift.

Truly. I'd seen the boy target magistrates and nuns.

Now, judging from the purposeful stride of his small, pumping body, Tommy had already picked out his next unlikely victim. I followed the child's line of sight. And then I *did* flinch.

Tommy was heading straight for the Queen's court.

More specifically, toward a hawk-faced scowler dressed all in black, bundled in a thick wool cape and in heavy trunk hose despite the balmy spring afternoon. I'd heard the man called Sir William, even as I'd brushed by him naught but an hour earlier. He looked like he was perpetually in a bad mood, as pale and sour as spoiled milk. The type of man who expected bad things to happen.

So I'd stolen his purse.

Sir William had been making a fine art out of flashing a

temptingly round money pouch, loosely attached to his belt. He'd displayed the heavy bag no fewer than a dozen times with a toss of his cape. It was a folly, of course, meant to draw the eye and the errant hands of a thief, whom Sir William could then catch in the act and punish publicly. Our new Queen, as it turned out, *hated* thieves.

Sir William's smaller purse, discreetly tucked against his side, was the real prize. Or it had been, until I'd nicked that pouch without the good lord realizing it . . . which meant that Tommy still had a gift for picking the wrong mark.

Figure it out, Tommy. . . .

A sudden spill of people jostled in front of me, blocking my view. For the first time ever I wished a teeming crowd had *not* turned out to watch our company's afternoon performance.

The Golden Rose acting troupe had become London's newest sensation—and not a moment too soon. Grandfather, God rest his soul, had always forbidden us to perform in any of the larger cities. But the young and dashing James McDonald was our troupe master now, and he'd seen the truth of things quickly enough: With the crowning of a new, triumphant Queen, no one much cared for traveling actors anymore. The village folk were giving all their time—and their money—to bards with stories of London and its new royal court. All eyes had turned to the capital city. To survive, that's where we had to be as well.

And without question, we'd never had larger crowds for our shows than here in Londontown, or riper pickings. Surely, Grandfather would understand.

Just today, in truth, as we performed in the sprawling courtyard of the White Lion Inn, we'd won the ultimate boon. The dazzling Queen Elizabeth and her court of fools had taken it into their heads to walk the city's streets and mingle with the common folk. Even now they tarried to watch our company shout our way through the second act of our most popular play, *The Beggared Lord*.

We'd felt the court's royal presence before we'd even been able to see it, like the quickening breeze of a seaborne storm. Gap-toothed urchins, worn-faced merchant's wives, even sharp-eyed hucksters, had all tensed with expectation, eager to see the new young Queen. I confess I stared as well. She was nothing short of awe-inspiring, our Elizabeth. Young and powerful. Radiant. Gloriously free to do whatever she wanted.

With her arrival the crowd had swelled to bursting. I'd caught Master James's knowing nod, and had set to work among the smug-lipped lords. In no time at all, I'd secreted away a fortnight's worth of their coin beneath my skirt's heavy cloth.

Master James would be proud. I smiled just thinking on that.

But if Tommy picked the wrong pocket, the blessing of the Queen's presence would become our curse. Even if the boy didn't come away with Sir William's purse successfully, he would be detained for trying. Searched.

And though Tommy wouldn't have Sir William's money on him, he'd probably managed to lift *someone's* silver this day. Which would be aught that was needed to doom us all. Unless I moved quickly, there would be twenty branded thumbs before the day's end—the Crown's punishment of choice for first-time offenders.

And that was if we were lucky. If the Queen *wasn't* feeling indulgent, our plights could be far, far worse. Gibbets. The stocks. The whistle of whip leather cutting into flesh.

My stomach clenched and I plunged forward into the crowd, locating Tommy anew when he stepped deliberately into the outermost ranks of royal courtiers. With a nonchalance I'd perfected over long years, I moved ever closer to him, my steps meandering and my manner harmless. This was an act I knew all too well.

Because I was female, I was forbidden to play a true role as a Golden Rose actor before the crowd. Instead, I'd honed my theatre craft *in* the crowd.

I was a fine and laughing lady, a guileless merchant's daughter, a scornful fishmonger's wife. I mimicked those around me easily, be they farmers, freemen, or fools. To a one I smiled, nodded . . . then picked their pockets.

By all accounts, you could say I stole the show.

I reached Tommy just as I saw his tiny hand flash out toward Sir William's false purse, brushing the man's coat but missing the purse entirely. Then I heard the turning harrumph of Tommy's target. The boy had committed no crime, yet that still might not save him.

Moving quickly, I yanked a heavy brooch out of my bodice and swirled forth in a fluster, praying that my carefully painted face still gave the impression of sophistication far beyond my seventeen years.

"What, ho, young man. You found it!" I cried, even as Sir William's head jerked up at the interruption, his cold gaze flashing over me as I reached out, clasping my hands over Tommy's and pressing the brooch into his dirty palm. "My sweet and heavenly days, this is some great luck. What a wonderful lad you are, for finding my lost treasure!"

Even Tommy realized something had gone terribly wrong. "'T-tis nothing, m'lady. I saw it shining in the dirt?" he said hopefully, his wide eyes desperate as he proffered the brooch back to me.

"And shine it would!" I beamed, taking the bit of jewelry with great show. "You've done very, *very* well. You should be proud of yourself."

Tommy nearly fainted with relief, his grin huge and heartfelt. God love the boy, he did try.

As I cooed and fluttered, however, I could feel the chilly grey censure of Sir William, hovering like a soft-gloved hand over my throat, ready to squeeze. Panic clawed through me, but I kept my voice steady, my eyes bright.

"There now. Off you go," I said, plucking a coin from the largest purse in my carefully sewn pockets, and forcing myself not to smirk. I was paying Tommy with Sir William's own coin, of all the grand irony. Swiftly I pressed the shilling into Tommy's hand. "Run along and get yourself a pasty, sweetling, and tell your mum 'twas a gift for being the smartest of boys."

"I will! I will, then! Thank you!"

As Tommy dashed away, shouting with his good fortune, I turned smartly in the other direction and clutched the brooch to my chest, a fine lady with her riches restored. I went five long paces, then stepped into a deep and shadowed doorway, holding my breath as I glanced back.

I needn't have worried. With *The Beggared Lord* to draw the people's attention, no one paid any heed to a little boy running through the crowd, or to the woman who'd rewarded him so generously.

Even Sir William watched the play now, a curiously soft,

secret smile on the man's thin lips. I offered him my own mocking smile from the shadows. *Look your fill, you old goat.*

I had no way of knowing his smile would be my undoing.

After allowing another few minutes to pass, I rolled out of the doorway, taking pains not to clink as I drifted through the crowd. Master James and I exchanged another nod as I passed, even as the crowd burst into rowdy applause. Had he seen me save Tommy's thumbs? Had I impressed him?

The sudden heat that swept through me at that thought made me wince, and I looked away hastily. Not for the first time, I decided that I cared too much what our new young troupe master thought.

I lifted my chin, once more immersing myself in my role as a worldly merchant's wife—whose husband was conveniently away on the Continent, and ergo not complaining night and day like all the husbands I'd ever seen.

Pish on Master James. There was no harm in being glad he'd noticed my accomplishments, but that was as far as it could go. Master James was smart and handsome, to be sure—particularly this day in his deep black velvet doublet and slashed trunks, with his roguish grin and curling chestnut hair and bright green eyes. And, yes, he was doing a fine job as Grandfather's replacement, safeguarding our traveling license and ensuring that our troupe of twenty-odd actors and their families did their jobs and ate their fill. There was much to recommend him, but he was still *male*. In the eyes of Queen and country, that meant he was my better. Should I ever be so stupid as to marry, my husband would own me like I was some prize goat . . . or, worse, a sturdy cow.

I'd lived my life more or less as I'd wanted these past

seventeen years. I could not imagine suddenly shackling myself to any man, for any reason. So, to me, Master James could only be a troupe master, nothing more and nothing less.

And he would owe me for this day's work. I grinned as I hauled my gold-laden skirts up a short stone staircase to gaze over the Thames, the last lines of *The Beggared Lord* booming out behind me. Grandfather had always worried too much about the dangers the cities held for our company. And for what? London had welcomed us with open arms—and pockets—and I'd never felt more right with the world.

As my skills had sharpened dramatically over the past several months, I'd proven my worth to the troupe twelve times over. Soon Master James would promote me to lead the street thieves, and then I could begin keeping a portion of our profits for myself. Within three years—fewer if we kept to larger cities—I'd have enough coin to live anywhere, *be* anyone.

That thought was almost too much to think about. I hugged it to me close, a hidden dream.

Then I straightened, pressing my hands to the small of my back to counterbalance my heavy skirts, as acclaim for the Golden Rose troupe thundered through the courtyard behind me. I had no time for dreaming. There were riches to be sorted and sold, and plans to be made for our next performance. Master James relied on me more with each passing day. And if he hadn't seen my work with Tommy, I'd be the first to tell him about it, and I'd bury my blushes in gold. Everything was moving forward the way it should, and I was at the pinnacle of my abilities: subtle, skillful, and—in my own way—wondrously free.

CHAPTER TWO

Two weeks later, they caught me.

CHAPTER THREE

"A moment, miss? A moment!"

I wheeled around, glancing back in surprise at the extraordinarily beautiful young girl who stood behind me on Thames Street. Her eyes were large and luminous against her fair skin, but curiously sad, liked bruised violets in the snow.

She stared at me expectantly, and I quelled my first thought, that she would make the perfect mark. Her dress was a vision of indigo pearl-sewn velvet, and her slippers—I would swear!—were made of satin, molded in a pristine dove grey as yet unsullied by the muddy streets. But young girls like her rarely spoke to me, especially when I was in costume. Today I was playing the role of a round and buxom washerwoman, certainly not the type of woman a well-bred girl would notice.

Why had she stopped me?

Quickly I checked to my right and left. A shadow passed just at the edge of my line of vision, and I narrowed my eyes at the lovely waif in front of me, guessing now that her pearls were made of paste and her dress was as mended as mine. *You'll get no baubles from me, gypsy lass.*

"Do I know you, miss?" I asked with a broad Westcheap

brogue, holding my heavy basket against my hip, well out of the girl's reach.

She watched my hands, not my face, another tell. Something was wrong here. "Am I interrupting you?" the girl asked. "I can take your basket."

Oh, I bet you could. "'Tis no trouble. How can I help you, poppet?" I needed to get back to my task. Today we were running a gambit to get into the back rooms of the Whitechurch Arms. Troupe Master James had petitioned for lodgings at the inn earlier in the day, and had been turned smartly away for his troubles as if we were common thieves.

Not every inn welcomed actors into their midst. They thought us cutthroats and vagabonds; ruffians, villains, and curs. Incensed, our company had decided to teach the innkeeper at the Whitechurch Arms not to judge his customers prematurely, by stealing from his till. I was on my way to put our revenge in motion. My role would be to distract the innkeeper with my loud voice and boisterous antics, showing him outfit after outfit that I'd supposedly either washed, beaten, or brushed clean for his patrons, while other members of our troupe snuck in through the inn's back entrance. But now this child stood before me. And she wasn't moving.

"Are you looking for someone, miss?" I prompted her, not bothering to hide my annoyance this time.

"Oh, no!" she said, too quickly. Her gaze darted up to my face, shifted away, then came resolutely back. "I mean, I'm looking for a place, not a person. Do you know where the Crow and Pony Tavern is?" Her eyes slid away again, but I caught a look of sheer torture within them. I almost felt sorry for the poor thing. She was truly miserable at lying.

I lifted my hand from my basket to tuck an errant strand of hair behind my ear. "Well, I—" I started, but no sooner had I begun speaking than the girl gasped like she'd been punched in the stomach, then buckled right in front of me. Quick as a breath her face went slack, and her body collapsed into the most awe-inspiring swoon I'd seen in the past five years.

"God's eyes!" Momentarily forgetting everything except that this girl was a child with no one to care for her, I dropped my basket with a *thunk* and dove toward her, barely catching her in time before she went facedown into the mud. As it was, I yanked the girl back so heavily that she crashed into me, her hands grasping for mine as her eyes fluttered back open.

The moment our fingers touched, I knew.

Somehow I'd just been marked.

Oblivious to my sudden panic, the girl caught my gaze and held it, her face quivering in distress. "I'm so sorry, I'm so sorry, I'm so sorry," she whispered, her voice broken with tears.

"Sorry for what? Who is doing this to you?" I jerked the girl to her feet, then shook her thin shoulders roughly, my lye-burned fingers looking painful and cracked against the fine fabric of her gown. "Who are you?" I demanded.

"Sophia!" she breathed. "But you must flee! I'd thought it was just a dream, but it's coming true! I would never— Please know that I would *never* have done this had I known what they would do!"

It was already too late to ask her what in the bloody bones she was talking about, because steps were even now sounding around me. The fleeting soft strides of someone else slipping away, and then the *thunking* crunch of authority.

"Unhand the girl," came the terse command behind me, puffed with the weight of nobility. That'd be Sir William, sure as I was born.

Damn my eyes.

I carefully made sure Sophia, if that was truly her name, was steady on her feet, then turned to face Sir William, ready to spin myself out of whatever trouble I'd stumbled into. I could play the role of a rollicking washerwoman as well as any other part I'd learned. It was something of a specialty of mine.

I opened up my mouth to let fly a string of expletives, but Sir William raised his hand abruptly, cutting me off. "Your presence is demanded by the Queen," he said.

Hadn't expected that.

"The Queen!" I burst out, masking my alarm with a roughneck London cackle. I raised my brows and thrust my hip out, eyeing Sir William up one side and down the other. "The Queen 'erself, 'e says. Well, I doubt that, I surely do. Wot would the Queen want with me, eh, bonny?"

I beamed at Sir William with a gape-mouthed grin, wishing for all the world that I'd lost a few of my teeth already. "But what a *fine* man you are, my lord. Do I know you? Might you simply 'ave a fancy to buy me an ale—is that what this is about?"

Sir William took a step back. "I beg your pardon?"

The guards that were with him tried to remain unperturbed, but I caught a stifled laugh, a nervous shuffle. I bore my gaze down on Sir William and took a long step forward, jamming my fists onto my padded hips, amply stuffed with rags.

"It is, isn't it!" I crowed. "You 'ad but to ask, my lord. Ol' Sally is always thirsty." I grinned back at Sophia, only to find that she was also staring at me, stupefied.

This might actually work.

I returned my attention to Sir William, advancing on him with a wide smile, making a show of adjusting my apron over my round belly before I reached out to squeeze his arm. "What a right strong man you are." I grinned. "I'm happy to spend an hour chattin' with you."

Sir William was looking at me with growing alarm. "I am *ordering* you to come with me to the Queen's court," he intoned harshly. "Or failing that, to her Tower. It is your choice."

"The Tower!" I threw up my arms at that, thrusting my padded belly forward like I was going to dissolve into a puddle of jollity. This was going to be one devil of a costume to flee in, but one did what one had to do. "There's no need for any of that. You can tell me everythin' right 'ere. What is it then, eh?" I winked broadly, reaching up to chuck him under the chin. "What stories do you want to whisper in my ear?"

"I *beg* your pardon!"

"You won't be the first, love, an' you won't be the last." I fluttered my hands at him with an indulgent chuckle. "But carry on! We can talk where'er you like. Just be sure there's a pint of ale for ol' Sally when we get there, will you, my lor'?" I stooped to pick up my wash.

"Leave that."

"Leave it! Leave it, 'e says," I protested, to mask my growing alarm. "Then you'll be 'avin' both ale *and* shillin's for me, you better believe. Orderin' a good, honest woman to leave her clothes in the middle of the road where any sort of unnatural people might come across them. As I live and breathe, the Queen 'e says. As if the Queen would 'ave anything to do with the likes of ol' Sally—"

I kept up my grumbling as Sir William turned, scowling, to lead us through the courtyard. The guards fell into a loose phalanx around me, but not so close that I couldn't make a dash for it when the opportunity arose. I felt like I was being watched, but the panic-stricken Sophia had fled, and there were only the stares of the curious passersby.

We turned into the rough-and-tumble New Fyshe Street just where the lane widened into a town square of sorts, and I made a slightly wider arc than the rest of them did, so that the structure of our group got even looser. And that's when I saw him.

Troupe Master James McDonald was leaning up against a market stall, looking for all the world like he was the proprietor of a cart of trenchers, pots, and wooden spoons. He glanced over at our group lazily, apparently not even registering my presence. But I knew better, of course. When I hadn't arrived at my appointed place for our ploy against the Whitechurch Arms, Master James had doubtless come looking for me. That was just his way. He took care of his own.

And even though I hated for him to step in to help get me out of this mess, I couldn't deny my pleasure at seeing him there. Together, we'd beat this snare. Together, we'd find a way out. And together—

Then the stall next to Master James suddenly went up

with a blazing whoosh of fire and the *ratatat* of fireworks, setting the horses in the square to madness and the stall-keepers to screaming hysteria.

It took only a second for me to realize what had happened. And then I was running too.

"Fire!" I screamed, diving through the guards, loosening my girdle beneath my skirts as I galloped in huge, lurching strides. I whipped around a corner and tossed my padded false stomach into a doorway. I rued the loss of the disguise, but there was nothing for it. I had to move.

I heard the guards behind me, and knew I'd never beat them in a race of sheer speed. My skirts were too long without the padding to billow them out, and my legs were too short. But while I was new-come to London, I wasn't without resources. I already knew places nobody wanted to go.

I pounded down another passageway and out onto a narrow street that backed up to the Thames. Gutted, rotting fish carcasses pooled in narrow ditches, waiting for a good rain to carry away what the street cleaners always missed, and I rushed along the foul-smelling passage without a moment's hesitation.

Where had I gone wrong? My costume had been perfect and my manner carefully honed. Out of all the Golden Rose actors, I'd been the one Troupe Master James had chosen to approach the innkeeper, after all. So how had that chit of a girl known who I was?

I didn't stop until I reached the Thames proper, my long dark hair flying freely now, my wig and cap long gone. Then I heard a sound rife with wrongness. It was naught more than a whisper of movement, but enough to cause me to immediately shift away—

And then I was facedown against the stone ledge of the river wall, a wickedly sharp blade a bare inch from my eyes. My neck was locked down so tightly, I feared it would snap like a chicken's.

"Sorry, but I canna chase you all day." It was a girl who held me down, her voice as plain and flat as a board. She came from Wales, from her accent, and she sounded younger than I would have expected, for hands so strong and cruel. Perhaps eighteen, but no older.

"Who are you?" I gasped, my body tensing to flee at the first opportunity. Could I bribe the woman? Somehow break away? Would Master James find me in time?

She grunted as she positioned her knee more squarely into my back. "They'll be angry enough that you gave them the slip, especially one Sir William Cecil. I don't need him mad at me, too. You would have made it, though, if I hadn't been watching." She sighed, a soft whisper of regret in the sound. "I didn't have the sense to run when they came for me."

"Let me go!" I tried again, but the girl just clamped harder on my neck, cutting off my breath.

"I canna do that," she said, reasonably enough, as my sight dimmed to a pinprick. "You sealed your own fate when you lifted Cecil's purse a fortnight past. *He* might not want anything to do with you, but the Queen does. And she's what counts." She hesitated, and when she spoke again, her voice sounded like linen washed too often over the rocks: thin, cold, and resolute. "And I'm Jane, by the way. Beggin' your pardon again, but this is the only way."

I heard the *whoosh* of something slicing through the air, ending in a curiously loud *thunk!* against my temple.

And then there was nothing.

CHAPTER FOUR

THREE MONTHS LATER
WINDSOR CASTLE, WINDSOR, ENGLAND

I'd never hated words before I'd been brought to Windsor Castle.

Here, they'd become a plague.

"Again, Miss Fellowes," Sir William Cecil snapped, his voice striking out at all angles into the cramped room. He shoved the book at me, and I leaned over it dutifully, dread balling in my stomach. *Bahrrrr . . . barrruuss . . .*

I'd never really hated Mondays before Windsor Castle either.

On Mondays, the most loathsome day of the week, we studied and translated texts in Latin, French, Dutch, and Spanish. Tuesday, the subject was politics. Wednesday, social graces. Thursday, observation skills.

On Fridays, we learned about poisons. Strangleholds. And less dignified ways to die.

It seemed like a lifetime had passed since I'd first been hauled to the Tower and charged with stealing royal gold. That first day, I still thought I could escape. That first day, I'd been astonished, then furious with myself at my own stupidity for being captured in the first place.

Sir William had marked me with ridiculous ease, as it turned out. Using a trick so old and tired that I'd stopped looking for it in any village with more than two goats to its name.

Apparently assuming that his riches would be lifted the moment he stepped outside, Sir William had etched a secret symbol into his coins before leaving the safety of the castle. He was a skulking coward, I'd decided, a panic-stricken fool.

Well . . . perhaps not a complete fool. Because before night had fallen on that accursed day, Sir William had found me out. After waiting the shortest of whiles, he had sent men to follow Tommy, and they'd trailed the boy to the pasty stand. After that, it had been a simple thing to ask the stand's keeper to hand over the coin Tommy had just used to buy his treat. The shilling had borne Sir William's mark, of course.

I secretly prided myself that it had taken the Crown nearly a full fortnight to lay hands on me after that, and in the end they'd needed two maids to achieve it.

Or had they? Was that a lie too? In the long days of my captivity, I'd had ample time to learn the depths of Sir William's cunning. After three wretched months in his questionable care, my life with the Golden Rose was naught but memory, a freedom I feared I would never fully grasp again.

Gone were the days of shouting lines back and forth over the morning fires, of sewing late into the night to stitch back together costumes that had become more thread than cloth. Gone was the unfettered joy of sleeping under the summer stars, or bundled together in pitch tents while a child exclaimed over the first snowfall. Gone was little towheaded Tommy Farrow.

Gone was Master James.

Acting, thievery, and deception, however, were still very much a part of my life.

I'd carried nothing with me to the Tower but the much-mended clothes on my back and my two precious gifts from my grandfather, hidden in my shift. On his deathbed, sick and pale with fever, my grandfather had given me a slim book of verse and a set of golden picklocks—without ever explaining why. For luck, I'd sewn those gifts into my shift just hours before I'd been arrested. And as luck would have it, they now were the only possessions I still owned in the world.

That first day, as I'd woken up in my cell deep in the bowels of the Tower with a lump on my temple and my ears still ringing with pain, I'd prayed they wouldn't take my clothes from me. But I'd been prepared for it.

In fact, I'd thought I was prepared for anything. As a first-time offender and a woman, I knew I would not be killed or visibly maimed. But I'd expected their questioning to be painful—perhaps involving thumbscrews or white-hot tongs. And when they'd yanked me from my cell and marched me into to the foul-smelling heart of the Tower of London, my hands and feet bound with chains, I'd fully believed I would be humiliated, reviled, and left heartily wishing I was dead.

What they'd actually done was much worse.

In a dank and barren corner of the Queen's dungeon, they'd . . . sat me at a table. Served me spiced wine. And explained my new life to me in clear and simple terms.

If I did not do exactly what they told me to do, exactly how they told me to do it, it would not be merely me who suffered.

True, I'd be imprisoned for the rest of my life. But more to the point, Master James and the other principal actors of the Golden Rose would be hunted down with whips and blades, paraded through the city as thieves, and then left trapped in the stocks for five whole days, at the mercy of any Londoner with a stone to throw.

The news of their arrest would be spread throughout England as fast as a horse could ride. The troupe would be ruined.

They would all starve.

Alternatively, if I performed my duties well and honorably, if I completed my assignments and served the Queen as a loyal subject and spy, then perhaps—just perhaps—I would be allowed to go free, eventually. I could return to the Golden Rose to live out my days, with a small purse of coin besides, a token of the Queen's thanks. So my options were these: imprisonment, ruin, and the starvation of my troupe . . . or service to my Queen as a spy.

I knew I was missing some hidden deception in their words, but what choice did I have? After that miserable morning, I'd done everything they'd asked.

I'd learned to eat with silver utensils without palming (nearly) a single one. To laugh at every courtier's joke. To find the Queen's bracelet in the far corners of Saint George's Hall and slip it back into her hand with no one the wiser. Just three months in, and I also already knew how to kill a person six different ways. Which, despite my colorful upbringing, was six more ways than I ever planned to use. I would never kill anyone. I would never even *cut* anyone. I was a thief, not a common thug.

As it happened, the art of thuggery was the specialty of another maid in our less-than-merry troupe: the plain-voiced girl from Wales who'd walloped me with her dagger hilt the day I'd been caught. Jane wasn't stuck in the room with us this day, at least. Cecil had sent her away on some errand. Now, she was probably out somewhere sharpening her knives. I'd nicknamed her "the Blade."

"Miss Fellowes," Sir William prompted. "Repeat the passage Miss Knowles just completed. Only with better form."

I sighed and looked down dejectedly at the book before me. Despite all my newfound abilities, there was one skill that I could not seem to master, no matter how I tried. It was the one skill I most craved to possess too, since I could then read for myself the words of bards and playwrights. And yet . . .

"Say the *words*, Miss Fellowes." Sir William—or Cecil, to those who knew him well—jabbed his thin finger at a passage of finely wrought letters that mocked me from the page. I tried to sound them out in my head: *Bahrrrr . . . barrruus . . . hick . . .*

I could not read.

It was the one indulgence Grandfather had never allowed me, though he'd taught me how to speak all the words in the world, with the richness of speech favored by the noblest of men. *We doona have the time to read, lass,* he'd tell me when I'd ask and beg and plead. *I doona have the energy*. So it was all the more ironic when, on his deathbed, Grandfather's first of two gifts to me had been . . . a book.

A book I could not read.

"Sometime before I grow old and die, Meg," came the irritated whisper behind me.

Beatrice Knowles, dressed in a spectacular gown of dawn-pink silk, sighed dramatically to underscore her taunt. With her shining blond hair and sky-blue eyes, her gorgeous clothes and flawless skin, I'd been tempted to hate Beatrice on sight. Then she'd opened her mouth, and I'd given in to the temptation. Proud, haughty, and mean-spirited, her head filled with court gossip and very little else, Beatrice would have made a grand character in a play . . . as long as she ended up dead by the third act. Or at the very least married off to some pompous old fool.

But of course, Beatrice the Belle had not been chosen to join our group because of her sweet and sunny disposition. She'd been chosen because she possessed an uncanny ability to convince *any* of the male species to do her bidding, whether he was a six-year-old stable boy or a sixty-year-old lord. She cooed and fluttered, simpered and preened, and flirted outrageously at every turn.

Beside her, the quiet Anna Burgher shifted her feet. Currently clad in a sturdy overdress of soft yellow wool, with a high collar and heavy sleeves that tidily covered her plain white smock, the green-eyed, ginger-haired Anna the Scholar could be excused for having no patience for idiots. And sure enough, as I hesitated, I could hear her grinding her teeth.

The more I tried to actually read the words before me, the longer we'd be forced to stay in class. So I alone was causing their discontent. Though usually only reasonably tolerant of each other, Anna and Beatrice were now clearly united in their desire to escape this airless room. Even with my eyes trained on the page, I could feel them both from the side. Glaring at me.

"Miss Fellowes?" There was neither scorn nor pity in Sir William Cecil's voice as he watched my struggle—only cunning. He undoubtedly knew I could still not decipher those strange tracks marching across the page. He probably preferred it in some devious way, if only to keep me under his boot heel. Cecil did not relish spending time on a ragged, scrappy thief who'd fooled him once—and nearly twice. I suspect he would have kept me in the dungeon without a backward glance, if it hadn't been for the Queen's demand that I be trained as a spy. He made no secret of the fact that it was Elizabeth who had selected me for this service, not him. He did not trust me, he did not like me, and he did not want me here. And I, for one, did not blame him. I didn't want to be here either. I far preferred the swiftness of the chase, the swish of stolen silk, the cool feel of silver in my palm.

Barbaruuuss . . . hick . . . ehhgo . . .

But I feared that Cecil was *also* beginning to suspect I could do something far better than read, something that might be of particular and unexpected use to him and his Queen. And now he wanted me to show my hand.

Under the weight of the girls' combined stares, and Cecil's insistent tapping, I gave up the pretense of translation. I had other options.

Beatrice had been the last girl to translate, and her words still hung low in the air like overripe fruit. Without lifting my head, I opened my mouth, taking those same words and making them my own, as I'd done countless times while working with my fellow actors. Since Grandfather had never taught me to read, I'd learned to play the world by ear, and had become the perfect mimic to help the troupe's actors learn their lines. Now, after more than a decade of practice, I had only to hear an entire three-act play spoken aloud one time, before being able to repeat it back word for word.

One short passage of unintelligible babble was child's play to me.

"Barbarus hic ego sum," I began, careful not to repeat Beatrice's cadence exactly, faltering just enough that it seemed like I was, in fact, reading something of what lay in front of me. I knew Beatrice had made errors, so I would be making the same ones as well, but I added a few additional smell variances just to keep Cecil guessing. The Latin flowed like music, and its companion English translation sounded harsh, almost unnatural in its wake. "'. . . understands me,'" I completed the translation triumphantly, and then I finally saw a word I could decipher—one that Beatrice had not spoken. I looked up to meet Cecil's gaze. "By Ovid."

Beatrice clapped her hands in mock applause, and Cecil raised his brow, a sour-eyed owl.

"Exactly so," he murmured. "You are next, Miss Burgher. Turn the page and begin."

Anna Burgher recounted the new passage in her precise, learned voice—first in Latin, then in Spanish, then Russian, German, and what I suspected was Greek, of all things. All the while, Cecil continued to stare at me. No doubt calculating the likelihood that I had somehow achieved spectacular literacy since the preceding Monday.

I graced him with my most serene smile. Grandfather may have failed me on the art of reading, but he had more than made up for it with his lessons on voice, listening, acting, and persuasion. Let Cecil wonder just how deep that training went. *Old goat.*

After a long moment, Cecil gave a sniff of dismissal, then turned his full attention to Anna.

Left alone again while Cecil and Anna sparred in five different languages, I shifted in my ill-fitting gown of dull grey silk, and strained to pick up any sound beyond the walls of this makeshift study, tucked away just off the Queen's Privy Chambers. It was impossible, of course. These walls were as thick as a yew tree, and lined with heavy tapestries over panels of carved wood, rendering the room virtually soundless. As a result, the classroom always struck me as a half-open tomb.

Fitting, really, for what was to befall the five girls who took our instruction there.

While the other young women and ladies who served Her Grace—a swirling mixture of "ordinary" maids of honor and the older and usually married ladies-in-waiting—sewed and gossiped, knelt and processed, and learned the finer points of dancing and court etiquette, our little company was daily summoned away for "advanced" studies; a separate, secret sect. And here, in this tiny, overstuffed chamber that had become my own personal circle of hell, amid rustling skirts and thick, musty texts and the high, strident voice of our peevish instructor—here the true Maids of Honor were being taught how to spy for the Queen.

Perhaps that sounds exciting—even fun. A grand adventure to serve the most extraordinary Queen of any country, as bold and dashing protectors of the Crown.

It hadn't been exciting so far.

I'd been in the Crown's employ for three months now. It'd taken the first week for my jailers to simply get me clean, it seemed, though I never felt that way after I'd been perfumed and pomaded, powdered and pinched. They'd outfitted me in dresses of high—but not too high—quality, and assigned me the royal identity of an orphaned ward from a distant duchy. I'd apparently come to court through one of the many generous acts of Her Majesty, and should act at all times both grateful and painfully shy. This bit of business was designed to cover up my abysmal lack of social graces, as Beatrice was always quick to point out, but it suited me well enough. Being ignored was one of a thief's greatest assets.

Weeks two and three had been spent on manners and food, especially manners *with* food. It seemed the nobler I became, the longer it took before I could actually eat my evening meal. The sewing wasn't so bad, as I'd had plenty of experience mending the clothes of the Golden Rose players. The dancing, however, nearly killed me; as did the endless rounds of prayers, catechisms, and sermons I had to endure.

To assist me with my reading, I had *Lily's Latin Grammar* textbook, as well as hornbooks and spellers to keep me company. And, of course, the Bible. Needless to say, they didn't help much. Anna extolled the virtues of the philosophers she favored. In addition to Ovid, there was Plautus and Horace; Virgil, Cicero, and Seneca . . . but those texts were well beyond me even after three months of intense instruction. And none of them helped me understand my grandfather's tiny leather-bound book. Which was the only book I truly wanted to read out of all of them.

Finally, starting at the end of the first month, we got to the business of spying. At first I'd embraced the change. We learned how to move quietly, to observe keenly, and to kill or maim without creasing our skirts. The other maids were forced to repeat lessons they already knew as I caught up, which earned me no friends among them. But eventually, even for me, the study of deadly weapons became, well . . . deadly. And then there was endless instruction on elocution, languages, and court behavior. This included whole days spent on the proper timing and depth of curtsies, complete with accompanying drills that ran so far into the night that I couldn't pass a field mouse without instinctively dropping to the floor.

Yet even with the exhaustive training, I still felt so behind. The other girls had all been in service to the Queen four more months than I had. Elizabeth had selected her troupe of spies the moment she'd ascended to the Crown the previous fall . . . but no one would talk about why she'd suddenly decided to add me.

"Meg Fellowes!" Cecil snapped, startling me. His voice was always too loud for whatever space he occupied. "Repeat the passage Miss Burgher just shared."

He did not even allow me the pretense of reading it this time. It was a direct test of my secret skills, but I dared not pass it. "My apologies," I gasped. In truth, I could have recounted anything that had been said within the past hour, even though I'd been only half-listening. Anna had just said, *"Parve—nec invideo, sine me, liber, ibis in urbem."* I had no idea what it meant, but could have repeated it verbatim (a Latin word I actually knew!) just the same.

"I was not paying attention," I said instead.

"You were not . . . paying attention?" Sir William's icy gaze spoke volumes when his words would not. He likely knew I was lying. But that was a chance I was willing to take. I could not betray the full extent of my mimicry skills, not to him—not to anyone. I'd reveal enough to keep them happy, but nothing more. Certainly not the whole truth: that a word, once spoken, was forever in my mind, repeatable to anyone, at any time, with the same vocal inflections and tone. I liked having a skill that was not fully understood by the Crown; perhaps I could use it one day to get myself out of trouble. Besides, I could only imagine what the Queen's advisors would do if they knew my secret. Probably force me to listen to one of the archbishop's interminable sermons and recite it to condemned prisoners until they begged for death. It wouldn't take very long, trust me.

Cecil smiled thinly into my continued silence, and a whisper of warning snaked through me, recalling me to my present danger. "Then," he said, "I'm afraid Miss Burgher will have to repeat the passage for your benefit—"

"Oh, no, Sir William. Truly?" The ordinarily stoic Anna had now clutched up one of the small, ornate wooden puzzle boxes she always carried with her, her voice heavy with strain. I glanced at her in alarm, sensing disaster.

"I can repeat it," I said hurriedly, but Anna paid me no heed.

"I pray you reconsider, Sir William," she said, nervously twisting the small cube on its silver chain. The puzzle box was painted in gold, silver, red, and yellow, and featured a delicately illustrated cover of a Japanese princess, with its sides made to look like woven wood. Anna had told me that the box required more than four hundred steps, executed in the right sequence, to reveal its inner contents. She'd been given the box as a gift from the Queen's astrologer—as another test for our resident puzzle-solver, I suspected. Anna hadn't yet been able to open it, but that didn't stop her from trying. Now she twisted and turned the little box's moving parts so hard, I feared that it would break in her worrying fingers. "The Spaniards are at our doorstep, and they will not be speaking the language of Ovid, but Spanish, or possibly Dutch!"

I bit my lip in consternation. It was always reckless to object to Cecil's training, even politely—even (or especially) if he'd just ordered us to eat our fifth tureen of soup. But Anna, in her distress, was not noting Cecil's swift, cold smile, or did not recognize its danger. Her green eyes were large and pleading, her cheeks rosy with determination, and the loose strands of her braided burned-spice hair nearly stood up in agitation as she bobbed her head for emphasis. "Dutch is something on which we have spent far too little time. In fact, I—"

"I can repeat the passage!" I tried again. "I can!"

"Yes, surely, Sir William, you *must* see the folly in this." Beatrice's well-bred voice layered silkily over Anna's and mine with the imperious sneer of the soft-palmed rich. "Teaching Meg to translate is like teaching a fish to walk. It cannot be done, and 'tis a waste of all our time." Beatrice gazed at Cecil with her dewy eyes, now as wide and innocent as a wolf's. "Especially *your* time, Sir Wil—"

"No, no, you misunderstand! I take no issue with the *translating*." Anna's voice had a new note of earnestness in it, as if she sensed the shifting current of the conversation. "But while I have no end of interest in the classics, I fear our time for study is growing short. I urge you, please, Sir William: Have us decipher a report—a dockmaster's bill of lading from a Spanish galleon. A *contemporary* court conversation. Surely that would be more relevant, given our present needs?"

Beatrice pursed delicate lips. "It seems to me our most pressing need is to find a way to ensure Meg does not embarrass us all."

Anna turned to Beatrice, dropping her puzzle box to let it dangle from its chain at her waist. Her eyes now flashed with protective fervor, still more wisps of her hair slipping loose from her braids. "Beatrice, that is unfair," she said. "Surely you know that Meg would never *shame* us."

"I'm afraid that when it comes to *Meg*, I don't know anything at—"

"Enough."

Cecil's soft rebuke may have sounded calm to the untrained ear, but it masked a pit of outrage, like branches over a trap. I glanced over at him, biting my lip. The muscles in his jaw were tight, his eyes jaded and expectant, as if he'd seen this play unfold before. *Everyone be quiet,* I implored silently, the words of one of the Golden Rose's plays sparking in my mind. *Be mindful, still, and wary, for there is danger here.*

It did no good. Beatrice could never tell when she was baiting a bear beyond its patience. "But, Sir William," she whined, rounding on him. "You can *hardly* expect me to not wish to forestall the kind of social scandal Meg will undoubtedly bring upon me—upon us all. I have certain standards to uphold. My aunt, shall I remind you, is second cousin to—"

"I said, *enough*."

Cecil didn't shout the word, or even raise his voice. In fact, he spoke not quite above a whisper. Still, I felt like I'd been punched in the chest, suddenly unable to breathe. Beside me, Beatrice and Anna froze, but it was too late. Because Cecil wasn't finished.

"You've not been brought here to *uphold standards*," he said, slicing the air with his words, quiet and deadly. "You have not been brought here—any of you"—and he eyed each of us for a single moment that lasted half a day—"to *think*. I don't care if your aunt was Cleopatra. I don't care if you do aught but recite ancient poetry as the castle burns to the ground, if that's what you've been told to do. You have been brought here as tools for the Queen, utensils she can bend and shape as she wishes or throw into the trash heap without a backward glance. That is the *sum total* of your purpose, and you forget it at your peril. As long as you are a part of this group, you have no individual identity. You have no role beyond that which I assign to you. You are not free to speak or dance or prattle, or 'respond' or 'take issue' as you choose," Cecil spat. "You are the Queen's property. And, by her proxy and command, *my* property. Do you understand?"

Beatrice's mouth was still hanging open, but no more words came out. She somehow clamped her lips closed, too flummoxed even to nod. She'd be angry later—but not at Cecil, I knew. Somehow this would all be my fault.

"I said, do you under*stand*?" Cecil thundered.

"Yes!" Beatrice squeaked, and beside her Anna nodded hurriedly.

Cecil paused a moment, his scowl so deep, I feared it might be fixed upon his face forever. He shifted his gaze to me. "And you, Miss Fellowes. You will do what you are told, everything that you are told, and no *less* than what you are told." He paused for emphasis. "Tonight you will be called on to make your first official report. You will make that report specifically, in detail, and without missing a syllable of what you hear. Always observe. Always remember." His eyes narrowed. "And if you so much as pocket a thimble without my express instruction, you will be returned to the embrace of the cellar room you love so well. Do I make myself clear?"

He clearly expected an answer, and for once I gave him what he wanted to hear.

"I will not fail the Queen, Sir William," I said, and I meant the words with all my heart. "You can tell her that, for me."

His face did not change, but his gaze seemed to intensify. Somehow he was no longer looking merely at me—but into me. And in that damning silence we heard the only sound that ever dared penetrate the walls of our schoolroom. The castle clock struck, chiming the tenth hour with a steady, rhythmic cadence, as fell as the march of doom.

Cecil's mouth curved into a hard, mocking smile.

"You may tell her yourself," he said. "She awaits you in the Privy Garden. With your first assignment."

CHAPTER FIVE

Gloriana, her most high majesty Queen Elizabeth Regnant, stood magnificently in her private garden, surrounded by her attendants like stars around the sun.

She was spectacular in the morning light—tall and fair and flame-haired, her strength and vitality positively glowing beneath the deep red satin gown she wore. The dress framed her graceful neck and shoulders in a square-cut collar edged in snowy lace, and its wide-set sleeves were strung with pearls and ended in narrow, bejeweled cuffs. The entire gown was embroidered with heavy golden thread against its crimson silk, and must have weighed four stones. It would have overpowered most women, but not our Elizabeth. With every movement the Queen commanded the eye; each word from her lips pricked the ears and sent a shiver down the skin; each glance could send a heart aflutter or a stomach plunging in fear.

Her face could not be called pretty, exactly, though she was favorable to look upon, with high cheekbones, dark flashing eyes, and a firm jaw. But she possessed a hardness, a power in her very bones that transcended feminine beauty.

Even at a mere twenty-five years of age, she was both King and Queen in one resplendent form.

She'd saved me from prison, when Cecil had wanted me banished. And now she would give me the means to achieve my freedom.

My first assignment! Nimbly my mind jumped ahead days, weeks—months even—directing a play as yet not fully cast. If I carried out my charge well, what would the next assignment be? How soon would I complete my service and be allowed to return to my troupe?

Leading the way with his usual brisk stride, Cecil barreled through the garden like a bull among chickens, scattering the squawking women as he led us toward the Queen. Behind him, I exchanged glances with Beatrice and Anna. Even in the Queen's private garden, we knew what we had to do. We'd been trained to watch and report.

With an artful turn of her head, Beatrice began scanning the women arranged around the Queen. She was more than just a flirt, no matter my disdain for her. She had memorized a complicated map of the current alliances among the nobility, both temporary and entrenched, and she was ever adjusting that map according to the shifting tides of favor that seemed to rock the court. She knew more about how the women of the court ranked, whether by birth or by subtle court power exchanges, than they probably knew themselves, and she narrowed her eyes slightly as she watched, concentrating on two ladies at the far end of the garden who apparently should not have been standing together.

Anna, for her part, was to provide a simple accounting: who was there and who was not, from monarch to maid to serving girl, complete with names and what they were wearing or carrying. This work was not as intriguing to her as deciphering codes or playing with astrolabes or translating ancient Greek, but Anna enjoyed the game of numbers and descriptions very much. Even now, her cheeks flushed with excitement as her gaze discreetly swept the small space.

My role, in turn, was to learn the unspoken secrets of the players around me, simply by observing how they conducted themselves upon this royal stage. I noted who was leaning into intimate conversation, and who was being rebuffed. Who had curiosity or anger or delight or dismay writ upon their faces, and who was watching whom. After three months of this constant assignment, I could no longer enter a knot of people without systematically tracking the cues they gave, which announced their intentions before they ever opened their mouths.

Still, my stomach tightened as we approached the Queen. I didn't know what to expect from her, and I didn't like surprises. Surprises required improvisation. Improvisation worked far better in a play than in real life—and even then, only with the most skilled of actors. Would I be convincing enough to carry the day, if my assignment proved to be beyond my skills? I put on a smile of confidence like a mask, and made ready to say yes to anything.

Seated beside Queen Elizabeth were three ladies-in-waiting, who in turn were attended by the youngest member of our special group of maids, Sophia Dee.

Yes, *that* Sophia—whose touch had been my undoing, three months ago in the marketplace.

Orphaned when she was very young, Sophia was both

ward and niece to the Queen's astrologist, John Dee, and the dark-haired, violet-eyed girl was believed to *almost* possess the Sight. It was beyond ironic to me. A hundred years ago—or even more recently, in truth—an ability to foresee the future might have gotten Sophia burned at the stake. But here, with this Queen and in this court, the idea that she might serve the Queen in much the same way John Dee did had made Sophia a commodity of highest value. And her gift was going to manifest itself with clarity *any day* now, everyone was certain.

I, for one, suspected it already had. Cecil had forced Sophia to stand in my path that day in April, to confirm his suspicion that I was the thief that he sought—and with her touch she'd condemned me. I'd forgiven her for her part in taking me down, but only because she was so distraught for days after, swearing she did not know *why* I'd filled her with such fear, or *how* exactly she'd known of my crimes. Sophia had mentioned a dream to me that day in the marketplace, but when I'd asked her about it later, she'd said I'd misheard her. This of course was impossible—I misheard no one. But at the girl's obvious distress, I didn't press the point. Perhaps she didn't trust her dreams as yet; perhaps all of her dreams weren't accurate. Or perhaps she was simply scared. I know I would have been. It could not be easy to see the future, especially if it came true.

We'd talked more since that day, and I quickly realized that Sophia felt a certain kinship to me. Not because of our backgrounds, since Sophia had been born to wealth and had never roamed the streets and countryside as part of a laughing crowd. But simply because I was the new member, the slow learner, the sharpening stone on which the other girls honed their wits. Before, that role had been hers. I did not quibble with Sophia's camaraderie, though. I was glad to call anyone an ally. I thought of her as "the Seer."

Now, as Sophia sat quietly beside the Queen, her quiet blue gown of stiffened lace doing nothing to dim her ethereal beauty, her role was to watch the space between the spaces around the women gathered here, in case their spirits spoke to her or she was given some clue as to their future actions. It was a fruitless chore, in truth. Sooner or later, I felt in my bones, Sophia would gain real command over her sight. And then she would truly shine.

Hopefully, it would be sooner rather than later. The poor girl was already *betrothed*, and to an old man at that! I couldn't imagine a worse fate. Invariably, when I'd played the role of the wife of an older man as part of my "acting" duties within the Golden Rose, it had called for sarcasm, anger, and a surfeit of grief. From everything I could tell, in observing both the members of our own troupe and the lives of the villagers and farm people who made up our crowds, marriage was the lot all women hoped for . . . until they found themselves enmeshed in it. Yes, of course there were exceptions, but they were precious few. For most women, marriage was like a yoke hewn from a sturdy beam, something to be endured for the security it provided. But my aim in life was freedom, not endless servitude; joy, not misery. There would be no husband for me.

That left only one member of our small band of five maids a-spying who was unaccounted for this morning: Jane Morgan, the Blade.

The most secretive spy among us, Jane was probably

hiding not ten feet away, watching us all. She had a knack for that sort of thing, as well I knew. Invariably her role, no matter the setting, was to be ready to kill someone—or at least horribly maim them. She could recognize the tensing of a body, the stealth of a step, the shift of the eyes. An attack on the Queen was not a likely concern when she was surrounded by women in her own Privy Garden, but Jane never knew when she'd be called upon to act. Especially in a castle as full of mayhem as Windsor.

In the short time I'd been here, there'd been no fewer than a dozen odd court disturbances, from the theft of the ladies' precious gowns—later found floating in the Thames—to the string of English roses painted around the rim of the Round Tower, to the enormous wharf rats that had been released into the kitchens, setting the entire staff of cooks and servants into a screaming fury. The Queen and her court were irritated, and all of Windsor was abuzz with the outrage of it all.

Cecil halted in front of me with a brief bow to the Queen, and I forced my attention back to my royal obligations. In unison, Beatrice, Anna, and I curtsied deeply to Her Majesty, then stood straight. Each of us, if asked, had already observed enough in this small garden space to give a full report.

Sadly, in all the time I'd been in the Crown's employ, nobody had asked.

Perhaps now that would finally change.

Queen Elizabeth eyed us with approval. Given that Her Grace's gown was studded with jewels along both sleeves, it was plain she had not dressed merely for her ladies this morning. She must have just left her enormous Presence Chamber, where she routinely heard her subjects' requests, resolving everything from village conflicts to tax relief to marital negotiations for the most minor of nobility. Having lived with the Golden Rose the whole of my life, I'd never realized how much a monarch could govern the daily lives of her more dignified subjects.

Now this monarch turned to Cecil, fully ready to govern mine.

"Good morrow, Sir William," Queen Elizabeth said, her voice filled with proud command, causing everyone in earshot to turn her way abruptly. "I trust your morning lesson has gone well?"

Cecil bowed slightly, his response measured and equally firm. "Very well, Your Grace," he said. Something passed between them, riding the innocent words, but I could not puzzle it out. "Your maids are ready to serve you."

The three ladies-in-waiting behind the Queen tried to appear bored but failed miserably. I could sense Beatrice snapping to attention as they eyed us with furtive attention. They wanted desperately, I knew, to gather some idea of why the Queen concerned herself so much with the separate studies of five young maids, but so far they had been unsuccessful in that attempt. According to Cecil, not even the Queen's closest confidantes were privy to our exact purpose, other than that we were being taught "advanced etiquette, comportment, and grace." As if we were rather slow and needed extra instruction. Considering the curious backgrounds of most of us, this seemed eminently logic to all, and we were all glad of the covering story. Except Beatrice, of course, who remained constantly indignant about the perceived slight to her reputation.

Then something moved near the hedgerow, the subtlest shift of shadows, and I hid a smile. Jane Morgan had finally made her appearance known. At least to me.

Dark and fluid in her somber grey shift, sharp-featured but oddly striking, Jane was the grimmest member of our small group of spies in many ways, but she was also the easiest for me to understand. Her skills were straightforward, and exceedingly useful, though to my knowledge they hadn't yet been put to the test under the Queen's command.

Jane had been found just after Christmastide, I'd been told, when the Queen's Guard had been sent to arrest a traveling group of marauders who'd attacked a small hamlet in North Wales.

Jane, whose family had been killed in the attack, had gotten to the marauders first.

"Leave us," the Queen now said abruptly, interrupting my reverie, and it took me a moment to realize she was commanding her ladies-in-waiting to depart. It took them a moment to realize it as well, which made Beatrice stand particularly straight as the three older women rose to their feet—Kat Ashley, the Queen's oldest friend, who had the grace to not look annoyed; and Blanche Parry and Lady Knollys, who left no question of their disdain for us.

I watched them go, then glanced back to the Queen, somewhat startled to see that her gaze had fallen on me.

"You have been with us three months, Meg. Sir William tells me you've progressed well enough for your first test."

"Your Grace," I said, curtsying again under her watchful gaze. I was getting very good at curtsying.

The Queen swept forward, her skirts brushing by my forehead, catching at my hair. Even in the midst of the garden, she smelled of lavender and something else, a sharp but pleasant spice I could not identify. All of the castle was like that, aswirl in pomanders and scents that I encountered at every turn. I had begun working with Anna to sort them out, but I was still a hopeless novice.

"Walk with me," the Queen commanded, and I popped up so quickly, I felt dizzy, stumbling forward as Beatrice shoved me.

"Go!" Beatrice hissed. "And try not to embarrass us!"

I nodded tightly and hastened after the Queen, who was already several steps ahead.

The Queen set out at a fast pace, and I carefully remained just behind her. We were of a height, which made it easier for me to match her stride, though her heeled slippers made her seem taller. At the far corner of the yard, the Queen still did not look at me, but glanced out across the garden as we turned, never slowing. "So, Meg, tell me," she said, her words almost casual, but not quite. "What have you learned in your three months of training?"

"Your Grace?" I asked, surprised by the breadth of the question. "Ah, I have learned a great many things." She did not reply, so I blundered on. "I have learned the family lines of all political houses in England and the rest of Europe. I have learned to dance the Almain, and I have—"

"And what have you learned about your fellow maids?"

I hesitated again. *Where is this going?* "Well, Beatrice's mother is from the house of Winterton, and is married to the Earl of—"

"Beyond that." The Queen silenced me with a wave of her ringed fingers. "What is Beatrice's best ability?"

"Manipulation," I said, without thinking. Then I rushed to soften the words, lest they seem uncharitable. "She is perfectly placed in the court. Everyone knows her and her standing, and she makes alliances with ease and elegance. She is one of the most sought after young women of the land, though far below you, of course, Your Grace."

"Of course," the Queen said dryly. "And her flaw? What is her greatest flaw?" The Queen was walking more swiftly, and I was forced to keep pace, my heart now beginning to beat a little faster. I tried to choose my words carefully, and the Queen's lips pursed. "Don't try my patience, Meg," she said, the words a slap.

"Her pride," I bit out, cringing at the betrayal, even though it was just Beatrice and she richly deserved it.

Rather than ask me to explain, the Queen moved on. "Anna, then," she prompted.

"Anna's best skill is her discernment—she can see hidden patterns in events, encoded letters, or even in mechanical things," I said, thinking of Anna's fascination with the puzzle boxes. I swallowed, knowing the next question. "Her flaw is her innocence. She believes the best in everyone, even when there is naught but evil there."

It was only the truth, but I still felt wrong in saying it. Before the Queen could speak again, I hurried on. "Sophia's gift is the Sight, of course, or at least the promise of the Sight. Her flaw is her lack of confidence." I blinked at that, surprised at my own assessment. "Jane knows what it is to take a man's life without remorse, and it has turned her heart to stone." My words sounded curiously sad to my own ears. "And that is both her gift and her curse."

Time seemed to hold its breath as we stood there, and I saw my fellow maids line up before me in my mind's eye: Sophia and Anna, Beatrice and Jane. The Seer and the Scholar, the Belle and the Blade.

And as for me? I had a nickname too, of course. As the Maid whose job it was to ferret out secrets, I'd received my nickname the very first day I'd arrived, when the others had not realized I could hear them whispering. Now they didn't even bother to hide it from me. My esteemed partners in the Queen's service called me . . .

The Rat. And I had just proven their case.

But what should I care? They'd done nothing to help me, either.

Other than Anna, of course, who'd tried to help me with naming herbs, and who *would* gladly teach me to read, if only I could admit more fully that I needed help. . . . And Jane, whose words before she'd bludgeoned me had at least given me hope. . . . And Sophia, who'd truly seemed distraught even as she'd identified me to the Queen's guard.

Of course, Beatrice deserved my harsh words without sanction. But then, Beatrice cared even less for me than I did for her.

The Queen's next words jolted me back to attention. "And you, Meg? Do you know your greatest skill?"

I opened my mouth to speak, but the Queen raised her hand, effectively silencing me.

"No." She shook her head. "We cannot assess ourselves as easily as we might think, so I will tell *you* the answer. Your best skill is not your thieving, though you consider it so, or even your stealth. It's your ability to play whatever role you must, for however long you must, to live a life of secrets and lies." She grimaced. "I know that skill very well. It serves me more faithfully with each passing year."

Then she flicked a sharp glance at me. "But unlike me, Meg, you have not learned to master those roles and rise above them. To know that they are *roles* alone. Your flaw is that you have spent so long being who you are not that you have no idea who you are." She shook her head, her judgment swift and complete. "And until you do know who you really are, you will *always* be someone else's servant."

That isn't true! The words sprang hotly to my lips, but I knew better than to give them voice. *I know myself, of course I know myself. I am seventeen years old. How could I* not *know myself? You are completely wrong,* I wanted to say, right to her face. *Completely.*

"Thank you, Your Grace," I said instead, my voice as flat as the Thames in full summer. "I will think carefully on your words."

She nodded, taking my agreement as her due. "Now," she said, glancing back to where Cecil stood in the middle of the Privy Garden. "We do not have much time, so I will be plain. Sir William believes I am telling you about your assignment for this evening, and to give truth to that lie, here it is: Tonight we will dine in the Presence Chamber, and a ball shall follow to honor our guests. There will be a new young courtier with the Spanish delegation, whose conversation we wish to know. Rafe Luis Medina, the Count de Martine. I am told he is attending as a nobleman and a flatterer, but I suspect he is something more—possibly an agent of King Philip, possibly an agent of the pope. He will be dining with Ambassador de Feria as they prepare for the rest of the Spanish delegation to arrive. You are to listen to their conversation and report it."

She stretched out her fingers then, studying them with impressive interest. "You have been chosen for this assignment because with your acting skills, you can comport yourself like an established lady of the court, yet you are unknown to the delegation." Now she flipped her hands over and regarded her palms. "Further, if Cecil is to be credited, your recall is exact, even if you don't understand at all what you are hearing. Is this so?"

Cecil! Annoyance rippled through me as I recalled all those days of translations, the endless books and languages. The old goat had known all along, and had still made me stumble through the lessons until I'd relied on my memory to save me. He'd been testing me from the first moment.

The Queen was waiting for a response, and I nodded hastily. "Of course, Your Gra—ma'am," I said, remembering the next stage of honorifics in a conversation as long as ours.

She smiled faintly, and while I was certain she had to be bored with her hands by now, she continued to observe them with great solemnity. "Good. But now I will give you a second order to follow, one that is between us alone. A secret order. And one only you can complete."

Yes. My nerves tightened in anticipation, but I kept my voice steady. "Yes, ma'am," I said.

The Queen raised one of her hands to fuss delicately with her crown, and finally, I understood. She was hiding her mouth, ensuring that her words could not be deciphered by prying eyes.

"Look down at your hands," she directed, and then continued once I did. "You have noticed, without question, the distractions of the court these past months," she said. "The outbursts among the courtiers over some secret revealed or another, the petty thievery, and all of that."

I nodded, biting my lip. In truth, it had been great fun to witness the frequent disruptions, to realize the court was not just made up of perfect little puppets. *And if I'd contributed to a few baubles being temporarily misplaced, well . . .*

The Queen's next words caught me up short. "The Crown is under siege, Meg. From those who wish to see me fail."

I froze, still staring at my hands. "Your Grace?"

"These disturbances to the court began when I formally rejected King Philip's marriage proposal, and not a moment before." She paused, pursing her lips, and I attempted a sage nod. I knew the history well enough by now.

King Philip of Spain had been married to Elizabeth's half sister Mary, the former Queen of England. The two women had not been friends. For one, Elizabeth was Protestant, and Mary had been Catholic. For another, their father, King Henry VIII, had divorced Mary's mother so he could wed Elizabeth's mother. The fact that Henry had gone on to *behead* Elizabeth's mother, so he could marry his third wife, hadn't seemed to mollify anyone.

But the third and perhaps most damning reason for the two royal sisters' enmity was this: The devoutly Catholic Queen Mary had been very ill. She'd feared she would die before having the one thing that could keep the Protestant Elizabeth off the throne forever—a baby. All of the Catholics in Christendom had prayed for Mary to conceive, but it was not to be. Queen Mary had died childless, leaving the throne to Elizabeth.

The staunchly Catholic King Philip had immediately proposed marriage to the new Queen, which had made perfect sense to everyone . . . except the new Queen. Instead, Elizabeth had ascended to the throne alone, had declared Protestantism the official religion of the land, and had dashed the hopes of Catholics everywhere.

"First the disturbances were benign enough," the Queen now said bitterly. "The ladies' sodden gowns, the accursed rats. Soured milk in the evening's ale. But it has gotten so much worse. Royal missives finding their way into the wrong hands. Brutal attacks on members of the court. The burning of Protestant vestments in the Lower Ward. It is not to be borne."

I looked up sharply. "Brutal attacks?"

The Queen ignored me, her words dry and stony. "If I were a young and callow girl, I might think that I could not manage my own court. That I have need of a husband to help me rule. Such a course would be the safer choice, I am told; such a course would please the people."

She turned to me then, her eyes hard. "However, I am neither young nor callow, and the people need only a *strong* monarch to rule them, not a male one. And I need no one but myself to rule."

"Of course you don't," I breathed. I may as well have not been there, for all the notice she paid to my defense of her Queenship.

"As an actress, you are a trained deceiver," she stated instead.

This was starting to not sound very good. "That is correct, ma'am."

"And you can discern the lie on another's lips, I wager?"

I began to find my own fingers fascinating again. "Yes, ma'am."

"And you have no fast friends among the court."

I winced. "No, ma'am." My fellow maids were not my enemies. But no one could truly call them my friends.

"I thought not. Starting tonight, then, you will watch the Spanish delegation for Cecil," the Queen commanded. "And you will watch the whole of the court for me. If you find the cause of the disturbances, you are to follow it to its core and root it out, quickly, quietly, and completely. And then report the transgressors to me, and me alone. Do you understand?"

She waited until I'd nodded. "Do not tell Cecil of this," she said. "Nor anyone else." Her words were clipped. Certain. And I felt a chill roll down my spine. "Start by watching the women of the court. You will find, however, that any trail that begins with them will ultimately lead to a man." She sighed. "It is always thus."

My ears pricked at that. "Is there any one man you believe is a particular threat?" I asked. The words "brutal attacks" kept swirling through my thoughts. *Brutal attacks.*

A moment passed, then a second. I swallowed, finally

daring another glance at the Queen. And what I saw . . . shocked me.

In that moment, in the full blush of youth and strength, Queen Elizabeth Regnant looked as old as my grandfather had lying upon his deathbed. Weariness had drifted over her face like a pale sheet, and her eyes glittered with dark knowledge I could not hope to understand. She placed her hand on my shoulder, as if to sear her royal decree into me. "All men are a threat to women, Meg, no matter if she is maid or monarch," she said. "Especially those men we most want to trust. Don't ever forget that."

And just that quickly the moment passed, and she lifted her hand away. I felt the weight of sovereign command lift with it. Then the Queen turned, and our audience was at an end.

I don't know how I made it back to my group waiting at the garden's edge. The rest of the Queen's maids of honor and ladies-in-waiting had flooded the garden by then, a virtual sea of linen and lace rustling in the morning breeze. The Queen had set up court again near the central fountain, but I'd had enough of her company to last me a month.

I drew up next to Beatrice and Anna, feeling suddenly out of place standing beside them. Unbidden, the beginning of a couplet sprang to mind: *Two maids of quality, one but a thief.*

"Well?" Beatrice demanded, tossing her blond curls. "What is it the Queen thinks a rat can do that better-trained spies cannot? Or have they asked you to pick de Feria's pocket?"

Jane had decided to join the rest of us too, her interest plain. Sophia, her eyes luminous with distress, drew in close to Jane. The two of them made an even odder pairing, and the couplet completed itself: *One maid of spirit, the other of grief.*

Shaking myself to attention, I sectioned off the Queen's orders neatly in my mind. "No," I said. "I'm to report on a conversation between the Spanish ambassador and one of his men. Nothing more."

"You?" Beatrice's laugh laced the syllable with pretty disdain. "Why you?"

It was Anna who replied. "Meg has not circulated through the court," she said, as if it were obvious. "She can act like a lady of court, with de Feria not yet realizing her station. He may be freer with his words around her."

Jane nodded, even as Beatrice rolled her eyes.

"But even after three months of training, Meg can barely speak Spanish," Beatrice snipped. "Heavens, what am I saying? She can barely speak English."

I shrugged. "So you can look forward to my failure."

"But they have no *reason* to give you the honor of their trust," Beatrice said, pouting, clearly not willing to let it go. Then her eyes went crafty and narrow. "Or maybe they've chosen you for this fool's game precisely *because* they don't trust you. They trusted Marie, after all, and look what that got them."

My brows shot up. That was a new name. "Marie?"

"Beatrice," Jane said at the same time, the word a quick rebuke.

"Who is Marie?" I asked again, looking around the group. To my knowledge there were only the five of us who were spies. *Brutal attacks*, the breeze seemed to whisper, and I tried to shrug the words off.

Beatrice sneered at me, ignoring Jane's quelling hand on her sleeve. "So Sir William told the Queen you were ready to serve, and the Queen gave you an assignment, yet they haven't told you yet about poor Marie?" She tsked in false dismay. "You'd think that would be the first item to share, given you were brought to court to *replace* the girl not a fortnight after the scandal."

"It is forbidden to discuss this," Jane warned, glancing around.

Anna hugged her arms to herself, rocking slightly. "Forbidden!" she agreed.

"I don't know anything about a scandal, or this Marie," I said, staring at Beatrice. "I was brought here because—"

"Oh, please," Beatrice scoffed. "Tell me you are not that stupid. Did you really believe that all of us have been here since the Queen's coronation and then, for no reason at all, she decided to add *you*? That your skills as an actress and cutpurse were so *amazing* that she couldn't have found a dozen more like you in the five months before she stumbled across your little acting troupe?"

"But I . . ." My words trailed off as I was struck by the accuracy of Beatrice's words. Of course I was not the only thief in London. So why had I been chosen?

Beatrice's smile was cold. "That's *right*, Meg," she said with exaggerated patience. "There must have been *somebody* in your position before you, don't you think? And whyever would we be forbidden to speak of her, unless she had done something terribly wrong?"

"Beatrice!" Jane's voice was hard. "You go too far."

Beatrice shrugged. "Either you tell her or I will."

A long, terrible moment of silence stretched between them. Then Jane spoke at last. "There was another of our number, Meg, before you," she said without looking at me, her voice like chipped stone. "Marie Claire could ingratiate herself into any group, and gain information from them. She was known as the Queen's ears before Beatrice usurped that role."

"She was a thief, too." Beatrice sniffed. "Not that she ever stole anything of value."

I stared at Beatrice, then Jane. "What happened to her?"

Jane grimaced. "She died."

"She got herself *murdered*." Beatrice's gaze, as cold as a snake's, flicked from me to Jane, then back again. "She'd—"

"That's enough, Beatrice," Jane said.

"But she was *attacked*. Her ears—her eyes—"

Jane turned sharply toward Beatrice, lifting her hand in warning. "Say one more word, Beatrice. Just one, and you will regret it. You will not speak ill of the wrongfully dead."

Jane's tone was lifeless, but her body was vibrating with dark energy, and I felt a cold certainty slide through me. No one knew how many men Jane had attacked that day in North Wales; no one knew precisely what had happened. But I no longer doubted that she'd done something terrible to them. And permanent.

"Tell me what happened to Marie!" I protested now, looking from one to the other of them, desperate for the full story. *What about her ears—her eyes?* my mind demanded. *Brutal attacks!* came the response.

Jane turned her glare from Beatrice to me. "You don't

need to know the details now. Just keep your wits about you tonight, and try not to do anything stupid."

The mother of the maids called us all to attention from across the garden, just as Beatrice scoffed, "Well, *that's* going to be an impossibility for Meg."

And for the first time since I'd been brought to the Queen's court, I agreed with Beatrice completely.

CHAPTER SIX

The corridors that led us to the Presence Chamber were lit up like full day, and I clung to the back of the Queen's retinue. I'd been to the Presence Chamber before, as had all her ladies, but as a maid of fairly modest (which is to say no) standing, I'd never been asked to *do* anything when I'd been called to the chamber, merely to look presentable. Which inevitably involved yet more uncomfortable clothing than any one person should ever be forced to wear.

The attire for all of the Queen's maids this afternoon was stiff white gowns with modest square-cut necklines and miniature neck ruffs that were apparently meant to mimic the Queen's more elaborate court ensemble, only I suspected ours were made with far inferior cloth. These torture devices had been visited upon us as we'd been leaving our chambers—and thus we'd had no time to alter them. It was the height of summer! As pretty as the ruffs looked against bare skin, they would become unbearable in the heat and closeness of a crowded Presence Chamber. I tugged at mine, hard, and felt the lace begin to stretch. I noticed Jane tugging at hers, too, and I hung back with her.

Jane eyed me with grim tolerance as we processed through the corridors to the Presence Chamber, two long lines of girls rendered silent by our mass discomfort. "What do you want of me, Rat?" she asked. Her fingers moved swiftly beneath the hard planes of her jaw, loosening her ruff a bit more every time we passed through shadows.

"Breath, for one," I said, ignoring the insult of my nickname—I'd earned it, after all. "And I want you to tell me about Marie."

Jane's mouth tightened, but she stopped, dropping us both out of line. "Lift your chin up and away." She narrowed her eyes at me even while she deftly pulled at the fine laces of my ruff. Her hands smelled of honeysuckle, heather, and sunlight, reminding me of open fields. "I'm telling you this not because you've asked, but because you need to know. For your own safety. But you didn't hear it from me."

"Agreed." I would have agreed to anything at that point, as long as she kept loosening my ruff.

"Marie Claire was the first spy chosen for our group. She considered herself above us before we ever set foot in the classroom. Her role as our chief ears allowed Marie access to every courtier in the castle, and we were at Whitehall then. With the Queen coming to power, there were too many courtiers to count. Marie did her job well. Soon she began slipping away at all hours of the day and night, on her 'missions,' as she called them. She didn't share them with us, of course, but went straight to Walsingham."

"Walsingham?" The Queen's spymaster, Sir Francis Walsingham, was a man I'd heard of too much, and seen too little. Whispers of his ruthlessness swirled about him like smoke in a smithy, black and foul. I put that thought away. "When did she die?"

"April. It was after the Saint George's Day ball, sometime after midnight but before dawn. That morning, there I was coming up over the seawall from the Thames, and I saw her straight away, crumpled in her finest gown. She'd been killed by a professional. By someone who'd known what she was."

"By a professional?" I frowned at her. "How can you be certain?"

Jane shook her head. "This was more than a jealous suitor, Rat. Marie's clothes were torn, sliced to ribbons in places. As if her attacker thought she'd hidden something in her pleats." I stiffened at that, thinking of my own picklocks and book, now carefully hidden away in our chambers, no longer sewn into my clothes. "But more to the point," Jane continued, "both of Marie's ears had been cut off." She touched a fingertip to my own ear. "And her tongue as well."

I gasped. "Her tongue?"

But Jane wasn't finished. Her voice had taken on that curious flat tone again, and I steeled myself against her words. "Her tongue. And her eyes were nothing but empty sockets, completely hollowed out. It was the most gruesome thing I'd ever seen, and I've seen my share. There was blood all down her neck, and on the collar of her gown." She frowned. "Now here you are, Elizabeth's newest maid. Her newest ears. Be careful to keep yours."

She pushed me forward then, seeming suddenly angry. "They're waiting for you."

I could only lift my own skirts and hasten forward, my mind churning, as the maids wound their way into the Queen's

Presence Chamber. Ears, tongue, and eyes. Everything a spy used in the course of any assignment.

Everything that had been taken from maid Marie.

What was going on here? What secrets were hiding from me in these castle walls?

I was scarcely in place before Cecil glanced back to make sure we'd arrived. We'd all been given assignments by then. I was supposed to watch the ambassador and Count de Martine, but each of the girls in our band had similar tasks for the ball—to witness conversations and report. Not to do anything about the information we learned, of course. Not to draw conclusions and act upon those conclusions. Just to watch, memorize, and report. What had Marie seen that had ended her life so abruptly?

"Don Gomez Suarez de Figueroa, le Conte de Feria," the Queen's steward proclaimed. And the procession of courtiers began.

Even though the Queen made no secret of her disdain for the Spanish ambassador, as the highest-ranking foreigner in the procession, the much-maligned de Feria mounted the steps first and swooped a deep bow to her. The ambassador's doublet, trunk hose, and cloak were black, his ruff simple, his belt an understated silver chain. I'd seen the Count de Feria before, of course, though never this close. He seemed practical and prudent, and looked far older than the twenty-five years I knew him to be. As much as Anna and Beatrice gossiped about his dreary temperament, he did not appear to me a bad sort, if a bit disapproving. He did strike me as shrewd. I'd always tried to stay well away from him.

But I could no longer stay away from de Feria or his fellow Spaniards, I thought grimly. I was, for good or ill, officially now the Queen's eyes and ears. The keeper of her secrets.

After de Feria another Spanish courtier was announced, a laughing rogue dressed in peacock blue, with rich caramel-colored hair, golden eyes, an easy smile, and a smooth unshaven face. I noted more than a few sighs among the ladies-in-waiting as Nicolas Ortiz made his bows, and I fought to keep from rolling my eyes. Whenever there was a new man in the court, half the women fell in love. My lips twisted into a small smile. How Master James would have laughed to see them swoon.

I felt a strange tightness in my chest as I realized I hadn't thought of Master James—or the troupe—at all that day. Not with the excitement of my first assignment and the horror of Marie Claire's killing. Was I forgetting them?

Never! I thought, hastily calling up image after image. Fat, jolly Meredith, our finest cook; glowering Matthias, her husband. Geoffrey, the best bard in all of England; wool-headed Tommy Farrow, still a little boy. But three months was a long time in a little boy's life. How much had he changed?

Have they forgotten me?

After what seemed like hours, Ortiz finally moved to the side, and the steward spoke once more. I attended him half-heartedly, then realized I recognized the name. "Rafe Luis Medina," he'd proclaimed. "Le Conte de Martine." I stood on tiptoes to get a better look at my mark.

Then I blinked. Hard. *Sweet mother of angels. They have to be jesting.*

Rafe Luis Medina was . . . astonishing.

My heart seemed to stop working quite right as the young count approached the dais with the poise of a monarch himself, then spoke in a rich, flowing dialect while bowing elegantly to the Queen. The Count de Martine was tall, more than six feet, and his thick dark hair fell over his forehead in a graceful swale. His eyes were a vivid blue, the color of sunshine on water. His smile was quick and broad, his skin as golden bronze as a sailor's. He carried himself with strength and poise, nearly but not quite overwhelming the dark seniority of de Feria—and completely eclipsing Ortiz.

Once his initial introduction was complete, the Count de Martine stood at his ease, and I was struck all over again by his beauty—and, I realized, by his *youth*. Surely he was not even twenty years old, though experience gleamed in his flashing eyes, and practiced effortlessness in his smile. He spoke again, responding to the Queen, and his words danced upon the very air like a silken sail.

I forced myself to pay attention to the details, which was no hardship. First, de Martine's clothes were nothing short of exquisite. His deep crimson cloak was thrown back from his shoulders, revealing a doublet of stiff cloth-of-gold, sewn with pearls at the waist and the wrists. Rubies sparkled on his fingers, and matched the color of his trunks and hose. His hose, in fact, looked like they'd been spun of the finest thread, and they showed his well-muscled legs to such perfection, I could not avoid staring. The young lord had to be rich. Richer than de Feria, certainly, whose somber disapproval even now bracketed his stern lips as he watched his own countryman preen before the English Queen.

Who was this dashing count, so bold as to murmur endearments to the Queen in front of us all? I didn't know all of what he was saying—he slipped through languages in a blur, flattering the Queen's acknowledged penchant for translation. But his manner caused Beatrice to hum with calculating interest beside me, no doubt plotting how to use the young man to her advantage. And his words caused Anna to emit tiny gasps of surprise; brief, strangled puffs of air.

I frowned, considering that. Maybe Anna should be the one to follow Rafe, since she would at least understand him. Then I glanced back at the beautiful and bold young count.

No, I decided. I'd just have to work harder to learn Spanish.

The Queen responded regally to yet another sally by Rafe de Martine, but she, too, was clearly charmed by the young man. Who wouldn't be?

A soldier or a courtier or a sailor was he? *All of these and more,* I thought. And even at the end of his presentation, the count did not disappoint. He did not turn from the Queen but backed nimbly away as tradition demanded only of Englishmen, and he did it all with a flourish, bowing to Her Grace with flamboyant style.

Her eyes now merry, the Queen bowed slightly to him in return before turning to her next sycophant. The Count de Martine had won the Queen's favor with little more than a smile. What secrets would that same smile reveal to me tonight?

I narrowed my eyes at the flattering Spaniard, as if to pry out his thoughts, and in just that moment he turned his head, and our gazes met.

God's breath.

I almost staggered back, the force of our sudden connection like a physical blow. My heart seized in my chest, my eyes flared wide, and my feet were rooted to the rush-strewn floor. It seemed as if time itself held still for a moment, waiting in frozen anticipation alongside me. Had he caught me staring? Did he know my heart was about to burst?

Then there, across the crowded Presence Chamber, the impossibly gorgeous Rafe Luis Medina, Count de Martine did the unthinkable: He raised his brows at me, tilted his head . . . and smiled.

Finally remembering myself and my role, I smiled archly back.

This was going to be some assignment.

CHAPTER SEVEN

Nobody threw a party quite like the Queen of England.

The night's revel was a glittering triumph, with music, dancing, and huge trenchers of food. I turned one way, then the other, surrounded on all sides by laughing women and sharp-eyed men, every sense assaulted.

And if the crush of bodies hadn't been enough to make me dizzy—the overwhelming scent of musk and sweat and perfumes—I needed only to consider the *food* of this feast to be pushed to the brink of a swoon.

Thinking of how we'd scraped and struggled to put food on our acting troupe's table, I watched course after course pass me by—pickled eggs and steaming quail, sweet rolls and meat pies, fish stew and sugar tarts—all with plenty of ale to loosen tongues. I'd heard nothing yet of import, but I'd seen enough food to make me queasy.

What were the Golden Rose players eating this night? And did they know the price I'd paid for them to laugh and dance and talk, sharing their flagons of ale? Their evening would be mild as well, I thought, but with the warmth of a bonfire, not of too many people in too close a hall. The troupe would be on the banks of the Thames, fireflies dancing just out of reach of the smallest children, a sweet song wafting over the water from one of the bards. Winters could be hard for the troupe, but in the summertime, with fruit hanging low on the trees and crops in the fields and gold in every merchant's pockets—summer was a magical time, of fresh air and simple joy.

Here the air was stifling, and joy was just another mask worn by the swirling, whirling nobility.

And then there was the sheer *noise* of the ball. Gold and pewter clinked and crashed, music thundered, and voices rose and fell in ever widening arcs as the ale and wine began to tip from urns and cups. The laughter was the most shocking of all, as it sprang up from nowhere in sharp, percussive bursts, at constant odds with the melodies churning forth from the sweating musicians. Only when the Queen was dancing did everyone fall silent, and this evening the Queen was in the mood to watch, not to partake. But she smiled easily and well, and her manner drove the entertainment to higher and higher levels of frolic. Women in their bold satin gowns, with plunging necklines and wasp-waisted bodices, careened into the arms of their male companions, who spun them around with laughing ease. The noblemen, for their part, looked like hunters prowling through a stand of excitable rabbits, picking one, then the other just for the sheer sport of it. The heat of the night flushed through the hall, and hands strayed to waists, to breasts, to cheeks, all in the crush of too many people wedged into too tight a space. It was . . . just too much.

"Oh, pish, Rat, you look a fright."

I jumped at Beatrice's sudden, too-close words, my stomach

slewing sideways. I had not heard her creeping up. I truly *hated* surprises.

She looked satisfied at my reaction. "So, have you seen aught of de Feria yet?" she prodded, as she and Anna took their places to watch the dancing.

"No," I said. I didn't bother to remind her that it was de Feria's new courtier that I was to focus on, not the thin, dour ambassador himself. Count de Feria was almost an afterthought anyway, as he'd announced today that a new ambassador was on his way from Spain to replace him. The new emissary could come none too quickly, I thought. We'd all grown tired of de Feria's pale scowl.

Beside Beatrice, Anna was pink with excitement, and up on her toes in a charming white satin gown. She did not carry a puzzle box with her for once. To Anna, this entire ball must have seemed a puzzle.

Jane, of course, was nowhere to be found; but then, Jane was good at hiding. Doubtless she was in the crowd somewhere, staring down some unfortunate soul.

Only Sophia had managed to escape the ball. She claimed illness, but I knew the truth.

Poor, distraught Sophia. She feared that her betrothed, Lord Brighton, would be here tonight, his dark eyes watchful, his lined face fervent. I shuddered. She didn't fear Lord Brighton himself, she insisted. She feared what she sensed *around* him. As if the man were ringed with danger. I allowed her the lie tonight to cover her fears. After all, while the eccentric Lord Brighton seemed to give no indication of wanting to marry her soon, Sophia was only fifteen, and her freedom was already lost.

"Isn't it a sight," bubbled Anna, catching our attention now with her excitement. "I've never seen so many dancers, not even on Saint George's Day, and that's the truth. What's brought them all out, I wonder? The new Spaniards in our midst? The good crops in the fields?"

Beatrice actually smiled at Anna in genuine warmth, and I caught my breath at the sight. Beatrice was truly a lovely girl when she wanted to be.

Tonight she was dressed in a whisper-light gown of palest sapphire, which set off her blue eyes and soft pink cheeks to perfection. Certainly it was more eye-catching than my own dull grey. I pressed my fingers against my stiff bodice, my fingers brushing against my grandfather's book and picklocks, which I'd taken out of their hiding place and sewn into my shift for luck. They did nothing to improve my mood, however. Unlike Beatrice, I had no desire to catch the roaming eyes of the courtiers, and my role tonight demanded that I blend in with the stones.

But seeing Beatrice now, so slim and straight, her fair blond hair crowned by tiny roses and her ruff a mere puff of silk, I felt like a swineherd beside a princess. As I watched, she parted her lips in a calculating smile. "Lady Amelia seems quite taken with one of the Spaniards, I see," she said.

I glanced toward the dancers to see the lady-in-waiting in question being twirled across the floor by Nicolas Ortiz. That worthy Spaniard was dressed in a doublet and trunk hose of rich cream silk, the color making the most of his honeyed good looks.

"The Queen will not mind?" chirped Anna, ever aware of our sovereign's dictates on the actions of her attendants.

"She's probably asked Lady Amelia to put on a show, though perhaps the woman's choice in partners is questionable. Ortiz is only a minor noble, but he clearly outshines Amelia. And she's nearly to her twenty-fifth year," Beatrice said, and sniffed. "It's well past time she were wed."

I frowned at Lady Amelia, lovely with her white-blond hair piled high upon her head, her ornately embroidered white satin gown wreathing her in wealth. She didn't look like any old crone I'd ever seen. Why should she be so quickly consigned to marriage?

"Lord Cavanaugh is watching *you*, I see," Anna said beside us, but Beatrice didn't turn.

"He is?" she asked, and the faintest blush crept up her cheeks, her eyelids dropping in an artful display of modesty.

I looked between Beatrice and Anna, utterly confused. "Who is Lord Cavanaugh?" Beatrice's entire existence involved men staring at her. What made this pair of eyes special?

"Lord Cavanaugh, Marquess of Westmoreland," Anna informed me in an impatient whisper. "You must start paying more attention, Meg. He'll be a duke, you know. 'Tis said he wants to marry Beatrice, and oh, wouldn't that be a coup. He's the richest man in court, and the most powerful. 'Twill be a wondrous match. The Queen is considering his suit as we speak, or so they say."

"Really?" I stood on my tiptoes for a look at the future duke. He was tall and as thin as a whip, with sharp-bladed features and a shock of black glossy hair. He wore his rich emerald-green doublet and trunk hose with flair, I'd give him that. And even from this distance, I could see that he moved like a rich man. Instinctively I looked for his money pouch, then caught myself.

Sometimes being a royal spy was truly a chore.

"Oh, Anna, you overstep," Beatrice said coyly, in that way she had when she didn't at all mean what she was saying. "Lord Cavanaugh is merely being kind."

"Well, his kindness knows no bounds, then." Anna giggled.

But Beatrice's attention was already wandering. "In truth, the Spaniards are outshining most everyone in the room, except my Lord Cavanaugh, of course," she murmured, her gaze level across the floor. "Look there, in fact. Now, that's a worthy competitor for our attention, wouldn't you say?"

I blinked at Beatrice, marveling anew at the flush in her cheeks, the sparkle in her eyes. She was undeniably beautiful, I thought again as I turned to follow her gaze—

And then I saw him, too.

The bold, exquisite Rafe Luis Medina, Count de Martinc, stood casually beside the thin and disapproving Spanish ambassador. Rafe carried a goblet of hammered gold in one of his long-fingered hands, his grin broad, his manner relaxed. As we watched, he leaned back his head and laughed heartily, the gesture so full of life and vigor that even the Count de Feria twitched a smile. Beatrice fanned herself, without artifice. I felt strangely warm myself.

"I'm going to dance with him," Beatrice declared.

"Beatrice!" Anna blinked rapidly. "You dare not ask him! Lord Cavanaugh is watching."

"Silly girl, I won't do the asking. And it's precisely *because* Lord Cavanaugh is watching that I will indeed dance. So attend and learn." Beatrice smiled, and her gaze darted up to meet mine, a challenge. "You too, Rat. Though I cannot imagine you'll have need for lessons such as these; beauty and grace will never be your stock-in-trade."

And she was off, sailing through the crowd like a swan. Self-consciously I straightened my own neck, squared my shoulders, and lifted my chin in mimicry of Beatrice's studied elegance. I watched her pause and engage in what looked like completely spontaneous conversation with Lord Radcliffe, then turn the heads of four young courtiers, her shimmering form in Rafe's direct line of sight.

The music changed at exactly that moment, and the young count looked up and saw her. In another breath he'd neatly excused himself from his conversation with de Feria. He then took no more than a half dozen steps and was at Beatrice's side. He drew her away from her crowd of admirers, curling her arm into his as if she were his alone. Then he turned her toward him gracefully, the intimacy of a kiss upon the air between them, though they were barely even touching.

It was nothing short of masterful.

"Oh, my, then," Anna sighed deeply, and I nodded, also impressed. But when I opened my mouth to agree, Anna continued, "Did you ever see such a godly man?"

That stopped me, and I glanced her way. Of all the terms I'd use to describe the young Count de Martine, "godly" wasn't one of them.

But Anna wasn't looking at Beatrice and her conquest—or even at Lord Cavanaugh, who was now watching the proceedings with a decided frown on his aristocratic face. Instead she was gazing at a young man in long robes who stood against the far wall of the hall with other men of the cloth, his strawberry blond hair tousled around his ears, his eyes wide and inquisitive. He twisted his floppy hat in his hands, and his attention seemed pulled in a hundred different directions. He was—attractive, I supposed. But . . . "He's a priest, isn't he?"

"The son of a vicar, of the Church of England," Anna corrected me. "And the finest of scholars."

I goggled at her. "You know him?"

"Oh, aye," she sighed, her eyes as soft and wide as a doe's. "I've known Christopher Riley since he was eight years old. And have dreamed of him as my husband since I was twelve."

What was with this talk of husbands? Did these girls not understand that marriage was not the answer to every question in their heads?

Suddenly desperate to serve my purpose here, I shifted this way and that, finally locating the Count de Feria again. By now, ale flowed from vast pitchers into mugs and goblets; even the ambassador had finally indulged. I watched him stare almost forlornly at the swirling ballroom as the Count de Martine and Beatrice danced. De Feria had been married just this past year, I'd learned, and his wife was now nearly full-term with child. He would be impatient with the Queen and her revelry, eager to return to the Continent as soon as the new ambassador was in place. Was this what his conversation would hold tonight?

After bidding good-bye to Anna, I moved through the crowd, flushing with embarrassment at the ever more personal conversations that reached my ears. To steady my nerves as I walked, I drew out my short blade. I cut a loose brooch from one courtier's sleeve and slid a hairpin free of a lady's elaborate wig, then slipped another woman's jewel-studded cuff off her wrist as she pushed by me, intent on her laughing quarry. As I tucked my plunder into the wide band of cloth at my waist, I caught sight of Jane.

She was striding away from a side table, a flagon of wine in her hand, with three leering, hungry-eyed men staring after her. *Oh, no.* The last time Jane had been bothered by the men of the court, she'd practiced her poisoning skills on their fish pies. I eyed the flagon she now held snugly, then looked back at the men quaffing their drinks from newly filled goblets. This would not go well for them, I was sure.

By the time I reached the far end of the hall, de Feria was leaning up against a thick stone column. I crept up alongside it as near to him as I dared. I felt his glance, so I stood on tiptoe as if to watch the dance progress, a young noblewoman at her first ball, eager for love.

De Feria huffed a short, disgusted breath, and I hid my smile. Let him think me a fool. As I watched the dancers, I found my eyes drawn again and again not to Beatrice and Rafe, but to the Spaniard Nicolas Ortiz and Lady Amelia, laughing and intimate in their too-close embrace, the courtier as dark and intense as she was fair and earnest. I blinked. Was Lady Amelia in love as well—and with a Spaniard? Had everyone lost their minds?

The musicians wound down their dance to silence at last, and Rafe de Martine elegantly took his leave of Beatrice. She nodded to him with sophisticated reserve, too smart to swoon, and his smile broadened further. He seemed to be a young man who enjoyed life with great fervor, and he fairly bounded over to the Count de Feria, taking up his post beside him.

"¿Haya Terminado de bailar?" de Feria inquired, and their conversation launched into an animated debate. My vantage point gave me an excellent view of them both. I frankly had no idea what they were saying—my Spanish was as bad as Beatrice suspected—but after the young count's easy reply, de Feria seemed to respond with anger and frustration.

Their words flowed like music, and I stared at them discreetly, my heart in my throat for the whole of the quarter hour that they spoke. Fortunately, though they tried to converse quietly, they were still a bit flamboyant, giving me visual cues to attach to words so that I could memorize their discussion as easily as a dance. I sensed their conversation was ending as the young count lapsed into smooth and placating words, but I remained in place, gawking at the dancers over the heads of the assembled crowd.

At long last, de Feria and Count de Martine took their leave of each other, and I felt my shoulders relax. I held my position another ten minutes until I felt Jane move up beside me. Of all the maids, her walk was the most distinctive, no matter her gown. Her gait was long-limbed and fast, but with a strange efficiency that seemed the exact opposite of Beatrice's elegant extension. Jane always seemed to be prepared to leap from a crouch, even when she was standing still.

She stood surveying the dancing couples alongside me for a moment before she spoke. "You cannot find this as fascinating as you appear to," she said.

"I don't." I shook my head. "Has de Feria left the room?"

"Not yet. He's now talking with Cecil and Walsingham."

"Walsingham?" I half-turned, but Jane's warning hand made me swivel my gaze back to the dance floor. "And Count de Martine?" I asked.

"Charming his way through a gaggle of lords and ladies as we speak. Beatrice is about to eat her own ruff, even with Cavanaugh panting after her. It almost makes the evening worthwhile." I felt Jane's glance upon me. "Did they say anything of import?"

"I couldn't say." I gave her a weak smile. "How well do you know Spanish?"

"Not as well as Anna," Jane admitted. "Should you speak to her before you meet with Cecil to gain an understanding of what you heard? Can you remember all of it?"

"I can remember it, yes," I said. "Still, Beatrice is right. It's foolish for me to eavesdrop on a conversation I cannot understand."

"Foolish like a fox, perhaps," Jane murmured, narrowing her eyes at Cecil. "And the fox shouldn't be the only one to know what the Spaniards are planning. We should know, too."

I hesitated, welcoming her camaraderie but still unsure of my place even after three months in the Queen's service. I could not afford a misstep in my role as spy, not with my troupe hanging in the balance. "But . . . that wasn't part of our orders, Jane. Cecil said nothing about me sharing what I learned."

"Of course he didn't. But he didn't say you couldn't, either. And some secrets are not worth keeping." She looked at me hard. "Marie told us nothing, Rat, and look what that got her, on a night just like this one."

A chill shivered down my back. I swallowed. Nodded. And Jane nodded back. "Wait here," she said.

Within moments she'd returned, dragging a protesting Anna behind her. Jane set the three of us up in a row, her body blocking Anna and me from view. "Now," Jane commanded to me once Anna was in place. "Speak."

I leaned forward and began whispering into Anna's ear.

"You go too fast, you go too fast!" Anna gasped, but then she stilled until I was done. I rocked on my heels and drew in a heavy breath, the words circling back on themselves in my mind, the lines of a play ready to be run again.

Anna looked sick, and Jane prompted her. "Well?" she demanded.

"He . . . the Count de Feria . . . he said terrible things about the Queen," Anna breathed, her voice hollow. She blushed. "He called her—a *whore*."

My eyes went wide, but Jane merely grunted with amusement. "He's a Spaniard. What do you expect him to say? Was there anything of import?"

Anna frowned. "The young Count de Martine is to give de Feria letters—from the pope, he said. He has these letters with him now, but de Feria said no, he would not take them. And de Martine had to convince him to do this 'one last time,' and to pass them along as he normally did."

"Pass them along?" I frowned. Letters from a zealously Catholic pope being sent into the court of a fiercely Protestant queen could only spell danger. "To whom?"

"That part apparently did not need explanation," Anna said. "The ambassador finally agreed, but he still would not take the letters here. He said for Rafe to meet him at the Norman Gate."

"The Norman Gate and not Winchester Tower?" Jane mused. "Then de Martine doesn't plan to flee after he hands off his information. A hundred steps down from Winchester Tower, and you're practically at the Thames. Beatrice will be so relieved."

"Flee?" I asked as I searched the crowd. "How could he leave the castle? Wouldn't he be questioned?"

Jane shook her head. "Not tonight. No one expects anyone to leave a ball so grand, I can assure you."

Anna agreed with a sharp nod. "De Feria said the same thing, that the guard would be lax on the night of a grand revel." She beamed, happy to be in on a secret. "De Feria knows the castle well, it seems."

"The walls of this old wreck are filled with holes," Jane said with disgust. "And the guards don't do a good job filling them."

"There's Cecil!" I warned, as he turned and caught my eye.

Instantly Jane hissed "Get down!" to Anna, who obligingly dropped to a huddled ball, remarkably flexible in her heavy gown.

Jane turned and gave me a blithe smile. "Did he see Anna?" she asked through her teeth, as if we weren't hiding a full-skirted maid behind our own stiff gowns. I stared at Cecil another moment while he stared back at me, and I shook my head uncertainly.

"I don't think so," I said. Cecil scowled with even more disapproval. "But it seems he wants something from me, so I, uh—I'd better go to him."

"Yes, you'd better," Jane said. "But you won't say anything about Anna knowing the Spaniard's conversation, no?"

"Oh, no. You mustn't!" Anna squeaked from behind us.

"Of course I won't," I said, even as Jane ordered Anna to be still.

Then Jane met my gaze, her eyes lit with a grimly satisfied light. "It looks like we have our first secret to keep—but not our last," she said. She smiled tightly. "The Queen's new ears are a lot better, it seems, than those we had before."

She gave me a gentle push toward Cecil. "Be careful, Rat."

CHAPTER EIGHT

I left the brightly lit hall and slipped into the torch-lined corridor that led away from the Presence Chamber. In the sudden silence my ears pounded with sounds from the ball, the laughter, the music, and the swirling conversations. I pressed my hands against the sides of my torturously-tight corset. It was not difficult to act the part of a maid needing to catch her breath; I could have easily crumpled into a big ruffed heap, right there against the wall.

Over and over the words that de Feria and Count de Martine had spoken replayed in my mind, along with Anna's rapid translation. Then came Jane's chilling words about the maid Marie, found with her ears sliced away, on just such a night as this. Her ears had not saved her. Would mine save me?

I came around the corner so quickly that I nearly knocked Cecil down. He lifted his hands hastily to stop me.

"Are you ill?" Cecil asked sharply, and I pulled back, unnerved by the irritation in his tone. He was always so *cross*. Among the Golden Rose players, no one ever berated me. You either succeeded or you starved. There was no emotion attached to it. "Breathe, Miss Fellowes!"

I hadn't realized I'd been holding my breath until it all came out in a rush. Cecil rolled his eyes, and I found myself wringing my hands against my skirts with embarrassment, like a child reprimanded for sneaking an extra meat pie. The blasted old goat had that effect on me.

He knew it, too. "What did you hear?" Cecil asked, his censure plain. "You seemed most inattentive every time I caught sight of you. Did they speak?"

I nodded, not willing to admit how I had felt at dinner, dizzy with disorientation at the laughing, gorging people all around me. "I have to tell you exactly, Sir William. In Spanish."

Cecil shifted with impatience, then understanding lit his eyes. He nodded. "Follow me."

He led me to his official chambers off the Queen's Privy Chamber and lit the candles on the writing desk. He sat down at the desk, lifted a quill, and dipped it in ink. "Begin," he said.

And once again I let the words take over me, rolling through the quiet chamber like music on the wind. I felt the cadences and styles of both men—the harsh and angry de Feria, the wry and amused Count de Martine. It took nearly as long to recite as it had to hear the Spaniards' conversation, but Cecil stopped me only twice, to ensure the inflection I used meant whatever he thought it did.

When I finished, Cecil's manner appeared quite changed, excited even. He put his quill down and stretched his fingers in the candlelight.

"Now that, Meg, is a faithful retelling. Please be aware that I know the difference."

I colored, not sure exactly what he meant, but accepting his comment as equal parts approval and criticism. "Yes, Sir William."

Cecil harrumphed and sat back in his chair. "This is very good," he said, and he slanted me an approving glance.

"May I ask what they said?" I asked quietly, praying I did not sound false. "My . . . Spanish is not yet skilled enough to—"

"Of course it isn't," Cecil said, far too happily. And then to my astonishment he proceeded to *lie* to me about everything except de Feria's mockery of the castle guards and his shocking words about the Queen, and the fact that the two men were to exchange letters. Only, in Cecil's retelling, they were letters from *King Philip of Spain*—not the pope, as Rafe had claimed. Why the lie? The Spanish had no long-standing grudge against England—especially given that King Philip had still harbored hopes of marrying Elizabeth until she'd rejected him scant months earlier. The Catholics and the Protestants, however, were very much in the midst of an unofficial war that had lasted for years, worsening now because a new Protestant Queen had taken the throne of England. Mary Tudor's reign of persecution had been considered by the Catholics to be an act of God. Now Elizabeth's rise to power was an affront to that same God. Whisperings of a Catholic plot to dethrone Elizabeth had started buzzing even before she had been crowned Queen. For the pope to take part in that plot would make a certain deadly sense.

So why was Cecil lying about the origins of the letters? Was it merely to catch me out should I share the tale with others?

I studied Cecil closely, memorizing his face and his eyes as he gave me his completely false accounting of Rafe's and de Feria's conversation. I'd recognize that deceiving look when Cecil lied again, without question. "You may rest assured that the guard will not be slack tonight," he finished, ripe with satisfaction.

I decided to test my newly minted skills at identifying his deceit. "Was the guard slack the night of Marie Claire's death?" I asked.

Cecil paused a moment, the distant sounds of the revel wafting toward us down the long hallway. "What do you know of the maid Marie's death—and who told you?"

"Two ladies were talking at the ball," I said, shrugging. I could lie better than he. "They said she was found lying against a wall on Saint George's Day, after a ball not unlike this. Strangled." *And mutilated.*

"Not strangled, precisely," Cecil said, his tone hard. In this, I knew immediately, he was not deceiving me. "Marie Claire was killed by garrote, a very effective but particularly brutal way to die. You should be familiar with it by now."

I nodded. Garroting was silent and quick, and did not require as much strength as ordinary strangulation. In truth, Marie's attacker could have been a woman, with a weapon like that. But no woman, surely, would disfigure another woman's face so horribly. I shuddered. *Would she?*

"But we're not here to discuss Marie." Cecil sat back in his seat, his attention shifting back to my report. "These letters the young count is carrying could be of import. Rafe Luis Medina is the son of Marquess Juan Carlos and the Marchioness Isabelle. We know that Isabelle spent two years in King Henry's court as an attendant to Catherine of Aragon. She would have made friends here, Spanish sympathizers. Some of the letters could be from King Philip to Isabelle's friends. And they could contain information that would harm the Queen."

But once again, Rafe had said the letters had been from the pope—not the king. Still, I couldn't betray that I knew that. "Surely Isabelle would not have any friends still in the court," I protested.

He tapped the pages. "Not directly, perhaps, but where there is money, there are always friends. And we know nothing of this Count de Martine, other than his parentage and his schooling."

"He is a nobleman."

Cecil snorted. "He is perhaps more than that. Think on it. The Queen has been in power since late fall. Yet suddenly this young man arrives, highly placed in the Spanish delegation. Where did he come from, and why is he suddenly here?"

Unbidden, the image of a maid slumped against the wall flashed across my mind, her face bloody, her gown torn. But Count de Martine had only just arrived from Spain. He could not have had anything to do with Marie Claire's murder.

Could he?

"All courtiers, whether Englishman or foreigner, have the potential to be enemies to the Crown," Cecil said, as if he'd read my thoughts. He hesitated a beat, then faced me square, his eyes now fully on my face.

"You have done well, Miss Fellowes. So well that you will now have another assignment, of utmost secrecy, to be carried out within the fortnight," he said. "You may not share this information with anyone."

I nodded, fully expecting him to reiterate the Queen's command from this morning, to ferret out whoever was behind the disturbances within Windsor Castle, and I was impatient to be gone. I didn't care that the Queen had decided to include Cecil in her plotting after all. That made perfect sense. Instead I thought of the maid Marie, and how her journeys for Cecil and the Queen had been secretive too. And how she was now dead.

"Yes?" I asked. The silence was somehow worse than being bored by the repetition.

Cecil still did not speak, and for a moment I thought that he might have decided against this additional request, that perhaps I had not impressed him with my first assignment after all, and this further charge would be, in his mind, too much.

Well, he could go sip his sorrow with a long spoon. The Queen had already given me the task. I didn't need his approval to serve her. Nevertheless, just for practice, I held myself perfectly still for a moment more, waiting him out. He finally spoke.

"As I said, all courtiers, no matter their country, could be of risk to the Queen," Cecil began again with his customary care. "And not only to the Queen, but to England. We, as the Queen's protection, must serve her even when she might think our service is unnecessary. We cannot fail her, in any hour—especially when she might rather that we did fail. Do you understand?"

I gaped at him. This was *not* what I'd expected him to say.

"When would the Queen ever consider our protection of her to be unnecessary—or want us to fail to defend her?"

The question seemed to pain Cecil, and deep furrows appeared between his brows. His face sank into a scowl. "The Queen is new to her role, and after all the strife and struggle of her early years, she has embraced her royal station with enthusiasm—and all the luxuries and perceived freedoms it affords her."

"As well she should," I protested. I did not like where this was going, not at all. The Queen had made allusions to those who might not consider her fit to rule, but surely Cecil was not one of those ingrates. "She was held prisoner in the Tower, Sir William, when she was only a girl! She was kept under house arrest for months, not knowing her fate. Her life was filled with one prison or another since she was but a babe of three years old. She is entitled to all the luxury and freedoms the Crown brings her. She is our *Queen*."

"And if those freedoms put England herself at risk?" Cecil asked.

He had taken the stance of an instructor now, and I pulled my emotions back, wary. "The Queen would never put England at risk."

"Not intentionally, no—"

"Pray, Sir William, not ever," I said. "It is her entire *life*; her people are her only concern." I found it unnerving to say these words to one who should already know them better than I did.

Cecil's eyes narrowed in the semidarkness. "Then you are in luck. The assignment I am giving you will prove your point masterfully."

There was danger here, and I waited, not wanting to commit myself. Cecil had no idea that the Queen had given me a private commission, of that I was certain. What possible assignment could he have in mind—and would it counter the Queen's own commands? Surely not.

After a moment he went on. "I am concerned that the Queen may be . . . endangering herself with the personal company she keeps," Cecil said heavily. "I would like to be proven wrong in this concern. Accordingly, you will uncover the Queen's most intimate secrets and report—"

"Sir William!" I jerked back, aghast. "You cannot be serious."

My shock seemed to irritate him further. "You will be given access to the Queen's most private conversations to learn what may be learned. I want to know exactly who is with her and when, and what they say—to the word, to the exact word, and not as a general recollection."

"But I could never—"

Cecil's voice was merciless. "You will furthermore complete this assignment once within the next fortnight by being placed in the Queen's bedchamber, and then again as often as I have the need for you to do so—"

"But she will know me, Sir William," I argued, grasping for reason. "She will know I am in her chambers."

"Of course she will know you are there!" Cecil snapped. "You are an *actress*, not a ghost. And as an actress your role is to make sure the Queen trusts you implicitly—that she doesn't suspect for a moment that you are watching her, or that you would ever betray her, no matter what she says or does."

Betray her! How could I ever betray the Queen? She was the one who saved me, when Cecil wanted me locked away without a key!

Again, as if he read my thoughts, Cecil provided the answer. "And if you dare speak a word of this to her, to anyone, I will not waste my time with a public humiliation for your precious Golden Rose." He spoke the name of the troupe with deliberate disdain, as if my friends were beetles beneath his feet. "They will be hung on the gibbets to die as common traitors. All of them." He scowled at me. "Starting with the boy."

"You would not do that!" I gasped, too shocked to couch my words in careful phrasing. Cecil was not a madman. He would not do such a thing—he *could* not do such a thing. He wouldn't!

Cecil leaned forward in his chair, his body tight with purpose. "I would do *anything* for England," he said, his bland words a frightening counterpoint to his intense glare. "The Queen brought you here to serve her, Meg, and serve her you will. But you will serve England, too. Otherwise, you are useless."

I stared at Cecil blindly, but he said nothing further, busying himself instead with the papers on his desk. Silence stretched out before me, a pit of darkness that threatened to swallow me whole. Somehow I managed to nod, to mumble something, and I dropped to a curtsy as my only means to tear my eyes away from Cecil's hard, implacable face.

As I came up again, he was still there, his dark eyes boring into mine as if he could see all the way down to my heart.

"You dare not fail in this, Meg," he said, and there was real menace in his voice. The menace of a man who would care nothing for an actress and a thief, were she to lie crumpled against a low stone wall, her eyes sightless, her dress torn, and her face and neck streaming with blood. The menace of a man who, if I did not follow his orders precisely and do exactly as he said, would simply find another thief to do his bidding. He had been willing to let me rot in the Queen's dungeon when he'd first caught me out as a thief. He was willing to put me back there now if I fell short in this new charge. Or even . . . do something far, far worse.

I turned from him and fled.

CHAPTER NINE

I know I started by walking, with careful measured steps as befitted a maid of honor. But as I turned the corner and realized that Cecil was not giving chase, I allowed my pace to quicken until I was in a full-out run through the castle, desperate to escape the Queen's advisor and his harrowing words.

Spy on the Queen! In her own bedchamber! The thought roiled through me like a sickness, leaving me at turns hot and cold. I needed to get out—needed to think. How could I do this, commit this crime against the Queen? And yet, how could I not? Cecil's orders had been plain. I was here to serve the Crown, and if the Queen was . . . somehow being led astray? By a man she trusted? Then surely . . . I should help her? And did she realize she was in danger? Is that what she had meant by every man being a threat?

My face flamed at the very thought, and I came to a halt quickly in the shadows of the corridor, slapping my hands to my cheeks to cool them. My palms gave little comfort, as wet and clammy as they were. I forced myself to step farther into the murky darkness, pressing up against the paneled wall.

Nervously I passed my hands over my hair, which was fairly standing on end, and tried to loosen the stranglehold of my neck ruff. *Accursed scrap of material!*

With a yank I wrenched the tiny ruff away and balled it up—then just as quickly I smoothed the ruff out again, my fingers trembling at my indiscretion. I would never be able to reattach it, not by myself. But I couldn't lose it either. My clothes were not my own here. Nothing here was my own. I clenched the thin ruff in my fingers. There would be time to reset the fool thing in the morning, if I managed to survive tonight.

I needed to find Jane. She'd been here longer. She would know what to do. Then again, Cecil had forbidden me to speak of my assignment, so I couldn't tell Jane. Or anyone, not if he'd find out. Not even the Queen. *Especially not the Queen.* But Jane—Jane wouldn't say anything, would she? Not about this. Not about—

My thoughts were cut off as a gust of conversation tumbled into the hallway ahead of me.

I froze.

I knew that voice. Knew the rise and fall of the words, the laughing, musical cadence, at once indolent and on edge. And instantly I grasped at a new thread of hope.

Perhaps . . . perhaps if I learned more of what Count de Martine was doing at Windsor Castle, maybe that would distract Cecil from his task of madness. I could not *spy on the Queen*, but I was not *useless*. My ears could still be bent to her service. I could still gather secrets.

I crept forward slowly, along the wall, and the talk grew more distinct but still curiously muffled, as if the young count and his partner were speaking behind their hands. I came to the small, pretty antechamber we called the Blue Room, a sitting area for lords and ladies to refresh themselves, with its newly cut doors opening onto the crumbling North Terrace. I slipped inside and scanned the room . . . only, it was empty. Frowning, I reached out to the tapestry-hung wall to steady myself—

And felt my ruff-clutching fingers connect with a broad, firm, and decidedly *male* chest.

“What’s this?” Count de Martine’s words were amused as his hand swiftly closed around mine, capturing my hand against him.

I could feel the searing heat of his chest through his thick doublet, and I struggled to free myself. “My apologies! I am so sorry—” I blurted, but my frantic movements pulled him out of his shadowed hiding place. Behind him, a young woman in long rustling skirts followed.

And my misery was complete.

Beatrice.

I flushed crimson in the semidarkness, grateful I could not be fully seen. “I am so sorry to have disturbed you,” I said hurriedly, holding myself upright even though Rafe still imprisoned my hand. “I thought this room was empty; I needed time away from the crowd.”

“What has troubled you so, fair maid?” Rafe asked, still amused, as if I were some grand joke presented for his entertainment. His hold on my hand was light but firm, and his fingers kept *moving* upon mine. I pulled again, and still he held. I decided a little honesty was necessary to fire my lies.

“Forgive me. I’ve had a terrible shock,” I said, staring desperately at Beatrice. She stepped forward, and as she moved, Rafe turned to her. I took the opportunity to wrench my hand free from his grasp. To my dismay, Rafe still held on to my small ruff. He tucked it into his sleeve with a dexterity that would've marked any other man as a thief.

"What sort of shock?" Beatrice asked, plainly irritated. "Were you assaulted?"

"No!" I protested, but as my mind caught up to my words, I realized Beatrice had just given me the perfect excuse for my disarray. "I mean, not exactly. You know I am not used to crowds."

"Meg is here on the charity of the Queen," Beatrice explained. A new wave of mortification washed over me. *She didn't need to put it quite like that.*

Smirking, Beatrice sidled closer to Rafe, and I stepped away. I had no designs on her conquest for the evening, even though my hand still burned from his touch and it felt like a flock of butterflies had taken flight inside my chest. For his part, Rafe wrapped one arm over Beatrice's shoulders, the gesture entirely too intimate for their short acquaintance. I absently wiped my hand upon my skirt, and saw his quickly suppressed smirk. I hastened on.

"Yes, well, I am not used to the rush and flurry of the revelers, and one man, I do not know who—I thought at first it was Lord Bensman, or perhaps Lord Wallace . . ." And here I was making up names completely, but I needed time to think. "In truth I could not identify him. He came up behind me and placed one hand upon my neck, the other around my waist."

"Enterprising of him," Rafe drawled, while Beatrice now stared at me, wide-eyed, no longer sure I wasn't speaking the truth.

"Where is your ruff?" she demanded, leaning closer. Rafe still had my ruff, blast him. "Tell me you didn't lose it!"

"I don't know!" I shook my head hard. *This was all wrong!*

"The lecherous lord must have pulled it away from you," Rafe supplied, and I shot him a glare.

"All I could think to do was flee," I said. "I do not think the man knew what maid he'd caught, for he didn't call my name, but in truth I was hurrying so fast, I doubt I'd have heard a baying hound." I blinked at Beatrice, and her eyes narrowed again, her mouth turning down at the edges.

"That lord has your ruff, Meg. How will you explain that?"

"Or perhaps it's not as bad as you think," observed Rafe genially. "Perhaps the cur simply loosened it and it fell away as you ran?" I scowled at him. He was not helping matters, and even as he spoke, he curled his fingers to tease a lock of Beatrice's hair next to her cheek, distracting her. It made my stomach twist. *I don't belong here, in this castle of lies and games.* In the streets, at least, I knew my . . . my role! I reached for that idea. Held on to it.

"I apologize again for interrupting you," I said with just the right mix of embarrassment and distress. I was an *actress*, playing a *role*. "I stopped running as soon as I realized that I wasn't being chased. I just wanted time away."

"And so you shall have it," Beatrice said, her patience with this interlude at an end. "Rafe and I will leave you to your sulk."

That brought my head up again, but Beatrice was already tugging at the Spaniard. "Come, then, Rafe. I would like to finish our conversation, if we could."

"And I am glad to hear it."

Rafe stepped forward then, away from Beatrice, and I lifted my hand to ward him off. Instead he deftly caught it and lifted my fingers to his lips. "I will pray for a more satisfactory end to the evening for you, fair maid," he murmured. "May you find all for which you search."

He brushed my fingertips with his soft lips, and it was all I could do not to yank my hand away. Instead I bobbed a half curtsy, because that's apparently what I did when I was flustered, and by the time I'd risen, Rafe had moved back to Beatrice's side.

She, for her part, was staring daggers at me, a reaction that was wholly unwarranted. But as she pulled at him, Rafe went willingly enough, without a backward glance.

I stood in the center of the Blue Room a moment more, cupping my fingers to my face.

My cheeks were burning hot, of course. Stiff with embarrassment, I turned and moved to the doors to the terrace and pushed the nearest one open.

The night air welcomed me, beckoning. Calling me home.

I stepped outside, and something hard shifted in my chest. The Queen might have thought I didn't know myself, but I did know this: I could not stay trapped inside these walls. I could not spy on the Queen, not in the way Cecil needed. And I could not put my own people at risk with my undoubted failure.

Beyond the terrace, I could almost see the distant river through the nighttime murk. There were plenty of boats clustered upon the Thames, merchants heading into London or back again north. I leaned upon the stone wall, looking at nothing, pulling in deep breaths. The brisk night air had now replaced my heat with an unnatural chill. In my borrowed ball gown I was not dressed to be out of doors for long. But I could make it to the Thames. I had my grandfather's book and picklocks tightly sewn into my shift—all that I owned in this place. And the jewels I'd secreted away in my waistband this evening would more than buy me safe passage.

London was only a short boat trip away, and then . . . I swallowed. Surely the players of the Golden Rose could be found again. It was still high summer, and the money had been good in London; perhaps they hadn't yet left. I would find them. Cecil would quickly tire of looking for me, realize I was no threat. He would convince another hapless spy to serve the needs of Queen and country. And then I would be free.

I began walking, slowly and idly, sidling into the Middle Ward and past the Round Tower, keeping to the shadows. Far below, the Lower Ward was more boisterous, a large open yard where the servants and merchants and townspeople gathered, their lighthearted revelry a bright mockery of the ball that went on within the Presence Chamber. Still, they were intent upon their own celebrations, and I was intent on not being seen. I touched the jewels snugged against my waist. I could do this. I could escape.

I slipped back onto the North Terrace of the castle as soon as I could, my pace quickening.

Winchester Tower loomed ahead of me, just as Jane had described. The Hundred Steps leading down from the Tower marked the break between the castle and the town, the threshold between the world I could never be a part of, and the one that was welcoming me back into its embrace.

I'd just set foot on the third stair when I saw him.

Sir Francis Walsingham, the Queen's spymaster, leaned against the thick stone wall of Winchester Tower not ten paces ahead of me, his eyes dark as thunder, his face implacably set.

Waiting for me.

CHAPTER TEN

"'Tis a fine night for a walk, isn't it, Miss Fellowes?"

Walsingham's words were as quiet as his person, a mere whisper in the oppressive gloom. An unusually tall man, he seemed to draw the shadows around him like a second cloak. Though I knew his hair to be the color of russet hounds, in the night it looked nearly as black as his habitual attire. His white ruff was pristine and almost shockingly bright in contrast. He was slender but not gaunt, and he carried himself with both grace and power. He watched me with flat eyes a moment more as I stood on the third step, transfixed. Then he pushed off from the wall.

"I've seen many members of the town stumble down these steps tonight, after taking their fill of the enjoyment in the Lower Ward. But—it's interesting, this—you are the first—the very first member of the actual *court* who has passed this way. Could that be because if members of the court come down these steps without an escort, they know they are leaving the Crown's protection? Surely that is it. And yet, I do not see an escort with you, Miss Fellowes. How can that be?"

The question was rhetorical, but I willed myself to respond with the kind of prim superiority with which the well-bred ladies of the court seemed to be spoon-fed from birth. "Indeed you startled me, Sir Francis," I said. "I am but on a walk to clear my head. You're out late yourself—and also without an escort, I see. Perhaps we shall escort each other?"

Walsingham's eyes flared with what might have been a spark of humor, then narrowed again at his momentary lapse.

"Verily, if I did not know any better," he said, "I would say a young woman leaving under dark of night, with nothing on her back but the gown given to her from the Crown, I would say that such a young woman rather thought she would be fleeing the court this eve."

"Without a cloak or bag? And by herself?" I challenged back, as if the young woman in question were anyone but me. "That would be an unwise course, even on so fine a night as this."

He tilted his head at my rebuttal, considering me. "Pray, then, where were you heading just now?"

"Naught but down the stairs and up again, to take in the night air in relative peace." I waved vaguely behind me at the revel still going strong in the Lower Ward. "'Tis too close within the castle, and too loud without. I craved solely my own company for a time in the open air. A foolish caprice, I'm sure you would think."

He smiled, but there was ice in his bantering tone. "You sought to daydream in the nighttime?"

"A folly, to be sure."

"Naught but a fancy?"

"Nothing but a whim."

Walsingham folded his arms, leaning forward, his brow furrowed. "And yet," he said, with the first fell hint of rebuke in his tone, "I rather doubt such bursts of whimsy would be regarded favorably by the Queen. You shall have to educate me on why this act of yours could not be considered treason."

My eyes flew wide. "Treason!" I said, making my shock sound like laughter. "Surely you jest."

"Treason," he confirmed. "And surely, I do not. Walk with me."

Walsingham stepped close and grasped my hand as he turned me smartly back up the steps, folding my arm into his. Every bone and muscle in my body cried out that I was heading the wrong way, back into the castle of noise and intrigue, of scandal and embarrassment, and I hesitated even as his hand tightened.

"Oh, come now, Miss Fellowes," he murmured into the night air, not looking down at me at all. "You have already so much to explain—"

"I was simply on a walk," I scoffed, trying not to sound desperate. I committed to my words even as I spoke them. I had been, in fact, simply on a walk. What was the harm in that? The words that came to mind could have been spoken by a Golden Rose player: *The best of our lies are those we believe true.*

"And what a dangerous walk it could have proven to be," Walsingham said. "You are a member of the Queen's most trusted corps of maids. If you were caught out here by her enemies, unprotected as you are . . . Well, you can see how it would go. It would put the Queen in a position she would not care for."

"But I am the very least of all the maids," I said reasonably, even as he persisted in carting me off in the wrong direction. "I am of no consequence." *I must first convince* me, *and then play to* you.

"Well, of course Her Grace would be devastated at the loss of one of her maids, but your point is well taken, Miss Fellowes," Walsingham said. "Unfortunately, that's not precisely the issue here. If you were taken by an enemy of the Queen, and made to share details of Her Grace's private life—"

I blinked at his profile. Did he know what Cecil had already asked of me? "Details of her private life? I would never do that. And I know little of her life in any case—"

"You and I know that, true enough. But the Queen, well, she could not take the risk. What if you were to be tortured into revealing some detail, some sight, or perhaps some *words you'd overheard*?" His emphasis on the phrase was deliberate, drawing it out like an accusation. Clearly, everyone knew of my mimicry skills. It was the worst-kept secret in Windsor. "Well. You see it's simply something that we could not allow. And then there is the treason of any who may have helped you form this foolish plan to escape. That is a concern as well."

"There was no 'plan to escape,'" I said stiffly, recognizing the trap of his words. "No one even knows I am gone."

Walsingham nodded as we strolled on. "And I would believe you, if it were in my nature to do so. But unhappily for us both, it is not—particularly not when your situation presents such an intriguing possibility to set a few court issues to rights."

I frowned. "What is your meaning, sir?"

He patted my hand again, like I was a favored pet. "Well, in orchestrating your downfall, I can take down others of your station as well. Sophia Dee, for example. She defied her orders this eve. Again."

I glanced up at him, wary. "But she is ill!"

"Sophia is ill every night that she might be presented to her betrothed," Walsingham said dryly. "Or hadn't you noticed the correlation?"

I drew back as far as I could with his arm locked on mine. "I know little of her betrothed."

"Lord Brighton is a good man, a favorite of the Queen's, and he would solve the dilemma of John Dee's perplexing niece quite neatly. If Sophia's abilities manifest into something palatable, such as astrology like her uncle, or something useful like keen intuition, her place near the Queen is assured for the balance of her life. If her abilities do not manifest at all, then marriage to a Queen's man is her only chance for a secure future."

"But Lord Brighton is old enough to be Sophia's father!"

"Lord Brighton has rich lands in Bristol, and coffers of gold, and a willingness to share his bounty with the Queen. That matters more." He cocked his gaze at me. "Remember, Miss Fellowes, it's considered the Queen's duty to marry off her maids of honor in good faith. You should recall that your own marriage question will someday need to be settled."

I refused to give him the satisfaction of knowing how much that line of conversation made me ill. My own marriage question had already been answered. With a resounding *no*. "Pray do not trouble yourself on my account," I said through my teeth.

"I assure you, it is no trouble." He patted my hand again, letting me stew in my own indignation for another moment. Sophia would become my personal crusade, I decided. She should not be forced to marry *anyone* she did not wish. "I do say, though, Miss Fellowes, you are taking a rather narrow view of these proceedings."

"I rather think that being asked to do atrocious things or to allow harm to come to those I care about is sufficient cause for narrow-mindedness. You've made my situation plain."

"Too plain, it appears," Walsingham observed. "As tonight's events show. We cannot have you thinking that the best course of action for you is flight. That wouldn't serve any of our interests."

"I assure you," I said grimly, "you will not catch me attempting to leave this place."

Walsingham chuckled at my deliberate choice of words. "But you see, I have no wish to spend my time trying to catch you at all, Miss Fellowes. Rather, allow me to give you a better reason to stay."

"You do not need to threaten me further—"

"No, no, not a threat." Walsingham's words were quiet, soothing. "There is a value to the work you do. The Queen herself would not gainsay it. Depending on what you bring her, she would return that boon to you several times over."

I frowned even as my treacherous ears pricked up, the promise of freedom sweet on the air. “A boon?”

He nodded. “Riches enough to set you up in quiet comfort, in some small town far from London.”

“You cannot make such a promise.”

“Oh, but I can. And I will, for the right level of service, Miss Fellowes. The Queen is already your champion. Swaying her further in that direction would be easily done. What say you to that—a lifetime pension, enough to purchase a small cottage and see you safely settled if you guard your coins? Never having to thieve again? Or is the act of thieving so much a part of you that—”

“No,” I said hurriedly. “No, it is not, Sir Francis. But how— I mean, who is to say what is worth such a pension? How would I know you were sincere in this offer?”

He glanced at me. “Do you wish a contract?”

I shook my head. “No,” I said. My grasp of written text was improving, yes, but no matter how much I studied, I would never be able to understand the kind of subtle wording that I suspected Walsingham and Cecil could employ without a moment’s thought. I’d likely be trading away my life for a brace of chickens, were I to sign any contract of his. “Only your pledge as a man of honor.”

Sir Francis nodded in admiration, seeing through my ploy while acknowledging its worth. He was a proud man, if nothing else, and I had challenged his sense of nobility. He would keep his word.

“I do so pledge to pension you off, Miss Fellowes . . . if your work saves the Queen’s life, her throne—or her reputation.”

I winced. He had to know of Cecil's request of me, and now he'd given me incentive to complete that horrid charge. There *had* to be another way.

We were now walking back along the North Terrace, and my eyes strayed to the terrace doors, tightly shut against the night. Had I shut them? How had Walsingham known I would flee—and down the Hundred Steps? I hadn't known myself until my humiliation in the Blue Room.

Suddenly everything came together for me.

"You were *there*, weren't you?" I said. "In the Blue Room."

"I assure you, I took no joy in that task," Walsingham returned, another flicker of humanity in his words. "But as you'd occupied Cecil for the moment, I thought it would be more fruitful to keep tabs on the boy. I'd no idea he'd spend his time behind the tapestries with Miss Knowles."

My cheeks burned, but my mind leaped forward as I thought about Rafe and his impending conversation with Count de Feria. There *was* another way I could serve, I thought. I did not have to betray the Queen.

"I saw Count de Martine with letters," I said, delicately treading around the transcript of my report. "He flashed them to the ambassador, but they did not get a chance to make an exchange. I suspect they will tonight, though."

Walsingham had stopped, eyeing me with interest. "Did de Martine say where they would make the exchange?"

The snake was testing me; he knew I could not understand Spanish without assistance, and he doubtless knew Cecil wouldn't have told me. "I . . . I don't know," I said, letting just enough frustration shine through. "I could not understand their words. But if we could read the letters now, before de Martine and the ambassador have a chance to exchange them, would that not be of service?"

Walsingham looked down at me. "And how would you propose to come by those letters?"

I rolled my eyes. "I am first and foremost a thief, Sir Francis. The pocket in which Rafe de Martine carries the packet is not so well hidden that it cannot be picked."

The smile that creased Walsingham's face curled into a deeply contented grin. "You can lift—and return—these letters?"

"Of course," I said. I might not have been able to understand the Spaniard, but I could certainly pick his pocket.

The Queen's spymaster stared at me a moment more. Then he nodded. "Then so you shall. But first," he said officiously, and he reached into his doublet and took out a modest—but barely crumpled—ruff, shaking out the narrow linen folds. My hand flew to my neck.

"How did you—"

"I saw the lout take it from you and sent a servant to fetch another. Turn around." He slipped the new ruff around my neck and tightened it so firmly, my eyes watered. "You should be more careful, Miss Fellowes," he said, his words clipped.

"I'm sure the count will return it—"

"And I am sure he will do no such thing, at least not in a way that won't cause terrible embarrassment to the Queen. Now this removes the temptation for him. Let me look at you."

I turned to face him, my chin held high, and he considered me closely. "You can do this?" he asked, his words unexpectedly gentle.

"Yes, Sir Francis, I can," I said, confident in my restored costume. What a difference the right clothes could make.

"Good. Then let us begin." Sir Francis Walsingham smiled genuinely at me then, his teeth gleaming in the torch-light. "We'll make a spy of you yet."

CHAPTER ELEVEN

"He is there, to the right of the grand table," Walsingham murmured as we paused in the shadows before the Presence Chamber's huge double doors. I caught sight of Rafe, resting easily against a table, looking smug. What had he done with Beatrice, I wondered. And why had he chosen *her*? A stupid question, I supposed. Beatrice was beautiful. And noble. And rich. Everything I was not.

Walsingham lifted a hand, and a page scuttled up to him, the boy wide-eyed and sweating in his miniature doublet and breeches of red velvet. Stooping slightly, Walsingham delivered his orders, and the servant rushed off.

A terrible thought struck me. "What if Rafe has already handed off the letters to de Feria?" I asked, even as I scanned the room for the Spanish ambassador. The Count de Feria was looking a bit shakier than when I'd seen him last, his eyes sunken and his skin unnaturally pale. I grimaced as I watched him set down his goblet. Had Jane spiked his wine as well?

"Cecil will advise me if so, but I do not think so. I'm not sure how long the young count chose to dally with Miss Knowles, but I suspect he has only just returned. It would not be seemly for him to rush off again so quickly, even for a Spaniard."

The music changed, with more players joining the fray.

"Go dance with him," Walsingham said, but I shook my head, eyeing the musicians.

"They are playing an Almain, and that doesn't serve me," I said. "Wait for the music to announce a Trenchmore. Where will you be?"

He nodded, following the logic in my choice of dances. "By the second column near the head of the line."

I followed his gaze. It would do. "Very well," I said. "You'll have exactly the length of one rotation to read the letters. Is it enough?"

"It will be enough."

"You'll have to break the seal on the packet," I mused, even as I straightened my gown. I felt the familiar pull of excitement, the same I felt when plunging into any crowd, seeking the day's marks. Rafe Luis Medina was a dandy; he would not hide a packet of letters in his close-fitting doublet. They would be in the side slash pockets of the flamboyantly puffed slops that flared out over his silk-clad legs. His very *well-muscled* silk-clad legs, I noticed again. "He'll know they've been read."

"Or think that the packet had been jostled open in the midst of his revelry," Walsingham countered. "In any event, it is not your concern. Just get the packet to me."

I walked out into the ballroom, slipping between two couples engaged in conversations so intimate, it made my ears burn. How could the nobility be so loose with words and deeds? Ale flowed freely, and the food was now all but forgotten, heaped in great piles on the wide tables of the Presence Chamber. The revel had taken on the aspect of a barely controlled bacchanal, the Queen nowhere in sight.

I surveyed the crowd, picking out the faces that I knew. If I was to become the Queen's spy as well as Walsingham's, I'd need to begin recognizing faces better, knowing names. I pursed my lips at the thought. In a court such as this, it would be no easy task. The nobility all looked alike in their overstuffed doublets and vividly colored capes, with their sly smiles and yearning eyes. But I would need to learn.

I positioned myself where I knew that Rafe de Martine would see me, and clasped my hands in front of me as I went up on my toes. The mere act of it made me cringe, but I was here to look like a young woman in desperate need of a dance. He'd seemed willing enough to flirt with me while dallying with Beatrice, so I just needed to show the proper amount of interest. I'd seen the hopeful gazes cast at the men by the women at court. I knew how to mimic them, to tilt my chin just so, to widen my eyes, and to sigh with abject longing.

Still, it galled me to play the fool in front of him, of all people. Which was ridiculous. He was a Spaniard and my assignment, nothing more.

The Almain finished, and a Measure started up next, with the music—and dancers—growing more relaxed with every turn. I added a not-too-subtle sway to my movement, keeping my hands held high, the epitome of the country girl gone to her first ball. *If Troupe Master James saw me now, he'd double over in laughter*, I thought grimly. The image of Master James made me suddenly sad, however. Would he be plotting the next triumphant run of the Golden Rose this night?

And did he ever think of me?

Shoving that thought away, I kept my pose through an interminably long refrain, even edging closer to the dancers in excitement.

Then the music shifted subtly, and I swallowed, glancing over to where I'd last seen Rafe. He was still there. Only now he wasn't dancing, or even talking to anyone else, but held a goblet in one hand, a lazy grin on his face.

And he was staring directly at me.

I did not have to feign the rush of color that came to my cheeks, but surely he could see my reaction to catching his glance. And just in case he didn't, I brought my hands up to my cheeks, like a milkmaid caught dreamy-eyed.

It did the trick. Rafe raised his brows, set his cup down on the table, and straightened.

Then he started walking toward me.

And I . . . froze like a rabbit.

Now, I could tell you that I froze because it was all part of my carefully scripted plan. That the play had been blocked to proceed as so: I catch the eye of the gallant mark and appear completely entranced, the gallant mark asks me to dance, and I divest the gallant mark of all his worldly goods.

But in truth, as I watched Rafe Luis Medina approach me, I could not have moved even if Walsingham himself had been bellowing in my ear for me to run.

For his part, Rafe never took his eyes from mine the whole of his brief saunter across the floor. His smile was easy and teasing, his skin burnished bronze and lustrous. He looked like a dancer. He *moved* like a dancer, and I allowed myself a silly grin. Which was all part of the role, of course.

Finally, the reality of what I was doing struck me.

I was about to do something that could very well spell disaster.

Not the thieving; that part I knew how to do. But—*dancing*?

Then Rafe was in front of me, and suddenly I couldn't breathe. He bowed in perfect deference. "You've returned to me, fair maid, complete with a new ruff, I see."

I lifted my hand self-consciously to my neck. "Ah . . . Yes. I couldn't very well reenter the Presence Chamber without one."

"And that is to my advantage. I'll be rather glad to keep yours." He grinned, and held out one elegant hand. "Shall we dance?"

And there it was. I was going to dance the Trenchmore with the Count de Martine.

I curtsied (why stop now?) and lifted my hand to his. Heat blazed between us at the touch, but if the young count noticed, he gave no indication. He raised me out of the curtsy and folded my arm into his as if we'd been dancing together for years, and moved us into place on the floor as a couplet facing each other.

"I confess I do not know this dance well," he said as he took my hands to perform an elegant Honor, the step-and-bow flourish favored before every courtly dance. "Is it challenging?"

"I don't think you'll have any difficulty, Count de Martine," I said, surprised at the strength of my own voice.

The play had begun now, and I scanned his clothing. He was right-handed, and I expected the letters would be in the right-hand slash pocket of his heavily embroidered slops.

We moved up two steps and back two steps, and then cast off, walking down the length of the long line of dancers before meeting up again at the bottom of our row. I saw Walsingham position himself in the shadows of the column he'd specified, but Cecil was not with him. Instead, Walsingham was apparently having a conversation with a bland-faced man, who seemed to turn away just as I glanced at him. *Another of his spies?* I wondered. What other secrets did Walsingham keep?

As I took my place opposite Rafe, I did finally catch sight of Cecil—in earnest and back-slapping conversation with the increasingly ill-looking Count de Feria, both of them turned away from the dancers. Walsingham must have told Cecil to keep the ambassador occupied.

The second verse began, and more complicated steps with it. I held hands with the women alongside me, and we faced the men across the patch of floor. We all took a step toward our partners, and suddenly Rafe's face was before me, his eyes merry and his lips curled into a soft and knowing grin. I realized with a start that I was nearly close enough to Rafe to kiss him.

Where had that thought come from?

Just as quickly we stepped back again, and Rafe and I joined hands. The heat of the dance must have been getting to me, because I suddenly felt flushed, almost dizzy. *Focus!*

This portion of the dance required couples to make arches with their arms while other couples went beneath, and then the first couple would similarly duck through another couple's arches. It was a fast-paced process, involving tight turns and a fair amount of laughter, and it presented the chance I was looking for. As Rafe and I pressed up together to slip beneath the arms of a very short couple—no easy feat, that—I sidled my hand along his ornate slops, and slipped it into his slashed pocket.

My fingers instantly found what they were looking for, a tight packet of papers with a rough wax seal. I slipped the packet out adroitly and—

Nearly stopped dead.

I was not wearing my own familiar thieving gown, riddled as it was with enough custom-sewn pockets to store half the ball's finery. Instead I was wearing a very proper costume befitting a maid of honor, nary a slash pocket to my name. And my waistband was already full of stolen jewels. Only my bodice allowed me any room at all, as it had originally been sized for a much more well-endowed maid.

We turned again, and I palmed the letters, whirling with a grand flourish. There was nothing for it, and as I lifted my hands above my head, I quickly shoved the letters down the front of my bodice, before turning again to clasp Rafe's light fingertips in mine.

"You're flushed, fair maid. Is everything well?" Rafe asked.

"Oh, *yes*!" I responded with perhaps a touch too much intensity, my gaze darting to his. Did Rafe suspect? But no, there was nothing but laughing amusement in his eyes. His thumb flicked along the palm of my hand as we allowed another couple to move beneath the arch of our arms, and I glanced at him nervously. *Had he caught me out?* "Count—" I began.

"You may call me Rafe, fair maid," he said. We were now doing our part to thread beneath other dancers' upstretched arms. "Would you do me the honor of your name as well? It is Meg, I believe?"

I jolted, to hear my name on his lips, but of course he'd heard it before. Beatrice had called me by name. "It is, and I give you leave to use it, in appreciation for this dance. It has been a long time since I've enjoyed myself so much."

He gave me a teasing smile. "May it be only the beginning of many dances to come."

I blinked at his flirtatiousness, but fortunately, the third verse was beginning. We stepped toward each other and back, then toward the dancers on either side of us and back again, which gave me just enough time to collect my thoughts. Then we paired with other partners on down the row, twirling and whirling our way through a complicated series of figure eights that brought us all the way to the end of the line. We cast off again, to walk the length of the row of dancers and eventually resume our regular spots.

As I walked, I clasped my hands to my breast as if to quell my beating heart, and plucked the packet of letters free. Walsingham stepped just into my path at that moment, a specter in the shadows. I slipped the stolen letters to him as easily as if we'd been thieving together for years.

I regained my position next to Rafe, my stomach now as tight as a drum. Walsingham had disappeared back into the throng, and I prayed the man could read quickly, or had collared Anna to do the reading for him. She could decipher hidden messages in text with almost unnatural speed. The next rotation would be our last move down the line, and my best chance to fetch back the letters. Even now, I was desperately trying to remember how many verses remained in the Trenchmore. After the next stroll down the line, were there two more verses—or three?

"I seem to be making you unaccountably nervous," Rafe observed, startling me as we stepped forward, then back, following the steps prescribed by the dance.

"Not at all, my lord," I said, raising my chin as I scanned the crowd. *Where was Walsingham?* "I am only worried about my footwork. I have managed the dance so well to now, 'tis merely a matter of time before I miss a step."

He chuckled. "I get the distinct feeling that you do not often misstep, fair maid."

I looked at him sharply, but we were now turning to our partners before us and behind us, and we cast off again, beginning the long walk down to our original spots in the line. During this walk I was to intercept Walsingham and reclaim Rafe's packet of letters, with just barely enough time left to return them to their rightful owner before the dance came to an end.

Only . . . Walsingham was nowhere to be found.

I passed our appointed rendezvous point, and my heart was in my throat by the time Rafe and I arrived back in our positions. The dance was speeding up, in anticipation of a grand finish, but I did not have the letters!

I replayed my instructions again and again in my mind. I had told Walsingham specifically that he would have very little time to read the letters. He knew that. He knew I had to get the letters back into Rafe's pocket *before* the end of the dance. Which was now bearing down upon us like a mad bull.

"Breathe, fair maid," Rafe whispered into my ear as we came together then to duck under another couple's lifted arms. "You'll faint if you keep this up. Should we retire?"

"No!" I said. My mind clamored with thoughts, possible new gambits, none of them any good. This was why I didn't improvise. I did not have the stomach for it, let alone the heart. The moment Rafe patted his pocket, he would realize that the letters were missing. Would he immediately suspect me, a country lass with no formal education? Beatrice had given him to understand that I was here on the Queen's charity. Would that be enough to save me?

I realized he was waiting for me to speak. "I'm sorry, my lo—"

"I said, call me Rafe."

"Rafe." I blushed, and it had nothing to do with the role I was playing, but it was masterful timing nevertheless. I'd have to call upon these memories if I ever had to play the awestruck girl again. Assuming Rafe didn't have me thrown before the Queen as a petty thief, of course. Wouldn't that be quite the irony. "I'm sorry," I said again. "The dance is coming to an end, and I want to savor every moment of it."

"Perhaps we—"

His words were lost to me as we began the complicated handoffs, swirling through the other men and women who danced alongside us in figure eights. I brushed by Rafe's side a half dozen times before the refrain was complete. Any one of those times would have been enough for me to slide the letters back into his pocket, but where was Walsingham?

And suddenly the spymaster was there. His face implacable, his position just outside the whirling rows of dancers. He was no longer hiding in the lee of the column but out in plain sight, just close enough for me to reach him. He was talking to a young woman in apparently earnest conversation, but his body was angled so that he was just open enough . . .

The music picked up speed, and laughter rippled through the lines of dancers. We all swirled yet more vigorously, and I threw my arms out in an expression of exultation just as my turns flung me farthest from the line, as near to Walsingham as I ever hoped to get.

He turned in just that moment, and I felt the whisper of pressure on my fingers, even as his short cloak glided over my outstretched arm in a careless whirl. I had the letters!

Hurriedly I pulled my arm back and pushed the papers into my bodice again, success sparking through me like a leaping fire. I turned to face Rafe, a grin on my face, triumphant.

And then the music stopped.

But I still had the letters.

CHAPTER TWELVE

I stared at Rafe, actually feeling the blood drain out of my face. He backed away neatly from me and bowed, like the proper gentleman he was. I curtsied as well, like the well-taught maid I was trying desperately to be.

The music was shifting into a Volta, but I could not risk that dance. It was too intimate, and required the man to lift the woman off her feet. In lifting me, Rafe's hands would be positioned directly on the waistband of my dress below my bodice—exactly where I didn't want them to be. He would feel the lumpy weight of the stolen jewels immediately, and I could not run the risk that he would begin wondering what else I might be hiding beneath my skirts.

I needn't have worried that I'd have to endure another dance with Rafe, however. Immediately upon my ascent from my curtsy, Beatrice appeared at his side.

"You are kind to favor poor Meg with such a dance, my lord," she cooed. I felt myself grow hot, and even though it added to my disguise, I was infuriated that she could nettle me with such ease.

"The favor was hers to bestow, my lady," Rafe said in

return, smiling at me even as Beatrice swanned in front of him, turning smartly so as to block me from Rafe's view. If it hadn't been such an elegant move, I would have been outraged by Beatrice's audacity. As it was, she played it off as if it were merely part of the dance.

"And will you take my favor now?" she asked him, holding out her hand.

Knowing I should retire to figure out how in the name of heaven I was going to get the letters back into Rafe's pocket, I nevertheless lifted my chin, sliding to the left even as Beatrice shifted to the right, striking her pose for the Honor to commence the dance.

"It was a pleasure, Rafe," I said with a gentle incline of my head, using his first name quite deliberately. No "my lords" or simpering curtsy this time! "But I suspect you will be far better matched with Beatrice. Her skills at all manner of dance have captured many a gentleman's fancy at court. Her experience is much remarked upon."

Rafe's brows lifted ever so slightly, but Beatrice narrowed her eyes, clearly unsure about whether or not I'd just insulted her. I smiled at them both serenely. I hadn't *really* just intimated that she'd bedded half the male population at Windsor Castle, not exactly.

But it was close enough.

The music crashed to mark the opening strains of the Volta, and Rafe smoothly swept Beatrice away. I turned as well, and therefore only imagined that her eyes were burning two smoking holes through the back of my gown. For just a moment, I was almost cheerful.

Walsingham was waiting for me before I even cleared the first row of columns.

"Well?" he asked without looking at me.

I stopped, making as if I were straightening my hair after the rush of the country dance. Half-turning, I caught sight of Beatrice's soft blue dress swirling as Rafe lifted her into the air. I was taller than Beatrice, and more fit, but she had the kind of lithe beauty that men could not resist. I strained to see whether Rafe looked like he was enjoying himself. Surely he could see through Beatrice's game and—

"Your *report*, Miss Fellowes." Walsingham's biting tone cut through my thoughts, and I looked up at him, suddenly peevish.

"Ah, yes, my *report*." I barely constrained myself from spluttering the words. "Where shall I begin? You dallied during your act of the play, despite my express warnings, and returned too late to the stage." And now, I realized, I would have to betray yet another secret to this man. I had to transfer the packet of letters from my bodice to my waistband, since that was the easiest place for me to hide the letters so that I could quickly retrieve them and return them to Rafe. Unfortunately, my waistband was already weighed down with my spoils from earlier in the evening, which meant I needed to empty it. Now. In front of Walsingham. I'd been warned not to pick-pocket, but . . . there was nothing for it.

"Oh, very well," I huffed. I shoved my hand into the tight wrap of my waistband and pulled out the offending jewels. A brooch. A cuff. A hairpin with a stone the size of an egg. I thrust these at Walsingham, and he took them without a word. "Since I was not of a mind to be discovered, I abandoned my role," I continued. "I now find myself still with a final act to complete and no idea what lines I will say."

Walsingham frowned at me, clearly confused. I got the impression he was not much one for the theatre. "You still have the packet of letters," he said dourly.

I pulled the papers out of my bodice and brandished them at him. "I do."

"I was afraid of that." Was that an eye roll? My blood began to simmer in my veins. I'd like to see *him* try to light-finger a set of papers both into and out of a man's trunks, verily I would.

"You'll need to intercept the boy before he reaches Ambassador de Feria," Walsingham continued, scanning the ballroom. "De Feria is already making noises to Cecil that he must needs retire, and the moment he leaves the ballroom, you can expect the young count to follow him. You won't have much time."

I shoved the letters into my newly emptied waistband. "And how do you expect me to get close to the Count de Martine again if we are not in the midst of a dance, Sir Francis?" I asked, my words tight. "It's not as if we're countrymen, nor even well acquainted."

Walsingham gave a short, derisive laugh. "You are a young woman of the court who has just had the pleasure of dancing with a bold young count from the Continent. I'm sure you have enough experience with the *theatre* to imagine how the next scene might play out, Miss Fellowes. Count de Martine won't be so eager to meet with the Spanish ambassador that he won't take the time to tip the chin of a wide-eyed and willing maid."

I stiffened. "Tip the chin?" I repeated. *Tip the chin!* "Surely you can't mean what I think you do." *Had the whole of the court lost all sense of decorum?*

And just that quickly, Walsingham's humor turned to irritation. "Do not try my patience, Miss Fellowes. You are seventeen years old, not ten. I'm not asking you to tumble the boy, just get him to tarry with you down a dark hallway long enough for you to set everything to rights. You cannot tell me that your training with your acting troupe did not include how to make eyes at a man. I won't believe it."

I bit my lip, but the man had a point. As soon as I could easily pass as a woman and not just a girl, Grandfather had made sure I was taught enough tricks of fluttering femininity to make a man think I was interested in him for something other than his money. Still, could I use those tricks to fool Rafe? I somehow didn't think he'd be pulled in simply by my blinking a great deal and giggling into my hand.

"It's time," Walsingham said abruptly. "De Feria is leaving the ballroom now, and de Martine is tracking his departure. You can rest assured your young count will take his leave of Beatrice the moment the music ends."

I glanced to where Walsingham gestured, and caught sight of just the hem of de Feria's dark cape as it sailed through the west entrance of the Presence Chamber. Rafe would exit through that same doorway, and there were any number of long corridor-like antechambers in which he could meet with de Feria. The castle was a rabbit warren of intersecting rooms, and I'd have to move quickly if I planned to intercept Rafe before he reached the Spanish ambassador—or before he realized his letters were gone.

I left Walsingham without another word, nimbly threading my way through the crowd. I cleared the west entrance to the Presence Chamber just as the Volta came to a close, to the enthusiastic applause of all those watching. I'm sure a good portion of that applause was for Beatrice, fluttering and simpering and cooing simpleton that she was.

Focus. I couldn't go too far outside the Presence Chamber. There were too many possible corridors Rafe could take.

I moved down the hallway with purposeful strides, glancing into this room and that. What would a young woman do if she were waiting for her would-be lover? Where would she go?

And what would she do once she got there?

"Don't even think about it," I muttered, poking my head into an antechamber. *Would it suit? No. Only one entrance. I'd feel trapped in a room such as this.* "The game is the letters, nothing more."

"Talking to yourself, fair maid?"

I squeaked and whirled around, doing such an admirable job of sounding like a startled little girl that I would have commended myself, had any of it been on purpose. I looked up to face the Count de Martine, who was lolling in the doorway, his eyes glittering in the half-light. A single sconce in the room lit his face, making him look almost saturnine. "My lord!" I breathed.

"I thought we'd decided on 'Rafe.'" He smiled, shrugging himself off the wall and stepping toward me. Trapped,

trapped, I thought. *Trapped*. "What brings you to such a dark and silent room? Did the dancing fatigue you after all?"

"I . . ." I swallowed, feeling seventeen inches the fool. I knew what had to be said, and I gathered up my skirts in my fists, willing the words to come out. "It's just that . . . I saw that you were heading toward the west entrance, and I went out ahead. I'd hoped we could . . . talk."

It was honestly the lamest speech I'd ever contrived. I could have died from shame right there on the spot.

But Rafe merely smiled.

"You wanted to . . . talk with me?" he asked, taking another few steps forward. At least, I assumed he took actual steps. Somehow he'd glided toward me far too quickly, and he was now near enough to touch. I felt the heat radiating from his body, sweeping over me in a rush.

"Yes, ah . . . to talk," I said, my words barely more than a whisper. I took a step back.

He took another step forward. "And what did you want to say to me, fair maid?"

My smile faltered, and I stepped back again. "I thought we'd agreed upon 'Meg,'" I said, playing for time.

"So we did," he said, his words low. He stepped forward again, even as I moved yet farther back from him—and I came up hard against a damask-covered wall. Rafe stopped in front of me and rested one hand on the wall over my head. He suddenly seemed . . . very tall. And very close. "So, Meg," he said quietly, smiling down at me. "What did you want to talk about?"

My head was swimming, but the nearness of him at least helped to instill the urgency that had been sorely lacking in my playacting up to this point. A voice shouted deep inside me to get this task over with already. So I tilted my head up in the semidarkness, the movement positioning my lips only inches away from his. Exactly where they should be.

I think . . . I think I should like you to kiss me, Count de Martine, I said, my words soft and subtle and full of promise. *I think you should do that right now.*

Well, that was what I wanted to say, anyway.

Instead I opened my mouth—and stopped breathing.

Rafe's gaze seemed to swallow me whole, his dark eyes intent, his own breath suddenly quickening. "I think that's a very good subject to discuss, sweet Meg," he murmured.

And he leaned down and pressed his lips against mine.

The touch of his mouth was a sparking flint strike, and suddenly heat flooded through me like mead drunk too fast, burning its way through my body and lifting me along a current of excitement and urgency unlike anything I'd ever felt before. *I was kissing Rafe!*

Lest you think I handled the rest of that moment well, let me assure you, I did not.

This, of course, was not my fault. Despite the very generous nature of my fellow actors in the Golden Rose acting troupe, up until the moment I'd been unceremoniously hauled off to the Queen's dungeon, I'd had yet to have any success in getting any of the men to kiss me. First, of course, there had been their fear of my grandfather—and I could understand no one wanting to run afoul of the old man. But Grandfather had passed away in the early fall, and I had increasingly been asked to act like an experienced woman as I moved through the crowds. How was I to act like I was knowledgeable in the ways of women and men if I'd never been kissed? I'd demanded. It was just a kiss, for heaven's sake!

Still, no one had been willing to indulge me. Not even Troupe Master James, who'd looked positively sick when I'd asked.

All of this is why, I am sure, I was so unforgivably *pole-axed* by such a straightforward event as one young Rafe Luis Medina, Count de Martine, pressing his soft, luxurious, heavenly lips against mine. It felt dangerous. It felt glorious.

But mainly it felt like I was going to die.

I think I may have swooned.

In any event, I did find myself falling forward, a bolt of sheer fiery bliss shooting through me, starting from my mouth and coursing all the way to my toes. Rafe caught me easily, and somehow managed to wrap his hand around the nape of my neck in the process, moving his lips to my cheek, my jawline, and then . . .

He kissed my *ear*.

(!)

Somehow my right hand moved up Rafe's chest to press firmly against him, and I felt Rafe's warmth through the gold brocade of his doublet. My mind was consumed with that heat, overwhelmed with it. I felt stricken. Delirious. Fevered.

Then my left hand dropped to my waist. With a thud.

And, to be wholly honest, that's the only reason why I remembered that I was still carrying Rafe's letters on my person.

I stiffened reflexively, and Rafe chuckled against my ear, which made me dizzy all over again. "If you're only now surprised at my kiss, fair maid, I must not be as skilled at this as I am told."

What? "N-no," I said quickly as Rafe moved away from my ear to trail a line of kisses down my jawline. The fire in my toes went screaming back up my legs and coiled in my belly. God's teeth, somebody should have prepared me for this! If this was how it felt to have one's ear kissed, what would I do if he ever touched my lips again?

At long last, the logical part of my mind finally awoke, and my left hand dipped inside the waistband of my gown, even as Rafe seemed to find my neckline above my ruff to be of excruciating fascination. He lifted his head slightly and drew his tongue along my earlobe, and I felt all coherent thought fleeing me. Struggling to breathe, I fumbled the packet of letters out of my waistband, even as Rafe began to whisper something to me in Spanish that was lyrical and lovely and impossible for me to understand. I sighed heavily, pressing my full weight into him on the right side, which allowed my left hand to have free access down the length of his torso.

Rafe shifted into me as well, whispering another round of Spanish that I wanted very much to understand. I only prayed I would remember it, but I couldn't focus on his words. Instead, as stealthily as a cat, I drew my left hand down his doublet, found the slash pocket in his trunks, and slipped the papers inside.

The moment I did so, I pressed myself to Rafe as if I'd been rapturously swept away by the heat of passion. . . .

And Rafe immediately pulled back.

"What ho! What's this?" he asked. His grin was victorious, but his gaze was filled with curiosity at my apparent forwardness. "I suspect you are not the innocent girl you first appeared to be."

Had he caught me out? I blinked at Rafe, barely recovering in time. "I am so sorry, my lord," I said, opening my eyes wide, my embarrassment wholly unfeigned. He was grinning, though. A man wouldn't grin if he thought he'd been duped, would he? *How could I salvage this?* "I overstepped my place. I cannot apologize enough, I—"

"Shhh," he said, pressing a hand to my lips. "I rather like it. It would not do for me to be caught out with an untrained maid."

A what? Did he know I was a spy . . . or did he simply suspect that I was a trollop? And which was worse?

"I—I don't understand," I whispered, and that was true enough. Instead of explaining, Rafe kissed me on the forehead.

"And that's to my advantage." He chuckled as he stood back from me. "We'll see each other again, sweet Meg, fear not. But now I must be off. Be assured you've given me plenty to think about this eve." He grinned again at my expression. "All good things, I promise you."

"Oh," was all I could manage as he bowed gracefully to me in the semidarkness. Then he was turning and out the door in three long strides.

And I was left alone, completely unsure of what had just transpired.

But the letters had been delivered successfully, it seemed. Which meant I was safe, for the moment. Wasn't I?

And just as quickly I thought of Marie Claire. Had she too thought she was safe, fresh from her secret mission? Had she been similarly threatened by the Queen's own advisors, even as danger stalked her steps? Had she known that death surrounded her, before it was suddenly too late?

I swallowed, taking one step toward the chamber door, then another. I had to get out. I had to *move*.

Rafe de Martine's kiss had been a distraction for him, a wayward moment before he moved off to some dark intrigue with the Spanish ambassador. My kiss back to him had been a different kind of distraction, solely intended to misdirect him while I replaced what I had stolen.

Secrets and lies surrounded me here, and death and darkness waited just outside the door.

Until I found Marie Claire's killer, I would never be safe at Windsor Castle.

CHAPTER THIRTEEN

"Oh, now then, you are doing so well! In truth I am surprised, Meg, even with you trimming the candle late every eve. You've quite mastered this piece, to be sure!"

I smiled weakly at Anna, my eyes bleary from lack of sleep. It had been a full week since the reception ball, and I'd been studying nonstop. "I read it correctly?"

"Oh, aye, you did. A few troubles with the conjugation, but true enough, what expectation can you have of reading Spanish better than English? And your English reading is coming along even faster. You've much to be proud of, Meg. Sir William will be pleased. A pity he did not come to lessons himself today but left us to read on our own."

"Don't let him know you've been teaching me," I said quickly, and Anna puckered her brow at me. Unconsciously, her hand drifted to the puzzle box on its chain, and I smiled to ease her nerves.

"I just want him to be surprised." I forced the words to sound as bright as I could manage. I'd been thrilled beyond measure that Cecil had stayed away from the day's classes. Mondays were bad enough without his scowling countenance.

He'd also absented himself from Friday's lesson, another session with the herb mistress on the fine art of poisoning. After learning about how many revelers had come down with a terrible ague after the Queen's ball, I had a new respect for these lessons. I couldn't say for certain that Jane was behind the courtiers' sudden illness, but it seemed a safe wager.

"Ah! Well, then, anything to surprise Sir William will be a treat." Anna grinned back at me. "But you need to be getting some sleep then, Meg. Your eyes are as red as poppies."

"My thanks, Anna. How fetching I must look."

She shook her head. "Naught but what a good nap will fix. There comes a time when learning too much can be detrimental to the health. Believe me, well I know! When first I sought to translate Homer, I came down with a cough so deep . . ."

I let her prattle on, grateful for the distraction. I was exhausted, but conquering the struggle of reading was only the half of it. In the past week I'd mapped out the castle like a battleground, memorizing its every twist and turn. I could not afford to be surprised again by unseen eyes tracking me in the dark, like Walsingham had done. And I could not afford to be attacked unawares, as Marie's killer had done.

But now there was another problem. Rafe had undoubtedly handed off his letters from the pope to Ambassador de Feria. If so, de Feria would have passed them along to his English contacts by now. Did that mean another "disruption" was in the offing? Walsingham had said the letters contained no instructions regarding disruptions, but could I believe him? The Queen had strictly enjoined me to root out the cause of any disturbance to the court and eliminate it. That meant I needed to find those letters—and be able to read them once I did.

My rumination was cut short as Beatrice stormed into our sleeping chamber.

"He is impossible!" she wailed.

I stared at her. "What happened? Who is impossible?"

"Oh, Beatrice, if it is what I think, he is simply being a man," Anna chirped, and I shifted my gaze to her, goggle-eyed. What had I missed? "You cannot expect Lord Cavanaugh to take advantage of one of the Queen's favorites."

"He should be so enamored of me that he can't help but take advantage!" Beatrice flung herself down onto her bed, her skirts billowing out like a whey-colored cloud. In keeping with both the current Sumptuary Laws as well as the unspoken order of the Queen, none of Elizabeth's maids or ladies should ever outshine her, particularly in dress. As maids we were expected to make do with greys and whites and pale colors—including Beatrice. Yet somehow, Beatrice always managed a way around the strictures. How she found cloth that shimmered with just a hint of color—not so much to be inappropriate, but enough to make her stand out like a nightingale among crows—I could not fathom. Of late, I'd taken to wearing even drabber colors than usual, just to avoid notice. It had been working admirably.

Beatrice continued her lament. "I wore my best gown, my family's own treasures." She shoved herself up onto her elbows, and I noted the white-green jade stones that hung from around her neck, strung together in a nest of fine golden wiring, and offset by flashing blue sapphires. A matching bracelet adorned her wrist, and a hairpin besides. I'd never seen anything like them. "He may be rich, but so am I. We are a perfect match."

"Of course you are," soothed Anna. "He is just being careful. And I've not seen the hairpin before. 'Tis glorious!"

"Of course you haven't," grumbled Beatrice. "It took me half a year to track that down."

My ears pricked at that, but Beatrice's moan distracted me. "I fail to see how the Spanish count can fall for me in an instant, and the perfectly English Lord Cavanaugh doesn't weep at the knowledge that I want to be his bride. It's simply not to be borne." Then she rolled over, eyeing Anna. "But say, Anna, did I see you speaking with the new ambassador's assistant? What news has he to share?"

"Oh!" Anna exclaimed, her eyes brightening at the gossip she'd learned. "You will not believe what they are wearing in the court of King Philip—especially with his new French bride! Her style of hood alone will not take long to reach our shores, he is certain, and the cut of a gown's very sleeves has now become a question of status and wealth . . ."

Mercifully, I made my escape.

I found Sophia not far from our chambers, hunched over her needlepoint. Her gown was of the finest wool, which ordinarily should have been too warm in high summer, but Sophia seemed perpetually cold. It was dyed a soft rose, the perfect color for her porcelain-fair skin and dark hair. I wondered, idly, where she'd gotten it. Was Lord Brighton supplying her trousseau? The thought made me ill.

"Sophia!" I called out, glad to see her. At least I knew for certain she would not drown me in talk of marriage. "You will go blind trying to sew in the shadows like that. Come walk with me."

"Really?" She looked up hopefully, her violet eyes wide. "Could we walk the cloisters?"

I smiled at her; I couldn't help it. After my conversation with Walsingham on the Hundred Steps, Sophia had gone from being a worrisome little sprite to someone I needed to protect. I'd been making it a habit to pay greater attention at mealtimes and in my rounds about the castle for any mention of Lord Brighton. The man truly did keep much to himself. Which was just as well, given Sophia's attacks of fainting spells whenever he showed his face.

And she had every right to faint to avoid him, I'd decided. I'd learned a great deal about the lord, and not just that his coffers were full of gold. Lord Brighton was forty years old if he was a day. He had a massive library of books on all manner of subjects, including, it was whispered, the arcane. Is that why he wanted to marry Sophia, I wondered? When Lord Brighton wasn't at the Queen's court, he locked himself up in his grand ancestral home in southern Wales for months at a time, with nary a visitor welcome. He scared me, and I wasn't even betrothed to him. No wonder Sophia was cold all the time.

"Yes, we'll walk all three cloisters today, the Horseshoe, Canon's, and Dean's, and you'll tell me which house you would pick out for yourself."

Sophia clapped her hands together and laughed, the sound of a happy child. I tucked her hand into my arm, and we set off.

The day was bright and sunny, and the sharp, fresh air chased away my sleepiness, at least for the moment. We passed the Round Tower with its thickly painted English roses, and I frowned at them as we walked. Although originally she'd been incensed by the unsanctioned decorations, the Queen must have decided the flowers were intended to honor her after all, or she'd have washed the cheap paint off long since. And they were rather festive, I decided, all bright red petals and dark green stems. We trooped down to the Lower Ward, passing under the archway into the Horseshoe Cloister to make our rounds.

"Well, none of these appeal," Sophia said solemnly as we passed the first set of houses, her gentle voice managing the finest thread of disdain. I glanced up to the timber-and-daub-frame homes that lined the semicircular yard. These homes were reserved for the priests of Saint George's Chapel, and had been restored by Queen Mary. But Mary Tudor hadn't exactly been known for her architectural daring. The homes marched in lockstep around the grassy space, and there were barely a few benches to break up the yard itself.

One of those benches was occupied, a welcome surprise. The Spanish courtier Nicolas Ortiz was bowed over a small leather-bound book, making careful notations in the margins with a finely feathered quill. He looked up, distracted for a moment as we approached, seeming confused as to why we might be there to interrupt his reading. Immediately, however, his dancing golden eyes cleared, and he stood up and greeted us with a courtly bow. "You honor the morning with your presence, fair ladies," he said in pretty, accented English, and I laughed. Sophia ducked her head, suddenly shy, as she was with most of the men in the court.

"Good morrow to you, my lord," I said, to cover Sophia's distress. "You are finding the day to your liking?"

"Any day that allows me to read in the shadow of a chapel so fine as this is a grand day indeed," Ortiz said, gesturing to the magnificent Saint George's Chapel that soared behind us. I glanced at his book and realized it was a Catholic prayer book. A tiny pot of ink rested beside him on the bench.

I found myself warming to the man. I might not have agreed with all of the teachings of his faith—and I might have been in service to a fiercely Protestant Queen—but I admired anyone's tenacity to serve God in his own fashion . . . especially if he did it quietly and with reverence, as Ortiz clearly did, despite his dandified airs. "Then I wish you all the peace the day can bring you," I said sincerely.

He smiled, dazzling us with the sudden beauty of his face, and raised his left hand in a gracious salute, his quill still in his fingers. By rote I noted the movement with Cecil's words ringing in my ears. *Always observe, always remember.* There were few left-handed men in the court, and I suspected Ortiz hid the condition as best he could, lest he be called out for having bad luck. The fact that he did not think we would judge him made me like him even more. There needed to be more grace such as this in the Queen's court, I thought.

"And to you as well, fair maids," he said, bowing to us. "The most gentle of days."

We exchanged a few more pleasantries, then continued on our way after he bowed over our hands once more. As we smiled our good-byes, I caught the scent of oranges and cloves about Ortiz, a fitting mixture for such a warm spirit.

The Spaniards most assuredly were not all bad.

The next clutch of homes on our tour was the Dean's Cloister, small cramped buildings fitted out for scholars around a square courtyard, and then the Canon's Cloister. We gazed around the pretty buildings lining this area, and I reminded Sophia of our game. "Which house, then, Sophia, would you choose to live in if you could?"

"That one, I should think!" she said, pointing to the largest home in the square. Number six of the Canon's Cloister was built against the castle's curtain wall, and likely had views out toward the Thames. The house had an extension that allowed it to reach farther out into the courtyard than its neighboring homes, and flowers spilled from well-tended boxes. It was pretty, without question, but it was something more than that.

I looked at Sophia, unsure if I should tease her, given what I knew of the home's current occupant. While typically the house was reserved for men of the cloth, Elizabeth wasn't much one to stand on ceremony, and she quartered whom she wished in the priests' homes. "And why do you like it so? Because it is the largest—or the finest?"

"Because it is the safest," Sophia said resolutely. "It has the best sense around it, a place in which I know I would always feel protected."

I immediately decided against teasing her. Had Sophia known that Lord Brighton currently made number six his residence, I suspected she would no longer take such enjoyment from the neatly kept home. Instead I squeezed her arm, and we continued on in happy companionship, emerging back into the Lower Ward a few minutes later.

As much as the walk invigorated me, I could already sense the fatigue of the past few days returning as we made our way back up toward the Middle Ward. I resolved to stop in at the herb mistress. Surely she had some remedy for drowsiness. I could not afford to be anything less than sharp, if I was to learn to read . . . and solve the riddle of Marie's untimely death.

I sighed in thought, and Sophia looked up at me, her enjoyment dimming.

"You're thinking of her again, aren't you," she said. "Marie Claire?"

I nodded. Sophia's Sight might not have been fully in flower, but her intuition was clear and sharp. She would be of use to the Crown no matter what. I remembered Walsingham's quiet words about the possibility that Sophia's abilities might not be strong enough to merit her place beside the Queen. That could not be. So our first step was to make sure the girl did not marry a codger. We could explore her abilities more thoroughly after that.

"It's all I can think of anymore," I said. So far, I'd not spoken of Marie to any of our small group except Sophia. Her death was a mystery I had to puzzle out without tipping my hand, at least until I had a real lead.

Sophia nodded. "I knew the guards would find her that night—or, I should say, I was not surprised when they discovered her," she amended quickly, her cheeks going pink as she caught me staring at her in surprise. "I dreamed it, I think. Before it happened."

I felt my eyes go even wider. This was new information

to me. "You dreamed it, Sophia? As part of your gift? Why didn't you say anything?"

She gave a pretty shrug, dismissing her own abilities. "Mine is no gift worth wanting."

I thought of my own skills, and the flaw that the Queen had so callously assigned me. "Sometimes we don't get to choose our gifts," I said, and she sighed.

"But my dreams don't always come true. They *never* did when I was a child. And most still don't, in fact, so it would do me no good to share what is so often false—or to claim a skill where none exists."

She fell silent, and we walked a few steps more. Then she continued speaking quietly, as if she were talking to herself, not to me. "I dreamed about Marie three days before . . . before it happened," she said. "A horrible dream that I remembered too well. I was so frightened! Then nothing happened for a bit, and I thought it was another false vision. I even thought to warn Marie, but . . ." She looked away quickly, and my heart twisted. When you couldn't trust your own instincts, what could you trust at all?

Sophia shook her head. "When the alarm went up that Marie had been found, I knew how it had happened exactly. Or I believed I did. But several days passed without any word on her killer. So once again I feared that I'd been wrong."

I felt my breath quicken. "Can you remember your dream about Marie Claire? Can you share it with me?"

She bit her lip. "Are you sure you want to hear it?"

I nodded. I'd never been more certain of anything in my life.

"Well, it's just . . ." Sophia stopped, her head tilted, apparently unaware of the odd pose she struck. I glanced around to see if anyone was paying attention, but the cloisters were blessedly empty. Then Sophia began to rock a little, and I looked at her in alarm. Rocking I could cover, even a little humming. But if she started screaming or bleating like a sheep, I didn't know what I'd do.

Then Sophia began to speak, and her voice was startlingly different and gorgeously lyrical, almost like a bard's. The words that tumbled out of her rooted me to the ground.

"Great excitement marked her steps.
She was moving fast,
The kind of pace that starts with ease
But can never last."

I blinked rapidly, focusing on Sophia's mouth, on the words washing over and through me. Something powerful was happening here, something almost magical. I knew I had to memorize Sophia's words exactly. There'd be time to understand them later.

"The darkness came down far too quick,
A light put out, she turned.
Her face, it spoke of sly delight,
The power of what she'd learned.
But then he bore down swift and still,
His hands about her neck.
His blade it flashed into the night,
No pity or regret.
His task was only that she died.

His cuts, howe'er, were those of pride.
And as he stole away, he smiled,
His light eyes dead, his dark hair wild."

Sophia stopped talking, and in the sudden silence I felt as if a chasm had opened up between us. She looked at me, a blush crawling up her cheeks.

"That's it, I'm afraid," she said quietly, her voice dropping back into normal cadence. "I know it makes no sense—it was a dream, nothing more."

I fought to keep the excitement from my voice, drew her hand back into mine, and started walking again with her. "You've told no one else this? Not Cecil or Walsingham?" I asked.

"No one at all," she said, biting her lip. "It offered no real clues, other than the light eyes and dark hair—and that could be any of a hundred men."

"But from what you say, she *knew* the man who attacked her," I said. "She smiled at him, let him get close. And she was clearly coming from somewhere specific, still flush with excitement from what she'd learned." *What had you overheard, Marie? What had you learned?*

Sophia was unconvinced. "There is too much that can be discredited," she said. "I can only recall it in verse. It sounds like a bad play. No one will ever believe me."

I snorted. "I know far more about bad plays than you do." I quirked a smile. "Heavens, I know a certain troupe master who'd put you to work tomorrow if he could get you to write whole plays in rhyming schemes. Much easier to memorize that way."

Sophia laughed wistfully, and the look she gave me was far too wise for one so young. "I'm afraid I'm not meant for traveling theatre troupes. You've no idea how lucky you are, Meg, to have lived the life you have."

"Your life's not over yet," I said, squeezing her arm. I thought of Cecil's excitement as I'd recounted the conversation between de Feria and Rafe. I thought of Walsingham and his careful eyes and deceptive manner, his many twisting demands. These were men who thought of us as tools, Sophia included. But neither the Queen nor her advisors would marry off a *useful* tool. "If your dream helps lead us to Marie's attacker, then your gift is something rare indeed. I doubt Cecil and Walsingham would allow you to leave the court for wedded bliss, with such a gift as that."

Sophia frowned at me, then sudden comprehension dawned, bright in her eyes. She clasped her hands together like the child she still was, and my heart twisted again. Who in their right mind could marry this girl off to a man such as Lord Brighton!

"I—I would do anything, Meg, anything to remain here, and not cause anyone harm." She swallowed, looking around. She moved closer to me, and I took her hand in mine again, two careless maids going for a stroll through the Middle Ward. "I fear for Lord Brighton's safety," she confessed in low tones.

I still could not quite reconcile this idea, and it made me impatient. "It's not Lord Brighton I'm afraid for. It's you."

"No, no." She shook her head resolutely. "He is in danger—I can feel it. But I just don't know why."

Maybe Jane is planning to poison him? The thought gave me

unaccountable cheer. "Well, do not worry about it," I said with conviction. "You won't be marrying anyone, anytime soon."

"You're sure?" Sophia asked hopefully, and I thought inexplicably of Tommy Farrow, all morning-bright eyes and tow-headed trouble. How long ago it seemed since I had seen the boy . . . or his gallant troupe master. And where would they be now?

We passed under the archway of the Norman Gate and into the Upper Ward, the more private area of the castle grounds welcoming us home. I realized that I was no longer sure of anything in this place, especially for a girl as remarkable as Sophia. I couldn't change her fate any more than I could my own. I should have told her she had better chance trusting in the stars than to trust me. I was only one petty thief, up against the whole Queen's court.

"I'm sure," I said instead.

CHAPTER FOURTEEN

"Go for his eyes!"

I heard the barked command, but I was already punching my assailant's nose. He deflected me with a grunt of anger and unleashed a torrent of blows. He was stronger than me by far; I would never win this. Instead I crouched low and leaped toward my attacker, wrapping my hands around his waist and slipping behind him in one swift move. I straightened, pulled my arms up and clasped tight, kicking out his knees. As he dropped, I repositioned my arms around his neck and clenched him in an iron grip. He flailed at me, fingers stretching for my eyes now, and I tucked my head down then tightened, tightened, tightened until he spit with rage and pounded the dirt floor.

"Again!"

I rolled away to the right and he to the left, and then both of us staggered up. The guard eyed me malevolently. His nose was already streaming with blood from the last round's direct hit, and I couldn't blame him for being irritated. In the corner, the short, stout fight master conferred with Cecil, then sent Jane jogging across the small space.

Wonderful. I blew a strand of hair out of my eyes, reluctantly getting into ready position. "What now?" I asked grumpily. Jane routinely beat the stuffing out of me, and I was already tired. It felt like we'd been at this for hours. I slid my gaze to where Anna, Beatrice, and even little Sophia were working on clawing their attackers' eyes out, the guards wearing protective masks against the girls' nails. "I'll go for his eyes next time, I promise."

"You never go for his eyes," Jane retorted.

"Attack!" shouted the fight master.

We came together then, blocking and thrusting with the short, jabbing punches that would be our only defense in a fight. We were strong, but we were women. We would neither outweigh nor outmuscle a man, but we could hold our own if we were shrewd.

Jane cracked me on the skull, making my head ring, then darted back again. She was faster than I ever wanted to be, I decided, but there was nothing for it. I was not a killer; I was not a thug.

You don't know who you really are, I heard the Queen's voice accusing me.

Jane came at me again, and I slipped away barely in time, managing to land a glancing blow as we shifted our positions once more. Breath was coming fitfully for me now, and I blew out hard as I lifted my arms, my wrapped fingers already swollen.

"You're distracted," she said harshly. "Drift, and you die in something like this, Meg. You know that."

Anger flashed through me. Since Sophia had told me about her dreams three days earlier, I'd spent every free moment listening at doors and skulking in corners, trying to find out more about Marie's untimely death. I now had several theories about who might have been staging the court disruptions that so irked the Queen: a member of the Spanish delegation, an Englishman with Spanish connections, an Englishman with Catholic sympathies, or simply an Englishman who intensely disliked his new Queen. That didn't much decrease my number of suspects, and I was no closer to finding Marie's killer. I felt time was running out, the sands in the hourglass at a constant pour. If I was going to put any of the girls in danger, it would be Jane. She could take care of herself better than most. "I have learned—possibly—some new information," I said, my words sharp whispers in between swings. "About Marie. And her killer."

Jane grunted, her swing going wide but the movement carrying her close to me. She went for my throat, and we grappled together until she slid around me. "Good. That death has gone too long un-avenged." She pulled me back, exposing my neck. *Uh-oh.* "We can talk here," she said. "What did you learn?"

"Wait!" I lifted my hands and gripped her shoulder while hurling myself forward. We somersaulted off the woven-rush mat and to the straw-covered floor, breaking apart easily. No one noticed, and we sat for just a moment as if we were merely discussing the finer points of strangulation.

"Two things," I said. "First, I've learned that Marie's attacker was in fact male, and I suspect he was known to her. He was aware of her work with the Crown, was possibly an informant. Light eyes, darker hair. Emotional. Proud.

Operating under some kind of vendetta against her or against . . . something. The killing was not strictly professional. He was glad to do it." I paused. "And this I'm less certain of but still believe to be true: I suspect that whoever did the killing is also behind the disruptions we've experienced in the court. Certainly the theft of the baubles and the soaking of the women's gowns."

"Why?" Jane asked, glancing to me sharply. "There is a fair distance between petty theft and murder."

"But the same result, in the end. The court in disarray, just to a greater degree. And it is the women of the court who were targeted." I paused, considering. "How many days did it take to quell the speculation about Marie's death? I certainly heard nothing of it."

Jane tilted her head, considering. "A fortnight, nothing more. The story was passed about that she'd been robbed by a townsperson." She pursed her lips. "They moved her body outside the castle gates to avoid suspicion falling on the court. That's why I found it where I did. Everyone was more than willing to forget."

I nodded. "And when did the small disruptions begin again after that?"

"Mid-May. They've been increasing in frequency but not severity, other than the vestments-burning." She shrugged. "And that could be something entirely different. It was so much more violent than the rest, just like Marie's death."

"So two violent acts bracketing many small slights," I said. "It's been more than a month since the vestments were burned. I fear our villain may strike again."

"Why now?" Jane asked. "Last week's ball would have been the best opportunity for him. A revel, the castle overflowing with guests and courtiers." She shrugged. "Perhaps it is all mere coincidence."

"Enough!" The fight master's command drew us up short, and we were instantly on our feet, back in ready position. But Cecil had left, and Beatrice was delicately picking straw out of her hair, while flirting with the guards. Our session was at an end. "You're to attend the Queen in the Privy Garden," the fight master announced. He nodded to the guards, who were paid handsomely for both their silence and their aid in this particular set of studies. "Clean yourselves up and begone with you."

We curtsied dutifully, then hurried out of the stable area into the adjoining privy, which had been substantially improved since we'd first begun our lessons. In addition to the close stool in the corner, which harbored a chamber pot that was now faithfully changed after every use, there was a series of water jugs and basins lining one wall. We took turns pouring water to clean our faces and arms and changing out of our practice kirtles and bodices, lacing up our finer gowns with speed born of long practice. We helped one another, despite any small annoyances among us. The object was speed and thoroughness, and we were judged on this as much as everything else.

Less than a quarter hour later, we were all in the Privy Garden, keeping pace as the Queen took her walk. After the flurry of the practice session, it was a welcome respite to be asked to do nothing but wander along aimlessly. Excitement flowed through the air around us. The Queen, her closest ladies, and her nonspying maids had just returned from London, where she'd spent the last several days since the ball, entertaining the Bishop de Quadra, the stout new ambassador from Spain. Today was the first time all of her ordinary attendants and we maids a-spying were together in this private sanctuary since I'd received my initial orders.

And how private was it, really? I glanced around. There were dozens of women here; that made for scant solitude. We rounded the next bend in the garden path, and my thoughts strayed inexorably to Cecil's heinous assignment. Where could the Queen have true privacy in the castle, if only for the briefest of times? Her chamber would seem a natural location for privacy, of course, except the Queen slept with a half dozen ladies in attendance just beyond her bed's ornate canopy. This garden was a lovely oasis, but still—out of doors, and open to prying eyes. She seemed to favor Saint George's Hall, of course. . . .

That tripped my memory. The large, drafty Saint George's Hall was a wreck and a ruin, built more than a hundred years earlier and never updated. But more than once the Queen had tasked me to find a dropped bauble or bracelet in that unwelcome space and return the item to her in secrecy. She'd planted other trinkets around the castle, in other places, but none so frequently as in Saint George's Hall. I'd assumed it was a silly test. But instead did she venture there to be alone? Was that her own secret hideaway, to escape her royal obligations? As if I were running lines for the Golden Rose, another couplet began dancing through my mind: *To slip away a-wandering without the world a-wondering . . .*

Perhaps there was not so much freedom in the Queen's world as I was determined to believe. The thought made me curiously sad. *A chain too tight for sundering, her royal gilded cage.*

We turned again, a river of muted colors flowing down another cobbled walkway. The Queen was well ahead, the deep emerald of her gown startling in the morning light. The rest of us followed en masse, both ladies and maids, like an extended train. I gazed over the women, taking in details with rote practice. A smile, a cocked head, a whisper. Hands fluttering or at rest, skirts swishing in hypnotic measure.

And then I saw it.

"What is it?" Jane instantly tensed, still attuned to me after following me so closely in our staged combat session. "What just happened?"

It had been only a flash. A hand gloved in milk-white satin secreting a folded square of parchment from her dress, then pressing it into the slim fingers of an ungloved hand, just at the turn of the cobbled walkway. The bare hand slipping the package into her waistband. Fingers both covered and bare now smoothed down skirts, and no one but me had seen the subtle movement. It had happened so quickly, but I'd just seen one of Rafe's letters get passed from hand to hand, I was sure of it. I grinned, triumphant. *Got you.*

"A moment," I murmured, memorizing every detail as we continued our sedate progress. The woman who'd taken the letter was a lithe figure in a soft green gown, a gown whose subdued shade perfectly offset an ornately styled pouf of white-blond hair. *Hello, Lady Amelia.* If I'd not been looking exactly where I had, I might have missed the exchange entirely. But then, that was my role here.

To watch—and to steal. And, apparently, to catch other light-fingered ladies.

Lady Amelia . . . she had been friendly enough with the Spaniards, but her family was old and well respected. Was this just an innocent transfer? And who was the other woman, who'd given the letters to Lady Amelia? I'd seen only her hand. Gloves were not much favored among the younger women of the court, at least not in high summer. I frowned, my eyes darting from hand to hand. Only the ladies of the bedchamber wore any gloves at all.

Could that be right? Those august ladies had been parted from us since the ball, but . . . a traitor in the Queen's own bedchamber? Among her closest friends?

"What is it?" Jane prodded me again. "You've seen something."

I nodded, still trying to puzzle it out. "I think I just found one of the letters Rafe gave to Count de Feria," I said.

Jane glanced at me sharply, a grin spreading over her face. "From courtier to ambassador to English lady? That's a crooked path. Which one?"

"Lady Amelia has it now. I couldn't quite see who gave it to her."

"Makes you wonder what's in these letters," Jane said.

"And who they're really from," I muttered. Was it the pope or the king of Spain? Or someone else entirely? And what did Rafe have to do with them?

"Shall we see for ourselves? Tonight?"

I felt excitement stir within me, and not just because the chase was on. In that statement, Jane and I had become partners, if only in so small a task as nicking a note out of a lady's chamber.

Perhaps the castle would not be so bad a place after all, with adventures such as this.

"Tonight," I agreed.

We turned the corner to take another lap around the fragrant space, and were startled by a page waiting at the doorway to the garden. His eyes lit up when he saw me.

"Miss Margaret Fellowes," he said in that too thin, too-high voice that plagued some boys who'd not yet reached their manhood. "I present you with a summons from Sir William Cecil."

He proffered a salver bearing an ornate card. With my name on it.

My eyes flew open wide, and I looked from him to Jane, then back down again. My hesitation must have seemed odd, because the boy's hand began to tremble.

But I knew that salver, and what it meant. I'd not been taking classes in court etiquette for more than three months now for no reason, after all. I just couldn't believe it was meant . . . for me.

"Take it!" Jane hissed, and I reached out for the card. The boy tucked the salver under his arm, pivoting to escort me.

I turned the card over, and the words swam together. Jane was at my side, pressing close to translate, but I did not need her to read the card for me. My reading skills had progressed well enough for this.

Cecil was summoning me to his office chambers. To discuss a betrothal.

My betrothal, specifically.

I looked at Jane. She blinked at me. Then a wry smile creased her lips.

"Beatrice will lose her mind," she said.

I stared back down at the card. "She's not the only one."

CHAPTER FIFTEEN

I don't know how I even made it through the castle, stumbling blindly after the page. What had I done to merit this terrible turn of events? Why was I being punished? Had I not acted promptly enough in finding the source of the castle disruptions?

And who was being considered as my husband?

I barely glanced up as I passed into the Queen's receiving room. Normally this space was reserved for visiting ambassadors as they waited to present their suits to the Queen. Of late it seemed like a second Spanish stateroom, filled to bursting with the newly arrived members of the Spanish delegation and their hangers-on.

I'd tried to avoid this area of the castle since the ball, because it only served to remind me of Cecil's terrible orders to spy on the Queen. But I knew my way to the advisor's official chambers by heart nonetheless. It was a simple room meant to impress upon everyone that the Queen's advisor was but a lowly servant to Her Majesty. Cecil had a certain reverse conceit in this fashion. He was powerful, yet strove to appear humble. It was the kind of falseness that seemed to assuage his piety.

The room was boisterous and relaxed, proclaiming the camaraderie of men confident in their positions. Rafe was in the midst of a laughing group of courtiers, each more handsome than the last. I had a vague sense of capes and long silk-clad legs, and brightly colored embroidered doublets over short, paneled slops. Every one of the Spaniards wore a long, slender—and unsharpened—rapier, all part of the show, but at this moment the men were little more than a blur to me. I felt Rafe's eyes upon me even as I trained my gaze forward, but I couldn't look at him. I suddenly wished for Beatrice at my side. She would have provided an ample diversion, and left me free to gain my audience with Cecil.

I'd barely made it halfway through the room, when Rafe stepped into my path.

"An unexpected pleasure," he said, reaching for my hand and bowing over it, the perfect gentleman. His touch still sent a thrill through my fingers, and I pulled my hand away just a bit too quickly. The page stopped in front of us, clearly annoyed at being forced to wait.

"What brings you to our quarters this afternoon, sweet Meg?" Rafe asked.

I clutched the card in my hand reflexively, but swallowed. I could not say that Cecil had summoned me, for no reason at all. Why would the Queen's advisor have need of a maid? Unless it was to discuss her betrothal? A horrifying thought struck me. What if my *intended* was standing in the room beyond? How had it all come to this?

Rafe's eyes dropped to my hand with its damning contents, then darted to the servant, taking in the page's salver. His gaze came up to mine with a snap, his eyes intent.

"Are there congratulations in order, fair maid? If so, you don't look entirely happy."

I smiled at him sweetly, my own eyes widening in a worthy approximation of girlish glee. "'Tis the most amazing surprise, my lord, and I am the luckiest of girls."

If anything he looked even more shocked. "In truth?" he spluttered. "Is this what I think it—"

"Miss Fellowes?"

I started, and it was Walsingham, not Cecil, who was smiling at me from Cecil's chamber, that same odd half smile that he'd worn the night he'd escorted me along the North Terrace. He gestured for me to come to him, and my body seemed bound to do his bidding. Even now I felt it, urging me forward. I bobbed a curtsy to Rafe to give myself another precious moment of time to gather my thoughts.

"I bid you good day, my lord," I said, and he bowed in response.

"Good day to you as well, Miss Fellowes." Was that chagrin I heard in his voice? Was he truly dismayed that I was being summoned to discuss a betrothal? And if so . . . *what did that mean?*

I moved with some reluctance past Walsingham and into the shadowy reserve of Cecil's private domain. Walsingham shut the door behind him, cutting off the rolling noise of the Spaniards.

I approached Cecil's desk and dropped a curtsy. Because, truly, whyever stop curtsying when there's another to be made?

I rose, and Cecil looked at me with genuine worry in his gaze. "Whatever is the matter with you, Miss Fellowes? You look like you're being sent to the gallows."

I frowned at him, mutely lifting the summoning card. He glanced at it, then looked at Walsingham in exasperation. "Was that really necessary?"

Walsingham chuckled. "Miss Fellowes, how else would you have summoned a maid into a private conversation, through a gauntlet of Spaniards who need a reason not to pursue her farther than the door? Do you have a better suggestion?"

I blinked at him, and Cecil shook his head. "She is a maid of honor, Walsingham. We can summon her whenever we like."

"She is an unmarried girl who's going to find herself in close proximity to a knot of Spaniards too free with their time for their own good. And we may be summoning her quite frequently for the next fortnight, as well you know. Let it be thought that her marriage negotiations are under way. I know how much she's looking forward to the wedded state."

"It's excessive," Cecil said, and rolled his eyes.

Walsingham shrugged. "It's done. Do you take issue with the subterfuge, Miss Fellowes?"

"I— No, Sir Francis. I don't." Too surprised to be relieved, I struggled to catch up. "So this was a . . . misdirection? You've chosen no husband for me?"

"Not yet, no," Walsingham said. Wait . . . not *yet*? But he continued, oblivious to my thoughts. "We brought you here to discuss your assignment regarding the Queen and her possible paramour. What have you learned? You've had more than a week since the ball, and yet I see no progress."

So here it was. Hastily I reordered my thoughts. I'd been expecting this conversation—just not layered in such deceit. "The Queen has been traveling since just last night," I said smoothly. "When at Windsor she rarely dines alone, and when she is not in her Presence or Privy Chamber, she's taking her exercise, riding, or spending time in contemplation. Always she is accompanied by her ladies-in-waiting unless she seeks real privacy; in which case, Kat Ashley attends her."

They knew all this, of course. "Your point?" asked Walsingham.

"The Queen's chambers are protected by a rotating guard, and her royal bed by another layer of protection—her ladies of the bedchamber. For her to slip away in the dark of night and tarry in another set of rooms would be difficult, but not impossible. Guards, after all, can be bought. I suggest that rather than push me upon Her Grace within her bedchamber, you add a new man to the guard outside it—a man you trust to follow your orders over the Queen's—and have him make the reports you seek. Not me."

I thought this had all been rather neatly done, but Walsingham seized on a portion of my speech I had not anticipated.

"If the Queen were to tarry in another set of rooms, as you state it, Miss Fellowes," he asked with genuine interest, "where would those rooms be?"

Instantly Saint George's Hall sprang to mind, with its moldering tapestries hanging from great stands and its dusty furniture and old rushes. It wasn't a pleasant room, but it would be private. And I would never suggest it to these two, that much was certain.

"There are several possibilities," I said instead. "I am ruling them out as I go. However, it is unlikely that the Queen would journey very far afield from her own bedchamber. There is too much opportunity for her to be caught out." I came to my second gambit. "So in addition to your bribing a guard, I also think I should simply narrow down the choices of rooms where she might visit, and then set a watch from a central vantage point."

"I see," Walsingham said. "And this will take some time, I suspect?"

I nodded gravely. "Indeed it will, to give the task its due. You would not want me to misstep in a matter of such vital importance."

"You've a fortnight, no more," Cecil growled from behind Walsingham. Leave it to Cecil to bring a ray of sunshine into the conversation.

"I will give you my report then." *Or come up with another excuse to delay you, most likely.*

Walsingham nodded, ready to dismiss me, but I could not let this opportunity pass me by. "Sir Francis, if I may, I have a question pursuant to my observation of the Spanish ambassador and his men."

Walsingham's brows went up. "Your report was successfully delivered on that subject, Miss Fellowes. You have no further assignment."

I kept my tone even, my words light. As if I weren't making up a wild accusation out of whole cloth. "Still, I must share this. I have reason to believe it was a Spaniard who killed Marie Claire. If I could prove that, would it not be of service to the Crown?"

That stopped them both. Walsingham crossed his arms over his chest, and Cecil steepled his fingers on his desk, leaning forward. "Proceed," Walsingham said.

"If my theory is for naught, I will not waste your time with it. But to determine its merit I have a question."

Cecil growled from the darkness. "Just tell us your theory, Miss Fellowes. You waste our time already."

I twisted my lips in not quite a sneer. "You are training me to be a skillful spy. I would learn my craft, Sir William."

Another pause. They knew the truth of my words, especially Cecil. "Then what is your question?" he snapped.

I started first with a question I knew the answer to, to get them conditioned to divulging information. Another ploy learned at my grandfather's knee. "The evening Marie died was that of the Saint George's Day ball, was it not?"

"Yes."

"And she had attended that ball throughout the evening?"

"Yes."

I nodded. "Did you send Marie out to gather information for you that night?"

Walsingham's eyes narrowed. "Marie moved freely throughout the court. She was our chief informant."

"But did you send her out for something specific that night?"

He nodded. "I did. She was to follow de Feria through the eve. She was a friend of his wife's, who still frequented the palace at that time. We suspected the Count de Feria to be passing letters through his wife and other ladies of the court, and wanted to identify who his contacts were, and what those letters entailed. Marie felt she was close to making a discovery."

Again with the letters! "And did Marie report to you, before she—ah—died?"

He shook his head. "No, Miss Fellowes, she did not. We did not believe she had even a chance to learn anything new that night. De Feria and his wife were absent from the revel that evening, claiming illness. It was unusual, and poorly timed, with his negotiations with the Queen still at a premium, but there was nothing for it."

"You did not check to see if de Feria was in truth ill?" I thought of Jane and her poisoned flasks. Had she drugged the Spanish ambassador that night as well?

"It was not *his* sickness that kept him away," Walsingham said. "His wife was in the third month of her confinement and came down with fever. He was at her bedside. There was no reason to intrude."

I puzzled over this. I was sure Marie had seen someone—or heard something—that had made her move with excitement that evening. I was also sure she'd known her killer. And, finally, there had been suspicious letters changing hands back then—and now we had another set of letters, circulating anew. Had the first set of letters led to Marie's murder? Were these new letters also worth killing for?

"Thank you, Sir Francis," I said, completely at a loss but smiling with confidence and secret knowing, as if he'd just handed me the key to solving the mystery of Marie's death single-handedly. "That gives me everything I need to know to move forward."

Walsingham snorted. "Indeed. And when may we expect your report on this personal investigation?"

"When I am—"

"No." He cut me off with a soft inflection of the word, raising his hand. "If you are to 'learn your craft,' Miss Fellowes, you must know the value of presenting timely information. A fortnight hence is the Harvest Ball. There will be a masque and a feast. In the days that follow that event, the largest contingent of the Spanish will leave England's shores—including de Feria, as his work as ambassador will be at an end."

I blinked. "A fortnight?"

He grinned wolfishly at me. "It's well-timed, is it not? You can provide us your report on the Queen's activities, should you uncover any details, as well as your findings about Marie."

Panic squeezed my throat. A fortnight. So little time to potentially betray my Queen. I felt the mantle of traitor settle around me like a heavy cloak, but I managed a graceful nod.

"Of course, Sir Francis, Sir William. You will have your report by then." I lifted my chin. "And what shall I receive in return?"

Walsingham chuckled, enjoying the game. He had expected this as well. "What boon would you ask?"

"My freedom," I said crisply. You did not know what you might receive, if you did not ask.

Cecil began to splutter, but Walsingham lifted a hand. "Your freedom?" he repeated. "Explain that."

"You said when last we spoke that if my work saved the Queen's throne, you would let me return to my former life—with the Crown's word that you will not harm anyone in connection to me, nor approach me again."

"You dare to make demands?" Cecil's voice was rising in both volume and tone, but it was Walsingham who held this particular key for me. And Walsingham was regarding me evenly, with no expression at all on his face.

"You think so much of your former life, and so little of this, Miss Fellowes, that you would return to the squalor from which we plucked you? Surely you have wanted for nothing here."

"The hospitality of the Queen is more than one such as me would ever need," I countered, not rising to the bait of his "squalor" reference. "I am a simple girl, with simple needs." *And I simply need to get out of here before I might betray my Queen.*

Walsingham appeared to consider the question seriously, which was more than I had expected he would. "If the caliber of your information is sufficient, Miss Fellowes, then you have the right to negotiate the terms of your departure."

That wasn't clear enough. Who was to determine "sufficient"?

"If I deliver you a Spanish murderer, Sir Francis, would you consider that sufficient enough?"

He nodded to me. "If he threatened the Queen herself, yes," he said, his mouth twisting a little around the words. "And if you deliver the villain to me no later than a fortnight hence."

I felt excitement catch at me, swelling me up, but before I could enjoy the moment too much, Walsingham continued. "And if you do not deliver the murderer, or you deliver him too late for us to be able to capitalize on his capture before the bulk of the Spaniards leave our shores, then you may *not* bring up the subject of your departure from the Queen's court again for a full year, on penalty of imprisonment. Agreed?"

All the breath died in my throat. *A full year?* A full rotation of seasons away from the Golden Rose. They would surely forget me then.

"Agreed," I managed with a confident shrug. "Sir William, Sir Francis. I bid you good day." I executed the perfect curtsy, then took my leave of them. With eyes straight ahead I breezed back out through the receiving rooms. I might have heard Rafe say my name as I passed, but I could not afford to stop. Not yet. Not now.

I had fourteen days to solve a murder. Fourteen days to prove my worth. Fourteen days to gain my freedom.

Fourteen days to fail.

CHAPTER SIXTEEN

As if the weather were in grim accord with the hopelessness of my cause, it rained for six solid days after that. And I don't mean the kind of rain that resulted in what my grandfather referred to as "soft days"—light showers drifting down from glowering skies to dampen the countryside, the sun peeking out, only to be nudged back behind the clouds. No, this rain was a torrent, bitter and unseasonably cold, chasing us indoors and keeping us there, musty, sodden, and foul-tempered.

Especially the Queen.

"I did not imagine I could hate this heap of stones any more than I already did," grumbled Jane, scowling out over the quadrangle of the Upper Ward from the archways of our training room. "Clearly, I need to work on my imagination."

We had not had the chance to search for Lady Amelia's letter that first night, nor any night thereafter. We had not had the chance to learn more about the Spaniards, sequestered as they were in their own section of the castle. Even our fighting classes had been temporarily halted, as it was just too oppressive in the castle for that much effort. While Windsor was one of the grandest homes in all of England, it still proved to be too small in a torrential storm, particularly when livestock was herded into the lowest quarters, their combined reek and bleating cries adding another layer of misery to the nobility and servants trapped above.

I blew out a frustrated breath. Another unexpected downside of the storm had been the impossible press of people roaming the castle's halls. Spying proved difficult when there was no place to hide. Even worse, the Queen had demanded that all of her ladies put forth their best efforts to entertain her. This meant endless hours of dancing, music, and acting in front of Her Grace, all of us tucked away in her Privy Chamber. These were command performances, which meant all five of her spies had to be there too, no matter that this was a colossal waste of time. My complaints to Cecil and Walsingham had gone unheeded. Indeed, I think the two advisors relished the rain, as it allowed them long days to sit and rifle through their papers and books, creating entirely theoretical conspiracies, only to devise ways to rout them out.

Finally, however, the Queen had claimed a headache, and we'd been set free to scatter as far as the rain would allow. Which, it should be noted, was not far.

"There you are!"

Jane and I turned to see Anna bustling up to us, carrying what looked to be a heavy stack of blankets, her eyes bright with excitement, her mouth stretched into a wide smile. She stumbled just as she reached us, and both Jane and I leaped for her, all of us laughing as she shoved her bundle into our arms. "I did not think I'd have a chance to try these out before the rain let up, but it looks like we still have time!"

I looked from her to the sheeting rain outside. We could barely see three feet in front of our faces. "I don't think that will be an issue."

"What are these things?" Jane lifted the garments in her hands. "Cloaks?"

"Not just any cloaks." Anna beamed. "I got the idea when they herded all of the sheep into the lower halls after the first great storm broke. They weren't wet."

Jane frowned at her. "Of course they were wet. They're the wettest, smelliest sheep I've ever been unfortunate enough to call my neighbors."

Anna shook her head. "Their *wool* was wet, but not their skin," she said. "I got the idea that if I could curry the lanolin from their skin and apply it to the proper cloth, we'd have waterproof cloaks—lighter than leather and cheaper besides, easier to pack and clean. I've tried a few different formulas, working with different tonics, and, well—here we are."

We stared at her, then back at the cloaks. "You have been experimenting with sheep sweat?" Jane asked.

"And it works?" I chimed in after.

Anna shook out a cloak and held it up high. "You want to wait here, or go out and see for yourselves?"

She didn't have to ask us twice. As one we donned the cloaks and lashed them to our bodies. They were lightweight, as Anna had promised, and only a little bit stiff. But the moment we ventured out into the Upper Ward, we gasped. Water bounced off the surface of our cloaks as if they were made of iron. "You're a genius!" Jane shouted from deep within her cowl. "I can't believe this!"

"Quickly! And keep to the walls!" Anna shouted back.

"We don't want anyone to look out and catch us actually having fun."

We ducked and ran flush against the walls, down past the quadrangle and through the Norman Gate. The sodden guards stared at us, bemused, but let us pass when Anna announced our names and claimed we were on an errand for the Queen. Used to Elizabeth's foibles, they didn't even blink, and if they noticed our miraculous cloaks, they were themselves too wet to care.

We ran around the Round Tower, and I felt my feet yearn to take flight, the whole of the Lower Ward yet to be explored. But beside us in the rain, Anna skidded to a stop, and Jane crashed into her. "What!" Jane groused, bouncing back. "What is it?"

"Look!" Anna pointed up to the rim of the Round Tower, and we squinted in the rain.

The heavily painted English roses were long gone, the cheap paints that had been used to craft them no match for the days upon days of downpour. But a closer look revealed what those heavy images had left behind.

There, etched into the stone, where one of the roses had been, was a symbol I had never seen before. An inverted triangle surmounting a cross. It was small, no more than a hand span in height, and looked like it had been pounded into the rock quickly. It was neither deep nor well defined. But it was definitely there. "Here's another one!" Jane announced, another quarter turn around the tower. We darted back through the Norman Gate and around the far side of the tower, and found four of the symbols in all—four symbols hidden behind what had been nearly two dozen painted English roses.

"Are they religious marks?" I asked as Anna stared hard at the symbol, committing it to memory.

"Possibly. The cross makes sense for that, but not the triangle. Either way, they do not serve the crown of England." She shook her head. "We'll need to tell the Queen. And Cecil." She peered through the pouring rain, her face upturned and surprisingly pretty beneath the cowl of her own creation. "They'll want these carvings gone before the rain lifts, whatever they are."

"You have the right of that."

We turned and fled into the castle, shedding our cloaks as we went. We agreed by common consent that Anna would get the role of telling the Queen, and Cecil after. Jane might have been the most ruthless of us, and I might have had the lightest touch . . . but Anna had seen these carvings in a driving rainstorm and had immediately recognized them as a potential problem. One day, I had no doubt, her sharp mind and quick wits would save us all.

The rain fell for fully six more hours, and by the time the sun peeked out at last and we ventured back outside, the work on the Round Tower was complete. Nothing remained of the four strange symbols cut into the stone. Instead Elizabeth's own shields had been carved over them, looking as if they had always rested there, high upon the walls.

Night fell hard that same evening, the moon partially hidden behind a drifting fog. By midnight the castle would be as dark as a shroud. It was barely ten o'clock, but we were all fast abed.

Good little spies that we were.

I sat up on my sleeping mat. Jane sat up on hers. Both of our gazes turned to the tinkling sound of bells as they shivered in a light fall of water that rained down from an intricate series of tilted flagons set up on a ledge between us. Over the past few weeks we'd observed the length of time that various flagons full of water took to drip out enough water to send it cascading downward over the string of bells, making a sound only discernible to us, as we slept closest to the apparatus. This eve we'd carefully set the musical timepiece with specific deliberation, and it had worked perfectly. "We go now?" Jane whispered.

I nodded. With the skies finally clear the ladies-in-waiting were to practice their night-goddess dance for the upcoming masque on the cobbled stones of the Queen's Privy Garden this night, so we'd have easily an hour to search. "Just one thing." I moved over to our community chest and opened it as quietly as I could. Rooting around beneath the dozens of wraps and boxes and packets of possessions that we each stored there, I finally found what I was seeking. I pulled out the waxed cloth packet and undid the intricate knotwork while Jane watched. She chuckled softly as she saw what the package held.

"Picklocks?" she asked. "Why didn't you bring these out when we covered that section in class? Those look better than anything they gave us to practice on."

"Because I wanted to learn on an inferior set." I held the picklocks up to the window, the thin shaft of moonlight making them seem like otherworldly creatures, at once delicate and strong. "My grandfather gave them to me, right before he died. Why, I'll never know." I shook my head. "We didn't have much occasion to pick locks on the stage."

Jane reached out and touched the tools almost reverently. "Maybe he knew you'd end up here?" Then her gaze dropped to the remaining item in the packet. "What's in the book?"

"Nothing," I said curtly. I slid the picklocks into my waistband and wrapped the cloth packet with the book up tightly, then picked up the binding strings. I didn't expect my paltry belongings would have excited the curiosity of the other maids in our small troupe, but I had nothing else that was mine alone. I reset the lock knot carefully.

"Anna could read it for you, you know," Jane said, and I tensed for a moment before shoving the wrapped book back into the chest.

"I know," I muttered. "But I want to read it myself." My grandfather's book remained an enigma to me. Ostensibly a book of verse, its words had yet to make any sense, despite my improving skill with the English language. I'd decided to stop looking at it until I could read an ordinary book straight through, but even though I'd achieved that feat, I still couldn't understand the little leather tome. It was infuriating.

We made our way to the sleeping chambers of the ladies-in-waiting. Luckily, there were no guards at their door. I'd been worried about this but had considered it a risk worth taking, since the room would be empty and the women doubtlessly needed protection from every available guard while they practiced in the garden. *The doors are locked,* they would have assured the guards. *Attend to* us *instead.* I shook my head. Locked doors made people lax.

Jane's laughter was soft as I put my left hand on the door, fishing for my picklocks with my right. They slid easily into my hand, as if coming home. "No one would believe you are using those for the first time," she said.

"As long as they get us where we want to go," I whispered back, working the delicate tools into the lock. The door gave far more easily than it should have, and I whistled low. "I don't think this lock would offer much resistance to anyone determined to get in."

Jane snorted. "I'm sure there have been many occasions for ladies-in-waiting needing to get in and out of their chambers with ease. There must be a passage out of here behind one of the panels in their chamber as well."

"You think?"

"Has to be. I'm surprised we haven't found one in ours. I'd wager the other chambers are riddled with them."

I thought about that as we slipped into the room, appreciating the warm fire burning low in the grate. Would the Queen know all of the passages within the castle? Could she find privacy anywhere within the very walls of Windsor?

"What are we looking for?" Jane's words were loud against my ear, causing me to jump.

"Lady Amelia's wardrobe. Particularly the dress she wore that day in the garden, or at least the skirts. She probably has a pocket sewn into them." The day clothes of the ladies-in-waiting were not dissimilar to our own—laced together in separate pieces to increase the number of times we could wear the outfit between washings. Amelia's soft green skirts would have been hung up and out of harm's way as soon as she'd returned from walking in attendance on the Queen in the gardens.

We found the garment easily, but a quick search of the pleats and hems therein was fruitless. So were our efforts to rummage through her collection of pouches, which would generally have been attached to a chain or sash around Amelia's waist. None of them contained any letters.

I stood, my head cocked. "Where would a woman hide a letter if not in her skirts or pouches?" Privacy was a virtually nonexistent luxury in the communal quarters we shared.

"Under her wig?"

I goggled at Jane. "Lady Amelia wears a wig?"

Jane shrugged. "She's not the only one. Her hair is as fine as corn silk and can't bear the torture of the braiding and stiffening."

"You cannot be serious."

"I am." She grinned at me. "I wore a wig, when I first came here."

"Whyever for?" I asked. "Your hair looks perfectly suitable as it is!"

"Well, now it is, yes." She bobbed her head. "But when I arrived, I'd shorn it close and tight. I looked more like a boy than a girl, they told me, so Cecil commissioned a wig to match my own hair—but appropriately long. I still have it," she said. "But Amelia wouldn't need her wig tonight. They're going to dress in cowls and long robes if they're practicing for the masque. No one will even see her hair."

I looked around the room, momentarily at a loss. The fire burned low in the grate, casting flickering shadows. Then my gaze lifted, and I saw what I was searching for, upon the high boarded chest. An elegantly poufed shock of white-blond hair.

"It doesn't look quite right, not sitting on a head," I said, and Jane followed my gaze.

"It doesn't look quite right even when it *is* on her head," she said. We dragged a stool over, and I stepped up on it, easily reaching the wig. I poked my hand underneath.

Nothing.

"This is beginning to annoy me," I said. "Lady Amelia isn't that smart!"

"And mayhap neither are we," Jane agreed, equally disgusted.

Time was now growing short. We rummaged through the interior of the boarded chests, and looked under the beds, through the sheets. We found two small coffers, of which my picklocks made short work. We spread their contents out on the hearth, careful to keep the two boxes separate. One was filled almost to overflowing with scraps of silk, broken bits of jewelry, and shillings. Jane frowned, looking at it, then looked at the box as well. "This could be the right box, you know. The lady who owns it is a bit of a scavenger."

I glanced at it, seeing it in a new light. "No," I said resolutely. "She may be a scavenger, but she is a poor one. Lady Amelia has a fine wig; I don't think that was purchased by the Queen's allowance." I lifted the gold-inlaid chest I held. "If either of the boxes belongs to her, it's this one." I frowned at it in my hands, testing its weight. Something didn't make sense. "There's a false bottom here."

Jane leaned close, and together we carefully pried up the thin wooden base of the box.

Beneath it was a packet of neatly folded letters, lovingly bound in a strip of lavender cloth. I pulled out the top one, the bold slashing script evoking a sense of passion and urgency. "This one's written in Spanish," I said. "These are the letters!"

"Who are they from?"

I peered at the letter in scant light. "Somebody named Dona Victoria. No last name."

Jane pulled one of the letters from the packet. "The tone of this one is familiar, like a friend or a cousin." She shook her head. "This one isn't even to Lady Amelia; it's to her cousin."

"And this one—to an aunt maybe?" I held it up.

Jane took the next. "And to Lady Knollys."

I froze. "Lady Knollys?" Why was a lady of the bedchamber receiving letters from Spain? "It's much like the others?"

"As boring as a box of sticks."

While Jane frowned at it, I turned to the next one. My pulse quickened. "Another one in Spanish." I realized. "But dated more than three months ago."

Jane glanced over, then frowned. "Some of those words in that one don't make sense to me. If it's Spanish, it's not very good." She pointed to the word "*muito*." "That should be '*muy*.' Even I know that."

I smiled. Jane had been in the court for only seven months, but unlike me she'd picked up languages quickly, despite her humble birth. I turned to the second page, scanning further. "Why would Lady Amelia keep letters written in bad Spanish?"

"Maybe she's learning the language?"

I bit my lip. "But it is a . . . love letter, I think," I said. "To Lady Amelia herself. The writer uses the word '*amor*' here, and here again. That's some Spanish lesson."

Jane snorted. "I'd probably pay more attention that way."

Then her eyes widened. "Tell me that one's not from Dona Victoria too!"

"No!" I said. "It's unsigned."

We burst into giggles, and it was odd to hear laughter on Jane's lips. Odd . . . but good. I shuffled through the rest. They were packed tightly together. "More letters to members of court—but some of these are sealed. Never delivered, do you think?"

"Or read and resealed. There are eight letters here, including the love letter." She pointed. "The one to Lady Knollys I find interesting. I don't know why Amelia would have that old bat's letter. They don't seem close."

I nodded. Could Lady Knollys be the traitor? Surely not! And another problem with that theory . . . "None of these are recent, either, from what I can tell. That means they aren't from Rafe's packet." I glanced up at Jane. "Should we have Anna look at all of them? In case they're . . . encoded?"

"She will love that, and I don't see why not." Jane pursed her lips. "You think Lady Amelia will notice they're gone?"

"Not if we can get them back in place soon. The ladies have more practices scheduled, after all. The masque is now only days away."

"Then take them we shall," Jane agreed. She tucked the packet of letters into her bodice and grinned at me. "I just want to be there when Anna starts translating, especially the love letter. She'll be in bliss."

I laughed, and we carefully rooted through the rest of the coffer. There was nothing else of import. We'd just decided to expand our search to the rest of the room, when the castle clock struck midnight, startling us with its intensity. Quickly we packed up the little boxes and put them back up on their respective shelves. We slipped out the door even as Jane was muttering again about looking for secret panels. But there was no time for anything like that, and well she knew it.

I worked the lock with my tools, taking a few precious moments to carefully reset it. Then we hastened toward our rooms.

We were only halfway down the corridor, however, when we heard the rapid footsteps of a dozen or more people bearing down on us—most of them women.

The ladies-in-waiting were returning.

CHAPTER SEVENTEEN

"In there!" I hissed, and we dove for a side chamber that was barely more than an indentation in the wall. Pressing up against one of the columns that flanked its entryway, I peeked worriedly out.

"Keep your eyes down!" Jane whispered fiercely.

I looked over at her, cocking a brow. "What?"

"Keep your eyes down—else they will catch the firelight of the torches as they go by."

I dropped my gaze, and not a moment too soon. A horde of feet walked by us, slippered women and booted men, in a knot of murmuring, exhausted people. Opposite me, I heard Jane tapping the wall panels quietly. The shallow room was something like a guard's sanctuary, I realized, meant to discreetly house the men assigned to protect the ladies' chambers without forcing them to stand directly in the corridor.

A . . . guard's sanctuary? Belatedly, I noticed the wooden stools on either side of the paneled alcove, and the ornate chest between them. The stools did not appear like they were included in the alcove for mere ornamentation.

I reached out and jerked hard on Jane's arm, gesturing

furiously that we needed to get moving. The women would enter their room quickly enough, and if the guards decided to return to this place as their evening resting spot, we would have nowhere to hide.

"A moment, just a moment," Jane muttered. She was running her hands along the wall.

"We don't *have* a moment!" I hissed. "They'll *be* here in a moment."

"There's something—not right about this." Her hands moved down the panels, pressing inward. She hesitated, but even I noticed the slight inward give to the wood.

The guards bid the women good night, and then we heard them discussing in low tones the details of the night watch. "Jane . . . ," I warned, just as I heard a tiny but distinctive crack.

"I knew it," she breathed, her words rich with satisfaction. "Do you have your candle?"

"Yes, but— What is *that*?" I tore my gaze away from the guards and stared down in horror. In the half-lit gloom, I could see a yawning black cavern beyond the knee-high panel.

"That," she said, "is the real way to get around Windsor Castle."

We both scrambled into the space, and Jane replaced the panel just in time as we heard footsteps passing outside. We could see the sconce light from the hallway beyond through two perfect circles cut into the panels—spy holes! I fitted my eyes to them, and was rewarded with a charming view of a guard's wool-clad calves. Rocking back on my heels, I saw identical spy holes above me. The panel opened low, but the holes had been hollowed out along the wall's entire length.

I stood slowly with Jane, both of us clutching each other. "We'll need that candle," she said, whispering into my ear.

I turned and squinted into the passageway beyond. It was dank and clammy . . . and as black as pitch. "We should take some steps away from the panel before we light it, though, lest they see us as easily as we can see them," I said. There was also the issue of the flint strike, which was quiet but not soundless.

Beside me, I felt Jane nod. "Never been in so dark a place as a castle, I will tell you that," she muttered. I thought again of what her life must have been like on the high plains of North Wales. I thought of my own life, in the village streets. We'd spent many a night camping in barns and open fields, but there'd always been music, dancing—and light. This darkness that pressed onto us seemed like an early death. "Off with us, then," I said.

We took one step, then another, cleaving together like sisters in the passageway. It was broad enough for two stout men to walk abreast, but after the faintest touch to discern the walls on either side, we kept our hands and bodies close to the center. Three more steps, and I felt the wall in front of me only moments before I would have smacked into it.

The corridor branched off to the left and right. Pulling Jane with me, I sidled to the left, then made short work with the flint striker, lighting my candle and holding it high.

"Charming place."

The corridor was lined with cobwebs and was filthy in an abandoned-looking way. "We've got three choices," I said. "To the left, to the right, and back to wait for the guards to leave."

Jane looked up at the bare, rime-encrusted walls. "We can't go back. They may be there all night."

"We can't get lost in here either," I pointed out.

"True." She seemed to be pondering a complex problem. "Let's just go down a few steps and see what we may find."

We prised a stone out of the wall and set it a few inches out into the corridor, to mark that we'd been by this turn. Then we set off down the corridor, Jane muttering that we were heading south, toward the quadrangle of the Upper Ward. Sooner or later we would get to an exterior castle wall, she reasoned, and possibly a staircase down to the ground level.

The passageway split, and split again, and we were moving down the third turn (each carefully marked) when something struck me as different.

I stopped, holding my candle aloft, staring at the corridor around me. It had broadened, and was almost spacious here, with high walls and ceiling, and even empty sconces at regular intervals. And there was something else about it, too. Something that made a knot of dread ball up in my stomach.

"It's clean," I said.

Jane, who'd moved a few paces ahead of me in the dancing candlelight, stopped as well. "You're right!" she said excitedly, her hands reaching out to the walls. They were as blank as ever, but they had been brushed down. No dust or grime coated their surface. I swept the candle low. The stone walkway had also been swept bare. Whoever had cleaned this route had stopped short of spreading the floor with rushes, but that was all that had kept it from being any other corridor in the castle. That, and the walls weren't hung with warming tapestries.

"We must be close to something important," Jane mused. "Except, if I'm right, we're near very the quadrangle." She turned to face me and peered past my shoulder down the wide, tidy corridor. "Should we go back the other way?"

That caused an even greater clutch in my stomach. "No," I said evenly. "We need to get out of here and back into our own beds before we are caught out."

She nodded, seeing the sense in that. We fell silent as we turned and proceeded down the hall, wondering where it would take us.

We didn't have to wait for long. The corridor ran in one long, wide swath, without turning. I could hear Jane count off measured steps as we moved forward, her mind—so indifferent in our classroom studies—now bent to a task for which it seemed to be made. The walkway was almost welcoming in its forthright direction too. Right up until it dead-ended into a wall that looked like it was made of solid yew. Clearly, the opening to this corridor had been paneled over—which meant it could contain a hidden doorway!

Jane clapped her hands together, as happy as I'd ever seen her. The flickering candle showed the eagerness in her eyes. "This is it!" she said. "A way out!" She placed her hands on the wall, then pulled them back just as quickly, then tried again, her fingers pressing against the wall, searching. "It's not an entrance to the outside, though. Given that it's night after days of rain, the panel isn't cool enough."

"Well, what folly would that be, in truth?" I asked. I set the candle at the base of the wooden panel, the better to search as well. "It's one thing to allow deeper access within the castle, but an outside entrance would be a threat."

"Hmmm," Jane murmured to herself. "But where is the fun in not being able to leave the castle proper? Surely there would be a secret escape passage *somewhere*, for the royal family if nothing else."

I nodded. That made eminent sense. "Still, we should consider ourselves lucky this isn't it, then," I said. "Or we'd likely find a guard on the other side of the wall."

That quieted us, and we searched in silence for a few moments more. Spy holes had once existed in this door, but they'd been covered over in thick pitch, at least the pair that we found at knee height. The pitch was old and brittle; it looked as if it had been there for years. Whatever lay beyond this door apparently hadn't needed scouting for some time. Eventually, my fingers came across a telltale edge in the rough-hewn wall, about shoulder high. "I've got something," I whispered, holding the place while I fished my picklocks out of my waistband.

Jane lifted the candle high for me to see, and I blessed my grandfather's memory once again. I was now using his gift twice in one night. Had he known the value of the picklocks when he'd given them to me?

The lock had been oiled recently, and the door as well. I heard the lock turn with a click. "Put out the candle," I directed Jane, and with a soft breath we were plunged into darkness again. I felt her hand touch my arm, and I drew the picklocks out of the lock and replaced them in my waistband. Without a word, Jane and I clasped hands, and I pulled the door inward.

It opened soundlessly . . .

To reveal an abandoned hall.

A hall that I recognized immediately.

"Saint George's Hall," I whispered. No one ever frequented this hall that I had ever seen, on my many treks to amuse the Queen with my skills at recovering her treasures and secreting them back into her hand.

We stepped quickly through the door, ducking out from under a torn but expensive-looking tapestry that hung off-kilter, into the large chamber. Jane pulled the door closed behind us, and the lock *snicked* into place. She eyed the hidden doorway, just visible in the thin moonlight that was peeking through the leaded glass windows. "Look, this tapestry is pulled just so that nothing might be disturbed if you were to enter," she said. "And the hall is clean enough—but jumbled enough—that there would be no trace of someone passing through. Just enough rushes strewn about to make tracking impossible, just enough light from the windows for one to not need a telltale torch, and no way to put anything out of place. It's the perfect place to misdirect someone!"

She glanced over at me, then stopped. "Is something wrong?" she asked into my staring face.

Jane was right. Saint George's Hall *was* the perfect place to misdirect someone—or the perfect place for a secret meeting. "All is well," I managed. "Just getting a feel for the place."

"I can help you there." She grinned. "The place is a wreck. And probably as haunted as they say."

We turned and scanned the piles of broken furniture and discarded or damaged tapestries, hanging down from enormously tall racks. From what I could see, this would not be a comfortable space in which anyone would linger, especially not a Queen. Far down the length of the room, I knew the hall opened onto a chapel, which would likely be in even worse repair. Surely there would be no sign of disruption there, would there? Even if the Mass was no longer celebrated in it—would that not be sacrilegious?

I almost thought I heard something creak, far in the depths of the hall, and I stilled. Was someone in the chapel even now? Even worse, was it the Queen?

I *had* to find out. And in this, I couldn't take Jane with me.

"We should go back to the rooms," I said, and Jane nodded, finally pulling her gaze away from the wall and the configuration of the secret doorway. She handed me the candle, and I pulled a bit of linen out of my waistband to wrap it, before tucking it safely away.

"We should," Jane said, her eyes straying back to the panel. "I want to get all of this down on paper. Start mapping it. Now that we know where to begin, imagine what other passageways exist in this old hulk of a castle." She was as excited as a child, I realized, and I smiled. She'd seen the maps I'd been drawing up of the castle; it now seemed I had a partner in the effort. Still, we couldn't tarry here.

"Do you think we should go separately, to be safe?" I asked.

"Mmm-hmmm," she said, still distracted. She lifted the fingers of her right hand to tap her mouth. "I wonder if this would be considered a main exit point," she mused. "Given how large the panel opening is?"

I gave her a little push toward the southwest doors of the hall. "You go that way. I'll exit through the chapel."

She wrinkled her nose, finally coming back. "There's an exit through the chapel?"

I had no idea. I just needed to see what was in that room. "There's an exit down through the kitchens," I lied convincingly. "I'll probably beat you back to our chambers."

"No chance, Rat," Jane scoffed. "But you can try. I'll see you in our chambers in a quarter hour."

"Done," I said. I watched her move swiftly down the long hall, disappearing in the gloom of the doorway. Then I turned toward the chapel.

And just like that, I saw it.

I blinked, squinted. And there it was again.

Ahead of me, in the reedy light, something shifted in the shadows.

CHAPTER EIGHTEEN

I moved forward through the room as silently as I could manage, my eyes adjusting to the murky light. Saint George's Hall had some fine bits of furniture still, but generally it housed the furniture and paintings not considered valuable enough to hang in the main castle chambers. The floor was covered in old rushes that were probably changed only once a season, and the air had the fetid smell of moldering hay and chimney smoke, doubtless from the enormous stoves that lined the undercroft below, where the kitchens were. This grand hall had fallen into disrepair in King Henry's time, and neither Edward nor Mary nor Elizabeth had seen fit to spend the extensive monies needed to refurbish it.

And as Jane had helpfully pointed out, it was rumored to be haunted.

Still, I rather doubted that whoever was moving around in the chapel this night was a ghost.

I passed a large painting propped up against a large, ornately carved chair, then paused, considering. The painting was covered in a dust cloth of plain linen. It was a little large for an apron, but it would do if I were seen at a distance. I slid the shroud off the painting in one light pull, and fastened it roughly around my waist. It covered a good part of my skirts, furthering my disguise. I almost looked like a chambermaid now. Almost.

"This had better be worth it," I muttered, suddenly feeling foolish. But I'd come so far. I couldn't turn back now. I schooled my features into bleary-eyed stupor, in case I needed to play part of sleep-addled maid, and moved forward on cat's feet.

I'd just reached the doorway of the chapel when I heard them: soft, lilting tones of Spanish, floating across the dusty air. My heart sank. I really needed to learn that language, and quickly. Memorizing was all well and good, but it was far easier to remember words that actually made sense, versus the hypnotic lifts and falls of a foreign tongue, as elusive as fading music. Two men were speaking, and I edged farther into the shadows, peeking around a tall screen as the conversation seemed to scale up a notch in anger.

I recognized one of them immediately, of course. Tall, slender, and sumptuously dressed, looking every bit as splendid as he had the night of the ball.

Rafe. My heart sank. Why couldn't he be fast abed this dark night, instead of engaged in conversation with another skulking Spaniard?

And why were they speaking here?

His partner was unknown to me, thick and bulky, his tiny pig-eyes squinting over an enormous nose that was roughly the size and shape of a turnip. Clearly the man had been on the losing end of several fights, though his clothes were certainly well made. If they didn't fit as well as Rafe's doublet and trunks, his silken hose and fine boots . . . well, what could one expect? No one could look as dashing as Rafe this night, certainly not a boorish Spaniard guard who seemed to vibrate with increasing anger even as Rafe's tones took on a placating sensibility.

I let the cadence of their words wash over me as I scanned the room. The chapel was almost devoid of furniture other than the pews and the glowering cross of Christ. It did not have the feeling of a Catholic chapel; there was no ornamentation other than the rather austere crucifix, and no tapestries lining the walls, which gave the room even more of a chill. As I'd suspected, the only other exit from the chapel was an archway built into the wall that led down a curved staircase to the undercroft. If I went that way, I would have to thread my way through the kitchens and storage rooms, then back up another staircase, which would take too much time. I could not afford to be caught by one of the castle guards—I was in no mood to explain to Cecil why I was roaming the corridors at this hour! Still, I was determined to stay and learn what I could from Rafe and the turnip-nosed Spaniard's conversation. Then I'd return to my chambers through Saint George's Hall.

The men's words grew quieter, but they were still clearly displeased with each other. Rafe trying to be diplomatic, the bulky Spanish guard having none of it. From time to time a word made sense: "castle," I recognized, and "lady." Even "Queen," although only Rafe used that term to describe Elizabeth. The other man's word for her was decidedly less flattering, and I recognized it from de Feria's speech of the other week.

I was getting a little tired of poorly bred louts calling my Queen a whore.

To stem my annoyance with Turnip Nose, I turned my attention more fully on him, trying to keep up with the flow of his words. Surely I'd remember him the next time I saw him, though other than his distinctive nose, he looked like many of the other Spanish guards—thick and unwieldy, almost laughable in their fine silks. The courtiers, at least the younger ones, were built generally like Rafe, strong and lean.

Why would Rafe be talking to a Spanish guard in the middle of the night? And in the middle of an abandoned chapel?

What *was* Rafe's role with the Spanish delegation, in truth? Had he just come across the English channel to seed a delegation of dandies paying court to a capricious Queen with another handsome face? Was he here to serve the Bishop de Quadra? Or was Rafe something more than a courtier after all?

Suddenly Turnip Nose thrust a small object toward Rafe, his words rising on a tide of disgust. Rafe reached out for it, and the object caught the light of the meager moonshine as the beams filtered through the dirt-clogged windows.

A letter!

I almost gasped out my surprise but managed to keep my peace.

Rafe tucked the letter into his doublet and patted Turnip Nose on the back, all forgiven between them, apparently. The guard grinned sheepishly in return, and they continued their conversation for a few minutes more, too quietly for me to hear. I seriously began to suspect I should be going, when Rafe turned away from the man.

Then Rafe whirled back in a blur of motion, so fast I could barely track him. Suddenly, his hands were on either side of the other man's head, which slewed sideways with a sickening wet crunch, shocking in the silence.

Turnip Nose slumped to the ground.

Rafe crouched over him, and I was gone.

Blind and deaf to anything but the sudden knowledge of my own danger, I started running like the armies of Satan were chasing me out of that chapel, headlong toward safety. A few moments later I heard rapid feet behind me, but the chase was abandoned quickly, and I didn't stop in any event until I'd gone almost the full length of Saint George's Hall. I ripped off my makeshift apron and threw it down, lungs heaving. I ducked out the door to the hall, then rushed through rooms large and small toward my own chambers as quickly as I could, my hands working furiously to reset my hair to at least some semblance of propriety, in case I ran afoul of a guard or servant. Heaven forfend! I had no desire to explain why I was out so late.

As I neared the maids' quarters I picked up my pace, and in my haste I wasn't looking as far ahead as I should have. If I had been more focused on what was ahead of me instead of what was behind me, I am certain I would have taken note of the faint prickling at my neck, the decided hitch in my stride as my heart began galloping faster than even my panicked run should have caused.

As it was, I was jerked off my feet by a powerful set of arms and hauled summarily into an antechamber before I even had breath to cry out.

"I thought I'd find you along this corridor." Rafe gave me

a shake. “Scream, and I’ll knock you senseless, like you so richly deserve.”

“What are you doing here?” I gasped. I jerked my head back, indignant at his hold, but he did not let go.

“I could ask you well the same thing.”

“I *live* here,” I snapped, and a cold chill bloomed in my chest. God’s hounds, had the castle become home to me? “You’re just an unwanted guest.”

Rafe grinned at me, too close. “An unwanted guest that you can’t seem to stay away from,” he said. “Why are you following me?”

I drew myself up. While I was still panting with the exertion of my run, Rafe looked as if barely a hair had been turned on his sleekly styled head. How had he made it to this part of the castle so quickly? If there was a second door in the chapel that I’d missed, how did he know about it? And more to the point: “What did you do to that man?” I demanded.

“You were eavesdropping on our conversation,” he said coldly. “I want to know why.”

I scowled. “I was just out walking. I do that. I heard voices.”

“You were just out walking. In the dead of night, in the middle of a deserted chapel at the far end of a ruined hall? I’m afraid you’re going to have to do better than that.”

“I don’t even understand Spanish,” I pointed out with exasperation. It was a convincing argument, and I shouldn’t care what he thought about my level of education. Really. I shouldn’t care.

That stopped him. “You don’t?”

Before I could shake my head, he spoke a torrent of

words, all of them rich and vaguely . . . intimate-sounding, but in truth I could neither follow them nor adequately memorize them, even though my name was sprinkled liberally throughout. All the while, he watched me closely. Whatever he saw on my face must have pleased him, because he finally stopped.

"What did you say?" I asked, making no secret of my annoyance. I was getting better at Spanish, true enough, but not Spanish that was spoken so quickly.

He tilted his head, considering. "You truly can't understand my words? And yet you continue to follow me?"

"I told you, I wasn't following you," I retorted. "I was out walking." I tried a different tack. "You killed that man, didn't you." It wasn't a question. Not even to me.

Rafe rolled his eyes. "I knocked him out. He will recover."

I narrowed my gaze at him. He most certainly had done more than knock the guard out. It had sounded like he'd snapped the man's neck. "Why did you strike him at all?"

"Why are you asking such questions?" Rafe frowned, and without warning his manner shifted into something almost . . . protective. "What is this about, Meg? Skulking around corridors pretending you're a spy is not a child's game. You could be taken for one in truth, and then where would you be?"

I stiffened at his tone. "I do not need your lecture, sir."

"No, you need a leash." His eyes narrowed. "Unless . . ." He shook his head. "Surely not. You cannot have been sent to follow me. That would not make any sense."

Uh-oh. "Don't trouble your mind with such a thought," I sniffed. "You'll hurt yourself."

It was too late. "But, wait. Perhaps . . . the night of the ball." A tone of wonder lilted his voice, and I hid my wince. I'd done too much, too soon. I'd overplayed my hand, but I didn't know how to turn him from his line of thought. "You were with me then as well," he said. "The night of the ball."

"As were about fifty other women, yes," I said. "What of it?"

"My packet of letters was opened."

"What packet of letters?" I asked blankly. "What are you talking about?"

Rafe shook his head again like a dazed dog. "No," he said finally. "I won't believe it."

Good. "Believe what?" I glanced at his clothes. They were not dissimilar from the outfit that he'd worn the night of the ball, and I would wager I'd find Turnip Nose's letter in the same place the other letters had been. Did I dare lift it from him now? I didn't have the opportunity of closeness like the dance had afforded me. I could embrace him again, but that thought sent me into a panic. It was once again too much, too soon.

Then all at once an idea sparked in my head.

I took note of where we were standing. This antechamber was used by members of the ladies-in-waiting and maids of honor when their families came calling. It was simply furnished, and exuded a comforting air. Shifting backward just a step, I sighed and sat down heavily on the nearest cushioned bench, leaving a space open beside me to my left. "I will tell you this," I said, my words small and forlorn. "I do not like this castle."

Rafe dropped down beside me, sliding into the role of

guardian so quickly, I almost felt bad. "Are you all right?" he asked, now all concern.

I smiled wanly at him. "I'm sorry. I shouldn't have said that. Yes, of course. I am quite well." I glanced away at the very end of this small speech. This really was too easy.

He leaned toward me. "You don't seem quite like the other maids," he said gently. "Are you from the countryside?"

The question sent a fresh bolt of panic through me. *How was I not like the others?* I needed to work on fitting in better. "I am from the country, yes," I said, with another shy glance to the side. "Is it so obvious?"

His smile was kind, and I felt a weird pang in my heart. Once again I was lying to him, though for a good cause. I let my hand sidle closer to his leg, inches away from the pocket in his puffed trunks. He would not even feel me lift the letter free, if I were careful. And I always was careful. Well, I usually was careful.

But Rafe was continuing. "You looked deeply chagrined at Beatrice's words the other night, and by your own admission just now that you don't know Spanish. There is no slight in coming from the country, Meg. Not everyone can be born into a wealthy family."

"I suppose." I moved my hand closer still. "You seem at ease here, though. Is this your first visit to Windsor?" I asked.

He leaned yet closer to me, and I found myself intensely *aware* of him. I needed to focus on my task, I knew, not on him. But he was making it very difficult.

"This is my first visit since Elizabeth has worn the crown, but not the first to England, fair maid." Rafe glanced up, as if thinking, and I made my move while he spoke. I nicked the letter from his pocket, palming the flimsy bit of parchment in a smooth, easy pass and shoving it into my waistband next to my candle and picklocks. *Time to sew more pockets.* I drifted my hand back down to the cushion while Rafe continued. "During Mary Tudor's reign, we Spanish considered England almost our second home. There's not a rock I haven't overturned in Whitehall or Windsor, so often have I roamed them both." He grinned at me. "But now that I've made your acquaintance, I'll be sure to return more frequently."

"And if I am still here, I'll be sure to say hello."

"I should like it very much if you were." He hesitated, dark eyes unreadable. "Your betrothal will not be brief?"

My what? I stared at him for a long beat before realizing what he was talking about. I would not be able to carry on that particular charade, I decided in an instant. There were some lies that could not be upheld. "Oh, that. It was a misunderstanding, I'm afraid—the Queen had chosen the wrong maid."

Rafe's brows shot up. "She cannot keep you straight?"

"She's very busy." I shrugged.

He shook his head, wonderingly. "I cannot think you'd be easy to misplace, Meg, whether by countryman or Queen."

"Are you always so good with words? Or am I just particularly blessed tonight?"

He grinned again. It looked good on him. "I've been taught my lines well. Not unlike you, I suspect."

"Your lines?"

He reached up to tuck a lock of my hair behind my ear, and his hand lingered on my cheek. "We all must play our roles, sweet Meg. Surely you understand what it feels like to not belong somewhere?"

"Well, yes, but—you're a courtier."

"And far from king and country, with no home to call my own."

His words were light, but the pain of them resonated through me, my own pain echoing in response. "You would find a home someday?"

His gaze held mine. "I go where my heart directs me. And there I find my home."

He was so close to me, his breath the scent of honey and cinnamon, his eyes warming me.

Kiss him! Kiss him! my own traitorous heart surged, and I blushed so thoroughly, he had to know, even in the darkness. "I . . . I should be going," I said, giving him a final shy smile.

"Of course, of course," Rafe said easily. We both stood, and I turned. I curtsied to him, and he bowed, gesturing for me to proceed him. I neatly transferred the letter to my bodice as I walked.

I'd almost made it to the door, when he laughed.

"You really are quite good, aren't you?"

Every fiber in my being screamed at me to flee, but a greater sense of gamesmanship held me fast. Rafe was beside me in an instant, turning me around. He held out a hand. "The letter, if you please."

I lifted my chin. "It is not yours. I'll not have any of the English caught up in your intrigues."

"*My* intrigues!" He protested. "If I'd not already been duped by you, I would not have checked my own pockets until well after you had left."

"Duped?"

"Don't be coy." Rafe scowled now. "The skills you possess are dangerous, Meg; I will tell you plain. Is thieving something you enjoy, or did you develop the skill by requirement?"

There was danger here, but I didn't know how to measure it. "You took a letter from the guard. I took it from you. There is nothing more to the tale."

"I see. And who else knows of your ability to light-finger a letter from an unsuspecting mark's pockets?"

I stiffened, feigning outrage. "No one," I lied succinctly.

"Not even your parents?"

For some reason that comment stung me to candor. "Certainly not them. My mother died in childbirth, not long after I entered the world. My father never recovered, or so the story goes. After that there was only my grandfather, and now he, too, is gone."

That made Rafe pause, and I silently commended myself. The words were painful—and honest fact; I'd heard the tale since I was little more than a babe myself. The admission added the necessary embroidery to make the whole cloth seem like it was woven in truth.

Rafe's next words were as unexpected as they were gentle. "Poor, sweet Meg, all alone in the world," he murmured. My heart slewed sideways, and I felt the danger prick my spine, but he began speaking again, almost more to himself than me. "But your skill is not inconsiderable, and your mind is as fleet as your thieving fingers." He rubbed his jaw. "There are those who would seek to use you, Meg, and not be careful in the using."

A bit too late for the counsel, I thought. Walsingham and Cecil had already claimed me for their own. "You should worry less for me and more for yourself, I should think. Whatever intrigues you're setting up for yourself within the castle, you will be caught out."

"And you would not see me hang, is that it?"

I instantly thought of Cecil's threats. "Do not joke," I said severely. "The Queen suffers no fools not of her choosing, and I cannot believe you set so little store by your own life to abuse her kindness so."

"Meg," he murmured, putting a hand over mine. I was held fast, like a rabbit in a snare, and he squeezed my fingers. "Your concern flatters me, but it is not I who am in danger here. You must have a better care for yourself. Whether you were out hunting for an errant letter or not, the castle at night is not safe for women alone; not even for the Queen's attendants."

The night whispered of Marie Claire, but I lifted my chin. "I assure you, you've no need to worry about my safety."

"After your demonstrations this evening, Meg, I'm afraid I'm not convinced that you have a care for it yourself. What if others learn of your abilities?"

"My abilities, as you call them, are not known, and shall not be known, lest I in turn know that you are the one who spread the rumors."

He shook his head. "I tell no tales that do not profit me, and your safety is not worth any price. But come." He stood and curled my arm into his. It felt right, somehow. Secure and warm. "We should return before your absence is made note of, by maid or master alike."

"No one would be looking for me," I assured him, but his laughter cut into the darkness.

"And that is where you are wrong, sweet Meg. That is where you are wrong."

We moved swiftly down the corridor, until we neared my chambers; gradually we slowed, then stopped. I thought he might lean into me then, a flash of knowing that startled me with its sudden imagery, at once intimate and foreign. *Would he . . . would he kiss me now?*

Rafe gathered me close, holding me in an embrace so soft, I thought I would crumple within it. Then his hands seemed to be everywhere at once, pressing me into the wall, searing through my skirts, hard upon my waist. He seemed to pause a moment, then redoubled in his intensity.

His hands crept up . . . up . . . and I felt suddenly dizzy, drunk on the moment with the sweetest of wines, yearning for him to touch me, even through the cloth of my gown. He did, tracing his fingers over the curve of my bodice, then brushing the tidy lacings that held the cloth together.

And just like that, I knew my mistake.

He pulled the letter out as quick as a breath, taking a sharp step away.

"You ingrate!" I yelped, clutching my hand to my bodice, though the letter was long gone.

"Sweet Meg, I can honestly say, I've never enjoyed my work more." Even in the darkness I could see the gleam of Rafe's teeth as he grinned broadly. "Pray feel free to steal from me at any time."

"I would not have need to steal from you at all, were you an honorable man," I said through gritted teeth.

"Spoken from the heights of your own inestimable nobility, I can see," he mocked back, then swept me another bow.

"Good night, sweet Meg," he said, and I murmured some semblance of good-bye, riddled with fury and embarrassment for being so easily duped.

We both turned at once, to retrace our steps to our separate lives. But before I turned into my chamber, I thought I heard his voice again, a whisper in the darkness.

"I'll be watching you."

CHAPTER NINETEEN

"Why do you suppose we've been canceled again?" Anna mused from her desk thc following morning, well after dawn had broken with no sign from Cecil or any other of our tutors. Her lips were pressed together. "Seems to me a briefing would be quite appropriate, with the Flemish court coming to England to pay homage to the Queen."

"The who?" I asked, as Jane straightened. Even Beatrice looked up at this new bit of gossip.

"The Flemish court?" Beatrice asked. "But the Queen despises King Philip, especially since he married the French child. She suffers the Spaniards because Spain is so powerful. But what need has she for the Netherlands?"

Anna nodded, setting some official-looking documents aside. "Well, she likes the Flemish painters well enough, and it is said Philip rules the Netherlands with a heavier hand than he does in Spain. Perhaps the Queen is looking to build alliances?" She pursed her lips together, thinking. "King Philip has not been idle, despite his love for his new bride, and with France firmly in hand, there now is whispering that he seeks to shore up his position on the Continent. The Queen will have to counter that with something. I've heard word that there will be visitors from the Ottomans as well."

"The Ottomans." I couldn't believe my ears. "But they're infidels!"

Beatrice snorted. "Elizabeth would allow the devil himself to pay her court, after what Philip did to her. He was still having de Feria beg for her hand on his behalf while he was finalizing his own marriage negotiations with France. There's nothing she wouldn't do to thwart him."

Sophia's voice piped up from the corner. "There is darkness coming," she said in her soft trill.

That, perhaps not surprisingly, froze us. We looked as one to Sophia, who was still focused on her embroidery. In the past weeks, she had taken to spending hours a day on her complicated needlework. Now she was working on a wide swath of black silk that Anna had whispered was part of her bridal ensemble. I was ever reminded of the tale we had read of Odysseus's wife, Penelope, weaving on her loom during the day, only to undo all her work every night.

Sophia ignored our stares and kept sewing, her needle flashing in and out of the expensive cloth. Jane broke the spell first. "What do you mean, Sophia?"

"Hmm?" Sophia looked up, plainly startled.

"You said there was darkness coming," Jane prompted. Her voice was surprisingly gentle, as if she were talking to a fawn.

Sophia colored. "I did?" She shook her head, pursing her lips. "I—" She floundered a bit, her hands clenching on the fine fabric. "I did not realize. I'm so sorry . . . but . . ."

Another pause ensued.

Beatrice opened her mouth, no doubt ready with a cutting remark, but Anna raised a hand. Shockingly, Beatrice remained still. More shockingly, Sophia did not.

"Darkness flows to Golden Splendor," she said, with just the slightest trance-lilt to her voice. She hesitated, but no more words came out. "That's it, I'm afraid. That phrase alone."

I glanced at Jane. "'Golden Splendor'?"

"Could be the masque," she reasoned back.

Beatrice nodded. "It will be the highlight of the season, another chance to assert the Queen's position." She smoothed her hair. "It would also be an ideal time to announce my betrothal, wouldn't you say?"

"Have you heard aught from Lord Cavanaugh?" Anna asked, her mind nimbly jumping to this newest bit of information.

"Cousin Henrietta could tell me only that he had requested a private audience with the Queen. But that was *days* ago. It's beyond time!"

I winced, thinking of the ball we'd endured just a few weeks earlier, and none too comfortable with the thought of anyone's betrothal, even Beatrice's. "A full house in just seven days," I murmured, feeling all of the intrigues of the court crashing in on one another. "The courts of Spain, the Netherlands, and the Far East all together." I glanced at Anna. "Surely the French will be here too."

"And the Italians," Anna said. "It will be a grand spectacle. And all in costume. So you really won't know whom you're speaking with, friend or foe."

"And yet we are not learning anything new, nor have we

received new assignments," I mused, "even though we all did exactly as we were asked during the welcome ball. It's all the same lessons, over and over again, and Cecil hasn't been here in days. Why?"

Anna opened her mouth, then shut it again. "I hadn't thought of it that way," she said. "That does make it even odder."

"Perhaps it is too dangerous?" Beatrice mused.

"Or perhaps we're ready, and our class time is at an end," I said.

"Or perhaps it's time we put our training to use, and discover the answers to our questions ourselves." Jane's gaze slid to me. We had held the letters in our possession for fewer than than twelve hours, but already they burned to be returned.

I swallowed. She was right. If only I'd managed to keep the letter Rafe had taken from Turnip Nose as well!

But first . . . "Anna, I know it may not be as interesting as political treatises, but how would you feel about translating a conversation I heard all in Spanish?" I asked, and Jane raised her brows in surprise. This wasn't exactly what she'd expected to hear.

I nodded at her, even as Beatrice turned to stare at me.

"What conversation did you hear?" Jane asked, her curiosity plain. "And when?"

"And where?" Beatrice's voice was pointed.

But I ignored them both as Anna held up a hand, gesturing me forward. "Speak on, fair maid," she said serenely. "I am at your service."

A quarter hour later she was not nearly as serene. None

of us were. *Five secret maids, all in disguise,* I thought.

Beatrice was wearing a line in the carpet. "Why on earth would two Spaniards be arguing over how much disruption they could safely cause in the Queen's court?" she asked. "You're sure you did not recognize either of them?"

"They were in full darkness," I lied. "And I only caught the haziest line of their bodies." *Hearts full of questions, words full of lies.*

"But they would only cause themselves discomfort," Sophia pointed out. She'd at last been drawn out of her fascination with her embroidery task and was now sitting by Jane. "Another disruption at court would mean a greater presence of the guard, fewer entertainments, tighter restrictions. We've only just been granted more freedoms with the rain coming to an end. You were not here, Meg, but we were practically confined to our own bedchambers in the days following Marie's death. That was no fun for anyone, especially not the Spanish."

"And they would be the first to be held accountable, would they not?" Jane put in. She'd taken out her knife and was polishing the hilt with a bit of linen. I could tell the movement soothed her. Sadly, it didn't have that effect on the rest of us, but Jane was oblivious to our discomfort.

"I should think yet another disruption would begin to make people wonder if the Queen were truly fit to rule," Anna murmured, and I shot her a look. I had not told them about the Queen's own fears about this exact outcome, but if Anna could puzzle it out on her own, I would not gainsay her.

"And that would help the Spaniards how?" Beatrice asked.

"It might push parliament to force a marriage, for the Queen's own protection," Anna said pensively. To suggest that anyone could force Elizabeth to do anything smacked of disloyalty, but the reality was plain. And, as I well knew, Anna was exactly correct in her fears.

"But to whom?" I put my chin in my hand. I had been racking my brain about this problem. "She could marry an Englishman, but how would that benefit the Spaniards? Or an Italian—or a Frenchman."

"She would not marry a Frenchman," Beatrice said with confidence. "She despises them."

"She won't marry anyone," Sophia said, her voice as clear as prophecy. We all looked at her, and she blushed. "Just a sense I get."

Jane snorted. "Anna, we may want to start writing down these 'senses' of little Sophia's here. You never know when they might become valuable."

Sophia smiled, the color still high in her cheeks. "Don't worry, Jane," she said, reaching out to pat Jane's hand, despite the fact that it was still holding the knife. "You will marry."

The moment she'd uttered these words, Sophia clapped her hand to her mouth, her eyes flying wide. Beatrice's jaw dropped, and Anna turned quickly to Sophia, all thoughts of Queen and country momentarily banished.

"How can you know that? What do you mean?" Anna gushed, and Sophia shook her head quickly.

"And what of me?" Beatrice demanded. "Surely I will marry before Jane! If the Queen would *only* give her consent, we could be married in one month's time." I blinked at her, but she was right enough. After three consecutive Sundays of her family Crying the Banns at services—and with the blessing of the bishop—Beatrice would be free to wed. "All the court is waiting for it. It needs to happen!" she cried, stamping her foot. She turned on Sophia. "How can you not know if it will come to pass?"

"I don't know—I don't know! I have no way of asking questions; answers just sometimes come." Sophia lifted her hands to forestall us. "I don't even know if *I* will marry." She sighed. "And I assure you, if I could call upon that information, I certainly would."

Jane chuckled, out of all of us the only one who seemed at ease. "Don't worry, Sophia. I won't be Crying the Banns anytime soon." She hesitated just a moment. "But if you ever do get a name to go along with this sense, I would appreciate knowing." She hefted her knife expertly before stowing it again in its sheath. "I may need to make sure that doesn't happen."

I pulled the letters from my skirts, where I'd hidden them all morning. "If we're finished with talk of marriage, we're not done with translations, Anna. Can you read these?"

"It seems you have been busy, Meg," Beatrice said, her eyes narrowing.

"Jane took them," I said, and Jane merely grinned. Anna took Lady Amelia's packet of letters from me. She scanned the first few of the open missives, then shrugged. "At first glance, they are the safest of letters," she said at length. "A discourse on the weather, and prayers for a rich harvest, and a lot of God saving the Queen . . ." Her voice drifted off, and Beatrice looked up.

"What is it?" she asked sharply.

"Just something . . . strange. The writing of this one does not quite match the others, though they are all signed by the same woman. Still, on these two . . . the hand seems to have shifted," Anna said, her voice taking on the air of distraction. "And some of these suggestions seem . . . a bit oddly worded."

I looked at her, knowing that if there were a puzzle to solve, Anna could do it. And additional words to my impromptu couplets sprang to mind, as if I was once again helping the Golden Rose players fix an errant line of a play. *All of them guessing, with questioning eyes. Five pretty maids, all of them spies.*

After a moment, Anna continued. "They look like they're written from a Spanish lady of some standing, this Dona Victoria, who is on familiar terms with various members of Lady Amelia's family." She frowned up at Beatrice. "Does that signify?"

Beatrice shrugged. "Lady Amelia's mother is Spanish, and she's well-placed at court. It's hard to turn around without running into a relation of hers."

Anna nodded. "She's mentioned several times here. There's a few strange phrasings, some more random girlish scribbling in the corners, but really . . . nothing I can quite . . . hmm . . ." Anna paused, reading further. "I wonder why Lady Amelia still had these letters? They appear to have been read and returned to her? And they seem all so . . . dull . . . Oh!" she exclaimed suddenly, her ears glowing bright pink as she held a letter up. "This one is a love letter to Amelia! In Spanish!"

Beatrice glanced at her, then back at us. "From Dona Victoria?"

Anna dimpled. "Ah, no."

"From a Spaniard, then," Jane said, satisfied.

"No . . . no, I don't think so," Anna said, and that caught both Jane and me up short.

"What do you mean?" I asked. "They're written in Spanish." But Anna shook her head.

"Yes, but," she mused, "it's a Portuguese man writing in Spanish. A few of the words are different."

Beatrice flapped her hands. "Well, close enough! Is there anything good in them?"

"A lot about divine love, actually," Anna conceded, wrinkling her nose. "An educated hand wrote these words, though they slant oddly, not far enough to the right for proper form. Hmmm." She fanned through more of the letters. "You want me to open the rest of them?"

Beatrice answered for us. "No," she said. "Just tell us if—" She stopped abruptly. "Now what is it, Anna? What do you see?"

I glanced up. Anna was now as white as a sheet.

"Where did you get these letters?" Anna asked Jane, her eyes wide.

Jane didn't even have to look to me for confirmation. "The chamber of the ladies-in-waiting. Why?"

Anna held up a letter. "Because this letter talks about Marie! And it mentions both her eyes and her tongue, as if as a warning." She shook her head slowly. "Nobody was ever told about that. Nobody knew."

We stared at Anna. I was the first to speak. "Except for the person who killed her." I swallowed. "We need to return these letters tonight."

"Hush!" Jane said abruptly. "Someone's coming. A lot of someones, in fact."

We surged to our feet, silent and intent, listening. Jane was right. At least twenty people, from the sound of it, were marching their way toward us. There was only one person in the castle who would command such an entourage as that, and my heart leaped to my throat.

"Hide the letters!" I blurted, and Beatrice and Anna scrambled to move. I snatched Marie's letter and had just tucked it into my skirts when the footsteps stopped outside the door.

We'd settled back in our seats, five maids conversing about the importance of the current political scene, when the door swung open and a magnificent portrait of color and opulence swept into the room.

The Queen had arrived.

CHAPTER TWENTY

Queen Elizabeth Regnant surveyed us with cool eyes as we lined up to curtsy low. When she commanded us to rise, we did so as one, a perfect line of maids, ready to do her bidding.

I looked beyond the Queen to Cecil and Walsingham, who flanked her on either side. Behind her, in the hallway, stood the royal guard. The Queen was dressed in high court finery, clearly on her way to her Presence Chamber. Interestingly, however, no ladies-in-waiting attended her. She scowled.

"They are not presentable," she said dourly. "Except Beatrice."

"You had only decreed their involvement this morning," Cecil said. "I do not think—"

"All you do is think," the Queen snapped. "We've discussed this. The time has passed for thinking."

I felt out of my depth. What had happened here? She viewed me next with a critical eye, then surveyed Anna. Disgusted, she glanced at Sophia, who seemed to shrink into herself but couldn't hide her loveliness. "She'll do. And you," she said, eyeing me. "Tell me you have something more appropriate than that sack you're wearing."

"Your Grace?" I managed, looking down at my dull grey frock, stung by the Queen's words. "I . . . I'm sure I have something finer," I said, though in truth my wardrobe was as limited as Jane's. We alone out of the five maids had not come from upperclass families, and so our clothing allotment was meager.

"She can borrow a dress of mine, Your Grace," Beatrice spoke up quickly. I didn't dare glance at her, but something unfurled inside me. Beatrice's clothes were her most prized possession! "We are of a height and nearly of a build."

"Good." The Queen nodded at Beatrice with approval. "Go now. I will be hearing petitions this morning and want you with me. You," she said to Anna, "need to start dressing at your station. I would like you at my side. For now, though, I have translation work for you." She gestured imperiously, and Cecil opened up the bag he was carrying and brought out a sheaf of pages. Beside me Anna nearly leaped with excitement. "You will await me in my Privy Chamber. And you," she said, pointing to Jane. "Go with Walsingham. He will give you instruction."

I glanced again hurriedly to Cecil, and the man looked positively morose. What had happened?

The Queen clapped her hands in imperious command. "Sophia, attend me now. Beatrice and Meg, present yourselves at my Privy Chamber in a quarter hour, then you will stand behind me in attendance in the Presence Chamber for the day. Yes," she said, nodding thoughtfully as she glanced between us. "This will do well."

And then she swept out of the room, a royal storm, with Sophia bobbing in her wake. The march of guardsmen's feet attended the Queen down the hall.

"Miss Burgher, please await me outside," Cecil said curtly, and Anna scurried out the door.

Walsingham gazed at Cecil a moment with hooded eyes, then gave Jane a courtly bow. "Miss Morgan?" he said, the perfect gentleman. He gestured ahead of him, and without a word, Jane moved forward. The two of them disappeared silently through the doorway.

"I need to speak with you both a moment," Cecil said.

Beatrice exhaled a long-suffering sigh. "Is the Queen not waiting for us?" she asked petulantly, but I was too amazed by her gracious offer of a gown to begrudge her. In truth, I was as ready to hasten off to primp as Beatrice seemed to be. I had never expected her to share so much as a hairpin with me, much less a gown, which in Beatrice's world was tantamount to being bosom friends.

"First, Miss Knowles, I would give you your charge." Cecil strode forward to Beatrice, took her by the arm, and turned her to the side. He thrust a small slip of paper into her hands, then stonily eyed her as she read it. I noticed, even in the dim light of the study room, that she turned pale, and he nodded once. "So you understand. Burn it." He directed her to the fire.

Beatrice curtsied, her composure not one whit dimmed by Sir William's tone. Then she turned and moved with grace to the fireplace. Without hesitation she cast the document into the flames, picked up a poker, and proceeded to beat the offending scrap to death. She looked positively ill. What had her assignment been?

Cecil turned impatiently and eyed me with some distaste. I could see the Queen had overridden his better judgment. Again. I did my best to look capable and eminently reliable. He had no other slips of paper; he merely approached me and turned me so my back was to Beatrice. "Lest you wonder why your orders are not contained in writing, rest assured, I would have done so, had I any trust in your reading skills."

Mortification rushed through me. Cecil's words had been low, but not so low that Beatrice could not hear, if she had any mind to be distracted from her desecration of Cecil's assignment paper. Cecil seemed to be waiting for me to say something, so I curtsied. Of course.

"I appreciate your kindness, Sir William." I said the words levelly and with neither rancor nor embarrassment, as if he had just told me that he had not written out my assignment because I was blue-eyed.

"You will see today the full contingent of the Queen's admirers, both within England and across the Continent," he said. "Watch them all, memorize them all. That is your role for her. For me—" Here he leaned down toward me, and I could smell the scent of parchment and leather-bound books around him, all wood smoke and gloom. "For me, I expect you to pay particular attention to the Queen's own attendants. Specifically, the ladies of the bedchamber who traveled with her to London and back again."

My tongue suddenly felt too heavy in my mouth, blocking both breath and speech. I stared at him, and he stared back, his eyes as flat and lifeless as river stones. I should have asked why he'd ask me to do such a thing, but I was afraid of the answer. It had been a gloved hand that I'd seen give Lady Amelia the letter. The letter hadn't been exchanged until the Queen had returned from London. And there were letters in Amelia's packet that had been addressed to Lady Knollys. Did Cecil know there was a traitor in the Queen's very midst?

Or was he still more concerned with the Queen's heart, not her head?

Suddenly, Cecil lifted his hand and snapped his fingers in front of my face. With my mind racing as it was, I didn't even flinch. He raised his brows in mock admiration. "Are you still attending me, Miss Fellowes?"

"Yes, of course, Sir William," I murmured. "I shall be honored to serve the Queen however she most needs."

"And England thanks you for your service," he said stiffly. He gestured to both Beatrice and me. "Now go find something to wear that doesn't make you look like a poor relation." And with that he was gone.

I turned to Beatrice at once, nearly overcome with gratitude at the loan of her fine clothing. The look on her face stopped me.

"Don't get too carried away, Rat, until you see the gown I will give you," she said with grim satisfaction. "I have a point to make as well. I apologize that I'll be making it on your back, but as I'm sure you'll appreciate, we all need to take advantage of our opportunities."

I stared at her, nonplussed. "You're not going to give me a dress?" I asked.

"Oh, you'll have a dress," Beatrice sighed. "You just won't like it."

We assembled behind the Queen not a quarter hour later, and I had to admit . . . Beatrice was right.

I was now clad in a charcoal-colored monstrosity of a gown with large slashed sleeves, a choke-hold of a ruff, a harshly pointed V-bottomed bodice that would have been tight on a sickly girl of ten, and skirts heavy enough to fatigue an ox. I think it was embroidered with lead. Just putting it on had required both of our greatest efforts, and all thoughts of secret orders and new missions had been crushed under its sheer weight.

"Who bought you this gown?" I'd gasped, once it was finally on my body.

"An aunt on my father's side," she'd said with disgust. "I got the distinct impression she did not care for me very much."

"Or wanted you dead before you were twenty."

"I never planned to wear it, because it is—as you see—horrendous," Beatrice had continued. "But to show the dress in public is to honor her, even if I'm not the one in it. And this keeps me from ever having to don the thing myself."

I'd sighed, refusing to respond, so I could focus on breathing. In truth, I didn't care so much, except for the discomfort of the gown. If it served Beatrice's purpose to see me in it, it was all the same to me. I rather thought she hoped I'd spill something horrible on myself.

Now we marched in silence to take up our positions on either side of the Queen, as part of a long, overly stuffed line of attendants. Beatrice, in her dawn-pink gown of gossamer satin, looked like the beginning of a radiant spring morning. I looked like the end of a long, hard winter.

But there was nothing for it. I straightened, raising my chin, and serenely considered the next supplicant for the Queen's favor. I was in for a trying day.

For the first hour, the petitioners were the villagers of Windsor. I watched them with a curious sense of detachment, which was only somewhat the result of my inability to breathe. These people were me—or who I had been, I thought, but my mind instantly rejected the idea. I would never have come to the Queen to resolve a dispute over grain or the local vicar. In the Golden Rose troupe, we had solved our problems ourselves, or had turned them over to Grandfather, and then to Troupe Master James after Grandfather had passed. It was all very civilized, and it had to be. We either worked together, or we starved.

Once the villager disputes were settled, though, an entirely different sort of crowd came to the fore, and Beatrice stirred to life with curiosity on the other side of the Queen. The Queen herself, of course, remained languid, but it was for these nobles that we had been brought here, I knew immediately.

She was approving the guest list for the masque. And giving us the opportunity to see the players before they were in costume.

Giving *me* the opportunity, anyway. Why were Beatrice and Sophia here? Merely for show? Or did she have some fell purpose for their involvement as well?

While I waited for the nobles to assemble, I turned to the assignment I knew would be most paramount in Cecil's eyes for me to complete. The study of the Queen's ladies of the bedchamber. This rotating favor was bestowed on the

Queen's closest intimates, all of them married ladies of the court. She had yet to choose any of the unmarried maids for the role, but it was rumored that that honor would be forthcoming. For now, however, there were six ladies, and I watched them under the guise of surveying the whole of the gallery. Two of them were so old as to be crones, their sharp features saved only by their bright eyes and laughing countenances. A third was equally old but looked like she hadn't laughed since King Henry had died. Her gaze darted around the room, taking it all in.

The remaining three women, including Lady Knollys, were not ancient, precisely, but they were not in the first blush of youth either, and one seemed slightly off in manner, as if she were somewhat slow. In addition, none of the women surrounding Elizabeth even approached true beauty. In their midst, Elizabeth shined like the sun. I watched the ladies interact with one another, picking out the alliances and rifts. These women had been with Elizabeth since she had become Queen. Who could be the traitor, if any of them?

I glanced back at Beatrice, who still looked peeved by whatever Cecil had asked her to do. I suspected she was being fobbed off on one set of nobles or another. There was no one as brilliant as Beatrice for holding the attention of a courtier.

The steward cleared his throat. The next stage of the assembly was to begin.

The first group of nobles seemed almost shockingly out of place, puffed up with earnest enthusiasm. Reading the roll, the Steward of the Chamber announced that they hailed from the farthest reaches of the kingdom: Wales. The lake country bordering the Scottish lowlands. Dover. The Queen had brought them to Windsor to symbolize the joining together of her great country, and they looked completely bowled over at the prospect.

Which was not to say that they were poverty stricken. If anything, as bolt after bolt of fine cloth was proffered and veritable chests of jewels were opened at the Queen's feet, this felt more like an ancient tithing to an overlord than a civilized tribute to a very modern Queen. I tilted my head, considering. After long years of financing wars on the Continent, thc Crown's coffers were bare, so Elizabeth needed their coin and jewels. But how much would tithes like this cost Gloriana in the favors she would eventually grant in exchange? When would she choose to repay those debts . . . and how?

The next group—far smaller—contained nobles I had not seen since my time in the Queen's primary residence at Whitehall. And once again, riches flowed. I watched the Queen's cool survey of the piles at her feet. She seemed on the surface to not be impressed, but I could sense the calculations churning in her head.

What was the Queen's purpose here? Was she seeking anything more than funding for her broken-down army and falling-down castles? Even her maids and ladies-in-waiting were dressed up to levels far beyond our typical state. Was it all a grand deception?

The doors opened again, and the Queen's own court processed in. I opened my eyes wide, grateful again for this rarified position to see them walk, talk, and interact together when all I was supposed to be doing was, well, staring at them. It was an unparalleled opportunity to match names with faces, and faces with intentions both secret and plain. There was even the slender and aristocratic Lord Cavanaugh, who despite Beatrice's belief that he cared naught for her, eyed her with an intensity that made her stand up straighter and even preen. I fought to keep from rolling my eyes. Love made simpletons of even the most sophisticated of women, I decided.

Then another English courtier walked in, and the entire hall held its breath.

Robert Dudley, Master of the Horse, carried himself with the same sort of easy charm as the Count de Martine. He was older than Rafe by several years, and he was married, but I'd not seen the man's wife when she'd visited in the spring. It was said Amy Robsart was quite pretty, but truly, how could one compete with the Queen of England?

In any case, Amy was not here now, a reality made painfully clear by Robert Dudley's bold eye contact with the Queen as soon as he walked into the room. The fact that she stared back was worrisome, too. I'd heard of this man, but hadn't had the occasion to see him in my work as yet. Now all of the court, from page to prince, watched them, and I began to worry my fingers at the edges of my sleeves. This was a man to give Cecil nightmares, if ever there was one. This was a man to fear.

No, no, no, I thought, earnestly wishing Robert Dudley gone.

Instead, however, he bowed to the Queen like a perfect gentleman, then backed away with a flourish. He eyed her with a burning gaze, but his manner was no less fervent than those of the families who had come begging for her charity.

The energy that leaped between them was undeniable, and yet eminently deniable.

Perhaps I was overreacting? I stole a look at Sophia, who was placidly watching the byplay as if it were not fraught with anticipation and danger. Her features were serene, her gaze almost blank. She looked perfectly normal. Then again, she'd been *sewing* when she'd had her vision of "Golden Splendor" in the schoolroom. Who knew when her next vision would strike?

Arrested by the possibility, I found myself surreptitiously glancing at Sophia as if she were a statue fixed in place there in the Presence Chamber, taking in every detail of her expression as she pursed her lips together in concentration. I noted her wide, watchful eyes, almost purple in their intensity, and the delicate color of her cheeks, blushed as pink as Beatrice's dress. I watched her so closely, I could practically count her breaths.

Which is why I noticed when Sophia jerked her head around, hard, and focused all her attention on whoever had just walked into the room.

Forcing myself to act naturally, I let my gaze drift back along the gallery of yawning nobles, until it reached the guards flanking the entryway. The guards were looking less bored. Foreigners must have just entered, I decided. Sophia was focused on foreigners. Unable to wait any longer, I triumphantly cut my gaze to the small group of men bowing before the Queen.

The Spaniards!

Wait . . . the Spaniards?

Why would the Spaniards cause Sophia to be distressed?

They'd been here for months. And if anything, her training would have demanded that she remain calm and unruffled in their presence, since they were the ones we suspected of giving illicit letters to Lady Amelia.

I barely kept from frowning, but it made no sense. Count de Feria, Rafe, and a half dozen of the slender Spanish nobles were there, putting on their grand show. None more so than Ortiz, whose laughing splendor was sending half the ladies into a swoon. The Queen beside me watched them with approval, for once not even bothering to scowl at de Feria. With the delegation now stood the rotund, smiling Alvarez de Quadra, bishop of Aquila, Spain's newest ambassador and the grim de Feria's replacement. I slanted another look at Sophia. Still rigid. Was de Quadra the cause? It was rumored that King Philip had sent the bishop to replace de Feria as ambassador, given the Queen's obvious disdain for the hapless courtier and de Feria's own desire to collect his heavily pregnant wife and depart for the Continent before she had the baby. I knew very little about de Quadra, other than that he was, if anything, even more ardent in his religion than the Queen was in opposing it. But he didn't seem a bad sort. The Queen, of course, would have no use for him, since he was a man of God—and a Catholic God at that. But she might tolerate him better than she had de Feria, so that was a boon.

I was watching the tableau the Spaniards made, bowing to the Queen, when I felt a hot gaze upon me. I shifted my attention to the right, and met Rafe's stare. We had not spoken since parting ways the night before, but my cheeks burned with that memory. And speaking of . . . where was the bulky Spanish guard whom Rafe had struck in the chapel? Was that who had captured Sophia's attention so completely? I scanned the small knot of men, but they were all slender and somewhat effete. No one looked like Turnip Nose. De Quadra was stocky, but not the slightest bit hard, and I'd already heard him speak. It was in soft, measured tones, not the guttural anger of the man I'd overheard in the chapel.

There was another shift, and a new nobleman stepped forward.

And then I understood.

I looked back at Sophia and sighed. She still hadn't moved. I was fairly certain she had stopped breathing.

"Lord Theoditus Brighton, Earl of Dawbury," the steward announced in sepulchral tones. Lord Brighton walked forward with the slightest limp. He paused in front of the Queen and executed a reserved and measured bow, the move so full of dignity and respect that it seemed almost, well—out of place in the hall, with its collection of fawning noblemen and poseurs.

"Your Grace, it is as ever a wondrous boon to be able to look upon your fair countenance, covered in the raiment of the sun. You are the Gloriana of England, and we bring you all the gifts of our devotion."

The words were deep and mildly accented. I looked at Lord Brighton more curiously. He was from Wales, wasn't he? But his accent seemed . . . different, somehow.

With a wave of his hand, Brighton signaled a footman. The young man came up smartly, bearing a silver and black chest, and knelt before the Queen. She leaned forward. Sophia leaned forward. I still studied Brighton.

He had the dark look of an aging gypsy, yet his clothing

was richly embroidered with silver, his trunk hose perfectly slashed with alternating stripes of silver and deep onyx. He was slender, and his hair was shot with grey. There were lines at the corners of his eyes. He was *old*.

But I couldn't bring myself to quite place him in Grandfather's sphere. This was not a grandfather, but a man still in his prime.

The box had been opened, and a magnificent necklace presented to the Queen, of onyx and hematite and pearls. "To protect you," Brighton said. The Queen beamed. She loved getting gifts, particularly from men, though I couldn't see how a chunk of twisted metal and stones was going to help her achieve new heights of security. Still, she nodded to Brighton, and sat back in her throne, well-pleased.

Brighton, for his part, straightened. Then he looked at Sophia, pure gentleness in his eyes, and I felt more than heard the girl's raspy intake of breath.

Irritation coursed through me. That wasn't the look of a threatening man; it was the look of a caring protector. But the man's very presence turned Sophia into a quivering mute. What was going on?

I risked another glance at Sophia. The intensity in her expression was gone. There was fear only, and her body had, in fact, begun to tremble.

The Queen made her pronouncement of thanks for Lord Brighton's gift of generosity, and he bowed again, backing away.

As soon as Lord Brighton returned to his station at the side of the door, the steward announced the next delegations. First came the courtiers of the Flemish court, then the vividly dressed delegates from Morocco. Beatrice outdid herself, making eyes at men of wildly different nationalities and styles, somehow managing to flirt with all of them just within the boundaries of each country's traditions of how women should behave. It was nothing short of masterful. There was some time for the whole of the Italian delegation to process through, including a gaggle of priests sent by the pope. I worried my fingers once more against my sleeve at their arrival. There were plenty of Catholic sympathizers still in the court, and having a faction of priests to help fuel their fire could not be safe.

Then the simpering fools from France took their position, and the Queen's demeanor grew frosty. She accepted their bows with cool repugnance, and I knew hatred stirred within her. She had been but a new Queen when the Treaty of Cateau-Cambrésis with France had been signed, and in gaining the peace she'd needed so desperately, she had lost Calais, England's only foothold on the Continent. She would never forgive them for that, just as she never would forgive Philip for marrying the child Elisabeth de Valois. I'd been shocked at Sophia's betrothal, but Elisabeth was only fourteen—three full years my junior. I could not even imagine how unsettling that would be.

Then came the Scots.

I stood up a little straighter when they entered the room, descending on the court with the air of brigands and thieves, despite their fancy clothes. Even though they marched along quite silently, they seemed a rabble. They were less refined than the other nobles, the material of their clothes thicker and more roughly sewn, although it was clear that they had dressed in their best for an audience with the Queen. The Queen had no interest in the Scots, I knew, other than the fact that she would use anything in her power against the French. And many of the Scots were at war with the French to boot, so they would be here seeking money, not giving it. Still, there was something so . . . authentic about this lot. They were proud that they were not as polished as the rest of the crowd, rough and tumble men with the kind of easygoing grins I hadn't seen since I'd parted ways with the Golden Rose. I rather liked the Scots, I decided.

I could tell Beatrice did not. As rigid as Sophia had been before, now it was Beatrice's turn to be caught in a thrall. She leaned forward slightly, clearly memorizing the features of the men young and old, as we had been carefully taught. But unlike her reaction to every other delegation, Beatrice did not slip easily into a flirtatious manner with the Scots. In fact, for one long moment she couldn't seem to do anything but stare. Then, at last she smiled—with coy and perfect grace, her eyes bright, her manner lively and feminine. And in that moment I realized that Beatrice's assignment from Cecil involved this crass, unlikely bunch. No wonder she'd been so quiet on the subject. The Scottish nobles were an entirely different breed of man from the English—barely civilized, and proud of that fact. If Beatrice's job was to beguile and bedevil this lot, she would have her hands full.

Even now the game was beginning, I could see. The light that arced in from the high windows caught the fairness of Beatrice's skin, and the Scots at once noticed the pretty young woman eyeing them so keenly. One of their number, a tall, powerfully built young man of perhaps twenty years, flashed a large, knowing grin in her direction. He was handsome in the way of a warrior, with sharp eyes and broad shoulders, but it was difficult to see what he truly looked like under his unruly hair and thick, braided beard. While I watched, he elbowed his mate. Both of them leered back at Beatrice and waggled their eyebrows. Beatrice stiffened, but kept her smile winsome and pretty. All of this happened while the Scots made barely deferential bows to the Queen, then proceeded to sneer at the Frenchmen who had come before them.

It was, in all, a hopeless mob, and a sudden thought struck me.

If ever England's enemies wanted to strike a blow to disrupt the Queen's court, it would be seven days hence, when the dignitaries from several foreign lands and the far reaches of the English court all gathered under one roof for the Crown's rollicking late summer masque.

Sworn enemies.

Desperate conspirators.

Fawning opportunists.

Cunning traitors.

And every one of them in disguise.

God save the Queen.

CHAPTER TWENTY-ONE

Finally released from the Presence Chamber, all I craved was the open air of the Lower Ward. I fled toward the outer doors, not even bothering to return to the maids' chambers to doff my gown. Beatrice wouldn't miss it. She'd been collared by Walsingham the moment the audience had ended and had been carted off to be introduced to a dozen dignitaries. I'm sure the Scotsmen would be in that group.

How she'd ever keep one overstuffed nobleman straight from another, I would never know. Still, that was part of her talents—her capacity to remember everyone, and everyone's position, and use them to her own advantage. That was a gift I would not want.

"A moment, dear?" The words jolted me out of my reverie, and I half-turned, sinking into a curtsy before I could stop myself. Then I realized it wasn't a member of the court addressing me but a small, wizened woman in a faded but well-made gown, her eyes rheumy with age. She might have been a gentlewoman or a highly placed servant, but I had no way of telling. I completed my curtsy anyway. There was never any harm in being polite.

“Ma’am?” I asked as she stared at me. “Is aught amiss?”

“No—no.” The old woman clasped her trembling hands together. “I came up for the presentation to the Queen and saw you standing again with the Crown—I couldn’t believe it.”

I frowned at her. “Do I know you?”

She cackled at some joke only she could recall. “You don’t, my dear, you don’t. I have not been here since King Henry died. I make my home in Bath now, near the old abbey. I did want to see his daughter, though. She makes a glorious Queen, a glorious Queen.”

I smiled and reached for the crone’s fluttering hands, cradling their frailness in my own. “She is blessed to have loyal subjects such as you to welcome her to the throne,” I said.

“Me!” harrumphed the woman, shaking her head. “Far more blessed she is to have you, my dear. As was her father before.” I frowned at that. Clearly the old woman was confused. She squeezed my hands then, her gaze now wandering as much as her mind, and I looked around for help. It came in the form of what must have been the woman’s granddaughter, bustling up with rapid apologies to claim her errant elder.

I watched the two move off, feeling suddenly, oddly alone; then I turned back toward the Lower Ward. As I walked, my mind turned over the events of the morning like a churning waterwheel.

Who had the old woman thought I was? And how many in the crowd today were proud of their new Queen, like she had been, while others angled for the Queen’s downfall? How many were heaping their treasures upon Elizabeth with one hand and aiming a knife at her heart with the other? Who could she really trust?

And what of Robert Dudley? The look he'd given Elizabeth had been mild, even banal, but his spirit had imparted something different entirely. He was both the figure of propriety and the soul of desire, like a man acting a play without words. To an untrained eye Dudley was just another flatterer. But to anyone who knew the Queen and could read her reaction truly . . . he was a threat. Why would the Queen choose Robert Dudley, though? Why did any woman choose any man? I thought of the men I knew, all so very different—Grandfather. Troupe Master James. Walsingham and Cecil. Rafe. Especially Rafe.

Rafe was a Spaniard, and I suspected he was a spy. In truth, more than suspected. And he was quite possibly a killer. He had bartered with Turnip Nose for the letter at the very least, and then he'd incapacitated him. According to Anna's translation of their conversation, the contents of the letter pointed to a disruption, but I didn't *have* the letter, so I knew no details. What was going on?

I looked to either side as I entered the boisterous Lower Ward. I'd been here dozens of times in the last few months, in full day and at night. Tonight it seemed more crowded than usual, the air richer with spices, the laughter louder. A large group of onlookers had gathered south of the King's Gate, out in the open space of the ward. The energy of the crowd was up, and I felt a tingle of recognition. I smiled to myself, a faint thread of excitement curling within me. If I hadn't known better, I would have thought the Golden Rose was playing here this day. The crowd had that kind of feel, an undercurrent of anticipation. A smell of money.

A familiar heat pulsed through my hands, and I suddenly

yearned to be among the crowd, back in my old role—with my patchwork gown and my hair caught up with broken pins, my "jewelry" of glass beads, and my careful makeup. The role I played now was so much deeper than anything I had attempted with the Golden Rose, however. Could I ever go back?

I smoothed my hands down my ugly borrowed gown. The silks and linens I wore now were far finer than anything I had pieced together as an actress. The jewels around my neck were simple—almost austere—yet they were of the highest quality, given to me out of the royal coffers that I might carry off the illusion of being a daughter of noble parentage.

An odd tug caught at my heart. My parents had not been noble, but that was all I knew of them. Grandfather had never spoken of them, no matter how I'd pestered him. He'd said they had been struck down when they were young, losing their lives in their prime, and leaving him with the "joy," as he put it, of raising me. He had never once complained, I remembered now. But he had never once explained, either.

Who had my parents been?

Again I thought of the old woman and her odd comments. Had she mistaken me for my mother? Had my parents ever performed before King Henry, just as I now performed for his daughter?

The Queen's accusation surfaced again. *You do not know who you are.*

Who am I, truly?

The thought made me unaccountably sad, and I turned away from the crowd. I was seeking passage along the outskirts of the throng to Knight's Gate, when I saw him.

Little Tommy Farrow.

Unbidden hot tears sprang to my eyes, and I lifted my hand to my mouth, stifling a cry. I stood stone still as I watched the small tow-headed figure march resolutely through the crowd, his breeches seeming a little shorter now on his pumping legs, his cheeks just the slightest bit leaner. Surely the boy could not have aged so much in just four months. I must have remembered him being younger.

I watched him another thirty seconds before the reality of his presence was brought home to me.

Tommy Farrow was *here*, in the *Lower Ward of Windsor Castle*.

And where he roamed, so roamed the Golden Rose players.

I whirled, scanning the crowd. Could it be? Were they here? Despite my height, I could not see through the crowd that thronged in the bustling ward, but the men gave obligingly when I pushed through them, willing enough to let a young woman enter their midst. By the time I'd pressed through the horde and into the small empty space of the makeshift courtyard, the play was just beginning. And I had the best view in the yard of act 1, scene 1 of *The Queen's Promise*.

I couldn't believe it. There was Marcus, and Thom Barrister, too. And George, Henry, and Leo, all dressed like high lords of the land. They were shouting through words I'd learned at my grandfather's knee, back when there had been no Queen of England but only a king—Henry VIII's son, Edward.

The pageant looked like it had been revised to reflect a Queen in command, and to the troupe's credit, I could see that the changes to the play had been thorough. So many of the lines were the same (which would please the actors, I knew) but there were new words around them, bracketing the phrases with additional story, now that all of London had become fascinated with the details of every move the Queen made. The cadence and flow of their dialogue were still richly detailed, redolent of the northern England brogue, but the words now spoke of a Queen who ruled king and country with her own fierce hand, and who loved England more than she even loved herself.

I thought of the Queen I'd seen today in the Presence Chamber. The Golden Rose had gotten that much right. This Queen loved England to the core. More than she could ever love any man. *The Queen will never marry,* Sophia had said. Could that be possible?

Then I saw Troupe Master James, his back to me, and my heart surged. How easy it would be for me to cross the line and fade back into the crush of players. They would hide me, smuggle me out of this place. And if we fled this night, we could retreat to the far reaches of England for a few months, until the Queen's advisors had tired of looking for me.

Another thought kindled inside my mind. Perhaps the troupe had come to Windsor with the express idea of freeing me? I'd gotten no word, but even that was not surprising. If the Golden Rose had levied this adventure into the castle grounds to get an initial feel of the Lower Ward and all her entries and exits, then they wouldn't even have tried to get a message to me. It would have been too soon. Hope suddenly bloomed within me, but it felt strange. More like a stomach upset than the elation I would have expected. What was wrong with me?

I felt the swish of skirts beside me, the lightest touch against my girdled pouch. Without hesitation I reacted, snaking my hand out and catching a small wrist in my iron clutch.

"What 'o, now!" Tommy Farrow staggered back, going up on his toes as I pulled him high. "Begging yer pardon, ma'am. I didna mean to run inta—Meg!"

His eyes goggled, and I laughed outright as I set him gently down. Clearly Tommy still had his talent for picking the wrong mark.

"Hello, Tommy," I said, crouching down to his level that he might not have to look up so high. "What brings you to Windsor today? Did you not expect to see me?"

"Not 'ere, no!" Tommy said. "Master James said ye'd been taken to Whitehall to serve the Queen. We assumed ye'd be inside *that* castle, not this one." He eyed me then, his gaze somewhat dubious. "Ye don't look like a maid, though. Ye look like a proper lady. Sort of."

My heart deflated. So the Golden Rose had not come to save me, had not even known I was here. Had they any idea how much I'd given up to save them?

I shook off the feeling of sudden despair that stole through me. *Poor, sweet Meg, all alone in the world,* Rafe had said. Once more, I felt like crying.

"Well, then," I said briskly. "You're playing here just to bring a show to the poor deprived townspeople of Windsor?"

"We tried to attract the crowds in the city proper, but everyone was up 'ere," Tommy said. His eyes brightened. "Ye want to talk to Master James? 'E'll have missed you! The day you were taken was a grim day for us all, I tell you that plain. 'E wanted to storm the castle for weeks after!"

I rather doubted that, but I grinned at Tommy's defense, and some of my dismay lightened. Still, Cecil and Walsingham had been quite clear. If my advisors so much as suspected my defection back to the Golden Rose, the punishment would be the troupe's imprisonment.

I straightened, ruefully rustling the boy's hair. "I don't think that is a wise decision, but I thank you for thinking of me, Tommy. Give Master James my love, will you? And tell him that I miss you all terribly."

"Why not tell him yourself?"

At the achingly familiar voice, it took every ounce of my spy training not to leap aside like a startled goat. Instead, I let my grin widen, and I turned to my right. "Master James!"

"At your service, madame." He executed a bow as courtly as any I'd seen inside the castle. "Or is it 'my lady' now?" He straightened and eyed me with a keen intensity. "You are well?"

Too many words rushed to be spoken, and I nearly choked on them. "Yes—yes, I am well," I said, tasting the faint lie on my lips, and realizing it was not such an untruth as it should have been.

"They are not harming you, or keeping you against your will?"

I blinked at him. How much did he know? "N-no," I said too hastily, and his eyes narrowed. I had the uncomfortable sensation that he was looking through me, not at me. "I am well, I tell you. They treat me like one of their own."

"They dress you like one, too. You cannot tell me *that* is a comfortable gown, but you do look like quite the lady."

My cheeks burned and I dropped my eyes, surveying my wreck of a dress. Could Beatrice not have found a more attractive gown for me? I felt deeply ashamed of the costume, though why, I couldn't say. "It—it was a gift from a friend," I managed.

"I'd consider cultivating more enemies, if these are the gifts your friends choose," he teased.

I twisted my hands in my accursed skirts. "It is not as though I came to the castle with a dowry, Master James," I snapped. "I'm grateful for what they give me."

"And what is the price for the castle's generosity, I wonder?"

"That is none of your concern!"

"Then perhaps it should be." He shrugged. "You were in my care until a few short months ago, Meg. Don't think I have forgotten it."

"I'd been in your care only six months prior to that," I countered. "I should not have been so difficult to forget."

"If that's what you think, then you've changed far more than in your appearance, and believe me, that's changed a great deal."

The words hung between us, awkward, and James paused another minute more, regarding me with his piercing eyes. I stared back at him, matching him scowl for scowl, and felt a curious shift in my chest.

There'd been only one other young man who had ever glared at me with such annoyance, and that had been Rafe. Who'd *kissed* me as well. Could Master James also . . . Did he actually . . . *Was that possible?*

"What is it, Meg?" Tommy interrupted my spinning

thoughts with real alarm in his voice. "Ye've gone white as snow."

I shook myself hard. Master James looked equally ill at ease. "I'm well, Tommy," I said, and lifted my chin, addressing James again. *Master* James, that is. "How goes the troupe? You seem to be drawing a crowd."

He smiled noncommittally. "When we go to where the crowds are, aye." He nodded into the throng. "We don't have your hands to help, but we draw the people to our cause well enough in more ways than one."

"Is Mary stepping up?" I asked, referring to a girl not even past fifteen who'd begun to show some aptitude at thieving.

Master James shrugged. "She'll do. I have to split my time between the actors and the street troupe. She's not quite good enough to take your place, I'm afraid, but she tries. So far, it hasn't cost us."

Tommy swiveled his head between us. "When are you coming back, Meg?" he piped up. "The harvest will come on soon, and with it farmers flush with coin and ale. We'll have all the money we can carry!"

"I don't know, Tommy," I said, looking down at him, if only to avoid James's—Master James's—eyes. "I have work here to do as yet."

"What sort of work?" Master James asked quietly. "What sort of work would the Crown need with a thief as good as any I've seen, and an actress better than half the men in our troupe? Work like that cannot help but be dangerous." He dropped his voice to an even lower tone. "Are you in danger, Meg?"

I lifted my head quickly, and met his gaze. Something

jumped between us like arcing fire. Then a cheer went up in the crowd, signaling the end of the first act of the play.

"Master James!" Tommy said, tugging his arm. "We must go! The second act is barely ten minutes hence, and I haven't changed!"

I blinked at Tommy, confused. "You haven't changed?"

"I've become an *actor*!" Tommy said in a rush of excitement. "Master James said I should focus on my lines, and 'e won't even let me lift the purses of anyone but women now. I'm an actor, Meg! Since right after you left!"

"Tommy is showing a talent for the stage," Master James said hastily, too sincere for believability. "I think he may serve us better on the stage than in the street."

Realization struck me, and with it a flood of warmth for James's adroit handling of the situation. Tommy was a hopeless thief, and I suspected he was an equally horrible actor. But as an actor, at least the boy would be safe from the branding irons of the Crown. *Since right after you left,* Tommy had said. The timing could not have been by accident.

"I'm sure you're a very fine actor," I said to Tommy, and he beamed. I glanced up to Master James, not bothering to hide the warmth of my words. "And you are—very wise, Master James, to see where his skills may best serve."

He shrugged and glanced away, and I saw the faintest flare of red climb up his jawline. Was he blushing?

Before I had time to think on it, Tommy started tugging on Master James's sleeve again. "We truly must go, Master James. I am already late!"

James resisted being pulled along for just one second more, and his gaze met mine. "As ever, Meg Fellowes, the

Golden Rose is at your service," he said, and he reached out his hand. "Should you need us for aught, you have but to send word."

Startled, I lifted my hand to his, curtsying. Because, after all, that's what I did when I was flustered. Master James took my hand into his and brushed his lips over it, his mouth warm even through my thin gloves. A skittering sensation zipped through me at the contact. It was nothing, the height of propriety, and yet . . . somehow, it wasn't. Master James was four years my senior, but the huge chasm that should have been between us suddenly seemed . . . less so.

I pulled my hand back with as much decorum as I could muster, and James straightened. "You never know when a troupe of rogues and villains might be of service to a fair lady," he said with a smile. "With words or blades to cut your enemies down."

"Then do not stray far," I said, surprising myself with my response. I looked at him, so fierce and sure, and I thought of Jane. Instantly, the cramping in my stomach stopped, a sense of rightness restored. *I should introduce him to Jane.* That was safe. That was better. That was . . . easier to think about. And yet . . . I suddenly didn't want what was safer or easier. "You never know when a fair lady might have need of rogues and villains. Or a lady who's a villain might have need of a rogue."

He blinked at me, but Tommy's desperate tugs won out, and the two of them were gone.

I allowed my gaze to swing lazily over the crowd, as if the chance meeting meant nothing to me at all, in case anyone were watching me. Not that I thought Cecil cared what I did with my days, as long as I stayed out of his way. Walsingham,

I'm sure, would have preferred me to be applying myself to one of my many assignments, but who was to say that I wasn't in the Lower Ward for exactly that?

A sudden fear stole through me, far too belatedly. If Cecil and Walsingham were watching, however, would they think I was plotting some escape with the Golden Rose? A midnight flight through the city, down to the river, and then off to Londontown?

The answer to that was chillingly simple.

Yes.

Fool, fool, a hundred times the fool! I kept my manner easy and light, desperately searching through the crowd for another familiar face, someone to explain my presence here in the Lower Ward, someone who would capture the interest of Cecil and Walsingham far more than my encounter with my old friends.

I swung my gaze to the right, and my concerns bloomed into horror. Cecil and Walsingham were out strolling through the Lower Ward as if they were bosom friends. Neither walked with a sense of purpose, but I knew them both well enough not to give their apparent meandering any weight. They could have easily been on their way to a beheading, and their easy strides wouldn't have faltered a half step.

Had they seen me with Master James or Tommy? Had I risked the troupe's safety with a simple conversation? And if they hadn't already, would Cecil and Walsingham realize who was playing to the crowd in the Lower Ward, and draw their own conclusions?

I felt a firm hand close around my arm, and I nearly screeched with terror, my teeth clamping down so hard on my tongue that my eyes sparked with tears. I whirled around, recognizing the familiar face immediately as my heart galloped with the nearness of Cecil and Walsingham's approach.

A cry of exultation went up from the crowd—act 2 was beginning—and I saw my next move as plain as if it had been written into the script.

I dropped like a stone into Rafe's arms, my body as limp as a rag.

CHAPTER TWENTY-TWO

Not even Sophia could have bettered that swoon.

"What are you about, Meg?" Rafe demanded, staggering back under my not inconsiderable weight. When he realized I was going to slide to the ground, unresisting, he cursed under his breath in Spanish. A few of those words I even knew.

I felt myself hoisted up into his strong arms. I flopped convincingly, and that earned me another curse. It was everything I could do not to grin.

Rafe turned and stalked away from the crowd, and I dared to open my eyes. I couldn't see much, with my head tucked into Rafe's chest, but I could reason from the slant of his stride that he would be walking right in front of Walsingham and Cecil. No doubt those two men would be far too curious about what I was doing in Rafe's arms to give any thought to what I'd been doing before those arms had obligingly shown up.

When Rafe had stomped another twenty feet, I stirred.

"Rafe?" I said weakly, fluttering my hand. I risked a glance, but saw only his jaw for a moment, and a large muscle twitching in his neck. Then he stopped, and I realized we were at a shaded bench, which had no doubt been cleared by his scowl.

"You'll sit here," he commanded, and he dropped my feet with surprising gentleness, easing me down onto the bench.

"I'm well, really," I began, surreptitiously glancing right, then left. A slash of black caught my eye, and I knew without looking more closely that I'd located Cecil. *I see you, old goat.*

"You are about fifteen strides away from being questioned by your keepers," Rafe said tersely. "What is the story here? Are you overcome with the heat of the crowd? Sick with the plague? Frightened witless by that man who just kissed your hand?" He quirked his lips. "In love with me?"

I blinked. "Those are my options?"

"Choose, or I choose for you. And that is a god-awful gown you're wearing."

"It was the heat!" I hissed at him, and he nodded, sitting down to fan me. I dared not wrench Beatrice's ruff off, though I wanted to, desperately. "And if you must know, they cannot know I spoke to anyone from the acting troupe. My even *being* in the Lower Ward with members of the troupe is the world's worst luck."

"Not so unlucky for me," Rafe said with a grin. "And you owe me." He reached out and clasped my shoulder, as if he thought I would collapse at any moment. "We are skilled actors, Meg. It's time to act the part." He snapped his fingers in front of my eyes, as if recalling me to life, and a flash of milky green distracted me. One of his rings?

Rafe glanced up, drawing in a quick breath. "Just follow my lead."

I narrowed my eyes. "Your lead?" I asked, but just then

Cecil and Walsingham were upon us, their censure as chill as death.

"What is going on here?" Cecil demanded. "What are you doing with Miss Fellowes?"

Walsingham spoke up, apparently unwilling to let Cecil steal all of the rebuke. "Should I summon the guard, Count de Martine, or would you like to explain yourself?"

I started to speak, then felt Rafe's hand tighten on my shoulder in a sharp squeeze.

"I confess, sirs, I don't know what happened to Miss Fellowes," he said smoothly. "I met her as she was crossing the Middle Ward and offered to escort her through the crowds here in the Lower. At first, it seemed all was well with her. But the moment we crossed into the Lower Ward, she grew concerned, as if she'd seen something to cause her distress. She asked to leave, but I confess I had caught sight of the theatre troupe and thought it to be a grand adventure." He waved vaguely to where the crowd had assembled, and I shivered quite sincerely. "She protested, and I am ashamed to admit I pressed on. I had no idea—" He broke off, sounding for all the world like a flummoxed courtier unable to figure out the wiles of women. "I had no idea that she would *collapse*!"

I had to moan to avoid bursting into laughter. Rafe might not have been an actor upon the stage, but he'd clearly had training somewhere. I brought a hand to my head, and I felt, rather than saw, Cecil and Walsingham turn to see the gathering crowd around the players. They made the realization immediately.

Cecil crouched down before me. I looked at him directly, all my feigned terror now gone. I wouldn't impress Cecil with hysterics. I would impress him by *acting* hysterical while operating in a coldly rational way.

"I did not realize whose troupe it was, Sir William, until it was too late," I whispered, barely loud enough for him to hear. Obligingly, Cecil leaned closer to me and made comforting noises, like a father might to his infant child. I would have laughed again at the irony, but I struggled to stay focused. Cecil raised me to my feet, and I did a credible job of looking unsteady.

"I appreciate your attention to the Queen's maid, Count de Martine," Cecil said, with just the right touch of frost. "I'll accompany her back to the safety of her rooms. She has need of rest."

Rafe looked like he was about to protest, but Walsingham didn't give him the chance.

"Walk with me, boy," he boomed to Rafe, turning him around in the opposite direction from the Upper Ward and the Golden Rose acting troupe. He clapped Rafe on the back hard enough to send a lesser lad stumbling, but Rafe had apparently braced himself for the blow.

Meanwhile, Cecil had curled my arm into his and was helping me back toward the Upper Ward. I wanted to shy away, but enough people had seen my inglorious swoon; we had to keep up appearances above all else.

All the court was about nothing so much as it was about appearances.

Still, as we turned the corner, I couldn't help but be pleased by my thrice-won escape. First from being rendered speechless and uncertain by Master James—then from being disgraced by Sir William and Sir Francis . . . and, finally, from the questioning I knew would have been forthcoming about the Golden Rose troupe from one very confused—but far too intrigued—Count de Martine.

In the space of ten minutes, I'd evaded them all.

But now Cecil was marching me forward with the grim determination of a man on a mission. He had another assignment for me, of that I was certain. One I was equally certain I would not like.

The man would be the death of me.

CHAPTER TWENTY-THREE

Close enough, as it turned out.

CHAPTER TWENTY-FOUR

"He wants me to do *what*?"

Beatrice regarded me with disbelief. We were sitting in the maids' chamber, and I'd just stripped off her hideous gown. I'd never been so happy to return a gift in my life.

Then again, I'd not exactly received a great deal of gifts to give back.

"Cecil said that the Queen has requested your elevation to lady of the bedchamber, in the very likely event that Lady Mathilde is unable to perform her duties," I said, indicating the lady Cecil had chosen as most replaceable. "She has not been feeling well."

This, of course, was a patent lie. The Queen could have had no intention of favoring Beatrice with this assignment, and Mathilde had looked as strong as an ox in the Presence Chamber this morning. Whatever her fateful malady was supposed to be, she'd not yet incurred it. But I continued on with Cecil's orders, to the letter, exactly as he had delivered them to me. "The Queen fears Mathilde will grow more ill before she gets better, and Her Grace is concerned that she will in turn fall ill if she remains in Mathilde's presence."

"That would be terrible," Beatrice breathed, though her eyes were bright with excitement. "And she asked for me? Why did Cecil not tell me himself?"

"He felt the request would be less unsettling were it from me." Another lie, and this even lamer. Beatrice didn't seem to mind.

"But why?" she demanded, fairly bouncing on her toes. "There are dozens of women who would draw blood to gain this role. Why did the Queen ask for *me*?"

I looked at her as if she were daft. "Beatrice, you're by far the loveliest and most noble of the maids, whether inside our select group or outside of it. You are the pinnacle of health and grace, and since you *are* a member of this inner circle, you are eminently trustworthy. Whyever would she not seek you out in a moment of need?"

Beatrice turned and stared at me wide-eyed. "The Queen said that?" she asked, breathless.

Whoops. No amount of flattery that I could spin would outrank the direct comments of the Queen. I improvised quickly. "That is merely the truth, Beatrice," I said. "Cecil said that the Queen herself intimated she would trust no one so much as you, to both step into the position and to step out of it again, knowing that your favor with her was constant." More lies, manufactured by Cecil to, he said, ease Beatrice's dismay about her "other" assignments. *Whatever those were*. I hated myself even as I said the words. But I wasn't done yet.

This part was the worst. "At first, Cecil wanted to put me in your place, but I said no—you are the best of any of us for this job."

"Oh!" Beatrice clasped her hands to her breast, positively radiant.

I felt like a worm. Suddenly, being a rat seemed . . . too clean for what I was right now.

Beatrice sighed happily as she turned away, absently putting the returned (and still quite ugly) dress back into its chest. I'd worn it less than a full day, and over my shift. It was a costume, nothing more. And despite my theatrics with Rafe, I'd not soiled it. I think Beatrice had been secretly disappointed about that. As I saw the gown disappearing back into the cupboard, I rather suspected I'd never see it again.

I let my gaze drift over to Beatrice's bed. Gowns still lay strewn there from when she'd pulled them out this morning. Her peacock-blue purse lay on top of the pile, its clasp of jade stone and sapphires winking brilliantly even in the indifferent light. Something about the purse nagged at me.

Beatrice cleared her throat, her back still to me. "I owe you an apology," she said.

I blinked. *What did she just say?* "You do?" I asked.

"I do." She stepped away from the cupboard, picked up another gown, and stowed it, still not looking at me. "I know Cecil favors you; he's never made any secret of that. So for you to position me before your own self speaks volumes of your character." She sighed as she lifted another dress, smoothing the fine silk beneath her fingers. "I do not know that I would be so generous, were the situation reversed."

"Beatrice, I—"

"No," Beatrice said. She straightened and turned her lovely face toward me, sincerity flowing from her in waves. "I do not deserve your grace, when I have given you none in return. I will resolve to trust you more, Meg. It means a great deal to know you have my back. There are so many in this place who are not true, who do things just because they may gain from them politically. Friends like you are very rare."

She honestly could not have twisted the knife any deeper if she'd tried.

I had hated Cecil violently over the course of my nearly four months in the Crown's service, but perhaps never quite so much as I did in that moment. I cleared my throat. "I thank you, Beatrice, but really—"

"No," she cut me off again. "You need say no more." She clasped the gown she was holding tightly to her, her eyes shining with emotion. "Thank you, Meg. Thank you from the bottom of my heart. I swear to you, I will not forget your kindness."

I felt sick. I wanted to tell her everything in that moment. Tell her of Cecil's orders, of his lies. Tell her that this entire announcement was being staged for Cecil to gain insight into the Queen's most private activities, so that I would know what to expect when I was set in place to spy. I wanted to tell her that I had had no intention of recommending her to Cecil, that he'd merely told me to act as if I had, to gain her gratitude and ensure that she would not plot against me. I wanted to tell her that I did not deserve her friendship, or her trust, that I had lied.

"You're welcome, Beatrice," I said instead.

The door to our chambers was flung open before I drew

my next breath, and we both turned, goggle-eyed, to watch Anna tear into the room practically shrieking with excitement.

"He's coming to the masque, he's coming to the Masque! Christopher Riley, he's coming to the masque!" Anna chanted, nearly bowling Beatrice over in her exuberance. "And it's all because of you, Beatrice!"

I hadn't thought I could suffer more guilt this day over what I'd just done to Beatrice, but I'd been wrong. I'd never seen such joy upon Anna's face, not even when she was translating myths back to the original Greek. I guessed what had happened, but I was forced to watch it play out, like a carriage toppling over a cliff.

"I told you he was going to attend, you silly goose!" Beatrice laughed, looking more like twelve than her eighteen years. She rocked with Anna back and forth, encircled by Anna's stout arms. "Whyever did you doubt me?"

"Because he is only a vicar's son! And I would have thought him too serious for such a trifle as this." Anna pulled back from Beatrice, turned to me. "Do you know? Did she tell you?"

"No!" I barely got out, before Anna began speaking again, her words a torrent of excitement and emotion.

"Well, it's like this—and I canna believe it, I tell you plainly," Anna began. "The masque that is coming up, half the world will be there, what, but surely not a vicar's son, with all the nobility from far and wide coming into town, you see?"

"I see," I laughed, enjoying Anna's happiness despite myself. "What happened then?"

"Well, Beatrice here," Anna said, casting adoring eyes at Beatrice. "Beatrice had her aunt put a word in with Lord Farley, whom you know is the patron of the vicar of Cleves, asking him to extend an invitation to Christopher. Lord Farley then proceeded to tell the vicar that his son could do worse than to consider marrying one of the young ladies of the court, especially a woman of gentle breeding and a scholarly mind. A scholarly mind! There would be nothing better to attract the interest of the vicar!" Anna fairly crowed. "Oh, Beatrice, it was masterful."

Beatrice smiled indulgently, and Anna rushed on.

"So there I am in the Middle Ward, translating correspondence for Sir William, and who should step up to speak with me but Christopher Riley! He asked with a smile should I know any maid with a scholarly mind, and told me the tale altogether."

Alarm flashed in Beatrice's eyes, and I also blinked. Why would Christopher be telling Anna all of this? Surely he wouldn't tip his hand so quickly regarding his intentions to woo her.

"We both got a fair laugh out of it," continued Anna, blissfully unaware of Beatrice's and my mounting concern. "An' because he does not want to disappoint his da, he will be at the ball. Dressed as a vicar, he told me! Can you imagine?"

I fought the temptation to roll my eyes, but Beatrice did not. Fortunately, Anna wasn't looking at her. Instead she had fallen silent, waiting for our response.

"That is a fine tale, indeed," I said, springing into the

sudden lull. "And do you think Mr. Riley realizes that *you* are the young maiden Lord Farley was recommending, the young woman of breeding and a scholarly mind?"

Anna stared at me in stupefaction. "Whatever are you talking about?" she asked. "I am hardly a young woman of—"

"Anna!" Beatrice blurted in astonishment. "You cannot be serious. Do you mean to tell me that you thought Lord Farley—at my direct request—would recommend someone *other* than you?"

Anna turned her gaze to Beatrice. "Whatever can you mean?" she asked again. "I—I just thought it was a ploy to get Chris to come to the masque."

"It was a ploy to get him to come to the masque to see *you*," Beatrice said, and moaned. "And now he must be thoroughly confused, because you played it off as if you had no idea what he was talking about."

"But I didn't know what he was talking about—I mean, I don't think he was talking about anything—certainly not about me!" She looked from one of us to the other. "Did I do something wrong?" Anna's soft face crumpled, and her large eyes began to fill with tears. I stepped forward quickly.

"This is the *best* thing that could have happened," I said firmly, with only the slightest sense of desperation.

That arrested them both. They stared at me.

"It is?" Anna asked in a tiny voice.

"Absolutely," I said. "If you'd simpered or blushed, Mr. Riley would have known his suit was already assured. By acting as if his attendance at the ball mattered not a whit to you—and in fact, laughing along with him at the notion of this mystery girl—"

"Well, not a mystery girl, precisely," Anna said. "I suggested two or three girls that might suit—"

I smoothly cut off both Anna's words and Beatrice's groaned response. "Then he has no reason to suspect you had anyone put in a word for *you*. And why is that? Because you are so confident of his attraction to you that you do not need to play such games. You will now both be at the ball, and in perfect accord with each other, easy in your shared confidences. Even better, there will be no question of your finding each other. You'll know your target when you see him the night of the masque. I cannot think there will be many other young men dressed like a vicar."

Beatrice stifled a giggle, but Anna twirled around, her skirts flying. "Oh, Meg, you have to be right. And better than any of that, Christopher Riley is coming to the masque!" She turned faster and faster. "It couldn't be more perfect!"

She collapsed in a heap on the bed and burst out laughing from the sheer joy of it. "It is almost as good as having deciphered your letters, Meg, verily I swear!"

Beatrice and I both froze, even as Anna continued chortling.

"Anna," I managed as soon as I could draw breath. "You mean that you've found the key to the letters?" This was a stroke of luck if so—though we'd had the letters less than a day, I needed to return them!

"Oh, yes. It wasn't so difficult as all that." Anna sat up on her bed, wiping the tears from her eyes. "Once I'd steamed open the wax seals of the rest of them—don't worry, they're back in place now pristinely perfect—it was easy to find the pattern. Deciphering a code comes much easier when you know that the code is there to decipher. I canna tell you the number of letters I've read that had no more code to them than cow's milk—"

"Anna!" Beatrice interrupted, sharply enough to stop even Anna's stream of chatter. "What did you find in the letters?"

She blinked at us. "Well, the ones I had were quite specific, to members of Lady Amelia's family. They spoke of 'waiting for the signal' to indicate that a major request was being made, but in the meantime to carry out some minor tasks." She grinned. "You remember the milk crate incident? That fell to Lady Agnes, Amelia's great-aunt. And the sour milk being stirred into the courtier's ale? That was Amelia's cousin Bailey."

Beatrice frowned. "Lord Bailey hasn't been at the court since midspring," she said. "He nearly died in that fall at the hunt in Shropshire."

Anna bit her lip. "Well . . . the letter was from about that time. Wait." She dove into our side cupboard, and pulled out the packet. "Yes, March. So it's possible that the writer didn't know of his fall. But still . . ." She regarded Beatrice thoughtfully. "The sour milk incident did happen. It caused quite a fuss."

"And I don't recall Lady Agnes remaining in the court either, given her son's injury." Beatrice tapped her chin. "So who could have carried out the requests?"

"Lady Amelia?" I asked, but Beatrice shook her head.

"Lady Amelia wouldn't have harmed Marie, though. Not so violently. And she wouldn't have set the vestments on fire."

"Oh, no," Anna agreed. "There was something in the letter about stealing vestments—but not burning them. And it was not even posed as a question, more of a 'if only we could . . . but it would be too dangerous.' That, too, was in the letter for Bailey. And that one was one of the letters I don't believe was truly penned by Dona Victoria."

"What about the love letter? Were there any codes in those?"

"Only the code of true love—and written in the same hand as Bailey's letter, I will say that." Anna sighed. "It's all so very tragic, in its way."

I grimaced. "Yes, tragic. Remember, that lovestruck swain knew information about Marie's death that only the killer would know. Why would he warn Lady Amelia about what happened to Marie?"

While we were considering that, a chambermaid appeared at the door. "Miss Knowles?" the young girl squeaked. "A Lord Cavanaugh is asking after you."

That arrested us all. Beatrice recovered first. "He must have heard of the Queen's intention for me to replace the ailing Mathilde," she said, and smiled. "La, how word travels fast."

"La," I agreed flatly. And then she was gone, leaving Anna and me to ponder. Me perhaps more than Anna.

I gathered up the letters from her and reattached the lavender ribbon. "Anna," I said. "The letters you think were not written by Dona Victoria, can you tell me anything else about them?"

"Well—I don't know much," she said. "He tried very hard to match Dona Victoria's writing, and he was quiet good. Still, the inconsistencies were consistent, if that makes sense?"

"It does." I nodded. "And it is definitely a 'he'?"

"Oh, yes. Men's handwriting has a distinctive feel even when it's trying to be otherwise. It's more . . . chaotic than a female's writing. Also, he was not a native Englishman speaking Spanish, nor even a native Spaniard, unless I miss my guess. Based primarily on the love letter, I believe he is Portuguese."

I nodded. "You'd mentioned that, I think before—"

"It only happened a few times, but he chose a word from that tongue in place of its Spanish cousin." She shrugged. "I could be wrong, but I don't think I am. And he wrote with . . ."

Her words tapered off as she gazed out the high window, over the quadrangle, and toward the Round Tower. "Oh, no," she breathed.

"What?" I looked over to where she was staring, but could see only the crenellated top of the Tower, striking in the afternoon sun.

"The Tower!" Anna gasped. "The symbols!" She pulled apart the letters again, rifling through them, folding two open that had the fancy girlish scribbling she'd remarked on before, when I'd first given her the letters. "Look here—and here!" She pointed, and there in the swirling, looping scrollwork I could see it too, buried in the design: the image of a cross, surmounted by an inverted triangle. Except here, surrounded by all of the twirling lines and swirling leaves, it looked almost like—"A thistle," Anna said. "It's a Scottish thistle." She stared at me, wide-eyed. "If this means what I think, then an alliance between Scotland and Spain is under way. And they are bold indeed if they sought to mark Elizabeth's own castle with their symbol."

"Beneath an English rose that would wither in the rain,"

I said. "They had to know that it would be found."

She shook her head. "The marks were faint—not many would have looked for them, or even seen them if the roses had faded with time, which I'm sure was their intention. Only if they'd known what they were looking for, would anyone have seen them at all."

"A symbol to put a new plan in motion," I said. "Another disturbance? An attack on the Queen?"

"Whatever it was, they missed their chance," Anna said. "The symbol never played out. Her shields covered it up before any could see it."

"And that is only thanks to you."

"And you." Anna blushed. "We are all in this together."

"As you say." I bit my lip, knowing it was time to take the next step. I'd gone too long trying to read my hidden book myself, I decided, and I simply couldn't do it. "I have a . . . book," I said. "That my grandfather gave me. But, well—"

If I'd expected Anna to be surprised, I was mistaken. Of course she'd known I had a book. There were few secrets we maids could truly keep from one another. In truth, Anna may have even undone the knots on my packet, just for the practice of doing them up again. Now she looked at me gravely, her green eyes gentle. "Would you like my help reading it?" she asked.

I burned with shame at her soft words. "I . . . Well, if you could take a look at it . . ." I went to my corner of our cupboard and fished out the package, then untied my lock knots carefully. The small, innocent leather tome gleamed in its cheap cotton wrapping, and with a sigh I gave it to Anna. "I can't make any sense of it at all."

"Well, I'm sure it's just . . . mmm . . ." She paged through it, her brows lifting higher in surprise with each turned page. When she looked up, she was grinning from ear to ear.

"Well, Meg, it's no wonder you couldn't read it," she announced in triumph. "It's all of it written in code!"

CHAPTER TWENTY-FIVE

Anna now had enough decoding work to keep her happy for days, but I couldn't rest until I'd returned Amelia's letters. I didn't even dare wait for night. Instead, I slipped out during the evening meal and placed the letters back safely in their coffer while Amelia was attending the Queen.

After that, the next five days flew by rapidly, and my fellow spies and I were pulled in different directions. Our formal instructions in the dark arts of spying, elocution, and courtly manners had ended, at least for the short term, and I couldn't say I missed them. Both Cecil and the Queen had me following around half the court, and reporting on their conversations. Further, just to be able to tell Cecil and Walsingham that I was in fact doing my best to secretly spy on the Queen, I'd stopped into Saint George's Hall a half dozen times—always, happily, finding no one.

Anna was making headway with my little leather book, though she'd deciphered nothing but a string of dates back from King Henry's reign. Secretly, I harbored hopes that the book was a diary of one of my parents, but I shared that dream with no one. After all, if this were true, why would Grandfather have kept such a thing from me?

Beatrice had been moved into her temporary role as a lady of the bedchamber within a day, the expected malady that befell the hapless Mathilde seeming suspiciously more like a mild case of poisoning than a true illness. Either way Mathilde had been relegated to the sickroom posthaste, and Beatrice put in place with a minimum of fuss. The official story was that there was no reason to bring in the next lady-in-waiting on the list for bedchamber duties, as Mathilde would be returning within a few days. However, there were plenty of women old and young to whom the honor could have fallen. That Beatrice had been chosen caused enough chatter to circle around the castle a half dozen times. Lord Cavanaugh was much in evidence, and rumors were flying that Beatrice's assignment was only the precursor to the formal engagement of the two.

Beatrice still considered me the reason behind her good fortune, and I could never find the right time to change her perception. She seemed so happy. And grateful. And, well . . . happy.

I tried to avoid her.

Instead, Jane and I had taken to splitting our time between following the Spaniards and navigating the secret passageways that led down and through the castle grounds. With as many passageways as we uncovered, I couldn't imagine how the castle could still remain standing.

Even now we paused in the entryway of yet another branch of the underground corridors. Jane bent over her parchment, and I held the candle aloft as she scratched the newest juncture onto the page.

"I just can't believe it," she said for what had to be the fiftieth time. "How could we not have known about these passageways? Cecil and Walsingham have to be aware of them."

"Remember, though, they are only just come to the castle this year. It's not as if they were welcome during Queen Mary's reign, and not during Edward's either." We'd discussed whether or not we should tell our advisors of our find. So far it had seemed wiser to keep the discovery to ourselves. "I don't think some of these corridors have been disturbed since King Henry's time. Like this place, for example." I shivered in the damp, reaching out to strike the loose strands of a spiderweb away from Jane's bowed head. "Not exactly the crossroads of civilization."

"We're right underneath the Round Tower, I think," Jane mused. "If we go that way"—she nodded forward into the gloom—"we'll still be east of Winchester Tower. It wouldn't surprise me if there is an exit there."

"And this way?" I asked, gesturing into the murk.

"Farther into the Lower Ward. But that's a great deal of wide open space to cover, and we've been gone for hours, with nothing to report." She grinned up at me. "Unless you've seen any Spaniards down here?"

"Not yet." I smiled back at her. "But we've still got time." An image of Rafe suddenly sprang to mind. Was he familiar with all of the secret passageways through the castle?

Jane stood, careful not to smack her head on the ceiling. "Let's go toward the North Terrace. I have a feeling that's where we'll find the dungeons." She grimaced as we moved forward. "I don't think they'd hide them under the visitors' apartments, and they won't be under the Lower Ward."

I nodded. It made sense. "If we come across any well-lit passages, that's likely to be our first clue."

"Our second will be the smell."

"You have the right of that." As Jane and I both knew from personal experience, dungeons were not known for their cleanliness. I had no doubt the dungeons of Windsor were equally as inhospitable as those of London. We didn't speak for another several feet. Twice there were branching corridors that she noted in her plans but we didn't pursue. Then we turned a natural corner in the passageway, and stopped cold. Before Jane even needed to tell me, I'd pinched out the candle.

A light flickered in the distance.

"Sconces?" I whispered. "Or torchlight?"

"Better hope for sconces," Jane breathed. "But the light grows no brighter. That bodes well."

"Go forward or retreat?"

"Forward," she said. "You come up with a good story if we're caught out."

I nodded. We'd fallen into this easy pattern between us, Jane mapping and me crafting plausible exit scenarios should we be discovered somewhere we weren't supposed to be. "If the corridor is well lit, the entryway must be close. It wouldn't be unusual for us to explore a lit passageway if we stumbled upon it. As long as the entryway was not impossible to find."

"And as long as there are no guards," Jane muttered.

"And that," I agreed. We crept forward, barely willing to breathe as the corridor opened up into a markedly different passageway from what we'd become used to beneath the halls of Windsor Castle. First, there were sconces (not actual torchlight, thankfully, since torchlight would entail someone *carrying* the torch) at regular intervals down the long hallway. Jane squinted into the distance to the northeast.

"That passage goes beneath the public receiving rooms of Windsor. Easy access to bring a prisoner down." She sniffed the air. "Do you smell that?"

"And I hear it," I said. "Running water."

"An underground aquifer?" Jane's disbelief mirrored my own. "A redirection of the Thames?"

"There had to be some reason they chose this location for the original castle," I said, but I couldn't wrap my head around it. How had they gotten water to flow *beneath* Windsor Castle?

Jane looked at me, and I could tell she wanted to explore the corridor further. "No," I said resolutely. "We can't afford getting caught there. And any Spaniard we'd find in the dungeons proper wouldn't be someone we could report on."

She sighed, turning the other direction. "Very well. But these sconces were lit recently. They haven't burned down much. Why?"

"Perhaps Cecil and Walsingham are expecting trouble from the foreign dignitaries?"

An uneasy chill slid through me as I said the words, and we both picked up our pace. Suddenly, sneaking around in the dungeon corridors didn't seem like the best of ideas.

We moved as one, bent over slightly in case the ceiling height suddenly changed. I held my hands out in front of me like a blind woman. I had gotten good at this process, which is why I went first, my feet somehow knowing where to go even in the blackest corridor. But I felt a newfound respect—

and horror—for those who had been truly blinded by accident or birth or injury. It would be no way to live.

I swiped the air just as my feet came into hard contact with a stair riser, and we both tumbled forward in a flurry of skirts. I smacked against the chiseled stairs with my hands, managing to turn my face only at the last minute to avoid cracking my teeth. As it was, I knocked my temple hard enough that bright lights exploded against the backs of my eyes, at the same time that Jane crashed into me, shoving me for a second time against the cold stone.

"Staircase," I moaned, smiling weakly as Jane giggled.

"Are you well?" she managed as she peeled herself off me and I struggled upright, half-crawling up the stairs. I felt my head and neck for blood, and found none. A knot was already forming above my ear, but at least my hair would cover it.

"I'll live," I said, still climbing. The staircase went straight up, ending in a wide platform and another door, but this one possessed no obvious peepholes to give a clue what might lie beyond. We turned around, and both of us slid to a seated position, catching our breaths before making the final run.

Jane laid her hand upon the door. "It's warm and it's full day outside, with a hot sun beating down," she said. "It's got to lead to the outdoors, but I don't remember any unaccounted-for doors in the castle's exterior walls."

I didn't either, and I'd paced the grounds often enough to know each stone by heart. "Are we up high enough for the North Terrace?" I asked. "It didn't feel like the stairs had gone up that long."

"No, but . . . there is something here." Groaning, Jane

stood, and I hauled myself up beside her. “Lock,” she said a minute later.

I took out my picklocks and bent to the task. A few moments later we were rewarded with a telltale click.

We opened the door a hair’s breadth, wincing as bright sunlight poured in.

“God’s teeth!” Jane hissed, pulling back as I also flinched away. Once our eyes had adjusted, we peeked out again through narrow eyes.

Wide, rolling grasslands greeted us, ending in a copse of trees.

We were outside the castle.

Free.

Jane and I pushed the door open a bit farther, meeting the resistance of some artfully placed bushes. Opening it just enough to escape, we peeked outside, then pulled back again, staring at each other. The sun still warmed our faces.

“Your troupe is still in Windsor,” Jane said, putting voice to what I had myself been thinking.

“It is,” I said. I smoothed my skirts and looked north to where the Thames lay, close enough to see the boats clustered upon it, Eton in the far distance across the river.

“You could be in London by nightfall,” she observed.

“I could,” I said. We fell silent for a moment, each lost in our own thoughts. I could leave, easily, with just the clothes on my back. I had no money that I was leaving behind, no belongings but Grandfather’s book, which Jane could secret out to me. I was far more adrift inside the castle than I was without.

“Why do you stay?” she asked, interrupting my reverie.

"Why do you?" I returned. "I'm not the only person who knows the world outside of these walls. You also were not born to castle life, in service to the Queen."

Jane chuckled. "True enough," she said easily, not affronted by my candor. "But I will die in that service." She spoke with far too much certainty.

"Why?" We'd pulled back inside the shadowed alcove more firmly now, and could see that the platform was broader than we'd first thought, almost a mini corridor. The sun was still upon us, and I looked at Jane's dust-smeared face, knowing that I looked scant better. We would have to find somewhere to clean up before we reentered the castle.

If we reentered the castle. I thought of all the people I had in the world; the thirty-odd members of the Golden Rose, who perhaps had not missed me, all of them, but who would still be happy to see me return, if only for my pick-pocketing skills. And some of them I'd be happy to see as well.

Jane had not responded, and I glanced at her again, even as her mouth twitched into a soft, inscrutable smile.

She shrugged as she noticed me watching. "I have nowhere else to go, Rat. No one to go home to, no one to care about." She sighed, glancing away. "I am better off remaining here."

Impulsively I reached out for her hand, and after a moment she took mine, still not meeting my eyes but instead gazing at the walls of our small alcove. In the light of the midday sun, I saw the fine scars that scored the backs of Jane's hands, speaking of trials I could only guess at. We were more different than ever, but we were forging a lasting bond, in our way.

Who am I, truly?

I was someone who could make friends.

Jane cocked her head, chuckled, then pulled her hand away to rap against another panel of wood. It sounded with a hollow *thwock*. "There's another door off this corridor, this one leading along the castle walls," she said, victorious. She looked back at me, her eyes now alert, her momentary sadness gone. "You want to see where it goes?"

And with that our decision was made. This day, we would remain in the castle.

Within minutes we'd sketched a new extension to our map, using the sunlight to get the proper dimensions of the entryway, and stepping quickly outside to get a fix on where it would be in the exterior castle wall, should ever we need to exit—or enter—the castle this way again.

It was always good to have an escape plan, I thought. Even one we were not quite yet willing to use.

We opened the new door slightly before we closed the external door, but it was as black as pitch beyond. I wasn't in the mood to run into another flight of stairs. "Candle?" I asked.

"Absolutely," Jane agreed. She too had no interest in worsening her appearance. There was no telling where we'd end up.

We relit the candle, closed both doors carefully, and found ourselves in a new passage that ran straight and true to the west. It was, we found, far less well-traveled than the corridor we'd just exited, but more hospitable to the creatures of darkness. Not entirely a pleasant discovery.

"This has to extend along the outside wall," Jane said

thoughtfully after we'd walked for some minutes. "We must be near the cloisters now."

"If so, I do not expect that the current residents avail themselves of this passageway to regularly escape the castle."

"I'm sure they don't know it exists." Jane sounded happy about that. Secrets held were always more intriguing than secrets shared.

We came to the first door a few moments later, and we stared at it, perplexed.

It was not really a door so much as a walled-off crawl space, a panel with a number inscribed beside it, carved into the stone. The number six.

"Seems an odd place for a back door," I said, and Jane cocked her head.

"Number six, number six . . . ," she murmured as I got down beside her. "I know that number, in the Canon's Cloister, the one with the flower garden. If it's the one I'm thinking of."

Recognition flooded through me. I remembered number six as well, from my walks with Sophia. One of the lovelier homes in this cloister, it was tended with care, and the flowers seemed to bloom more robustly even in the fading light of day.

It was also a home rented out to visiting nobility who found themselves in Windsor for an extended stay. And its current occupant was Lord Brighton.

"That's Brighton's residence," I said. "Maybe we should go farther along."

But Jane was already positioning her fingers around the panel. "We've been away too long as it is. We both know that Cecil will eventually come up with some pointless task for us to do, just to amuse himself. If this is number six and Lord Brighton is not here, we have a chance of cleaning up. Brighton should not be in his household midday; he should be at the Queen's court. We cannot say the same for homes with full families."

I couldn't gainsay her reasoning, and I bent to help her pry open the panel. It was old and encrusted, but it finally popped out with a snap, and we fell back upon her dress in the dust.

"We're going to need to get into a hair-pulling brawl in the middle of the Lower Ward to explain our appearance," she muttered. After wiping off her hands on her skirts, she leaned forward again.

This entranceway was lined in wood, not stone, and was just big enough for one person. The panel at the far end of the entrance, some three feet away, showed a soft rim of light at its seams.

"Locked?" I whispered, and she shook her head.

"As long as it's not blocked. Let's pray Lord Brighton didn't come to Windsor with a household of furniture."

She crept forward, then was out again a moment later. "Hinged and locked, but the lock is two-way."

We traded positions, and she picked up the panel we'd already pried free. It had handles on the inside that she could use to easily draw it back into place.

The lock itself wasn't even much of a lock, more a delaying tactic than something that could keep someone out. "It's free," I said a moment later.

"Any sound?"

"Not a whisper."

"There are times when you just do something," Jane said with a grin.

"And if you get caught, you get caught," I agreed.

I pulled the panel open, and we slid into the middle of Lord Brighton's study.

The house was fully silent, and Jane clucked with satisfaction as she pulled the panel back into the wall. It blended flush, almost inscrutable in the dull grey light filtering in through the leaded glass windows, and she gazed at it, serene. "Now that is a thing of beauty."

I caught sight of our reflections in a looking glass. "And we are not. We look like two cats far the worse off for the fight." I turned back to her. "You've got cobwebs in your hair," I advised as I pulled away the offending strands.

"And you've got three inches of dirt caked on your face." Jane looked around, blinking owlishly. "Let's find water—soap—something. There has to be something here."

"Agreed." We set off in search of water, and found two buckets inside the home's tidy kitchen, beside a large basin. Next to the kitchen sat flats of plants, thriving in the sunlight.

"We can water the plants with this after we're through," I observed as Jane dunked her head in the water. "And set the bucket aside with the others. With luck, he won't notice that it moved."

"Urghh," she said, the sound of pure pleasure in just being clean again. I grinned, looking around the room. There were some papers on the table, an open file of legal documents.

With the nonchalance born of long years of nosiness, I lifted a clean long-handled spoon and moved the pages around. I couldn't risk getting any of the castle dust on Lord Brighton's papers.

The second parchment I moved caught my eye. I thanked Anna a hundred times over for her time and patience in finally teaching me to read. But what I was looking at still made no sense.

"What is this?" I murmured, loud enough to garner me an answering noise from Jane, whose head was still buried in the water bucket.

It looked like a christening record, and I frowned at the names marching across the page. Lady Sophia Elizabeth Brighton Manchester, born 1545, was christened at the church of—

Lady Sophia Elizabeth . . . *Brighton*?

I shuffled through other pages, finding reference after reference that set me on my heels, even if I could not understand them all. One Lord Theoditus Manchester, Baron of Westchurch, a lost infant daughter, the death record of a young wife, the careful medical opinions of doctors throughout the English countryside claiming the mother's illness was born of a broken heart. There was a beautifully painted locket of a dark-haired woman with violet eyes. Instructions to the manager of Manchester's estate. And last, most chillingly, the baron's final will and testament.

I was still staring at the pages when Jane finally came over, availing herself of one of Lord Brighton's towels to dry her newly clean hair. "What is it you're looking at, Rat?"

"I know why Lord Brighton is so fixed on ensuring Sophia

is officially off the matrimonial market," I said, surprised I could even form the words.

Jane snorted a cynical laugh. "Because he's a lonely old man?"

"No," I said. "Because he's her father."

That stopped her. "Her father?" She shook her head in astonishment. "What are you talking about?" She looked down at the papers spread out in front of me. "This says Manchester."

"I think that's his real name. Look here—this Manchester had a wife who died, a daughter who was kidnapped. And then he died. Here's his signature on his will. And here's Lord Brighton's signature on his manager's statement."

Jane pursed her lips together. "They're the same hand."

"Yes. And now he's in the court, declaring his hand for a girl who could be his daughter . . . because she is his daughter."

"But he will be found out!" Jane protested. "He could be *hung* for a deception like that."

"Imagine yourself in his place." I shook my head. "Your beloved daughter was taken away from you when she was very young and raised as the ward of a court insider. You finally find her, only to learn she's in service to the Queen, with rumors swirling around that she's on the marriage block—and that, quite possibly, she may have the gift of the Sight. You know the Queen will never let her go, and will never believe you over the man who raised your daughter, a man who is her trusted friend. What would *you* do to protect your daughter?"

Jane blew out a long breath. "It's still a terrible risk."

"It is indeed." I thought of Sophia's fears for the man

who'd claimed her hand. Fears not *of* him, but *for* him. Had she guessed Lord Brighton was her father? Did she know the Queen would likely execute the man for treason should she ever learn that he intended to deceive the court in such a public and bold manner? And with her gift of the Sight beginning to manifest, did Sophia already know the outcome of her father's desperate ploy?

No wonder she kept fainting.

CHAPTER TWENTY-SIX

If I'd thought the midsummer ball was a grand affair, I was completely overwhelmed by the gaudy revel of the masque.

There were easily three hundred members of the court in attendance, and every delegate from across the Continent, it seemed. I suspected the inns in Windsor had no reason to stay open tonight, so many of their patrons were now drinking the Queen's ale. There was music at all four corners of the Presence Chamber, which gave the impression that one was drifting out of one room and into the next, without ever leaving the ballroom floor. The ladies-in-waiting had already performed their night-goddess dance, and it was every bit as tragic as I'd feared it would be.

I wandered through the Presence Chamber, taking it all in, my gypsy dress flowing around me like a costume fit for a fairy queen. Still grateful for her new assignment and believing I had helped her secure it, Beatrice had found the gorgeous gown in the depths of her endless clothes cupboard, the colors shifting from rose to crimson under the blazing sconces and chandeliers of the great hall, set off by soft black strips of cloth and dozens of appliquéd roses. I'd complemented the gown with my own handmade silk mask, complete with requisite eyeholes. The gown's roses roiled and tumbled with each step that I took, and I found myself admiring it more than paying attention to my long list of conversations to follow.

I'd already overheard the faintly annoyed censure of three clergymen in long, dour robes. Their conversation was not useful, fixed as it was on the state of Elizabeth's court, which we were now seeing at its scandalous best. I had sidestepped two conversations between prominent lords of parliament, who in their overweening—and loud—pride could have been tracked by anyone with an interest. My ability allowed me to memorize their words all of a piece, but it was clear that the Royal Marriage Question still hung heavily on the minds of the country's caretakers. And revels like these, as they showed the Queen as a wayward young miss and the bawdiness of her court as the height of impropriety, planted deep and festering seeds of worry in the minds of her more levelheaded countrymen. If the Queen wanted to demonstrate to the Catholics that the Protestants were a sensible and God-fearing lot, she was failing miserably.

And I was about to listen in on the most telling conversation of all.

Robert Dudley, Master of the Horse, was one of the easiest courtiers in the room to identify. Impeccably dressed in brilliant cloth of gold, his trunks slashed with velvet and satin, his hose of finest silk, and his short cape a rich crimson, he looked like a prince in the making, and several whispered words underscored that perception as I made my way across the hall. Robert Dudley had more idle enemies than passionate ones, but he also had more enemies of any stripe than friends.

As I walked, conversation wormed through the crowd that the Queen had fallen in love with Dudley, with others arguing surely not. I grew weary of the chatter, and wondered how the Queen herself must feel. Always on the edge of conversations about her—and doubtless vaguely disappointed when she realized the most fervent gossip was not about her politics, but about her potential paramours. Unbidden, the beginning of a new couplet came to mind: *All of them hunting for aught that's amiss.*

My thoughts had taken me forward until I was now almost upon Lord Dudley. He was a well-turned man, his manner as brash and young as that of a sailing captain indulging in his first race. Nothing about Dudley was ever done by halves. *The Queen's deepest secret, betrayed by a kiss.*

Now he was talking with Nicolas Ortiz, whom I hadn't seen in several days but who was well-matched to Dudley—two dandies out for attention, and gaining it at every turn.

Dudley laughed, and my attention was drawn back to the Queen's favorite courtier. He appeared to already be in his cups, but it was a popular affectation for many noblemen to appear feebler than they were, so as to justify their impetuous actions. Dudley was rambling on about the value of love in a loveless court, and how the Queen was in need of fresh air and time away. He was the burst of that fresh air, he declared, and he planned to be the Queen's right hand in any way she cared to define the term.

My eyes widened at his carelessness, and not just because he was speaking to a Spaniard. Robert Dudley was still a married man, his wife closeted away in some town far away from the intrigues of court. That he should speak so freely and in such earshot of the gossipmongers betrayed a curious sense of security that would doubtless irritate the Queen, no matter how much she enjoyed his company.

No wonder Cecil and Walsingham eyed Dudley with such concern. They didn't fear the Queen falling afoul of some random charmer. They feared Robert Dudley. Robert Dudley, the onetime London Tower–mate of the Queen's when she was but a princess out of favor, and now her bosom friend.

A scandal with another monarch was one thing, and easily explained. The affairs of heads of state were not something a commoner could be expected to fully understand. But for the Queen to be caught out with a man having no prospects but his charming face and pleasant speech? That would be an embarrassment of epic proportions. It was simply not to be borne.

Yet I feared it would be Robert Dudley whom I would find in the Queen's arms, if it were anyone. I prayed that Elizabeth would be smarter than that.

Mercifully, Dudley's conversation turned quickly enough to the Queen's horses, and the hunting to be had north of England. I began to search for my next targets, the Lord and Lady Bellencourt, late of Sussex. As I scanned the chamber, I felt a presence sidle up to me, and my heart quickened despite my determination to appear unfazed. How had he found me, in this terrible crush of people?

"The dress becomes you, sweet Meg," Rafe whispered, the words so low that I thought I'd imagined them.

I turned to him, offering both my hands as if we were old friends, not fully registering his appearance at first. "And you, Count de Martine, are looking . . ."

I blinked. "Well," I finished lamely.

There could not be any other word to describe it, since anything else I came up with would not be safe for polite company. Rafe was dressed like a seafaring rogue, his chest bared in a white shirt with its sleeves rolled up and its collar low, his well-muscled arms bronzed against the bright cloth. His cloak was thrown back from his shoulders, revealing richly colored breeches and stockings, ending in serviceable shoes that looked like they'd actually trod the decks. He had a bright gold medallion at his neck, and his eyes were covered by a black sash with cleverly constructed eyeholes. "You look like a pirate, come to steal the Queen's heart."

"The Queen has pledged her heart to far more courtly men than I," he said with a grin. "But is yours the heart of a gypsy, Meg? Or the heart of a noblewoman? That question holds far more interest to me."

I turned away from him, once more scouting the crowd. "I should think you would save your flattery for Beatrice," I said with a shrug. "She will be more receptive."

"And yet Beatrice did not hold my heart for longer than a dance. You seem determined to steal it away at every turn."

A warm rush of pleasure flashed through me at his weighted words. "You are very good at this," I said. "You must have begun practicing in the cradle."

"In my own mother's arms, in fact," Rafe teased. Then his eyes grew more somber as he gazed at me. "I cannot stay away from you, it seems," he muttered. "But I have no choice, this night. And you must promise me you will not follow."

I raised my brows to him. "Why? Where are you going?"

He shook his head. "I do not joke. You must know I'm aware of your presence now, and your threat. You and Jane and Beatrice and Anna . . . and even grave Sophia. I told you I would be watching you."

I stiffened. "I don't know what you're talking about."

He gave me a hard, cynical smile. "Worry not, sweet Meg. It is only in learning more of you that my thoughts turned to them. You all blend well enough. But now this game grows too dangerous, and you all should remain in the schoolroom, and not in harm's way."

Anger flared through me. "I have no need for the insults of a Spaniard."

"Then take them from a friend," he countered. "Do not try to follow me."

The dancers, laughing and rushing, forced us back into the press of the crowd, and we were jostled amidst the crush of people. I started to feel claustrophobic, and if anything, Rafe contributed to my discomfort, stepping close to me, his expression darkening.

"Do not try my patience. Your trick will eventually be discerned, as well as your secrets, by those who are not as forgiving as I am." Another burst of laughter from the crowd, and we were pressed closer together. I turned just as he did, and our bodies were flush—too close, too warm, our faces but an inch apart.

I pulled in an unsteady gasp of air, but the only thing I seemed to see was Rafe's mouth, his lips parted slightly, his breath honey sweet. My heart grew suddenly too full, and I jerked my gaze upward, only to find him staring at me. His gaze held mine fast, and his hand closed the space between us, his fingers grazing my stomach through its thick satin casing, then sliding around to my waist. His actions were protected from others' view by the depth of the crowd, but it was as if there were nobody there but us. "Know that I wish no enmity between us, Meg," he said, his words barely a whisper in the clamor around us.

He ducked down toward me, brushing his mouth against my hair, still shielded by the dancers. I froze as he touched his lips to my earlobe, worrying the heavy silver earring I had borrowed for the night. "I only wish to protect you."

My stomach curled into a tight knot, and heat suffused my entire body. Rafe moved his hands down the tightly fitted bodice of my gown, grasping my waist as if he were hanging on to it for memory's sake, breathing in the rose-petal fragrance that Beatrice had been kind enough to spare me. "I only wish to keep you safe," he said again.

"That is not your concern," I protested, but he lifted his head, his eyes suddenly determined, not a kernel of warmth in them.

"You'll forgive me in time, but know that I do not do this lightly. I must away, and you must not follow me."

The crowd suddenly broke, a fissure opening between us and the dance floor. The dancers were coming around again, arms and legs flying in circles wider and wider, not near enough to harm any onlookers, but enough to incite them into their own spontaneous jigs. Just as I began to question the firm set to Rafe's jaw, the calculation in his eyes, it was already over.

He pushed me, hard, into the roiling crowd.

I and my skirts went down like a woman drowning, and a great commotion arose around me, laughter and shouts of concern—even jeers about my gracelessness. Sound assaulted me from all sides, and as I struggled to rise, I had so many hands helping me that I was nearly torn asunder, a victim of the very Samaritans who'd rushed good-naturedly to my aid.

I finally regained my feet and whirled around to the great goodwill of those surrounding me, but Rafe was gone. I was alone in a sea of noise and color.

"God's bones, what was that about?" Jane hissed at my side. She grabbed my elbow and forced me along, none too gently; but I was so grateful, I didn't mind. "I would have been closer, but I expected you to be *embraced* by the Spaniard, not shoved to the ground."

"You were watching me?" I asked, shocked enough to turn to her despite the fact that she was still propelling me through the crowd.

She scowled at me in her mannish costume. "I watch everything. One way or another, I expected trouble to befall you this night. I just didn't expect it at the hands of your young count."

"Did you see where he went?" I asked. "He knows I will follow him; he goes to a meeting of some import. I must find him, but—"

"But he'll recognize you at a hundred paces in that gown." Jane narrowed her eyes. "I've never seen its like."

I gazed down at my gown, knowing her words to be correct. The gorgeous, distinctive pattern of the gown might as well have been a beacon in the night. Rafe would easily spot me if I approached him in this.

"Remind me never to trust a Spaniard, will you?"

She squeezed my arm. "You have my word. The moment I sense you going weak in the knees, I'll break his."

"You're a good friend."

"I try."

At that moment Anna rushed up to us. I'd opened my mouth to tell her I wasn't injured, when she cut me off. "The Queen! The Queen sent me to find you!" she gasped.

We halted, staring at her. "The Queen?" I asked. "Whyever for?"

"She's—she's just learned that Lady Amelia has left the masque—without an escort, at least not an English escort—and she, and she—"

"Anna, get a hold of yourself!" Jane snapped. "What is it you're trying to say?"

Anna took in a deep breath, her cheeks red with effort above her daffodil-colored gown. "Lady Amelia left with a Spaniard. I don't think she is fully in her right senses. Someone told the Queen and she told me to tell you, Meg. She fears another disruption, I think, and she can ill afford that."

Jane groaned. "Lady Amelia would have to be daft to leave with a Spaniard this night, I can tell you that plainly."

"What will we do?" Anna asked. "I can go, of course. Lady Amelia could be in danger!"

"You have to stay," Jane and I said at the same time.

"In fact, go back now, to the Queen," Jane said to Anna, and I nodded.

"Tell her that you've spoken to me," I said, "and that all is well."

"Are you sure? I can help, truly!"

"You can help more at the Queen's side," I assured her, not missing the disappointment in her face.

Anna stared at us another moment, then sighed and turned away, accepting our judgment. I breathed a sigh of relief. It was one thing to decipher a letter, but neither of us felt that Anna was ready for the challenge of following anyone. Beatrice was three men deep in a gaggle of Scottish courtiers, executing whatever fell plan Cecil and Walsingham had set for her, and Sophia was safely buried in the three rows of attendants that surrounded the Queen. Jane and I had not yet determined how to broach the subject of her father with her. How does one say, "We know your betrothed is actually your long-lost father in disguise, risking the wrath of the Queen to free you?" And what would be your follow-up line?

In any event, this night there was only the two of us.

"Go," Jane said to me, nodding toward where Rafe had disappeared. "I'll make sure Lady Amelia doesn't come to harm—or make any mischief herself—and I'll come back straightaway and report to Cecil after I find her. There will be no disturbances this night, I can assure you."

I looked at her. "My orders from the Queen were to ferret out the forces behind all the court disturbances. Lady Amelia is about to become a disturbance, I wager. I can't fob that off on you."

"No one but you can follow Rafe and report back what they say with accuracy. I can make sure a hapless maid doesn't get harmed. Now go, or you will lose him."

"But we've already discovered that I stand out to Rafe at a hundred paces. However can I find him without being caught out?"

The answer came to us of a moment, and Jane grinned at me. "Through here," she announced, and in another moment we were in a short outside of the Presence Chamber, and she was shucking her outfit. She was dressed as a sailor boy for the ball, with long, loose breeches gathered below the knee and thick woolen hose. Her cloak was black and her shirt a white tunic, blousy enough to hide any hint of the figure beneath. She bound my head in her wrap, and the mask fit neatly over my eyes.

"You'd never pass as a man up close, but in casual view, absolutely," she said with satisfaction. "All right, go. Rafe was heading for the North Terrace."

"He could have doubled back several times over," I said, dismayed. "The North Terrace extends the entire length of the building, and there will be others out taking their air."

"True enough," Jane said, fitting herself into my gown. I was slightly smaller than her, but the effect was breathtaking.

I stared at her. "Jane, you should keep that gown, if ever you want to catch the eye of a courtier."

She surveyed herself critically, then grinned at me. "Like you, I value my freedom from the marriage yoke too much," she said. "Now off with you."

I made my way through the laughing, too-intimate crowd. When I reached the North Terrace, I saw a group of courtiers and ladies clustered together, their conversation light and animated. Rafe would not be near here, but in a place of greater silence. Winchester Tower? I was still wearing my dancing slippers, and rushed along the crumbling terrace with an odd feeling of repetition. When I'd come this way last under cover of darkness, my future had still been my own, or so I'd thought. Now the walls of Windsor closed around me like a tomb, but I could not think on that now. I had only to hasten forward, focus only on this one thing. That would save me, I thought. Not looking too far forward.

I came around the corner, and the sound of conversation reached me. I had to stop and place a hand over my heart, so loudly and coarsely was it beating. Still, I had to move closer until I got a fix on the voices. I would be in their line of sight, but there was nothing for it.

Affecting a slight stagger, I rambled down just a few steps more, until I had cleared the last jutting rock of the abutment. I wandered over to the short wall. The Thames lay far down the slope, the inky darkness pockmarked with dancing torchlight, beacons in the darkness. The castle was not the only host to revels this night.

I threw one leg over the stone wall and sat down, straddling it. The breeches and hose provided an almost shocking ability to move, and I could well see why Jane favored this costume above all others. I put my hands down mannishly upon my thighs, leaning my weight forward, as if I'd stumbled down here in an alcoholic haze. Instead of thinking of my task, though, my thoughts held fast on Jane.

Could I truly be like her in sensibility as well as actions? Could I cut someone—could I kill? I grimaced, thinking on it, but the answer still was no. I'd not worked as hard as I had to become an expert at my craft, only to get into fistfights and knifing matches. I was not made to kill men—or to cut them. I was a thief, not a thug.

The voices had stopped when I'd lumbered upon the scene, but they started up again now, a full tear of Spanish, and I cursed my own lack of speed. How much had I missed?

I risked a peek at them. There were three Spaniards there. De Feria, a man I'd never seen, and another round man in long priest's robes. The Bishop de Quadra. The three bent together, words flowing rapidly, and I memorized as quickly as I could. I was improving in my Spanish, but I could only memorize, not translate, at this speed. For that, I'd have to rely on Anna.

The third, unknown man continued to move and gesture, and I studied him more closely. He moved differently than Turnip Nose, the man Rafe had spoken to in the chapel. And he looked different too, his face as wide as a full moon, with big eyes, full lips, and a round, puffy nose. How many Spaniards were involved in this plot? And where was Rafe?

De Feria, de Quadra, and Moon Face continued speaking for a few minutes more, their conversation growing more heated, with finger-pointing and gestures of great emotion. If nothing else, the Spaniards would make wonderful actors, I thought. I swung back off the ledge, then tottered back to the castle wall, once more out of sight. Then I edged forward anew, focusing again on their voices.

And just as I did so, a hand slipped over my mouth.

"Ah, sweet Meg, what am I to do with you?"

CHAPTER TWENTY-SEVEN

I tried to jerk away, but Rafe held my face, pressing up against my back and pinning me to the wall. He laughed softly at my sudden alarm, his lips brushing my ear, setting off tiny whirls of heat. "I should have known it was you on the terrace. No man walks like that, no matter how drunk." He sighed. "Though it is difficult to tell with you English what passes as manly posturing."

I gave a small inward groan. I would need to work on my walk if I wanted to make a habit of wearing men's clothes. I made again to move away.

"I don't think so, sweet Meg. And I've decided I don't like you very much in men's clothing. But—" He looked past me, down the North Terrace. "Why are you spying on my countrymen? Do you know what they are saying?"

"No," I said. "I'll have to get it translated."

"Can you tell me what they've said so far?"

He was still standing far too close, and at my nod he laid a finger on my lips. "Then tell me. But softly, softly. And not quite yet. They're beginning again. Can you hear them?"

I started to speak, but he pressed his finger again against my lips, silencing me. "Just listen."

I listened. The three men continued to argue, then de Quadra made a pronouncement and blessed the other two. Rafe stepped away from me as the men scattered, apparently to see if he could track their departure. Then I realized that not all of the men had left. De Quadra and de Feria were no longer on the terrace, but Moon Face had stayed. And another figure had joined him, a lean new shadow in the gloom. They began speaking, and one word they shared was instantly recognizable. I stiffened. *La muerte.*

Death.

Rafe returned after all of the men had gone. Had he realized that the players had changed midscene? "What did they say before I came upon you?" he asked.

I scowled. "Why should I help you?"

"Because we can help each other," he said, and tilted his head. "I will answer your questions and tell you what I know. But I am missing a critical piece to this puzzle, and I suspect it's held within the words of the men whose conversation I missed."

I stared at him skeptically, but I should have known he'd have another card to play. "And perhaps more important, neither de Feria nor de Quadra believes you maids are anything more than inquisitive girls with a penchant for finding yourselves in the wrong place at the wrong time. You would not want them to think otherwise."

I narrowed my eyes. "De Feria killed the maid Marie."

"Not him, directly," Rafe said, but he did not deny the accusation further. "De Feria's goals have been only to create a distraction—not a death."

I thought back to the mutilated face of Marie Claire. "I'm not sure I would agree with you."

He looked at me steadily. "You will share information with me, or I will go to de Feria and the new ambassador besides. This is not your battle to fight."

I let that one pass. "And what will I get besides your silence?"

He grinned, sensing he was wearing me down. "Why, Meg, you will get *me*. At your service, whene'er I am able."

"Small lot of good that will be. When this comes out, you will need to leave England as hastily as they do."

His grin only deepened. "Miss me already?"

I rolled my eyes, and he tapped my chin. "I will be an ally, Meg. And allies are hard to come by these days. I give you my word that I will do all I can to protect you, you and your small clan of spies. I will tell you what I learn, and find out whatever you wish."

"Then, what is de Feria's plan?" I asked baldly.

He nodded his understanding. He would have to give first, if he wished to receive. "Even more than de Feria is a man of Spain, he is a man of God, and the pope," he said. "He is helping to set up a network of Catholic supporters, supporters to whom he can convey the special blessing of the pope."

"The letters you carried when you first arrived," I said. "Those were from the pope?"

Rafe hesitated. "After a fashion, yes, but written as if from dear friends. The pope is no friend of your Queen."

"And what did these letters promise?" I asked, thinking

about the letters to Lady Amelia's family. All of those letters had contained suggestions on how to disrupt the Queen's court. Did Rafe's packet of letters include similar requests? "Do you know what the pope is asking of his followers in the letters you just delivered?"

"To know that, sweet Meg, I would have had to read one myself, which in this case would not only have been a violation of my orders but an offense against God. How base do you think I am?"

"Base enough."

He sighed. "You wound me. But if I *had* seen one of these letters, it *might* have said in coded terms that the recipients should be ready for a signal. I believe a Scottish thistle *might* have served as a choice for that code. Then and only then were those loyal to the pope supposed to carry out a simple task—nothing too dangerous. For now these requests are but to make small disturbances . . . but one day, perhaps, not so small."

"A death is not small. The burning of Protestant vestments was not small either."

A shadow passed over Rafe's face. "As I said, those were disturbances de Feria neither planned nor approved. I believe him, and I'm not the only one."

"And why are you telling me this?" I asked, suspicion blooming at his easy truths. But then I recalled Anna's words—that two of the letters had been written by a different hand. Had those letters contained the harsher requests?

His eyes betrayed nothing. "Spain does not endorse the murder of innocent girls, Meg, no matter what you think. And my orders come from Spain first, the pope second."

I pondered that for a moment, but another of Rafe's words caught my attention. "A thistle," I murmured, thinking of Anna and her ciphers. "But that means that—"

"That the trail of letters extends to Scotland, I should think, yes. Your neighbors to the north are more Catholic than England ever was."

I took in a deep breath, considering this. "So the Catholic plot exists." I thought again of Lady Knollys. Why would she be involved in any plot against the Queen—even a benign one?

"It exists, and will only grow stronger." Rafe huffed out an impatient breath. "Time is growing short, Meg. What did you overhear?"

I told him, reciting the complete conversation in Spanish. I didn't tell him that, after the men had seemed to depart initially, another man had arrived. I just continued the conversation as if it was all part of the same play and omitted the mention of death.

"You must translate for me what they said," I said when I finished. "What they were arguing about. I'll just get it from Anna later, if you do not."

He nodded, paraphrasing the conversation in rapid words. The three men had disagreed violently about a plan already set in motion. One of them—de Quadra, he suspected—advocating continuity; and another man who he believed was de Feria was just anxious to be done with it all.

"Do you think their plan would include murder?"

Rafe just shook his head. "No. A death would be too risky. De Feria understands that. Even de Quadra understands that." He frowned at me. "Why do you ask?"

I changed the subject hurriedly. "And the Spaniard I saw you speaking to in Saint George's Hall? What was his crime?"

Rafe shrugged. "He'd grown too careless."

"He had one of the letters." I slanted him a glance. "He was the one who'd been acting without orders? Who'd burned the vestments?" *Who'd killed Marie?*

Rafe's response was a snort of derision. "I suspect he couldn't drink a mug of ale without being told." He glanced at me, deliberately changing the subject. "How long have you had this skill of memorization, Meg? Another in your long list of talents, I see."

I hesitated, but in truth, I didn't so much mind the subject being changed. Within these walls my life was spent learning others' tales. It wasn't often that I got to share my own history. "I have had it all my life," I said simply. "Though it has been known by others only since I was three."

"So young," Rafe sighed. He settled against the wall, and despite the danger all around us, I thrilled to take this moment with him, talking in the darkness. "And how was this skill first discovered?"

I surprised myself again by wanting to answer. "I had wandered away from my grandfather's cottage to find him, far down in the peat. When I came upon him, he was singing a song that made no sense to me at all, but had a magical rhythm to it that I could not help but remember. He was surprised and a little frightened to see me—I'd no idea how far I'd wandered. Later that evening I sang his song back to him, and the reaction was swift and loud. Outrage among the women, ribald laughter among the men. Apparently my grandfather's song was not for a child's ears."

"And did he know right away the import of your gift?"

I nodded. "The next morning, as solemn and loving as always, he sat me down and explained to me that this was a skill that I'd best not share with anyone else but him."

"He was wise to do so." Rafe raised a hand to his face, and a ring on his finger caught my eye again.

"That's . . . jade."

He pulled it away, looked at it, and smiled. "It is at that."

I'd seen it before, of course, that exact setting. A jade stone caught up in a net of gold threads, offset by winking sapphires. It was an exact match for Beatrice's prized jewels. My throat suddenly went dry. "Where did you come by it?"

"A family bauble." He shrugged. "My mother brought it back with her from her stay in England. She would never show it to my father; only gave it to me when I was leaving to make my own fortune, in fact. I rather fancied it had been given to her by a man who favored her here at court, when she was but a maid herself."

I'd turned to him and was staring now. "You are flaunting an heirloom of your mother's—that she got in the English Court? Are you mad?"

He grinned. "It seemed to be the place to bring it out. My mother was ever so oblique about her time here, and I thought it might be interesting."

"But what if someone *recognizes* it? What if it was not your mother's to give?"

"Then they can steal it back. That would be a great game, would it not?"

"You don't seem distressed by the possibility."

He smiled thinly. "I rather suspect it will find its way

back to me. In all the time that I've carried it, it always has. I've been tempted to throw it into the ocean, just to see if it will swim."

"It's not something that you want?"

He regarded it solemnly. "It's pretty enough. But it's a question without answers, and I won't find those answers by keeping it in my pocket. And, too, my mother has never done anything in her life without specific purpose. I cannot help but think her generous gift came with a history I can only guess at." He looked at me. "There are many lies already in this castle. What's one more?" He slipped it off his finger and held it up to me. "Would you like to see it more closely?"

I hesitated, then took the unusual ring into my hands. The jade stone setting was exactly like Beatrice's family treasures. I'd been right. "I'd planned on stealing this, you know."

"I know," Rafe said simply. "I thought I'd spare you the effort." He curved his hand over mine, imprisoning the bauble within my grasp. "Keep it close."

CHAPTER TWENTY-EIGHT

I walked back to the masque so distracted, my head churning with everything I had learned, that I was amazed that I arrived before dawn. Certainly quite some time had passed since I'd left the festival's raucous revelry, but it seemed as lively as ever from the sounds that boomed forth from the great hall. Rafe's ring was heavy in my hand, and I held it tightly, like a talisman. Why had he given it to me? Had it been only to cause trouble? And what would Beatrice say when I showed it to her?

I'd just rounded the last corner before the grand Presence Chamber, when I encountered Beatrice. Before I could even speak, she shoved me back into an alcove.

"You!" she hissed, her face white with fury. "You are dressed like an imbecile. Where is my gown?"

"Jane and I switched clothing!" I retorted, instantly defensive. "Whatever is the matter?"

"You lied to me!"

Oh, no. My breath turned to ashes in my throat. "What do you mean?"

"Cecil said my services are no longer needed as a lady of

the bedchamber—that the Queen was displeased with me. And this never should have happened! He said *you* were the one intended to go to her bedchamber and listen to those insufferable biddies yap about the day's events, not me. He'd intended *me* to be the one following Rafe—not you. And you *lied* to me to get me to do it, telling me that the Queen had favored me when she'd done no such thing. And now through *no fault* of my own, the Queen is angry with me and has *dismissed* me from the chambers. If it ever gets out, my reputation will be destroyed, and it is *all your fault*!"

"I didn't! It isn't!" I protested, unable to keep the desperation from my voice. "Beatrice, it is true it was not the Queen's intention for you to be elevated to lady of the bedchamber this soon, but I have no interest in the role—it is not for me!"

"Enough with your lies!" she spit back. "I trusted you, and you turned on me like the rat that you are, greedy to get whatever spoils you could. Cecil told me what you did to try to scheme your way into Rafe's affections. You disgust me!"

"That's not true!" Even as I said the words, Beatrice snapped up her hand, cutting off my words.

"Tell it to the Queen," she said haughtily. "She knows how to deal with sluts like you."

"But I didn't—" And she was gone.

I could barely totter out of the alcove, a boat shattered on the rocks by a violent storm. *What had Cecil told Beatrice—and why?*

And what did he mean that Beatrice's services would no longer be necessary?

Cecil and Walsingham turned at the doorway to the

Great Hall as I approached, and they spotted me. Their faces were dark.

"What?" I asked. "What happened?"

"Where have you been?" Cecil demanded. "The Queen has summoned you for a private discussion."

"I—I was . . . ," I scrambled, trying to catch up. "She what? But why?"

Cecil took me by one arm, and Walsingham by the other. "It appears, Miss Fellowes, you will have the opportunity to explain yourself to her," Walsingham said.

We entered the half-lit Privy Chamber, and the Queen whirled around to face us, her eyes as flat as an asp's as she surveyed my manly costume. "Where were you off to this night, Miss Fellowes? And why weren't you reporting on the events that befell Lady Amelia, as I expressly asked of you?"

I blinked, stunned.

"Lady Amelia?" I offered lamely. I would have curtsied, but Cecil and Walsingham were still pinning me in place. Suddenly, I remembered: Jane was supposed to have found Lady Amelia and brought her to safety. "Say she's not hurt!" I blurted, the words more a statement than a question.

"And why would she be hurt? What do you know about her situation?" The Queen fairly bit off the last words, and I felt the blood draining from my face.

"I don't know anything." *Where was Jane?* She was supposed to have ensured that Lady Amelia had not come to harm. She was supposed to have reported to Cecil, no matter what she'd found.

Why had Jane not made good on her promise?

Had Jane been harmed? I rejected that notion immediately. Of all of us, Jane would not allow a Spaniard or any other man to get close enough to harm her. Or if she did, the ensuing row would have caused such a "disruption" that all thoughts of Lady Amelia's disappearance would have disappeared under a wave of blood and fury.

So then, what? Had Jane simply gotten distracted, not realizing that by her absence, she would be leaving me to swing in the wind?

Or was it worse than that?

I remembered Jane's willingness to change our clothes, leaving me in these ridiculous breeches and hose. I remembered her quick push to get me out of the Presence Chamber. Had she done that on *purpose*? To ruin me? Could that even be possible?

I felt my world closing in.

"Your Grace, this is my fault," I said, my voice lifeless. "I was supposed to take care that no disruptions befell the court. I—" I swallowed. "I knew that Lady Amelia left the hall."

"Of course you did," the Queen snapped. Her voice was pure ice. "Do you think I sent Anna to you for my health? You were supposed to follow Lady Amelia and bring her back to the masque. What part of that instruction failed to penetrate your feeble mind?"

This was getting worse and worse. My next words were so quiet that I felt Cecil shaking me. "Speak up," he growled.

"Two Spaniards left the Presence Chamber, Your Grace," I said. "The Spaniard with Lady Amelia, and Rafe de Martine. I chose to follow Rafe. Anna had no way of knowing that I would do such a thing."

"I would well think she wouldn't," the Queen sneered. "Disobeying a direct order from her Queen would never occur to a maid of quality like Anna Burgher."

Shame flared through me. She was right. Of course she was right. In my excitement to find the killer, I'd chosen the larger prey. But not the right prey.

And even that wasn't entirely true. I'd chosen to run off after the Count de Martine, a young, handsome courtier who could possibly have nothing at all to do with the plot against the Queen.

Walsingham was speaking, and Cecil shook me again. Hard.

"What?" I managed.

"I said, why are you dressed in men's clothes? Where did you find such a costume?"

"I bribed a servant to give them to me," I lied. I did not—could not—implicate Jane. I had already caused too much damage here this night. "I thought the Count de Martine—or whomever he was speaking with—might notice me, were I dressed as a maid."

"And what did you find?" Walsingham asked. My head felt muddy, but I still was able to lie. Some skills, it seemed, never failed me.

"I never did speak to the count but I stumbled across de Quadra and de Feria speaking." I brightened, snatching at the thread of hope. "I could tell you what they said?"

"This is not the point!" the Queen fairly screamed, and I whipped my gaze back to her face, my heart seizing up. Never had I seen her this angry. Certainly never at me. "You were given a direct order from *me* to ensure that Lady Amelia safely returned to the Presence Chamber with her skirts and her skin intact! You failed in that charge and instead took it upon yourself to run about the castle after a Spaniard—and do not think I don't understand the reasoning behind *that* little move."

She scowled at me from her dais, a goddess of wrath in her royal finery. Her gown this night was of gloriously embroidered heavy white silk, with a tight-fitting long pointed bodice circled with a jeweled girdle. Her skirts flashed like fire, embroidered with rubies, and opened in the front to reveal a cloth-of-gold lining beneath. Her ruff and wristlets were of finest linen, and her girdle and summer crown proclaimed her as the mighty sovereign she would ever be.

She was nothing short of magnificent.

And before her, I was awash in disgrace.

"You have proven yourself untrustworthy and false, the smallest, meanest creature in my kingdom, that you would fail me in such a way." The Queen's voice had grown quieter and, if anything, far more terrible. I felt myself at the edge of a very dark pit. "And to think, I *defended* you. Told Cecil you would be worth the months and months of training it has taken for you to even *act* like a woman of worth, to *act* like you have a shred of nobility about your person. And for *what*? You shame *yourself*, but it is clear that such disappointment would not trouble anyone so useless as you. But you shame England. And you shame *me*."

I opened my mouth, apologies bubbling up, but they did not come out. Somehow, even in the depths of my disgrace, I knew that words would not save me. I wrenched myself out of Cecil's and Walsingham's arms, stumbling forward.

I had seen others curry the favor of the Queen. I had seen her nobles ply her with gifts, the poor and meek kneel in front of her, wailing about their miserable plights. I'd seen the bold and audacious pledge to her the power of their horsemen and people. The rich offer her their coffers of gold. The churchmen promise her a very place in the heavens.

I had none of these to give to her.

And so I, who had nothing to recommend myself but my pride and my freedom, gave up everything I stood for, everything I was . . . and completely debased myself to my Queen.

Without uttering one word of excuses, reasons, apologies, or pleas for my safety, for another chance, for clemency, I sank to the ground at the Queen's feet, my arms outstretched above my head, my face buried in the rushes that lined her Privy Chamber floor, tasting dirt, and bile, and the tears I had not realized I was shedding.

I was undone.

CHAPTER TWENTY-NINE

There was complete silence in the room.

And still it continued.

And continued yet further.

When finally it broke, it was neither the Queen, nor Cecil, nor Walsingham who did the honors.

A footman rushed into the room, then knelt beside me, facing the Queen. If he thought anything of a woman dressed like a man lying in prostrate silence before his Queen, he didn't pause to comment on it.

"Your Grace!" he blurted, and she must have given him leave to speak, because he rushed on. "The Lady Amelia has returned to the masque, alone, Your Majesty. She appears unharmed and in good spirits."

"Thank you," the Queen said, and the man scrambled back, fleeing the room. I could only guess who he thought I was.

It no longer mattered, of course. Nothing mattered.

For myself, I lay completely still. Lady Amelia was safe, there had been no disturbance, but it was through no grace of my own actions.

The Queen seemed to stare at me from a great height, and I felt the cold chill of her gaze on my back. "You are indeed fortunate, Meg, that Lady Amelia is unharmed. And that you chose well in how you would account for your failings. But you receive only this one chance. Fail me again, and there will be no clemency."

She paused again, and I felt myself sink even deeper into the rush-lined floor, a worthless heap at her feet.

"But I am not without mercy for those who serve me well. Now that Beatrice has become indisposed, and until Mathilde recovers, you will attend me in my bedchamber. I will expect you within the hour."

She swept toward me, and I felt the pressure of her royal slipper upon my right hand. She stepped on me, not grinding her foot heavily, not intending to break the fine bones of my hand, but pushing my fingers deeply into the piled rushes, emphasizing the difference in our stations.

She was my Queen.

And I was hers to walk on.

She left without a word. One of the men left with her—but only one.

For another five minutes I lay there, as limp as a doll, wondering what would happen next. While I did, the most curious mix of emotions washed through me.

There was the aftermath of horror of what I'd just done—failing the Queen. There was also the misery of what I'd just been subjected to—shame, embarrassment, punishment. Though in truth I'd gotten off lightly. The Queen did not parcel out her punishments without careful thought. She'd chosen her actions deliberately, directing the scene with all the skill of a troupe master. And there was also my sick curiosity, left in the wake of her decision to assign me to her bedchamber—an assignment to replace one spy with another . . . but a spy with everything to lose. Was the Queen truly showing clemency, or working a strategy all her own?

And why did she say Beatrice was indisposed? What had Cecil told her—and why? Those questions continued to twist and burn.

But that was not all that roiled through me.

There was also the utter sense of loss that at first I could not place. Then it came to me in a sickening slap.

I had lost my friends.

Beatrice had shunned me, realizing me for the lie and cheat that I was. Sophia could potentially have warned me to follow Lady Amelia, not Rafe, but I had not asked her to use her gift on my behalf. I'd pushed Anna away pridefully as well. And then Jane had abandoned me, getting distracted or deliberately allowing me to face the Queen's wrath alone.

I felt . . . hollow. Like nothing I did would ever regain a trust so quickly lost.

"That, in the end . . . was well played." The voice belonged to Cecil, but it sounded oddly gruff. "I think now would be a good time for you to give me your report on de Quadra and de Feria's conversation, Miss Fellowes. You may stand."

I scraped myself up from the floor, and turned to face him, resolutely lifting my chin for him to rebuke me anew. Instead he eyed me with a look on his face that I had never seen before, exactly.

I had seen disdain, anger, irritation, boredom, indignation, and even disappointment in Cecil's gaze. I had seen calculation as well, and rest assured, that look was well in evidence. But I now saw something else, an expression that made me straighten, even as bits of straw tumbled from my hair and I fought against the urge to gag on the taste of salty tears and rock dust on my lips.

In the old goat's eyes I saw . . . compassion. And that was worst of all.

Numb with confusion, shame, and a weariness so bone deep that I did not think I would ever overcome it, I curtsied to Cecil, then stood straight. Without saying another word, he nodded at me to proceed.

I told him everything that I remembered from the conversation with de Feria, de Quadra, and the tall Spaniard. Even though it was all in Spanish, I realized with surprise that I was beginning to piece together a few of the words on my own. Anna's Spanish lessons, though infrequent, were finally paying off, and it was all too late.

I paused, and Cecil eyed me. "A guard went missing from the delegation a few days past. We sent Jane Morgan to find him, and she did—dead on the banks of the Thames. Did de Feria or de Quadra speak of that?"

I didn't have to feign my shock. "Dead?" I asked, thinking again of the words I'd overheard on the terrace steps. Was this the Spaniard who'd given Rafe the letter in the chapel, Turnip Nose? Jane had not shared this mission with me. *Had I seen Rafe kill a man?*

"I do not know, Sir William," I continued, shaking my head. "I do not understand all the Spanish that I hear, as you know. Not very well."

He nodded, remembering. "Proceed."

When I had completed my report on de Feria, I didn't pause for approval. I was somewhat beyond that, particularly now. I went on to describe all of the secondary conversations I'd overheard at the masque, detailing the castle's current round of petty jealousies and slighted hearts, scheming grandmothers and willful youths, and an endless round of intimacies, at once shocking and commonplace.

As I told my tale, I recognized the symmetry in everything Cecil had asked me to overhear. There was a string connecting them all—they were all of a piece of court life, a patchwork of English nobility. Except the de Feria conversation, of course. He ruined the whole cloth.

Throughout, Cecil said nothing. When at last I'd finished and folded my hands over my loose, rough trousers, he tilted his head and eyed me intently. "Is there anything you're not telling me, Miss Fellowes? Any part of the report you chose not to include?"

I fought against the blush that wanted to climb up my cheeks. *God's hounds.* I had included nothing of the Count de Martine. Rafe had not spoken to de Feria, but Cecil knew I'd followed the young courtier, and I was no slouch at the job. Surely Cecil also knew that I had tracked him down. He was the one who'd first given me the assignment to spy on Rafe and de Feria, after all. He would not be surprised that I'd continued to do so.

"Do you want conversations that are not pertinent to court business, Sir William?" I asked hesitantly. The only way out of this was through.

He raised his brows. "All of what you heard tonight is court business, Miss Fellowes."

I gave a wry grimace, artful in my disdain. "Not all of it. I also endeavored to hear the Count de Martine in his conversations with de Feria. Unfortunately, the two of them never met up. Rafe did, however, speak to a number of women as I tracked him through the castle, flirting outrageously throughout, I should say. I can recount his exact words if you would like. They tended to repeat in cycles."

"Cycles?"

"He would meet a lady and they would kiss. Then, heads together, they'd say—"

Cecil lifted a hasty hand, his lip curling in distaste. "That won't be necessary, Miss Fellowes. Thank you."

He paused, and I waited, happy to be still. I knew that my testimony alone would not be enough to damn de Feria; Cecil would need to catch him out in an actual attack against the Queen. But his mind was clearly working, and he seemed perversely pleased

The threat against the Crown was nothing compared to the fact that Cecil had been proven correct—the Crown was indeed at risk, and Cecil was pursuing that risk down to its heart.

He nodded then. "We will need to search out de Feria's confidant. Where did you overhear them?"

"The North Terrace, near Winchester Tower."

"Good." He eyed me stonily. "The ladies of the bedchamber have begun to prepare for the Queen's rest. You will report there within the hour, once you have changed clothing. Her attending ladies will advise you on your duties."

I sighed, miserable. "Why did she say Beatrice was indisposed? Why did she dismiss her?" There was no way that I could imagine even looking at the Queen, let alone speaking to her.

Cecil's words were clipped. "She did not dismiss her; I told her Beatrice had fallen ill. I know the Queen well. She punishes and then rewards. You were well set for punishment. It took only a few words to clear the path for your reward. A reward which meets our needs."

"What?" I whispered, aghast. "You lied to her about Beatrice . . . just to make it seem that it was *her* idea that I be installed in Beatrice's place?" I couldn't believe it. I was offended on the Queen's behalf, despite her disdain for me. "And then you lied to Beatrice?"

"How little you still know of the court. The Queen would never have chosen you first over Beatrice, Miss Fellowes. Beatrice had to be positioned first, and then removed." Cecil glared at me. "As it is, I expect you will be only granted one night in Her Majesty's company. Your assignment stands, however, as we discussed."

I blinked at him. "Surely you cannot think the Queen would see anyone tonight. Not after . . . all of this."

Cecil sighed heavily, and the first trace of humanity I'd seen in some time slipped over his face. "I truly hope not," he said. "For the sake of England and her Queen, I truly hope not."

Beyond us at the masque, a roaring cheer went up, announcing the Queen's departure for the night.

"God save the Queen," I murmured.

Cecil nodded grimly. "Or we will."

CHAPTER THIRTY

Even if I hadn't already memorized this area of the castle, I knew I'd reached the Queen's rooms when I heard the lively sounds of her ladies preparing her evening respite, their laughter and chatter loud and gay. They made no effort to hide their talk, and I slipped into the chamber, past the guards.

I looked around quickly. The Queen had not yet entered. I'd made it in time.

"You're Margaret Fellowes?" The voice was cold, and instantly steeled me. I made a hasty curtsy to Lady Knollys as she continued. "I see no reason for all of these changes. We can manage well enough without Mathilde for a few nights."

"Verily true," I said earnestly. "I believe I am here to see to your comfort as much as the Queen's, Lady Knollys. You do so much to ease her, I only wish to give aid where I may."

That seemed to mollify them, and even the woman who seemed slightly slow nodded gravely, her big saucer-round eyes sad but resigned. "Mathilde will be feeling herself soon," she promised, giving me a little wave.

I busied myself with hanging up the Queen's clothing, keeping well away from the others. "Did you see the Count of

Raybury," a lady asked to the room in general a few moments later. I felt my shoulders unknot. They were continuing their conversation. "He looked as if he'd split his doublet wide open, yet he never stopped eating, not the whole night!"

"He'll eat Her Grace out of house and home if she does not dispatch him quickly."

"At least he was willing to dance! Lord Sutherland sat like a stump beside his wife and eyed the whole of the revel as if it were a funeral dirge. And she was fairly up on her toes with excitement, begging to join the dance. I sent Lord Magwell over—"

"You didn't!"

"I did. And she almost fell over herself in her eagerness to be away from Sutherland's scowl."

"Hello, Your Grace!"

"Good evening, Your Majesty!"

As I watched at the back of the group, the Queen swept into the room, her color high, her manner almost girlish. None of her fury from earlier this evening remained. She pronounced that she was exhausted, though her eyes were bright and eager, and her ladies clucked and cooed over her like she was on the verge of collapse. I ducked and looked away. I set myself to putting out a few of the sconce lights and banking the fire, as Cecil had directed me to do.

"Meg Fellowes!" The Queen's command rolled through the chamber, and I turned quickly, curtsying low. The Queen did not approach me, but peered at me across the room from her seat at her dressing table, her other ladies gathered close. "Get up, get up," she ordered, and I rose again, not at all needing to affect a look of wan dismay. "You are fit to serve me?" she demanded.

"Yes, Your Grace," I said, and the words hung between us in heavy awareness, as thick as morning fog. "I live only to serve you."

She blinked at me, clearly surprised by my fervor, but in that moment I wanted only to believe the best of my Queen, that she had done this all to lift me up, after casting me down so low. I wanted to protect her from the trap that Cecil had set for her—even though I myself was that trap.

"Good," she said gravely, nodding. "It is well that you are here." And with that she turned away. A moment later, still shocked by the compliment, I turned away as well, my hands shaking slightly as I continued to trim down wicks.

And so it went. As we prepared the Queen for bed, the words of the ladies of the bedchamber tumbled over one another like water over rocks, the women secure that their gossip would go no farther than the privacy of their inner sanctum. I listened to them with half an ear, until an unexpected comment nearly shook me out of my role.

"The young de Martine had a finely turned leg, Your Grace, and he could not stop staring at you. 'Twas almost indecent!"

I barely kept from flinching and bent myself more earnestly to my task of preparing our sleeping mats for bed. I'd been watching Rafe for at least part of the night, and while he'd been as attentive as any other courtier to the Queen, he hadn't been what I'd call *indecent*. But the ladies were continuing.

"I overheard him talking to de Feria about you, clearly

smitten. The Spanish ambassador looked like he'd eaten lye, to hear your praises sung so charmingly. Had he not been forced into marriage so quickly, 'tis no doubt that he'd also be pressing his own suit for you, Your Grace."

What were these women talking about? De Feria would sooner spit on the Queen's slipper than kiss it—surely she knew that? But her answering laughter was light and unconcerned.

"Think you so?" The Queen laughed in return. "That would be a treat."

Oh, yes, they all concurred, and I was aghast at their flattering lies. There would be no way of telling truth from twaddle with these women. I dearly hoped the Queen did not rely on their accounts.

And in that moment I felt her staring at me, so I ducked again and turned away, this time busying myself at the fire. Did no one tell her the truth even in her own bedchamber? Could she trust no one at all?

I had no sense of time passing, bustling about as we were. The Queen's laughter flowed easily, and she seemed young and free and curiously excited, particularly as she donned a shimmering white gown, apparently something new. The ladies all exclaimed over her beauty, but my heart plummeted when I saw the gown in all its glory.

Why was she dressing up to go to bed?

They brushed the Queen's long hair and powdered her skin, detailing its perfection all the while, and the result at length was a monarch worthy of retiring, her bright new bedding gown setting off her porcelain complexion and reflecting brilliantly against her lush red hair.

I felt dread surge anew. Again, what woman dressed so carefully for bed, when she had to rise early the next morning for a royal hunt?

A chambermaid knocked, and the Queen whirled, bidding her to enter. The young girl crossed the threshold with a tray of seven goblets and a carafe of wine. One of the goblets, the largest, had already been filled.

"But come! We must toast another successful masque," the Queen said gaily, and the women clapped their hands in conspiratorial laughter. I suddenly felt like I was surrounded by children. Was all of this forced jollity an act? Or were they really this . . . carefree?

The servant departed, and we assembled around the drinks table, with me still hanging toward the back of our small retinue. The Queen did the pouring, despite our protestations. Then she lifted her own goblet.

I tensed, even as I obediently picked up my own goblet, staring at the deep red liquid within. The Queen's cup was distinctively different from our own, encrusted with jewels fit for her royal hand. The Queen's cup had also been previously filled with wine, while ours had been filled just now from a separate carafe.

We were going to be drugged.

I knew it as surely as I was standing there. Six ladies. Six empty cups. The Queen's wine in a separate goblet, ours poured later, by her own hand. Who in the kitchens had done the deed? And how much had they drugged the wine? I pried a kerchief out of my sleeve and edged behind the women. I needed time!

"Your Grace, you look so lovely!" cooed the woman in

front of me. Compliments immediately followed all around, giving me an unexpected opening. I turned slightly away, shoving my kerchief into my cup. The wine stained the linen like a crimson sickness, and I'd barely yanked the cloth out again before the Queen raised her goblet.

"To a successful masque!" the Queen cried out, and upended her cup. We all drained our cups, and I once again felt her eyes upon me, fever-bright. Despite my care I was still forced to swallow some of the wine, which tasted curiously sweet to my now trained palate.

The chatter between the ladies grew merrier, their voices too loud, almost jarring to my ears. We scurried around the Queen in our carefully orchestrated dance, but at my first opportunity I drifted over to the hearth to stoke the fire with a poking rod. In one swift movement, I dropped the wine-soaked cloth among the embers and watched it catch fire. No one noticed the sudden flare.

And then the Queen was in her bed with the curtains drawn and the rest of us retired to our sleeping mats, to give our monarch the illusion of privacy without risking her safety for a moment. It was, I thought as I laid myself down and willed myself to defeat the drowsiness clawing at my eyelids, a masterful game.

One by one my fellow ladies of the bedchamber fell asleep, emitting five sets of light snores. Only five, thank heavens, because I was still awake, though it was a close thing. Even with the very little amount of the sleeping draught that I'd ingested, I had to fight sleep off as though it were a smothering bear.

For her part, the Queen did not sleep either. She tossed

and turned in her bed, then became unnaturally silent, with the stillness of a crouching cat. And not two hours after we'd all said our good nights, I heard what I had most feared: the swish of bed curtains parting, the pad of careful feet, and finally the scrape of a panel moved aside—the same clicking rasp that I'd heard in Lord Brighton's house as Jane and I had unhinged the hidden panel in his wall. I kept myself locked in place, every nerve in my body wrapped tight.

The Queen was leaving her own bedchamber.

No, no, a thousand times no!

I peeked over the edge of my blanket, but she was already gone. I waited just a few heartbeats, then slid off my mat, bunching up my bedclothes to make it look like I was still lying fast asleep. I moved quickly across the room to where the panel remained ajar. The Queen had not tried to move it back into place. She'd done this before, I knew immediately. You did not grow lax the first few times that you duped your keepers, only after regular practice.

How many times had the Queen snuck through the castle's hidden corridors—and how had she learned of them without Cecil knowing as well? She had only been a baby of three when her own mother had been killed, and that had been long years ago. Had Edward told her of these passages—or Mary? Somehow, I doubted either monarch would have trusted their sister with such information. Then who—a servant? A craftsman, come to work on the castle renovation?

There would be time later to puzzle through that. For now, I slipped into the corridor behind the Queen, seeing her candle bob in the distance, which allowed me to follow her with ease.

The riddle of passageways should have confused me, but I'd been this way before. And when the Queen stopped and moved through a doorway set flush against the corridor wall, my deepest fears were realized.

Saint George's Hall.

I gave the Queen a moment more to move deeper into the room, while I hesitated in the corridor. Then I realized that I might not be the only person using this passageway, and I hastened forward and slipped into the abandoned hall like a ghost.

The Queen's candle had been extinguished, but I still saw her clearly, far down the hall, heading toward a sea of hanging tapestries bunched against the far wall. I had noticed the tapestries before, but now I saw them for what they were. A room within a room, all hung with ancient cloths and silks. With growing alarm I followed behind, careful not to get too close.

Then, ahead of us, the heavy draperies split wide, and a rough, sensual voice broke through the silence, quickening my heart even as I felt my stomach twist. It was a voice I'd recognize anywhere: the rounded syllables, the sharp inflections, the weight of double meaning in every careless phrase. And other than one gilded with a Spanish accent, it was absolutely the last voice I'd hoped to hear this night.

"My Queen," Robert Dudley whispered hoarsely.

CHAPTER THIRTY-ONE

Whole centuries passed before the curtains parted again, and I had died a hundred times over in my misery. How long had the Queen been in this room? A bare quarter hour? Half the night? There was no way for me to know. Time seemed to have turned around on itself, and even the faint tolling of the tower clock had begun to speak in riddles. Had it just rung two bells—or had I imagined it?

It mattered not, in any case. My heart was now a cold, wretched stone—my stomach so eaten with bile and anxiety that I thought I might never take food again.

What Cecil had feared was true. More than what he feared, in fact. More than he could ever imagine, I suspected, in his wildest, most worried dreams.

The Queen strolled by me close enough for me to touch her, then slipped back into the corridor. Behind her I trailed listlessly, too shocked to think. It seemed to take us far less time to return to the safety of her chambers than it had for us to leave it. As we approached our destination, however, I realized my mistake.

The Queen would return to her bedchamber via the

secret panel. She would go inside. And then she would close the panel behind her, and set its tiny clasp.

Locking me out.

Panicked, I cast about the corridor for a stone, a brick—anything I might use as some sort of distraction. There was nothing. The corridors were empty, as blank as a piece of parchment, and I dared not make too much noise here, lest she turn and catch me out.

I stumbled on the solution with only the greatest of misery.

With trembling fingers, I pulled out my precious set of picklocks. The treasure I had kept from my past, that had proven to be so valuable in my present. A gift from my grandfather. And now my best chance at survival.

No sooner had the Queen navigated the final turn in the corridor and begun making haste toward the entryway to her own chamber, than I made my move. I sidled up behind her, and just as she bent to duck through the opening in the panel, I hurled the picklocks over her head, far down the shadowed corridor. They struck a far wall and fell to the stone floor with a satisfying clatter, shockingly loud in the silence.

The Queen straightened so fast, I could hear the bones in her back crack. She held the candle aloft, the beginning of a sound on her lips. A haughty *Who goes there!* I was sure, or *Present yourself!*

Instead she fell still, and I tensed. A smart woman—or a less bold one—would have dashed back into her room and buried herself under the covers. The Queen, however, was the Queen. She had already proven herself audacious. And her actions this night had also proven that her better sense could be ruled by her emotions, at least in this one area.

She set off down the corridor, after my picklocks. I prayed she would not find them, but there was no time for me to see. As soon as her royal skirts cleared the opening in the corridor, I dashed up to it, flung myself through the hole, and scrambled across the room to where the ladies of the bedchamber lay sleeping off their drugged wine. Though my entire body shook with exertion and excitement, I slid onto my assigned mat and dragged the covers back over me.

A few moments later I heard the Queen enter the room, and my stomach tightened with worry. But nothing jingled in her hands, and I allowed myself the tiniest hope that my picklocks were still there, hidden in the darkness, waiting for me like a faithful friend. The only friend I had left in this place of stone and secrets.

I struggled to maintain measured breathing as the Queen made her way over to our sleeping group. She stood there, and I could feel her presence radiate around her, exhilarated and majestic. Proud. *She had won!* She had succeeded in escaping the clutches of her keepers for a few precious moments, to pursue her private agenda.

Whether she gloated over her ladies or silently thanked us for being so easily fooled, I couldn't say. But I was about to break in two from the strain of remaining quiet, when the Queen finally turned away and walked over to her own enormous bed, slid in between the covers, and dropped the curtains once more around her, safe in her royal cocoon.

Only then did she allow herself the smallest of sounds—her first in hours, besides the hushed and earnest talk she'd shared with Dudley, a conversation that would remain in my thoughts for an eternity. Dudley had pressed the Queen hard, suggesting that he might serve her not only as courtier and lover but as king and consort! And Dudley was married! It was an impossible thing, and she had rebuffed his pleas with gentle words that still left the door open wide for his continued suit to flourish. That had been bad enough. But what she expressed now was far, far worse.

It was the tiniest breath of happiness. A soft, wondering sigh. The kind of sigh that captured all of passion's sweet torment in its brief and fluttering hold, before letting it free once more.

The Queen was not just dallying with the wrong man at the wrong time, I realized, or entertaining a flatterer to ease the burden of her rule.

No. The Queen was deeply, hopelessly, irretrievably *in love.*

And I was no longer merely undone. . . .

I was lost.

CHAPTER THIRTY-TWO

Dawn finally stretched over the horizon. A servant slipped into the room, and I made as if I'd woken at once, leaping from my mat to serve and protect.

At my movement, the Queen swept back the curtains of her bed. "Yes, Meg?" she asked, a faint smile on her face.

"I, oh— I . . . My apologies, Your Grace," I said, stuttering. Behind me the other ladies of the bedchamber were stirring. "I heard a sound and—" I shook my head, hard, feigning that I was muzzy-headed. "I feel a bit . . . queer," I said softly.

She was watching me with keen eyes. "Did you sleep well?"

"Yes—yes, of course, Your Grace. I just . . . I feel . . . odd."

She nodded briskly. "It was a busy night for you. Go forth. You're relieved of morning duties, since you'd be no use at all in preparing me for the hunt. If Mathilde is not recovered, I will expect you here when I return at the tenth hour."

I murmured thanks far more sincere than she could have known, pulled on my skirts and kirtle, and fled.

But I did not go to Cecil's chambers. And I did not go back to my own room either. It was early still, the morning after a grand revel. The only focus of the guards would be on the hunters and their horses—not the guests who'd danced long into the night. There would be no one to track my movements. It would take only a moment to fetch my picklocks back. . . .

The doors to Saint George's Hall remained open, the only light to brighten the abandoned hall coming from the windows as before, this time a trickle of the sun's earliest rays over the walls of the castle. By this meager light I could easily see the panel set into the wall, now that I knew what I was looking for. I had only to pry the panel off once more, slip inside, and then retrace my steps back to the Queen's chambers and move several yards beyond. The picklocks would still be there, on the floor of the corridor. Waiting for me.

I'd almost reached the panel, when a flash of metal whisked in front of my eyes. "Looking for this?"

Rafe.

I stopped short, yanking the picklocks out of Rafe's fingers. "What are you doing here!" I hissed, turning sharply around. "Where did you find these? And where have you been?"

His grin was irrepressible. "I suspect I found them where you dropped them, in the corridor behind the Queen's chambers," he said, answering only the second of my questions. "And you should keep a closer eye. Royal picklocks are not tinkers' tools. These are among the finest I've ever seen."

"What?" I looked at him, then down at the gleaming metal in my hand. "These aren't royal picklocks." They were simply a gift from my grandfather.

"I assure you that they are." He plucked the picklocks from my hand and pointed to a tiny crest near the tip of the delicate keys. "Looks like old King Henry's seal, in fact, but it's too dark to tell. Either way, they're worth a royal ransom." He handed them back to me, and I stared at them in confusion, pulling myself back to the issues at hand only with extraordinary discipline.

"But how did you know where to find them—and how did you get into the passage in the first place?" I stamped my foot in utter frustration. It seemed to work for Beatrice. "And what *are* you doing here?"

My voice rose nearly out of a whisper with my last question, and he put a finger to his lips to quiet me. He nodded toward the chapel. "If you must know, I'm looking for someone."

At that moment a small, muffled cry came from the chapel, whether from pleasure or pain, it was impossible to tell. Rafe grimaced. "And I believe I just found him."

I froze, horror rushing through me. Surely the Queen could not be so bold as to meet Robert Dudley twice in one night—I'd left her with her attendants all awake! I looked at Rafe. "You cannot go in there," I said earnestly.

"I must." A brutal crack echoed on the heels of a muffled cry, both sounds emanating from the chapel. "And I believe that's my cue."

With that he turned and ran toward the chapel, with me hard on his heels. We rushed forward even as a tall, slender man burst free from the chapel and barreled through us, and another man's voice, low and guttural, shouted out in triumph from beyond the chapel doors. Caught between chasing the first fleeing man and saving the Queen, Rafe hesitated just a moment, but I did not. I sprinted by him and flew through the doorway.

The scene in front of me was clear. And it wasn't the Queen.

Lady Amelia lay collapsed on the chapel floor in a huddled ball, her face cut, her beautiful ball gown soaked with a tight arc of crimson. Standing above her was the moon-faced Spaniard I'd seen just hours before with de Quadra and de Feria, but now with a knife in his hand.

I barely heard a distant rousing cry well behind us. The fleeing Spaniard had doubtless alerted the castle to cover his own escape. We would be awash in royal guardsmen in minutes.

Moon Face looked up, apparently not having heard the cry of his comrade . . . but he seemed to recognize Rafe. He grunted in greeting, then looked at me, his face cracking into an unholy grin. *"¿Quieres que matar a ella también?"*

"No!" Rafe spit back, even as I realized that the Spanish sentence the man had just spoken had included the phrase "kill her too." "Kill *her*," as in kill *me*. Rafe reached out and shoved me behind him, and the two men began speaking in rapid Spanish, but I twisted out of Rafe's grasp. That was *Lady Amelia* lying there, half-dead, it appeared, her throat already purpling with bruises. I barely paid attention to them yelling at each other. I could not focus on their conversation, not with Lady Amelia harmed.

I moved to dash to her aid, but suddenly the man was right in front of me, his blade flashing out. I blocked his blow with a sharp upward thrust of my arm. The feint did little more than allow me to stagger to the side, but it startled Moon Face so much that he stumbled forward, missing me completely. Rafe hissed another command, but the man came at me again. I dodged once more, my training taking hold, and I rolled out of harm's way even as Rafe jumped into the fight.

Whirling around, the black-clad man threw his knife at Rafe, who ducked the blade and charged the Spaniard, his own rapier pulled.

"Run!" Rafe shouted, though I would do no such thing. I could not leave Lady Amelia behind!

The two blocked my path in a whirling sword fight. Rafe pressed forward against his attacker like a man possessed, his hands a rush of steel. In addition to his sword, he somehow held a second blade in his left hand, a short, thick dagger that he was able to wield with jabbing spikes whenever their battle brought the two men within a few feet of each other. Rafe connected once, then again, but Moon Face fought back with a fury borne more of desperation than skill. It was just a matter of time before Rafe finished him, I thought, but Rafe pulled back from the killing blow, speaking in rushed Spanish, as if he sought to get answers rather than blood from the man.

Moon Face responded with a feral bellow, and they came at each other again, finally opening a space for me to rush past them to Lady Amelia. I bent over her hastily, trying to determine if she still breathed.

Lady Amelia's eyes were open, but her mouth was slack. Only the faintest of heartbeats thrummed beneath my hand. Though she'd been sliced across the neck, the wound was not deep. Her throat was wreathed in dark angry welts, however, as if she'd been strangled by a man's bare hands. The killer had moved beyond garrotes, it appeared, to a more personal approach to killing.

I knelt, cradling Lady Amelia's head in my arms, still searching for injuries. Her right temple was already a knot of bruises, and I realized that the crack I had heard had likely been intended as her killing blow. The facial cuts were just for show, to shock whoever found the body. They certainly did the job.

"Don't die, Lady Amelia," I whispered as I lay her down again. "Don't you dare die." I did not know what had brought the woman to this dark, abandoned chapel, but she didn't deserve this.

Nobody deserved this.

A snarl from Moon Face ripped through the room, and I turned to see Rafe's attacker barrel forward with his sword held low and tight, preparing for a killing blow. Rafe whirled at the last minute, flipping around in a graceful arc, then plunged his short blade high into the man's left shoulder, angling down.

The man convulsed, then fell silent, slumping to the ground.

The sound of pounding feet rang through the castle, barely reaching our ears but coming fast. The guards!

"What did you do? Why did you kill him?" I nearly shrieked at him. "He could have explained what was happening—"

"He was a fool. He knew nothing!" Rafe shouted back, but his eyes were wild. What had he heard? *Why did I not know more Spanish!*

"You must go!" I said urgently. "They will never believe you are innocent in this, and I will not see you hang."

Rafe shook his head. "I cannot leave you here."

"Do you not understand? If you are found here hale and hearty with your own countryman dead and possibly an Englishwoman as well, you will be hung outside the Curfew Tower until you are nothing but skin and bones! It will not matter what is right, or true, or fair. Only that the death of an Englishwoman is avenged. And if we are both held accountable for Lady Amelia's death, no one will be left to save the other."

Rafe stared at me, then shook his head like an angry bear. "I cannot—"

A cry went up from the door of Saint George's Hall. They were so close! "You must!" I hissed.

Rafe set his jaw, the look in his eyes like ice. "Then, look sharp. It's time for you to play your part." He tossed his knife to me, and I caught it from long practice, stumbling forward as I strove to balance the bloody blade. As the guards pounded closer to the doorway to the chapel, Rafe yanked up a heavy canvas carpet from the floor, and disappeared beneath it. I stared, fully shocked.

He was going to *hide under a rug*? This was his grand escape plan? *Was he mad!?*

I lurched forward, aghast that he would try to hide under something so paltry, his name a cry upon my lips. *No!*

Then the heavy mat settled down on the floor . . . flat.

Flat!

I barely heard the telltale click as Rafe moved the floor panel back into place. Another accursed pathway—and this one through the floor!—that Rafe knew about and I did not! Was there no end to the damn things that the Spaniard knew?

"What, ho!" roared the guardsmen behind me, holding torches high.

I turned, holding the brutal dagger down and away. At my feet lay two dead—or nearly dead—conspirators, enemies of England.

Blinking into the torchlight, I was somehow not even surprised that it was none other than Cecil and Walsingham who rushed into the small chapel next, their mouths dropping in unison as they saw me standing there, a cruel knife in my hand.

I did the only thing I could think of, given the circumstances.

I curtsied.

CHAPTER THIRTY-THREE

Five hours later I was so exhausted, I could barely stay upright, but I was still in the midst of yet another round of interrogation. I'd recounted my false tale so many times, I was beginning to believe it myself, but when I launched into it this time, Cecil finally raised his hand.

His expression had ceased being one of patient support. Now he was angry.

He stood and went to the door. Opening it wide, he allowed the two guards to enter the chamber, their bulk and armor dwarfing him.

"Take Miss Fellowes to the dungeon—to the water cells," Cecil said. To me he said, "I will come to you before the water rises." He shrugged. "Or after, if you prefer."

"The dungeon?" I protested. My words were flat and dull. *Before the water rises?* my mind responded in return. "But why? I'm telling you the truth."

Vaguely I remembered the dank smell of the corridors Jane and I had explored, and the far-off rush of water. But I couldn't remember where those corridors were, precisely.

And I couldn't imagine why I would be taken there.

Cecil's tired words interrupted my thoughts. "What is truth and what people would believe are two separate things, Miss Fellowes. We need someone to blame for Lady Amelia's attack, and you were there. The Spaniard may have attacked you both in the height of your innocent exploration of the chapel . . . or he may have not. You may have wrested free his knife as he was attacking Amelia and killed him in a blind panic, as you so prettily convinced the guards . . . or you may have not. There are other possibilities. You are not so well known here that anyone would question your stumbling upon Lady Amelia and her paramour in a romantic tangle, and being overcome with jealousy. And the Spaniard died without telling his tale."

I blinked at him. "But I was not—"

Cecil cut me off. "Are you ready to tell me what truly transpired last night with the Queen?"

And this, really, was the rub of it. Cecil didn't care about another dead Spaniard—or even about Lady Amelia. He cared about the Queen. He suspected that I knew something.

And of course, he was right.

"I've told you everything," I lied, my words a bare, resigned mumble, the Queen's quiet sigh of stolen happiness in my ears. *Before the water rises?*

"Then you can rest easy with your conscience, even as the water surrounds you." Cecil nodded to the guards. "Remember, I could keep you down there for months, if it so pleases me," he said, almost as an aside. "I do hope you don't catch a chill."

He turned to go, and then we were both surprised as

Beatrice trooped into the room. She eyed me with frigid hauteur.

"I thought I would find you here," she said coldly. "Sir William, the Queen has summoned all the maids of honor and ladies-in-waiting to her chamber, now that she has returned from the hunt and learned of the incident with Lady Amelia. Of course, as usual, Meg was not among our number. I've come to collect her."

I stared at Beatrice in a daze, and she continued to sneer at me, but there was something . . . off about her manner. I'd been around her long enough to know her varying levels of sneering. This was . . . not quite right. She seemed almost desperate.

Cecil regarded Beatrice with level eyes. "I will bring Miss Fellowes when we have completed our questioning of her, if she is able to be presented. She is at risk."

"At risk?" Beatrice's tone was derisive. "At risk for what?" Beatrice asked. "Making even more of a fool of herself after last night?"

She sniffed at me, and if she noted my state of dishevelment, she gave no indication. "At least she's wearing proper clothing again."

"Miss Knowles, you may leave," Cecil said stonily. "Miss Fellowes will be returned to you when she is safely out of harm's way. You will be fully briefed at that time."

"More dramatics!" Beatrice pouted. "How you put up with her, Sir William, I swear I will never understand." She scowled at me. "And you sending Jane off on a wild goose chase, when you were the one who should have been seeking out Lady Amelia. It was no wonder she got turned around and *lost*."

My eyes went wide. Jane had gotten lost in the castle's secret corridors? Was that why she had not come back with Lady Amelia? But there was no kindness in Beatrice's eyes. If she was sharing a confidence with me, she was not giving anything away. Either way, I owed her one last favor for all of my lies. I lifted my hand to my waistband and palmed the treasure I'd kept hidden there.

"Oh, Beatrice!" I exclaimed, my voice nearly breaking on a sob. I rushed forward then and embraced her, sliding my hands along her opulently puffed sleeves even as she stiffened.

"Find Rafe," I hissed. "Ask him to explain."

Beatrice pulled away from me just as quickly, her lip curling in disdain. I had no idea if she'd heard me or not.

"You disgust me," she said, her voice cracking. Then she was gone.

And in her deeply slashed sleeves, she now carried Rafe's jade stone ring. I prayed she'd find it and understand. Rafe had gotten the ring from his mother—who'd doubtlessly gotten it from someone in Beatrice's family. It was too similar to the other pieces in her collection. Though I'd taken so much from Beatrice, I'd managed to steal back something for her too.

After that, things happened quickly. Too quickly. The guards blindfolded me, then led me down twisting passageways into the dungeon. They needn't have bothered with the blindfold. I was so disoriented from all of the lies I'd had to spin to cover the truth of Lady Amelia's death, if death it was, that I would not have been able to mark my passage either way. But they did not take the blindfold off until they had marched me into a cell that was more a pit than a room.

This carved-out well was about six foot square, with a single chair in the center. The walls on all sides were about fifteen feet up, and a guardsman lowered me down, letting me drop the last few feet. I could hear the water surging around the room, and the stones of the cell were already slick with drippings from unseen fissures. I remembered Jane and me exploring the dungeon corridors, the water we had sensed, and my mind shifted back to the events of this impossible night.

Had Jane truly gotten lost? Or had she abandoned me?

The guards left without a word.

I surveyed the small cell with growing trepidation. It was not simply a hole in the ground. The cell had a narrow lip of stone around its edge, enough for two men to stand at their ease. I assumed that was for people to come stand to watch me drown.

The thought was not a cheering one.

A quick scan of the cell walls yielded no hope. They were slick and without purchase. If the water rushed in quickly, I could potentially ride the surge to the edge, but I suspected that it would trickle in, not pour. Still, if I could float . . . or perhaps stand on the back of the chair when the water got high enough, leaping up to catch the lip of the stone ledge, hauling myself to safety . . . Perhaps that could be done?

As it turned out, I had plenty of time to test my theories.

None of them worked.

I was just a bit too short. Just a bit too weak.

Just a bit too.

◆ ◆ ◆

Cecil did not return until the water had climbed around my knees for the third time, and my body was now racked with shivers. The design of this cell was ingenious, I'd decided at length. The cell filled until approximately the seven-foot mark, when the water abruptly found four drain holes. When those began to allow water to pour out of the chamber as quickly as it had filled, some mechanism behind the wall churned, and drains in the floor opened as well, emptying the cell completely in a matter of minutes. It was a marvel—and curiously terrifying, as each time I found myself forced to stand on the chair in mounting desperation or—once—to tread water because the chair turned over, until I finally heard the water pouring out of the high holes. If any of those holes were stopped up . . .

I could not quell the hysteria that rose on my breath as the door opened; my head careened around. I did not know whether to beg for my life or beg forgiveness, but Cecil asked only one question.

"What transpired with the Queen last night, Miss Fellowes?"

The words died upon my lips.

"Do not make me do this, Miss Fellowes," Cecil said. "You are not supposed to think. Simply to act upon command."

I said nothing to that, either. There was nothing, really, to say.

The Queen had saved me once. Now I could save her.

Sometime later Cecil left again, when the water was now up to my chest. It was cold, cloying, but I could see the sluice in the rock, and knew in some dark corner of my mind that it would get no worse than this; the water could not rise beyond this mark—just enough to terrify me but not enough to kill me on its own. *It can get no worse*, I told myself. *It will get no worse.*

How many times Cecil came and went, I could not say. I turned every time he opened the door; not even my pride could forestall that reaction. But every time he asked, I denied knowing anything about the Queen.

In my mind, I saw only her soft, stolen smile. In my ears, I heard only her sighs. In my heart, I felt only the ache of her secrets. *She will never marry*, Sophia had said. *Never.*

Then the doorway opened again, but it wasn't Cecil who walked into my cell. It was Walsingham.

A heavy blanket fell to the cell floor. I stared at it as if it might attack me, but it did not move.

"Enjoying your stay, Miss Fellowes?" Walsingham called down cheerfully.

I stood in the corner of the cavern, my gaze constantly raking the floor. *No more water, please . . . no more water.* That was all I could think about, all that I feared. I didn't bother to respond to the Queen's spymaster, and was only slightly surprised when he dropped lightly down beside me, dark and resplendent even as I shrank away. He pursued me into the corner, picking up the blanket and putting it around my shoulders.

"Meg, make no mistake. I have no doubt in my mind that you know more than you are willing to say," Walsingham said. "You are nothing to us, naught but a tool that has been incorrectly forged, as evidenced by your failure to complete your mission to report on the Queen's whereabouts, actions, and company. But we cannot allow your insubordination. You must know that." His tone grew stern. "Lady Amelia has died, Miss Fellowes. We would avenge her, and yet you waste our time here."

"She's . . . dead?" That did penetrate my fog. Somehow, Amelia's survival had made my pain worth it. Almost. Somehow, I thought that by her living, by my having reached her in time, everything would work out in the end.

But now she was dead.

And Walsingham was still talking.

"I'm afraid we must make an example of you, Miss Fellowes. That's what we are doing here, as much as anything else. If you fail to complete your assignment, there must be repercussions. And they will only get worse."

I looked at him, unable to stop shaking, but my mind was not comprehending his words. "What more can you do to me?"

He laughed.

He actually laughed, and I thought I would never hear a more terrible sound.

Of course, once more I was wrong. Walsingham's next words were even worse.

"Why, I could blind you, Miss Fellowes. I think that would do nicely, for starters."

I opened my mouth to speak, but no words came out. Walsingham was more than happy to fill in the empty space.

"It is accomplished with a hot poker," he said, as if he were describing how to bake bread. "Placed against each eye, quite firmly, as you may imagine. Not a pleasant operation, but it is quick. And highly effective, I can assure you."

"You would—burn me?" I whispered, my voice hoarse. "Burn . . . my eyes?"

"Not just burn you, Miss Fellowes. *Blind* you. If you insist on betraying the Crown, then of course we would be forced to take action. You cannot act a role of any consequence if you cannot see. You cannot steal if you cannot see. You are no value to us if you are a traitor, and we must make sure you are no value to anyone else, either." His smile was almost kind as he looked down at me. My focus narrowed to a pinpoint on his eyes, but I couldn't block out his words, no matter how much I tried. "If you cannot spy for England, you cannot spy at all. Surely you understand that, don't you?"

"But I would never betray you—never." I must have said the words, though I couldn't feel my mouth.

In response, Walsingham leaned over and brushed my hair back from my eyes, tucking the lank strands behind my ear. He'd never touched me in such a way, almost fatherly but not . . . More like I was his property. I stood as still as a rabbit crouching beneath the hands of its killer. Walsingham clucked, turning my head this way, then that, a butcher inspecting his prime cut of meat.

"Don't cry, Miss Fellowes," he said, his words cracking off my nerves like a flint strike. Was I crying? "There are many roles in England, even for a blind woman. And you could even serve as a memorizer for your precious acting troupe." And here he spoke in a sneer. "Your ears will still be working. Assuming we don't take those as well. The Queen will I'm sure settle a fair stipend on you, for your troubles and your pain. Though she will not keep you here, of course," he continued, clucking his tongue. He reached out toward me again, and this time I did flinch. He was speaking of eventualities, as if nothing would come between him and his plan, as if he relished its execution. "She could not stand to have someone as maimed as you will be in her castle, where she might see you."

I could not say anything. My heart had stopped beating entirely as the full weight of Walsingham's vision crashed over me. I could not move.

"Guard!" Walsingham yelled suddenly, and the sound was like a striking whip. I stepped back as a ladder was angled down for him, and I was dumbfounded at the ease with which he could leave this place. His last words were whispered, and I'm sure the guards could not hear them.

But I could. For now, anyway.

"Think about it, Miss Fellowes," he said. "Your life is in my hands alone."

Then he was gone.

CHAPTER THIRTY-FOUR

I must have slept at some point.

I awoke with a start, clutching the coarse woolen blanket around me, consciousness slewing over me like a sickness. I sat up, but all was silent around me, and I sucked in a noisy breath—noisy. I was making a sound, wasn't I? Or was I simply remembering the sound that should go along with breathing? Could I still hear? Could I still see?

Who am I, truly?

Images swam in and out of my memory, of Cecil and Walsingham, questioning, questioning. Of water rushing around my ankles, then around my legs. Of the sound of laughter, and the hiss of a branding iron. They'd brought that, this last time, in a brazier of hot coals, so ready for its task that the rod was fiery hot all the way down to the—

I felt myself tipping forward. The room went black.

The next time I awoke, I was huddled into a corner, but more coherent. The water had not come in yet again; the blanket that had been dropped over me was still dry. The water seemed to flow in at regular intervals, every six hours, perhaps? I would have to pay closer attention to the bells.

To the bells.

I had not heard the bells in some time, I thought.

I tried to speak but couldn't. The hissing noise of my own breath was not proof enough that my tongue was still in my head. I sniffed, tentatively, and could not smell char upon me, nor the singe of burned flesh. Queasily, I lifted my hand up to my head—

Just as laughter floated down from above.

I jerked my hands down to clutch the blanket around me, and stepped quickly back from the wall, squinting upward into the darkness. That was not Walsingham's laugh, nor Cecil's. I shoved down my near hysteria at being able to hear at all.

"Who goes there?" I demanded, but my words came out as a death rattle, causing more laughter to rain down upon me.

"Oh, how the bold have fallen," came the voice, thick and mocking, but distorted to a harsh whisper. "Not quite so carefree as when I saw you last, I think."

I could not see anything but drew the blanket closer around me, as if the intruder could somehow see me. Where were the guards? Were the Queen's dungeons so riddled with secret entrances that anyone could wander through their corridors?

"Who are you?" I called out with greater effort, and this time the sound carried. My voice sounded as raw and broken as I felt, and I winced. What would my speech sound like, were I to lose my hearing? Would it gradually give way to awful, guttural noises, for lack of anything to compare it to? My stomach pitched dangerously at the thought, and my knees threatened to buckle. *Keep awake, keep aware,* I implored myself. *The Queen saved you once.*

"They say you know something of the Queen," the stranger said, and my focus was drawn back sharply upward. I said nothing for a moment, and he sighed with theatrical remorse. "I can get you out of here, you stupid girl. Don't make me think I've wasted my time. Your information could save not only your life, but the lives of your sop-headed friends. Or do you want them to die alongside you? Has there not been enough death in this castle?"

"No!" I said, struggling to clear my muzzy head. Was I talking to Amelia's murderer? And Marie Claire's, too? "Please, please. Was not Lady Amelia enough? You cannot kill again!"

"Lady Amelia?" The man seemed to move closer to me. "Lady Amelia isn't dead, more is the pity." He said the words with anger, and I blinked up. Not dead?

"But . . . ," I managed, trying to make sense of it all. They'd told me she was dead!

The man laughed, a cold and bitter sound. "Never fear, she will be soon enough. They say her throat is quite crushed, that she sleeps without waking. It will not take much to finish that task." He paused, and I sensed he was looking down at me, though I'd returned my gaze to the floor. "But if you help me, perhaps I will spare her life."

"How?" I croaked, before remembering his words of the Queen. I shook my head furiously. "I don't know anything about the Queen!"

"Then I am destined to be disappointed." Even though he tried to disguise it with his whispering, his voice wasn't cultured, exactly, but it was aristocratic. Foreign, I thought. A Spaniard? And there was something else about him I could not quite place. I heard the soft scrape of stone, and realized he was standing up. He was leaving.

Don't leave me! I almost cried out, and it was everything I could do not to scream the words. I licked my cracked lips, striving for coherence. "What is it that you want?" I asked, glancing up. I wanted nothing more in that moment than to keep him here, talking to me. "I truly don't know what you're seeking—you must believe me."

I knew better than to ever trust this man, even if he should offer to free me. He could be a spy sent by Walsingham, or worse—a true traitor to the Crown. But his laughter unnerved me, chilling me more than even the sound of water rushing through the walls.

The water.

Suddenly my mind was as loose and wandering as a child's, and I found it chasing thoughts that had naught to do with my safety or the words of my dark companion. What fiend had joined the cisterns of Windsor Castle to the River Thames, capturing and releasing water at such intervals as to drive its prisoners mad? Or was there some other fell waterway that wound its course beneath the castle—and if so, where did it lead?

The man above me sighed lustily, drawing my attention back to him with a jarring snap. There was a flare in the darkness, and he lit a small torch. The light made me wince away as it sent him into eerie shadows. Still, my training finally surfaced and I began to study the man more closely. He was tall, slender, hunching over just slightly as he watched me. "So this is how it will be," he said, with the same sort of whimsical good humor that had characterized

Walsingham's words. Had the spymaster sent this creature to plague me? "It's all so much a waste. 'Tis foolish enough to put yourself in harm's way—but to endanger innocent lives is shameful. I know you know something, you stupid girl. As much as it pains me, you are the only source that I have." He tsked. "And so another young maid will die—such tragedy is befalling your young Queen in the very first flower of her reign."

"Another maid." The chill I felt had nothing to do with my damp clothing. This *was* Marie's killer. Finally I fixed on him. "What do you mean?"

"My needs are simple." He pointed a long gloved hand at me, the gauntlet sticking out of his cape. Something about the way he was pointing bothered me. Something . . . strange. I could not fix upon it. "Tell me everything you know about your Queen—why you've been placed in this abysmal hole by your own countrymen—and no one else will die. Keep silent, and another maid will meet her end." He paused, and then he jabbed is finger again, as if poking me to response. "Do you understand?" he demanded.

"I—I must think on it!" I blurted. *Anything to keep him from going. Anything to give me time.*

"Whatever they've told you, they won't set you free. They'll kill you themselves before too much longer, or just leave you down there in that pit." He turned away as he spoke, and my stomach churned. *What would be worse, blinding or death?* They couldn't forget me forever down here—could they? They would have to decide what to do with me eventually.

Wouldn't they?

"Don't kill anyone else," I said miserably, and the man turned back. The flare of his cloak disturbed the air, sending down a faint warm scent that seemed almost familiar—like something I remembered as a child, so long ago I could not place it. But my mind was caught too quickly on the man's next words.

"I think I shall, my dear. You kept Lady Amelia from dying, and now someone must. I think the dark and silent one, who moves through the castle like a wraith. She'll do nicely."

The dark and silent one? *Jane?*

"You can't!" I blurted. "I will tell you—tell you everything—but you cannot kill again!" Even as I said the words, I knew they were insane. But he could *not* kill Jane.

Laughter again. He was enjoying this. "I shall have no need to kill again if you tell me everything. Why would I?"

"But how can I know you will keep your word?"

That stopped him, and something in my voice must have convinced him I was ready to break. I sensed him crouching toward me, studying me, and his breath came more quickly, excitement lacing it. "A name is all I want, a beginning place. A name linked to whatever it is they want you to share about your precious Queen. With that name, I will not only lift you out of this pit but I will leave off your maids as well. I will keep my word. I swear unto God. Remember that, Meg, when they put you to the question. What are they swearing upon? Naught but lies."

Far above us, another world away, the bells of the castle pealed. The man above me cursed in Spanish before leaning over the pit.

"I must away, but I will return here, or find you wherever they stick you. As many friends as you have in the castle, trust me; I have more. And when I do find you, you must be ready to speak, and to speak well. Or the blood of a young woman will be on your head."

And he was gone, the door shutting harshly behind him. A burst of rage and hysteria billowed up within me at the sound of that slamming door. I was forever being left behind in this pit! First by Walsingham, then by the mute servants who threw down skins of wine and day-old bread and cheese. I'd trapped five sacks now beneath my chair, so they would not float and possibly clog the sluice holes. Had I been here five days? Or were they not feeding me every day?

I awoke again, hours later. Or four rotations of water later, anyway. Three? Four. I thought. After the second flooding, I'd even begun to wonder if I'd seen the Spaniard at all. Memories of his presence in the darkness had begun to blend with a strange, spicy scent, and I no longer knew what was real and what was fully imagined.

More water came. I felt I was outside my body, watching me. I looked . . . old, I decided. No longer the girl for whom freedom was another few months of pickpocketing away. But the girl for whom freedom was forever lost.

Who am I, truly?

Nothing and no one.

The water receded. Again and again. I began to think of slipping beneath it.

CHAPTER THIRTY-FIVE

My first conscious thought as I awoke was *Voices*, and relief overcame me, the nightmares of my eyes being burned out dimming as I crashed toward consciousness. I still had my eyes! I still had my ears! They had not taken them from me yet. I was still untouched.

Bright light cascaded down, and I cried out, rasping at the pain. It was like I'd just been thrust into the sun. For a moment I thought I might be dead.

"Miss Fellowes, step back!" came the order, and I knew with a start I wasn't dead. Cecil would not be dead as well, I reasoned in my failing mind. Or if he was, he certainly wouldn't be joining me in heaven.

The man leaned forward over the pit, and the torch he carried obscured his face with a bright, impossibly harsh light, but I knew it was Cecil from just the impressions of his movement. Maybe I was becoming a better spy after all. "Attend, Miss Fellowes, and climb the ladder with haste," he ordered, as if he'd awakened me from my own bed. "You will come with us to the Queen." His voice was resolute, but even if I was disposed to argue, his next words cut me off short. "You have been summoned for a royal audience."

I stumbled up the ladder, and was briefed in transit. Once Cecil had told the Queen that I had fallen seriously ill, she had never questioned my disappearance and now only wanted to see me briefly, in her royal presence. For what reason, he did not know. But, he assured me, I would soon be returning to my cell.

They rather had to hold me up after that, I'm afraid to say.

"And Lady Amelia?" I managed when we were on our way again.

"She is not dead. Yet," Cecil replied frostily. "Your young count and the ambassadors have been closeted away in that regard, scrambling to explain her attack, and two dead Spanish guards besides." I frowned, taking that in. Moon Face and Turnip Nose were dead, but the danger still remained. "And my fellow maids?" I gasped. "Are they—are they all well?"

"Your fellow maids can be credited for this little charade," Cecil snapped, disgusted. "They have not ceased in their petitioning that you be brought before the Crown, pestering us at every chance, and daring to present their case to the Queen. They were only just short of joining you in the dungeon, so loud and long were their protestations."

I stared at him, a tiny spark of hope alighting again in my heart. "They . . . asked after me?"

"They *demanded* you, Miss Fellowes," Cecil said bitterly. "They will be dealt with accordingly."

Then just as it had when I'd been stuck into the dungeon,

everything happened too fast. Bandaged, bundled, bustled, and still reeling, I found myself a bare half hour later standing in front of the Queen in a clean gown and dry shift, my legs warm for the first time in what seemed like years. The Queen was dressed in full regalia, her black velvet gown beaded with pearls, and her glorious red hair flowing freely beneath her crown of rubies and gold. Walsingham was already there, looking like he'd just eaten nettles.

Cecil had made my position clear. I was on borrowed time. He and Walsingham had produced me only after the Queen had assured them I could return to my seclusion once she had seen me. The thought of returning back down into that hole was more than I could think about.

So I didn't think about it.

"Miss Fellowes, thank you for joining us," Walsingham said from beside the Queen. On the other side of her, my four fellow maids stood and stared at me. I struggled not to cry. "We are grateful that your illness has lightened sufficiently for this brief visit."

He smiled earnestly at me, as if he hadn't threatened to destroy my life in six different ways over the past—how long? I didn't even know how many days I had been in that hole.

I curtsied briefly to him on shaking legs, then turned to the Queen with another curtsy, this one full and deep. "I am honored to be requested into your presence," I said to her, "and gladdened beyond all measure to see you."

Something in my voice must have given more away than I'd intended, for as I straightened, the Queen regarded me curiously. She watched me with her dark, steady eyes, and my first and most powerful thought was: *She knows.*

"You are quite recovered, Meg?" she asked carefully, and I could only nod. She knew.

Knew that I had seen her, that night in her bedchamber. Knew that I knew her secrets. Knew that I had been punished for keeping my silence. Knew that I had protected her.

"I have never felt stronger, Your Grace," I said. I was *not* going back down into that hole. They'd have to kill me cleanly this time.

She nodded in return. "Walsingham tells me you have been confined to seclusion since Lady Amelia's . . . injury." Her eyes were watchful, questioning. The eyes of a monarch who'd dared risk her very kingdom for the pursuit of love. Had that been only a few days ago? It seemed like a lifetime. "Is that true?"

"No one could speak more clearly to my whereabouts of the past few days than Sir Francis, Your Grace," I said, my words unintentionally sharp. I felt Cecil's slightest movement behind me, the faintest warning breath. "But I am quite recovered. You can be assured of that."

"Good," she said, sitting back. "I am well glad to hear it. And to celebrate your recovery, I am pleased to share with you that the court will be graced with a very special production this evening. It will be just the thing to restore your spirits." Now she beamed at me, and I blinked at her in surprise. I noted Walsingham's and Cecil's stares upon her. This was a surprise to them as well.

"Your Grace?" I managed.

She smiled regally. "The pall that lingers over us with Lady Amelia's injury, even in the wake of the successful masque, is too dour to be endured. I have already granted some joy to the court, and now we shall have more, with the pleasure of your friends among the Golden Rose acting troupe."

My what? It was all I could do not to gape. The other maids just stood there, grinning at me. Even Jane, whose eyes were sharp and clear, and whose gaze was fixed upon me like she thought I would break at any moment, smiled.

The Queen was obviously waiting for me to say something, and I jumped into the breach. "I cannot tell you how pleased I am to hear it," I said, my mind scrambling for purchase. The Golden Rose acting troupe—here in Windsor? For a command performance? "The Golden Rose are renowned throughout all of England. You will not be disappointed."

"I am sure you are correct." The Queen sat back with satisfaction. "You will watch them as well," she decreed, "from a position of honor by my side."

No! My thoughts flew to Jane and the shadowy Spaniard. I had to proceed as if Jane—as if all of them—were still at risk. "Your Grace is far too kind. But I could not allow myself to rest in your company, when I should be serving you completely."

All eyes in the small room turned to me. The Queen's in sudden, curious expectation; Cecil's and Walsingham's in patent suspicion; and those of my fellow Maids of Honor in stunned surprise.

"What are you talking about, Meg?" the Queen asked.

"While I was . . . confined for my protection, I had the occasion to learn of a plot against the Crown—foiled once in the affair of Lady Amelia, but not yet put to rest."

The silence in the room was rich and filled with possibility, and I took the tiniest moment to revel in it. Cecil and

Walsingham had no idea what I was talking about, and the thought gave me far more pleasure than anything should have.

Perhaps I could excel at this game of spying after all. But only if I could stay ahead of my enemies. All of them.

"What are you talking about?" Walsingham finally demanded. His skin had gone faintly red around the edges of his mouth and eyes, as if his incredible fortitude was the only thing keeping a rush of anger from suffusing his face. It was quite . . . wonderful, actually, and I favored him with a gentle smile, which seemed to render him even more apoplectic. "I say, explain yourself," he blustered.

"Sir Francis." The Queen waved an airy hand, but her tone was more amused than disapproving. "We can but let Meg speak. You and Cecil have not brought a name to me for consideration, and Lady Amelia cannot name her attacker or her fellow conspirators in her current state. We have handpicked this maid for exactly this purpose, have we not? Perhaps we can be enlightened." She flicked her gaze to me, imperious and expectant. *I don't know what you are doing,* her eyes seemed to say. *But I know what you have already done.*

I straightened. "I was visited in my . . . confinement," I said, not able to resist the hesitation before the word, "by a man dressed all in black, whose voice and manner were completely muffled, both by his heavy clothing and, I confess, by my— How did you refer to it, Sir Francis?" I glanced to him but raised a hand at the same time. "Ah, yes, my delicate condition. However, I was not so ill as to not understand his purpose. My night visitor believed—quite wrongly, I should say—that I had gathered intelligence on you, Your Grace."

"On me!" The Queen's eyes flashed, and I held my chin

high. This was the ultimate gamble, and if Jane's life had not hung in the balance, I'm not sure I would have tried it. But Lady Amelia's injury had not been enough, and the next step for the Spaniard could be only death. It had to stop—and it could not stop if I was kept under lock and chain in a prison of Walsingham's and Cecil's devising. I needed freedom to move—to think—and to act.

And this was how I was getting it.

"Yes, Your Grace," I said smoothly. "I implored him to see reason, that I could not know anything about you that would be of interest to him, but he refused to believe me. He said if I did not provide him the information, another of your attendants—this time a maid—would be harmed. I urged him to give me time—in truth to come up with some falsehood that would satisfy him until I could seek the counsel of Sir William or Sir Francis." And here I favored them again with the sunniest smile I could muster. Walsingham watched me once more without expression, but Cecil's eyes looked like they might burst forth from his head. "And he agreed. Alas, I then, ah, fell terribly ill and cannot say what happened next, for I was next roused by Cecil, to bring me to Your Grace this evening—this morning . . . whatever time it may be."

"But you did not give him information about the Queen," Walsingham said, his doubt plain. "How can we believe that?"

I folded my hands over my skirts. "By the mere fact that I had no information to give. So he is, by all rights, forced to remain unsatisfied."

The Queen upon her throne straightened righteously.

"Then we are at an impasse?" Walsingham asked, the words a question, not a statement.

"Nay, Sir Francis, we are not. For I have a plan," I said.

Cecil made a rude noise, and the Queen snapped her fingers. "Leave off, Sir William. You have trained the girl, have you not?"

"Yes," he began. "But—"

The Queen cut him off. "Then let her speak."

I nodded. "First, in all truth, you must protect your attendants." I waved a hand to my team of spies. "Not us; you have taught us well enough. But your other maids should be cloistered, protected during this evening's performance. The only girls available as target should be the five of us."

The Queen looked at me sharply, and then at the four maids at her side. "You would use yourselves as bait?"

"There is no better way to ensure the safety of your other maids and ladies, Your Grace, and your safety as well."

She took a long pause, regarding me. Then she nodded once. "Agreed. And what will you do to capture this traitor?"

And there it was. I felt Cecil and Walsingham bristling, but I could not allow them to poke holes into a plan so recently hatched in my mind, particularly as it had been conceived under such duress. I could use the presentation of the Golden Rose to catch a murderer. In the midst of their amazing performance, the shadowy Spaniard would not be able to resist making an attack at the heart of the Queen's court. If he could take down a maid of honor with so many eyes watching—and get away with it—he would strike fear into the very heart of England.

I would give him that chance.

"Permission to speak to you in confidence, Your Grace?" I asked. The Queen's eyebrows shot up, but she beckoned me forward.

I reached her side, and bent to whisper into her ear. Whether the Queen could see evidence of my time in the dungeon, whether she knew that Walsingham and Cecil had been the agents of my downfall, I could not tell. But she listened as I spoke to her, in low and urgent tones, lengthening out my speech to an acceptable piece to give her time and space to nod, smile, and meet my eyes directly. The Queen did not interrupt me, nor did she ask for clarifications. She only had one request, in fact.

"Make sure you succeed," she ordered.

CHAPTER THIRTY-SIX

The silence that remained in the Queen's Privy Chamber after the Queen, Cecil, Walsingham, and all the guards swept out . . . was deafening. It seemed like so much time had passed since I'd been pulled out of that dungeon, and yet it had only been—what? Days? Hours?

"What is today?" I asked to the wall behind the now empty throne.

"It's Wednesday, Meg." And the voice gave me courage to move. To act. And to begin again.

Slowly I turned to see them, as if for the first time. Otherworldly, sensitive Sophia; brilliant, loyal Anna; beautiful, shrewd Beatrice; and brave, broken Jane. I found myself amazed that I had ever called them by such limiting nicknames as Seer, Scholar, Belle, and Blade.

Now they were so much more than that.

Now they were . . . my friends.

"Hello again," I whispered.

And just like that the space between us disappeared, and I felt Anna's warm arms encircle me, then Beatrice's surprisingly sturdy embrace. Then I sensed the fluttering warmth of Sophia. And finally, the last but not the least of us, Jane put her hand on my shoulder. Powerful, lost Jane. Her touch grounded me. For just a moment, I sagged against them all, exhausted.

"I can't . . . thank you enough for setting me free," I said, my words little more than a murmur, and wet with tears I dare not shed. "You don't . . . You can't know what it means to me, that you would do such a thing, take such a risk."

"Oh, pish."

Anna broke free first. "I have something for you. Something you look like you need, if your face is any indication."

She began rooting about in her skirts, and I shook my head, hard. I had no time for tonics or tinctures. We needed to prepare for the Golden Rose's performance. We needed to plan something—anything. And quickly.

"We can't— I mean, we must talk," I said.

Sophia reached out for me again, her gaze somehow much stronger than the last time I'd seen her. "I saw too many things when you were taken from us," she said, her voice strangely resonant. "Some that I could speak of . . . some I prayed were only my own fears."

I grasped her hand. Held it. "I am well, Sophia," I said. "You need not fear for me." I glanced at Jane, who shook her head slightly. She still had not told Sophia about her father. We could not find the words yet to share such life-changing news with her. We would. When we were all safe.

Safe.

I needed to think!

I turned to them, my heart beginning to hammer. "The killer will be here this night, at the presentation—the performance of the Golden Rose. He will be here, and he will be hunting us. We have . . ." I stopped. Swallowed. The gravity of it all struck me anew, and my throat suddenly felt as if it were closing up. Fatigue swept over me again. I grimaced, steeling myself to continue, but Anna gave a relieved "Finally!" and held up her prize. "Here it is!"

I frowned at her, recognizing the thin volume immediately. "My grandfather's book?"

"Yes," she said, looking pleased as she handed over the little tome. "It turns out you come by your spying skills honestly, Meg Fellowes. And here in Windsor, you are but coming home."

I snorted, opening the book and paging through its stiff pages, filled with garbled words I still could not understand. "My grandfather was a bard, Anna. And an actor. And, perhaps best, a thief," I acknowledged, trying to smile a little. "But he didn't know anything about spying."

"He may not have." Anna shrugged, but she couldn't quell her grin. The other girls were beaming too now. "But your parents did."

That stopped me. "What?"

"Those picklocks of yours, pure gold?" Jane asked. "Rafe told us they bear King Henry's seal."

"Well, he said that, but—"

"And your grandfather would never let your troop perform in major cities?"

"Well, no, but— What is this about?"

Beatrice clasped her hands together. "It's almost—but not quite—as exciting as my betrothal."

"Your what?" Had the whole world gone mad?

Anna laughed, then reached forward and tapped the book. "This, Meg, is one very long letter. A letter from your parents. Written in code. About their work with the king."

"The king."

"King Henry. Elizabeth's father. It's all in there. They wanted you to know their story, but they had to flee." Anna hugged herself, in love with her own tale. "They knew they could not keep you safe, in the end, and you were just a babe. They left you with your grandfather and asked him to give you the book when it was safe."

"Safe?" It had never been safe enough for Grandfather, apparently. Another thought struck me, hard and fell. "Are they dead?"

It was Jane who spoke into the sudden quiet. Jane, who knew more of death than any of us. "Don't think of it as death. They are travelers to a distant land is all," she said, her voice matter-of-fact. "You will meet them again, when your journey here is done."

I nodded, but I suddenly couldn't see. My eyes were covered with a dull grey film. "A distant land," I whispered. And I knew her to be right. They had passed from this world to the next. An emptiness opened up within me. I think it had always been there, but now it had a name. *A distant land.*

I folded my hands over the book. There would be time to read it later.

There would be time for everything.

After.

I blinked, hard, surprised to find my face was wet. "Marie's killer will be there tonight," I said. "He won't stop at just harming Lady Amelia. It's not enough for him. He demands another death."

Jane snorted. "He should be careful what he wishes for."

"We have to find a way to capture him."

Anna pointed to the book. "And so we shall. It's in your blood." My fingers tightened on the book, and I looked down at it again. *My parents* . . . A recent memory tugged at me, an old woman at the edge of the Presence Chamber, startled to see me at court again. "Again," as if she remembered me, from a long, long time ago. Had she known my mother? Could I seek her out? The thought was almost too much to bear.

"How did you know I was imprisoned?" I asked, trying to keep my voice steady. "How did you free me?"

Jane answered. "On any other occasion," she said wryly, "Cecil would have been proud. For Sophia found you with her visions, Anna thought of the plan to use the Golden Rose as an excuse to get you out of that hole, and Beatrice put the plan into motion. Well, Beatrice, Anna, and Anna's young man."

"Her young man?" I blinked at them both. "And you're betrothed?" I asked Beatrice. "Lord Cavanaugh, I presume?"

Beatrice fluttered her right hand at me. It was sporting a heavy gold ring with a ruby the size of a robin's egg. Though not every man pledged his suit with a betrothal ring, Lord Cavanaugh apparently wanted to claim his prize for all to see. "The Queen needed some good news to counter Lady Amelia's sudden . . . indisposition," she said. "I was handy."

"It helped that you'd badgered the good lord into a frenzy with your flirtation with Alasdair MacLeod," Jane observed dryly.

"Alasdair MacLeod?" I remembered the roguish Scot, with his thick beard and broad shoulders and hungry eyes. "But he's so unkempt!"

"And *big*," Anna sighed.

"And foul-tempered," Beatrice agreed grimly. "But at least he has the manners of a pig."

"And the tentacles of an octopus," Jane gibed back. "Lord Cavanaugh took one look at MacLeod monopolizing your time at the masque, and he made sure he was first in line to the Queen when she was looking for a distraction, with a ring for you and a coffer of gold for her."

Beatrice held out her hand, admiring it, all thoughts of the offending Scotsman gone. "My Lord Cavanaugh did do well, didn't he?" She sighed. "It was almost as exciting as finding Meg's old sweetheart."

That brought me up short and I fought to focus. "My what?" Ever since I'd crawled out of that pit, I'd had the feeling that the world was working at a pace far faster than I could manage. I looked from her to Anna. "My what?" I asked again.

Anna beamed at her role in the plot. "Chris Riley helped too—the vicar's son? He lives in Windsor proper, near the center of town. When Beatrice determined to find your acting troupe, I asked him first!"

"As if she needed an excuse to talk to the boy," Beatrice teased, and Anna blushed.

"He not only knew of your acting troupe, he knew where they performed!" she said excitedly. "His father is friends with the owner of the Fox and Hound, who'd been crowing about the Golden Rose for weeks by the time we asked about them. He took us to meet them! At an inn!"

I laughed at her excitement. How bold a walk to an inn must have seemed for a member of the court. "But what did you say?" I asked. "How in the world did you get this arranged?"

"Beatrice handled everything," Anna gushed. "She spoke with Master James and told him you'd *begged* her to come fetch him to Windsor, to perform for the Queen. And then she told the Queen that it would be such a terrible shame for you to miss the performance, that surely she could bid you to appear. And so she did!"

I'd stopped well before the end of Anna's tale. "You told Master James what?"

"Well, he *is* quite handsome, Meg," Anna said, her eyes wide and filled with romance, her favorite subject. "And he seemed quite taken with the idea. I don't think Rafe will be as pleased."

"He won't," Sophia chimed in. I looked at her in alarm, and she giggled. "A joke."

I rolled my eyes, but it didn't change the issue. "You told Master James that I'd *begged* for him to come?"

Beatrice shrugged. "I could hardly say you were a spy being interrogated in the dungeon. I wanted him to be excited about coming here, and to flatter the Queen outrageously, not accuse her of torturing one of her Maids of Honor."

I opened my mouth, then shut it again. Beatrice had a point, and she continued to press it home. "And I needed Master James to have a reason to ask for you specifically to watch the performance, so that it would seem the height of awkwardness if Cecil and Walsingham didn't produce you." She shook her head. "I think the Queen was looking for an excuse, honestly. She agreed before I'd even gotten out the words. I don't think she believed Cecil's explanation that you were merely . . . indisposed."

I frowned. "And Master James agreed to this . . . production. He didn't question it?"

"On the contrary, he was quite accommodating!" Anna enthused as Beatrice regarded me with amusement. "Beatrice was very convincing."

"I'm sure," I said dryly, and Beatrice grinned.

"Master James is actually an enigma unto himself," Beatrice said archly. "I would swear I've seen him before—or if not him then a relative of his. And I can assure you it wasn't in the open streets of Windsor."

"What are you saying?" I asked. "How can you know him?"

Jane chuckled. "Beatrice is convinced that your Master James is the by-blow of one of the highest families in the land. Don't get her started, or she'll begin hauling out enough family trees to seed a forest."

"Mark my words, I'm right," Beatrice insisted. "I know I've seen that bone structure before. He is not just some dockmaster's whelp, I am telling you plain."

"That's impossible," I said firmly, and Beatrice just laughed.

"Everyone comes from somewhere, Meg," she said. "Even you." She pointed to the book. "As we have all learned."

Who am I, truly? I tightened my hands on my grandfather's—no, my *parents'* book.

I shook my head to clear it. It was too much for me to take in—the Queen knowing why I'd been held prisoner, my fellow maids gaining my freedom, Master James thinking I'd begged for him to do *anything*, Beatrice convinced that James was some aristocrat's unclaimed son. Beatrice's betrothal. Rafe . . . That thought jogged another memory in my dungeon-addled mind. "Speaking of family histories, what of you?" I asked. "Did you talk to Rafe about his ring?"

Beatrice blinked at me. "His what? What ring?"

I grimaced. "The ring I gave you last . . . the other . . . whenever it was I saw you. What is today again?"

"Wednesday," Sophia said helpfully. "But what ring?"

Beatrice shook her head. "You gave me no ring—"

"I put it in the slashed lining of your sleeve, when I embraced you that night. When you came in and I was with Cecil."

She frowned. "You did?"

And suddenly I knew. I almost laughed at Rafe's audacity. "What happened, exactly, after you left me?" I asked.

"I returned to the Queen and told her you were being attended to by Cecil."

"And you saw no one?"

"No!" Beatrice said too quickly, then she paused. "I mean, not really."

I shook my head. *Damn you, Rafe*. "You saw Rafe." It wasn't a question. It didn't need to be.

"Only for a moment!" Beatrice protested. "He came up to me just outside the antechamber where you were being held. I just turned and—he was there."

"He has a skill with that," I said dryly. "And then what happened?"

"That seems hardly the question—"

"God's teeth." I looked up at the ceiling. "He lifted the ring from your sleeve."

"What *ring*?" Beatrice demanded.

"Why would he do that?" Jane asked from the side of the room. She seemed to be enjoying herself.

I shook my head. "Because he could." I looked at Beatrice. "He had a ring that I nicked from him, Beatrice, because it looked like your family's jewelry, same stone, same odd robin's nest gold setting. I wanted to show it to you." *He'd wanted me to take it.* "Apparently he saw me giving it to you, though I can't imagine how." *And now he has it back.* Insufferable Spaniard.

"But I don't understand," Beatrice said. "How did he come by a ring with that stone? They've been in my family for generations."

"He claims *his* mother received it when she was serving as a maid of honor to Queen Catherine of Aragon," I said. "So . . . maybe your mother must have given it to his mother?"

Beatrice shot me a look. "Have you met my mother? She wouldn't give another woman the time of day, let alone an heirloom."

Her eyes went wide at the same time that Jane said, "Uh-oh."

"He dared to send our treasure overseas?" Beatrice breathed. "That insufferable goat!"

"What?" asked Anna, her eyes wide. "What?" But Sophia knew, and her face seemed suddenly flushed with untold secrets. *What else did Sophia know?*

"That goat!" Beatrice said again, and despite my chagrin at Beatrice's mortification, I felt just slightly vindicated. This almost made up for Beatrice telling Troupe Master James that I'd *begged* to have him come to the castle.

Almost.

Beatrice pressed her hands to either side of her head. "Another slight. Another indiscretion. I thought we were done with him ruining my life," she muttered. "I thought . . . Lord Cavanaugh's mother would die . . . I will kill my father when I see him next. I will kill him dead."

"Have you, ah, seen Rafe?" I asked Jane as Beatrice got that faraway, calculating look on her face, undoubtedly plotting her father's untimely demise.

Jane frowned at me. "Cecil didn't tell you?" She sighed at my blank stare. "Since the moment Cecil took hold of you, Rafe's been secreted in council with the Spanish ambassadors." She tilted her head. "Though with tonight's production, he may be freed at last."

Sophia rustled from the corner. "When Rafe sees James, Meg, he may ask for your hand as well," she said. We all gaped at her, and her eyes flew wide. "No! No, that was not a prediction, I swear! Just a conclusion—truly, Meg, don't look at me like that!"

I flushed hot. "First, I have no need of a husband. Second, there is nothing between James and me," I insisted. I turned resolutely back to Jane. "What did they conclude about the moon-faced Spaniard's death?"

Jane's smile was approving. "That you killed him. Bravo, by the way."

"Me!" I blurted, unsure if I'd heard her correctly. "They believe that?"

"Everyone is doing their level best to act like they do, including the Spaniards, who are willing to concede that you may have been accosted and acted out of self-preservation. And if you didn't kill the man on purpose, then you *accidentally* stabbed him and he gave up the will to live. Cecil let slip that they discovered arsenic on his tongue. He apparently had a pinch of it at the ready."

"Arsenic." The Spaniard had not put arsenic into his own mouth. *Rafe, what are you about?*

"A moment here?" Anna asked briskly, drawing our attention. She had sketched out diagrams of the Queen's Presence Chamber on parchment and was making notations in the margin. "If we have to catch a killer in a few short hours, which is by far our most important assignment to date, we'd best be creating a plan." She eyed me. "I assume you have something in mind?"

I tightened my hold on my parents' diary. A love letter from my spying parents . . . to their spying daughter.

I straightened, feeling the strength finally flow back into my body. We could do this. We *would* do this. "I do have an idea, actually," I said.

CHAPTER THIRTY-SEVEN

Two hours later I knew *everything* I had to do and *exactly* how I should do it, but none of that eased my mind.

I made my way through the castle alone toward the quadrangle of the Upper Ward, trying to tell myself I wasn't actually fleeing the weight of the place. My head was ringing with too many plans, too many possibilities. And a nearly ceaseless stream of thoughts about my parents. Had they walked these same hallways? Had they seen the baby princess that I was now sworn to protect as Queen?

Was this truly my place, now?

I'd asked Anna for a special favor, to go fetch Master James to meet me in the Lower Ward. I'd even explained why I wanted to speak to him, but that still didn't quite stamp out the look of starry-eyed excitement Anna had turned on me before fleeing the room. God bless her, Anna would never stop looking for romance in every corner of the castle, even romance that was terribly ill-advised. Despite my heavy heart, I smiled to myself as I approached the wide doors of Windsor.

Then I stepped into the sunlight.

And almost burst into tears.

I'd been released from the dungeon hours earlier . . . but I'd been in that accursed hole for nearly a full week. It seemed like it had been years, however, since I'd felt the sun on my face, my hands. It was a fine August day, with the mist long since burned off and hours yet until the night drew down, and yet the air seemed filled with a fey energy, like there was magic sparking somewhere in the castle, an alchemist at his wheel. It was the most beautiful day of my life.

The Upper Ward was all but deserted, and I made my way down the quadrangle and through the Norman Gate to the Middle Ward without incident. I slipped into the Lower Ward, warming to the noise and life that surrounded me. It was Wednesday, market day, and the stalls in the Lower Ward were teeming with people. The smells of cooking meat and succulent spices filled the air, and I found my stride lengthening, my fingers twitching, the world striving to be once more at my fingertips despite all of the horrors of the last six days. *Spices . . . Spices . . . What was I trying to recall?*

Master James was to meet me in the sitting area of the Dean's Cloister, away from the market day festivities of the main ward. I just had to get to him and explain what I needed, and I was sure he would help. A rush of pleasant certainty flowed through me with that thought. Of course he would help; he was the troupe master. That was what he did.

I stepped into the marketplace, and was immediately caught up short. There was an odd energy here, a sense of characters being out of place, of a trap waiting to be sprung, and I frowned, trying to understand it. The townspeople of Windsor were all perfectly placed in their stalls of gaily colored ribbons and cloths, meats and sweets, so what was—

Then I turned the corner. Leaning against the first stall, plainly waiting for me . . . was Rafe.

Why did simply seeing him give me such a start? And why was I so glad when he stalked toward me like a victor claiming his spoils, when he took my arm with assurance and stared at me with a curious fire in his eyes?

Because I'm an idiot, that's why.

"What ho, Miss Fellowes, well met," Rafe said smoothly, the perfect gentleman as he turned me down the lane between the market stalls, forcing me to match his stride. I glanced at the cloisters, knowing my interview was drawing near with Master James, but unwilling to leave Rafe. Not quite yet.

"You're prepared to tell me everything?" he asked with deceptive calm. "From the moment I left you until now?"

"I am," I said, and he relaxed the tiniest bit.

"Then by all means, begin."

And I did tell him. Most of it. When I had finished, however, his face had darkened to a grim scowl. "It was all I could do not to free you myself, when Sophia told me what she'd seen. If your friends' gambit had not succeeded, we would already be gone from here." He sighed, a wealth of pain and frustration in the sound. "This is not over, no matter what happens today. This is not over."

"Rafe—" I began, but he cut me off.

"Anna told me this plan of yours," he said flatly. "I don't like it. I particularly don't like you dressing as Jane, and she as you."

"If the villain is looking for me, then Jane dressed as me

makes perfect sense," I said. "She's the better fighter. You know that as well as I." And if Jane was to be the target, as I feared, then she would be as far away from harm as I could set her, while still being close enough to give aid to me should I need her blade.

"You'll still be armed, I assume?"

"With Jane's own blades. They go with the costume. Though, mark my words, her knives will cause me more damage than any Spaniard could." I shook my head. The wrist blade was the worst, constantly nicking the base of my palm when I'd tried wearing Jane's weapons under her clothes. "And I won't be walking much, lest her wig falls off my head." I grinned to allay Rafe's fears. "I plan to stand rooted to the spot, trying to see everything."

Rafe nodded, and once again, I was struck with his seriousness. Yes, of course, I was in danger—we were all in danger—but that was almost to be expected. Why did he seem so . . . intent? "Are you well?" I asked carefully. "Those men were your own countrymen."

"Those men were no friends to Spain," he said briskly. "They were operating on their own, without official sanction of any kind. Any actions of mine taken to end the threat to your Queen—which shall never be proven, mind you—were met only with relief from the Spanish delegation."

"Even from de Feria?"

"Of course," Rafe said smoothly.

I quirked a glance at him. "So, um . . . you're a hero?"

He snorted. "I live to serve. I was sent here to stop anyone who would besmirch the reputation of King Philip, and stop them I did. But my work is not yet done. Cecil and Walsingham—and their guards—will be standing at the ready to come in?" he asked, changing the subject neatly.

"Yes. We can't have too many guards in the Presence Chamber, or it won't look right. But they will be lined up behind the right partition, against the wall. Which is where Jane will be as well." I shook my head. "I want this done."

"We all want this done," Rafe agreed. "How are your combat skills in tight quarters?"

I rolled my eyes. "Trust me, we will not need to find out. I will leave the fighting to the guards."

We argued back and forth before he finally took his leave of me, scowling at my insistence to be alone with my thoughts. I waved him off, and his elegant figure created a ripple of sensation through the market. After allowing myself a few additional moments to watch him cut a swath through a knot of sighing girls, I finally turned away.

Suddenly gloriously happy, I grabbed a meat pie from one of the stalls—I *was* famished, after all—and paid with the Queen's coin, happy to return some of her ever shifting wealth back to the villagers who adored her so. I looked into the blank, serene face of the woman who took my money as if I were seeing a merchant's wife for the first time. There was so much energy in the courtyard—so much noise and color and life!

I bit into the steaming pastry and wondered if I would ever fully recover from my days and nights in the watery dungeon of Windsor Castle. A chill stole along my skin even at the memory of it, and I resolutely shoved the question away. A thought for another time.

I entered the Dean's Cloister a few moments later, finishing the last of my small meal. I liked this place far better than the Horseshoe Cloister, I decided. That was a place for men of God; I felt unworthy there. But here, in this place of scholars and lore, I felt almost at home.

The lightest touch brushed my side, and I whirled to my right, feeling the pickpocket slide away—

And there was no one there.

"Looking for someone?"

It was a voice I knew all too well, laced with laughter. I turned to my left, and scowled at Master James.

"How long have you been waiting?"

"Long enough to see your exchange with your young friend in the Lower Ward." James laughed, the sound throaty and deep, his white teeth flashing. "So there's an admirer for my Meg?"

James's beard was closely trimmed, and he looked almost refined, with his dark chestnut hair curling against the collar of his doublet, which was stylishly slashed with alternating strips of black and silver. I blinked.

He was more than *almost* refined, I realized. His stockings were spun charcoal-grey silk, his shoes polished black leather. Even the hammered silver amulet that he traditionally wore under his tunic was out on display, now suspended by a fine black velvet cord. He could have passed for any nobleman in the court.

"Where did you get that clothing?" I asked, aghast.

"What, you expected me to come pay homage to the Queen in nothing but rags? I'm not a complete rogue, Meg."

I blinked hard again, trying not to stare. He could play a courtier anywhere, doing anything, and suddenly I realized how very little I knew of Master James. Where had he come from? "I never said— I mean, I never meant—" I shook my head, trying to reconcile this image of the perfect—and perfectly lazy—nobleman with the laughing, calloused-palm troupe master who had carried babies across flooding streams, built stage props out of falling-down barns, and chased down geese for dinner when the day's haul had not been enough.

"What are you about, Meg?" James asked, interrupting my thoughts. "You have more energy than a dormouse at dinnertime, and anyone who knows you will see it." Then he took my arm in his, as if he were a gentleman and not at all a troupe master and thief, and proceeded to escort me around the cloister. I tried to completely ignore the fact of him being so near to me, and focus on what I needed to say.

"I need your help, Master James," I said, and I felt the ripple of tension tighten his grip on my arm. An answering shimmer of awareness flowed through me, and I forced myself to steady my nerves.

"Anything you need, Meg. You know that," he said, his words warm and resolute.

All . . . right. "I—will be drawing out an unsavory character this night, who believes me to have information to sell." I drew in a breath. "He is targeting the Queen's maids for harm. I would hide all of the Queen's attendants away, but their complete absence would be noticed."

James slanted me a look. "How many maids are we speaking of?"

I nodded and smiled to a passing lady, who was doing everything she could not to ogle James. "I need six girls to be represented, as it happens. All from the ages of twelve to eighteen."

"Stout or slender? Tall or short? Or a mix such that a casual observer wouldn't notice?"

"A mix. I rather get the feeling we're not noticed at all by the nobility. Certainly not the younger maids. And none of the girls you've met, my friends, are a concern. I worry more for others."

"Yes, I rather think your Miss Knowles can handle herself." Ignoring my pointed look, James considered further. "I've seen the others of your company strolling through the wards. The bookish one wouldn't notice she was being attacked until it was far too late, I think. And the little one—who stands always at the edge of the conversation?"

I raised my brows. "Sophia? Dark hair, large eyes?"

"Her." He nodded. "Keep those two out of the fray. They are of this world, but not in it."

I frowned at the odd turn of phrase, but I took no issue with the directive. It had been ever thus with James. His stage management, whether for his actors or his thieves, was flawless. "Agreed," I said. "Jane and Beatrice and I will be in the main crowd. We just need a few others to round out the cast."

"Jane. The fierce one with the long stride. I got the sense she would as soon kill a man as talk to him." He nodded. "She would be an asset in any fight. Which turns us to that issue as well." And just that quickly, the tension returned to his body. We took another turn around the courtyard, and I forced myself to smile and nod, once more a proper English lady, out for a summer's walk.

"What is it you expect of this unsavory villain, who would target maids instead of men?" he asked when we were out of earshot again.

"I suspect he would hurt one of my friends, if we give him the opportunity. I'd rather his focus be on me."

James grimaced. "Of course you would." He tilted his head, angling it toward me. "They don't have guards in this place to do your fighting?" he asked in exasperation. "Or dungeons to hold enemies to the Crown?"

I smiled grimly, the shadow of the past several days catching up to me. Somehow James must have seen, for he stopped short.

"Meg," he said, turning me to face him directly. He stared closely at me, and if he saw anything in the pallor of my skin, the sunken-ness of my eyes, I could not have gainsaid him. "Tell me what is going on, plainly. What is this place you have come to? What is it they are asking you to do?"

His concern overwhelmed me for a moment, and an unwelcome rush of emotion rose within me, threatening to spill forth.

"That's really not at issue," I said gently. "It is the place I must be, for now. And the thing I must do."

Darkness flashed across his face. "We could get you out of here, if you wish it."

"James," I said, and I reached out my hand, touching his arm. A curious sort of warmth danced up my fingers, and I pulled my hand away from him even as he glanced at me in surprise. "What I wish is for your help in ensuring the safety of the Queen and her court."

Another moment passed as he stared at me, just a beat too long. Then finally James relaxed. "And I am just to sit by and watch? What of the young Spaniard who can't seem to leave your side?" He laughed softly. "He watches you even now, from the shadows."

He does? I steeled myself not to look. "He will be in the crowd. But he is too quick to rise to the fight, and it would not be wise for him to do so this eve."

"I see." James huffed a short laugh, then grinned at me. "Perhaps I should court *you* this eventide, then, and not the Queen? That will keep the Spaniard's mind off mischief, I wager."

I stared at him, my cheeks flaming. "Master James," I said severely. "Don't even think about courting me, not even in jest." *Which of course it would be. Would always be. Of course.* "There is serious danger within these wall this night. Distraction would not serve."

"Then I will play my part." James's voice was suddenly gruff. "But I'll watch out for you, and your other maids besides. You're all too pretty to be endangered." He winked at me, all levity again. "Especially your Jane Morgan, though she has not the sense to see it."

I raised my brows, remembering his earlier words. "When did you see Jane?"

"At my audience with your Queen. I turned as someone entered the room, thinking it would be you. Instead I almost felt as if a knife had been placed against my throat, though the girl was still half a chamber away."

I smiled. That did sound like Jane. "You would do well to remember that, Master James, and stay well clear."

He laughed. "I'll do well to remember it, and stay well close, I think."

"Just keep your wits about you and flirt with the Queen, not her maids, Master James."

He gave a labored sigh. "As you wish," he grumbled. "We'll have everyone in place when you arrive."

CHAPTER THIRTY-EIGHT

As in all things, Master James was true to his word, a master at preparing a production. By the time I arrived at the Presence Chamber, I was astonished at how perfectly everything had been arranged.

Rather than erecting a simple rectangular stage upon which the troupe would perform their play, Troupe Master James had chosen to build an octagonal platform, upon which actors were positioning themselves as if to play to the crowd from all sides—while still never turning their backs upon the Queen. *Best of fortune in achieving that miracle, James.* I smiled despite myself. Somehow I knew he would pull it off.

The Queen had not yet processed in, but there were several ladies-in-waiting now arranged on either side of her throne. I looked into the crowd and immediately saw my own group—Beatrice and Jane (dressed passably as me) conferring in one corner, Sophia and Anna nearer to where the Queen would be seated. Other young ladies of patent nobility, all round-eyed and excited, were milling through the crowd, looking every inch like the young maids of honor to the Queen.

I recognized them all, even in their wigs. I had not been

gone from the Golden Rose so long as all that, I was pleased to see. Martha and Gwendolyn, not-so-little Tommy Farrow (aghast at his girl's costume, I was sure) and Lettice, even little Sarah, who was but twelve years old. Each of them were outfitted in gowns that looked like they had come from the royal holdings, and perhaps had. I wondered how many of those gowns would be "mistakenly" secreted out of the castle should any amount of melee ensue this evening.

Not that there would be any melee, of course. It was my task to ensure we would capture the murderous Spaniard and give him over to the guards without anyone being the wiser. I'd promised the Queen no less.

According to our plan, the castle servants had set up grand tapestry hangings to surround the stage and crowd, creating a room within a room inside the Presence Chamber. If the Queen noticed the similarity to her own cloth chamber she'd constructed in Saint George's Hall, I prayed she would not mention it.

Behind the right edge of tapestry walls at the edge of the Queen's throne, a dozen guardsmen were already assembled. That side would be where Jane would stand, and I suspected Master James would be drawn to that side of the crowd as well.

After all, Jane was disguised as me, a fact that Master James did not yet realize.

I was standing on the left edge of the tapestry walls, facing the throne, near the servants' entrance to the Presence Chamber. From this vantage point, I could see the entire room, while noting who came in and out through the servants' entrance. Servants would be milling through the crowd with food and wine, and it would not have been reasonable to shut the entrance closed. In addition, guards at the servants' door would raise suspicion. Accordingly, I was to provide early warning to Cecil and Walsingham, who would be directly in my line of vision, should anyone suspicious enter the room that way.

Which assumed I'd know "suspicious" when I saw it.

I thought back to the shadowy man above me in the dungeon. He had not moved much, but he'd not held himself completely still, either. There was, in truth, a strong possibility that I would recognize him should he move among the crowd. I tried to comfort myself with that.

The Queen arrived in such shocking splendor that I found myself staring. Again. No matter how many times I saw Her Grace, she never failed to astound me.

First, a small group of ladies-in-waiting advanced in front of her, their gowns of pure white sparkling in the candlelight, and their hair hooded in pristine white as well, like priestesses to a goddess. Then the goddess herself arrived.

"Goddess" was not far from the truth. The Queen's gown this night was of an indigo blue so deep, it might almost have been black. The coloring made her fair skin shine, as it caused her glorious red hair, piled high upon her head and beset with glittering jewels, to look like a coronet of stars. She held herself with such backbreaking pride that all who watched her were nearly agape, though most of them had seen this woman every day for the past several months.

She was our Elizabeth.

She was our Queen.

Let anyone forget it at his peril.

The Queen reached her place and turned, settling in her

throne and leaning forward, eager for the play to begin. She surveyed the room with her cool, clear gaze, and I felt that gaze linger upon me. A wealth of satisfaction, power, and excitement poured into that glance.

And in that flash, I knew that once again she had not been fooled, by either Beatrice's gambit or mine.

She knew that the sudden arrival of the Golden Rose acting troupe had been no mere coincidence, just as she knew that I had been closeted away by Cecil and Walsingham for some fell reason that they would never share and that, for her own pride, she could never press them to reveal. She would not endure their censure, but she still needed their service. It was a delicate balance to strike.

Had she known I had learned so much about the Spaniard's attacks upon her court? Did she know that something deeper lay beyond the simple disturbances—a Catholic plot? Perhaps, and perhaps not. But at this moment, I would put nothing past her.

I found myself straightening under her watchful eyes, my chin tilting up in Jane's clothing, my head unusually still under the weight of Jane's wig. She was my Queen as well, and I would serve her this night. I owed her nothing less. I owed my friends in her service nothing less.

We would do this.

I would do this.

If God won't save the Queen . . . we will.

The Golden Rose acting troupe performed their special rendition of *The Queen's Promise* flawlessly, brilliantly, and with such aplomb that even I almost believed they had been playing to courts and kings the whole of their lives. The crowd was a pleasing, roiling mix of courtiers and their ladies, packed closely enough for comfort but not so tight that a phalanx of guards couldn't swoop in as needed. And by the end of the first act, the wine and ale and entertainment were beginning to fan the energy of the crowd.

Both of the Spanish ambassadors were in attendance—the outgoing Ambassador de Feria, all scowls and sour eyes; and the laughing, genial de Quadra, who seemed to be enjoying himself. Even Nicolas Ortiz made an appearance, and he was drawing the attention of many ladies despite the glowering disapproval of de Feria. I shook my head. The Spanish were such a motley mix of souls, at once romantic and oppressive, open and closed, rigid in their faith and loose in their bearing. Rafe was very much a product of his people, to be sure, but the entire lot could wear a body out.

The shadowy Spaniard would come to me soon, I thought, if he would come at all. I glanced at little Sophia and stalwart Anna, their heads together. No more than twenty paces from them stood Lord Brighton, his hawk eyes hooded but his manner intent. They would be safe, I thought, with him as their guardian. And for once Sophia seemed at ease with him nearby.

I glanced at Beatrice, ensconced four men deep in admirers—four *Scotsmen* deep, actually, more the worse for her—in the center of the crowd. Apparently, the Queen had not seen fit to invite Lord Cavanaugh, Beatrice's betrothed. *Interesting.* I watched as the bearded, burly Alasdair MacLeod tucked her arm into his, claiming her despite the obvious bridal ring. Beatrice looked ready to kill the man. He looked ready to let her try.

I looked again at Jane, who was in turn being watched by Master James with an intensity that almost bordered on the inappropriate. Surely he knew it was not *me* standing there, I thought. Yet still he stared, transfixed. Then again, if he was simply trying to be protective, I should be glad of it.

But still . . . had I imagined his interest in me?

A whisper of sound at my side was all the warning I received before Rafe began speaking. "Nice wig. Who is that man you're staring at? He looks familiar."

Was that jealousy in his voice? Could that be possible? "A friend, someone I've known far longer than I've known you, who's given me more reason to trust him than you have, I should say."

"I don't like him," Rafe huffed.

"You don't have to like him." I stared at Rafe, noting his fine garb and dangerous smile. Then I saw the familiar flash of jade stone on his right hand. I sighed, disgusted. "Again with that ring. You dare much, Rafe, wearing it in public."

He laughed, lifting the hand with the heavy ring and wagging it at me. "People see only what they expect to see, sweet Meg. There is no harm in wearing something no one will notice."

"Then why not let Beatrice keep it?"

"Because I didn't give it to Beatrice; I gave it to you."

I shook my head, glancing away from him in confusion, trying to calm the turmoil of emotions he set off in me. "It will be over soon enough, if we are lucky. But look sharp;

you're about to be collared." I shifted myself to the side, stepping back to not allow the two men bearing down on Rafe to have an easy look at me. My disguise as Jane was good, but not that good.

"My son, my son—we've been looking everywhere for you. Please say you are done dancing attendance on the English ladies, as lovely as they are, and can spare a few moments for your own countrymen?"

Rafe turned as de Feria and de Quadra stared him down, de Quadra with his usual open demeanor, and de Feria with his customary glare. "My lord ambassadors, what do you require? I am ever at your service."

"Just your time, Conte de Martine. You'll excuse us, Miss Morgan?"

I curtsied, keeping my head well low. As I came up, Rafe bowed to me, his eyes tight with frustration but his manner polished perfection. "Miss Morgan," he said with excruciating formality. Then the Spanish ambassadors drew him into their sphere like a spider draws a fly, and he went, unresisting.

I smiled at Rafe's stiff back, pitying him slightly. *We all have our orders to follow.*

I should have considered those words more carefully, in retrospect.

The play continued, and I expected I would see Rafe again within the half hour. I was wrong in that, and forgot all about Rafe as the minutes ticked away. Instead I idled my time watching Tommy buzzing through the crowd as an impish maid, mightily trying to keep himself from picking anyone's pocket.

Then time seemed to suddenly compress. The royal

production was building toward its climax, and there had been no sign of any Spaniard making his way toward me as I stood there in my Jane costume. I drifted back toward the wall of tapestries, scanning the room, but to no avail. Cecil and Walsingham now looked like they were arguing with each other. Jane was watching the play with rapt attention, as was the Queen. James was still watching Jane. Beatrice was trying to carry on three conversations at once with her Scottish admirers. The false maids were milling about with buzzing contentment, all without a care in the world. And the sands of time continued to spill through the glass at an ever more rapid pace.

He wasn't going to come, I realized with a shock. *I had failed.*

My thoughts crashed and tumbled. How had I miscalculated? The Spaniard had said his time here was short. He had sounded urgent, almost desperate. This was a scene given to him upon a silver platter, an opportunity for him to find the information he needed right under the Queen's very nose, or cause another terrible "distraction" to feed his lust for glory.

Where had I gone wrong?

Just then I felt the shift of bodies around me, and a presence came up behind me, to my right. A male presence, unknown to me. This was not Rafe. This was not Master James.

Everything settled into place, and a curious calmness stole over me. Here it was, then. At last.

And I hadn't failed.

I began to turn toward the man, then felt his left hand close over my fingers, crushing the bones. His voice whispered into my ear: "Make a sound, make a murmur, Miss Morgan, and I will kill your friend as well as you."

I nodded hastily, and allowed the man to draw me back toward the servants' entrance. Surely Walsingham and Cecil were noticing this. Surely Beatrice would—she'd been facing me directly, after all, and had begun to look desperate in the shadow of the burly MacLeod. Surely she could see around the heads of all the earnest men dancing attendance upon her.

But what if she couldn't? What if they hadn't?

What if I was in this all alone?

As soon as we were clear of the Presence Chamber, I expected the Spaniard to flip me around. If he got a good look at my face in the bright torchlight, it would be the end of my disguise.

Instead he shoved me, hard, into an access passageway off the chamber, where the middle courses were stored for the royal feasts. There was no royal feast tonight, of course. Tonight, the passageway was empty.

The door closed behind us with a thump. Wrenching away from the Spaniard, I stumbled forward into the pitch black room, and turned around to try to get my bearings. Rich, mocking laughter rolled over me like a physical weight.

"I've watched you, Miss Morgan," the Spaniard said. "Seen you practice your knife throwing as if it were some novel game. Seen you running in the park."

I frowned. *Jane ran in the park? When did she have time to run in the park? And how had she gotten the boys' clothes to do so?* I felt some sort of expression of Jane-like bravado was necessary, so I whispered harshly, "I'll kill you."

It . . . it felt rather good to say words like that, actually. But the Spaniard just laughed.

"No, no, Miss Morgan. I'll kill *you*. With pleasure. And before your body is even cool, I'll gather my information from your brave little friend, who will have no idea of your untimely death, and then your English whore will be off the throne for good." He was circling now, and I struggled to follow his movements in the darkness. I knew how men moved, how they should move. But I did not know this man. I pitched my voice low, keeping it a whisper. "What do you want?"

"To finish my task, for God and country, *meu doce*," he said. Something jolted in me, with those words. *Meu doce.* I'd seen those words before, in the letter to Lady Amelia, and I knew the trap had been sprung accurately. That wasn't Spanish. It was Portuguese. This man was Marie's killer, Lady Amelia's attacker. I almost felt both women in the room, watching us, and it was all I could do not to cross myself in superstition. *Think!*

"You cannot believe you can continue your game," I said. "Your pope's letters were passed to the wrong set of hands."

He laughed harshly. "The cause of God will always prevail, and there are many willing hands to come to its aid. Those hands that no longer serve, we simply cut off." He moved, and I moved with him, the two of us circling each other in the inky darkness.

"But yours are cut off as well," I pressed. "Even now, Lady Amelia recovers. She will betray you as soon as she has the strength to write. And Lady Knollys—"

His snort cut me off. "Lady Amelia will betray no one, lest she betray herself. And Lady Knollys—if that old crow were devoted to anything but assuaging her own private grudges, she would be a threat. But she hides behind her curtain of respect and leaves others to do the work. You will never catch her in the act of treason." I could hear the harsh smile in his voice. "Of course, *you*, my little fighter, will never catch anyone again at all."

He lunged at me.

I felt him coming through the darkness, and I turned to flee—though where I would go, I had no idea. Then the Spaniard—Portuguese—whoever he was—attacked, all strength and sinew and a scent of spiced oranges. Recognition sprang in my mind, unbidden, even as we tumbled to the floor. Spiced oranges? Where had I captured that scent before?

I lurched forward, but he hauled me back, his hands at my throat, his left hand pressing down. "No garrote for you, my dear Miss Morgan," he breathed into my ear. "I have grown accustomed to doing my work with my hands, not tools. Surely you can appreciate the difference."

And he began to choke me. Left hand harder than the right.

Left hand harder than the right.

My hands flew down to reach Jane's hidden knife in my bodice, but he kicked at my knees, and I crunched down, swimming in my heavy skirts. Unconsciously my hands reached up, grasping his thick forearms. I would never pry him off my back; I could sense that in a flash.

Even worse, my days of privation in the dungeon were taking their toll. I could not—I just could not *breathe*. Bright lights were flashing behind my eyelids. I saw spinning visions in my head. Beatrice, Jane, Anna, and Sophia. The Queen's garden. The chapel. Rafe. The Lower Ward. The schoolroom. The cloisters . . .

The cloisters.

Nicolas Ortiz, raising his left hand in salute in the shadow of the church spires. The oddly back-slanted letters that Anna had noticed, written in Portuguese. The scent of oranges and spices.

Ortiz!

Sudden panic consumed me as my lungs began to heave, even as my mind chanted Ortiz's name over and over again. I twisted my hands side to side, trying to improve my position—

And felt the nick of a blade against my forearm.

Jane's wrist blade. It was right there. I fought back horror as the breath was choked out of me, my chest beginning to burn, and focused only on the blade. The squat, fat, obnoxious blade that Jane herself had not yet mastered but had refused to have me leave behind. What had she said? What had she said?

And her words came back to me as clearly as the scent of oranges and spices. *You just flick your hand out, and it will slide into position, as easy as that.* As easy as that. I flailed my arm out in a panicked flutter, feeling the blade slide home into my palm even as Ortiz laughed.

"That's it, *meu doce*. Let me chase you down to death.

Don't give up too easily. Let me take you in a battle worthy of the name." He breathed in guttural excitement, knowing my end was drawing near.

The knife was in my palm.

But I could never kill a man, I thought, the words coming back to me like a distant roar. *I would never cut a man.* I was too smart for that. I was an actor and a thief, not a thug.

I was not a thug.

But who am I, truly?

Ortiz's fingers pressed hard upon my throat then. "Perhaps I should break your neck, my sweet? So fine and narrow in my hands?"

Ortiz would be wearing a stuffed doublet. Flaring trunks, puffed full of cloth and ribbons.

But Ortiz was also a dandy of the first order. Ortiz with his finely muscled legs and glorious silk hosiery. Ortiz with his well-turned ankles and flattering bows. Ortiz with his right leg pinning my hip, his thigh lined up alongside my right arm . . . just below the blade. Just below the blade.

Who am I, truly?

I struck.

I shoved Jane's knife deep into Ortiz's thigh, heard his high, strangled yelp as he leaped away from me. A skate of blood spurted across my hand. I'd not struck him deeply enough for him to die, but the blade was thick and true, and would slow him down. I pulled a second blade out of my bodice sheath, scrambling forward just as the door was flung open, and a dark shape barreled into the room, backlit by the passageway.

"Meg!" It was Rafe, and I gasped, waving him into the room, my mouth moving but no sound emanating from my bruised throat. Behind me I heard Ortiz unsheathe a blade.

"Guards!" I screamed in my tortured whisper, but Rafe was already past me, a wraith in the darkness. A knife clattered against stone wall, but there was no accompanying grunt of pain from Rafe. Ortiz had thrown, but missed. A thud and a gasp later, and Rafe was back.

"I'm so sorry, sweet Meg," he said, cradling my face. I lifted my fingers to his cheek, frowning at him. His hands felt as cold as ice. *Sorry?* I wondered. *Why sorry?*

"Guards!" I managed, my voice finally coming back in a desperate croak as my fingers curved over Rafe's hands, feeling the weight of his ring against my palm. I shook my head, confused. "Guards!" I hissed again. "They will want to—talk to him. He knows—about Amelia. The letters, Rafe. Lady Knollys," I babbled. "The—plot! He knows!"

"I know, sweet Meg, I know," Rafe murmured, his voice soft and pleading. "Which is why I did what I had to do, and why I was never here. Forgive me?"

I looked at him, sick comprehension dawning. "What!?" I tried to scream, and inside, my mind was wailing, *Rafe, what have you done?*

I clasped my hands around his, trying to hold him to me, but I was too weak. He sighed and pulled his hands away from me, rolling to his feet. Then he was gone, leaving me to flop in my sea of skirts back toward Ortiz, barely reaching the man to hold up a hand to his sagging, foaming mouth. Foaming? Arsenic! Rafe had drugged the last man standing who could implicate the Spanish Crown in this treacherous plot. Ortiz still breathed, but not for long.

Rafe had completed his assignment.

Then pounding feet echoed through the passageway and I was enveloped by my friends.

Soon Ortiz would be dead. And all of his and Rafe's secrets would die with him.

Well, not quite all.

I let myself be hauled up, clenching my hand around Rafe's jade stone ring.

CHAPTER THIRTY-NINE

Things got a little complicated after that.

CHAPTER FORTY

It was a full twelve hours later before I could break free from the castle, and I breathed in the crisp cool air with satisfaction as I watched the far boats of the Thames begin their journey down to London, and then away to the sea. I relished my privacy, seated against the castle walls. I'd not been alone since the melee of the night before, a melee the Queen had noted with appreciation had taken place in a passageway and not her Presence Chamber.

The Queen's appreciation had shown no bounds, in fact.

I glanced down at the etched gold ring now gracing the longest finger of my left hand. She had called this ring "the Queen's Grace," announcing to all and sundry among her advisors and guards that I was never to be questioned or held without her express presence, that I was in her highest confidence, the first among her Maids of Honor to receive this award.

The first, but not the last.

The Queen was no fool, and she had ordered similar rings be given to Beatrice, Jane, Sophia, and Anna as well. Before the night was through, we'd all knelt before her to receive these boons, no one understanding their importance perhaps more than I. If Cecil and Walsingham understood that same import, or the Queen's motivation, they gave no sign. Nor did she give any sign of suspecting me of having eavesdropped on her in her bedchamber. I prayed it would never again be an issue. Elizabeth was too young to give up flirtation—even love. But if she needed to be protected from herself, then I would do it. While I served Her Majesty, I would do anything she asked.

Beatrice had already leveraged her part in the plot to get her wedding date set for a few weeks hence, but I half-suspected she'd hastened the happy event to keep a certain Scotsman at bay. As the marriage talk had then turned to the next eligible maid, Sophia had fainted with her best swoon yet. Anna—and the vicar's son—had helped her to her chambers . . . and then Anna had returned more than an hour later, her eyes alight, her cheeks flushed.

Only Jane and I remained to talk with the Queen's advisors.

We had recovered the letters from Amelia's coffer and given them up. Most of them, anyway. At Beatrice's insistence, we'd kept Lady Knollys's letters for our own use later.

At first, the advisors refused to believe what we'd found for them.

Then, in the way of elders and men in general, they were angry that we had found anything at all.

But at length, finally, they'd realized the truth for what it was.

Here is how it all unraveled:

Ortiz, an agent for the pope, had two fatal flaws. The

first: He was too zealous in his passion for his church. And second: He was too careless in his affection for the women of the English court.

His fervor as a Catholic had moved him to go beyond his assignment of merely receiving letters from de Feria and handing them off to English sympathizers, letters that gave suggestions of how members of the court might disturb and distress the new Queen, giving rise to discussion that she was not fit to rule. No, he'd had to do more. So he'd opened the letters, read their instructions, written two new letters of his own, and even set some of the disruptions in place himself—including those that went far beyond what the pope had ever intended. Eventually those disruptions had turned deadly, when the maid Marie had discovered what he was doing.

And that took us to the second error in judgment Ortiz had made. He'd fallen for the easy smiles and winsome beauty of the maid Marie, not realizing she was spying on him. When he realized, too late, that she had figured him out—he'd had to kill her. But rather than making it seem like an accident, he'd done so ruthlessly and with pleasure. He'd then been careful for the tiniest of whiles, but all too quickly the fair Lady Amelia had caught his eye. He'd known she was no spy; she was merely a zealous Catholic, and a willing hand in his plot. He'd even written her a love letter, which Amelia had kept like a victor's spoils. But the woman's very lack of cunning proved a liability to Ortiz when Turnip Nose was killed.

The letters Rafe had given to de Feria were not truly from either the pope or the Spanish king. They were crafted by the new ambassador, Bishop de Quadra, to ferret out the conspiracy—and positioned Rafe to get rid of the rogue conspirators quickly and quietly. De Feria had handed these letters off to Ortiz, as was their custom. Then Ortiz read the new letters, which named Rafe as a potential comrade in arms. He instructed Turnip Nose to contact Rafe, to bring him into the fold. When Turnip Nose had met with Rafe, however, he'd summarily died—but it wasn't clear if Rafe had killed him. And that's when Ortiz had gotten nervous.

Ortiz realized that Lady Amelia, if questioned, could betray him. She had to die. He chose Moon Face to do the killing, but in the end Ortiz couldn't stay away. His thirst for murder had grown too strong. When Rafe and I arrived and disrupted Ortiz and Moon Face's attempt to kill Lady Amelia, Ortiz had known he'd need to leave Windsor Castle . . . but he couldn't quite bring himself to do so. He wanted something else before he departed, one last piece of information to further the Catholic cause and hasten Elizabeth's dethroning—or, failing that, another death.

He got what he wanted, in the end.

So there it was: the very first Catholic plot of the Queen's reign, doomed from the beginning by the main conspirator's own zealous hand. And though Rafe had set his own gambit in motion at the same time, the Maids of Honor had found the original letters Ortiz had given to Lady Amelia, and had understood them for what they were, deciphering the mark of the Scottish thistle, connecting it with the disturbances, and identifying the writer of the letters as a Portuguese man—who later turned out to be Ortiz. We'd discovered the threat to the Queen, and we'd destroyed it. We'd proven our worth a dozen times over. And our work was just beginning.

My individual work too, it seemed. Although we'd saved

the Queen, I had not, in fact, delivered Marie's killer to Walsingham and Cecil in time. Dead spies were of no service to the Maids of Honor, they had informed me stiffly. Nor were they of service to the Queen, nor to England. In Cecil's and Walsingham's eyes, I had not fulfilled our bargain, and so I would remain in service to the Queen until I had.

I found that, for the moment, I could live with those restrictions.

My parents had been spies for King Henry, my Queen's beloved father. They had left the court under cover of darkness and had hidden deep in the countryside. They'd remained with my grandfather only long enough to have me, then had pushed on. According to a note he'd penned himself on the final page, he'd later received their precious diary from a courier who'd explained only that their death had been swift and without terrible pain. Out of fear for my life, grandfather had never told me the first word about them, and yet here I was . . . so much my parents' daughter that I was standing in the Queen's court, ready to serve and protect.

Who am I, truly?

I am a Maid of Honor.

Beside me in the castle wall, a door scraped and swung open. Suddenly, I was no longer alone on the green hills rolling away from Windsor.

"Good morrow to you, Meg Fellowes," said Rafe Luis Medina, Count de Martine. He'd become many things in the short time I'd known him. A mark. An assassin. A friend.

Perhaps, something more.

I stood with him against the cool stone castle walls as

he gazed out over the wide rolling plain. It was not even a quarter-hour walk to the Thames, and he would need to make haste. There would not be time for much discussion.

Where he'd disappeared to last night, I had no idea, but under the remarkably polite questioning accorded to royal ambassadors, de Quadra and de Feria had stoutly protested that Rafe had been with them since the moment he'd left my side. They'd had enough to manage, with having to explain to the furious Queen about Ortiz and his letters. They claimed that Ortiz had acted without sanction, from either the pope or King Philip. That Spain had no part in a Catholic plot against the Queen or any other Protestant monarch. That King Philip was Queen Elizabeth's brother, not her enemy. Ortiz was dead now. The other guards in his employ were dead. Everyone else was protesting their innocence with loud and long lamentations.

No one believed them, of course, but it was a battle for another day.

My battle, I realized now.

"Good morrow, Rafe Luis Medina," I said. I nodded to the door he had carefully shut behind him. "Did you know that particular passageway before this morning?"

He smiled, eyeing me warily. "I did not. Jane was kind enough to accompany me. I think she expected the request." At my smile, he chuckled. "I thought as much. It is time for me to leave if I have grown predictable. She guards your safe passage back just inside the door."

I nodded. "You'll be in London long?"

"Not at all. I leave on the first ship out."

"That is wise, I think."

We stood there, strangely awkward in the shadow of the castle.

That was it, then. Rafe had to leave, and summarily, before Cecil and Walsingham came up with something specific to question him over. He was still at risk, remaining here. He was not an official ambassador; he was a spy for King Philip. The rules of polite questioning did not apply to him, and Cecil's or Walsingham's frustration would eventually play itself out.

"You'll be safe?" I asked, glancing away, hating the stupidity of the question. For everything else I could do, I still could not make intelligent conversation.

"Probably not," Rafe said with too much gravity. "I suspect I'll be dead before nightfall."

I looked at him sharply, and his teasing grin finally chipped away a piece of my armor. I opened up my mouth to speak, but found the words would not come. I pulled up my arms to cross them under my chest. I shrugged. After a moment I tried again. "Well, if you must go, then you must go. 'Tis the way of a spy, I suppose one could say."

He ignored my prattle, his eyes searching mine. "I would ask a boon of you, sweet Meg, one spy to another, then?"

I tensed, not backing down as he took a step toward me. "I should think my allowing you safe passage from the castle would be gift enough," I said. "Even though you deliberately thwarted my own attempt to secure Ortiz alive. You were rather quick with your poison."

Rafe dismissed that with a careless wave of his hand. "Ortiz was mine before he was yours. 'Tis the way of a spy, as you say."

I let that comment pass. For now. "You should go," I said heavily. "The longer you stay here with me, the more risk you take. You should—"

"And you should be still and let me speak," he said, and chuckled. He lifted a hand to my face. I jerked away, but he followed the movement with his usual grace, capturing my chin with his hand.

It was a simple, almost inconsequential move, and yet it more effectively trapped me than anything Cecil and Walsingham had ever visited upon me. I could not move. I could not speak. Rafe held me with his eyes, and I longed for this moment to stay exactly so, forever keeping precious what he was and what I was and what we had been together, if only for a moment.

"What else do you want from me?" I asked with, I thought distantly, a pleasing amount of exasperation in my voice. Never mind that my feet were rooted to the ground, a nervous tremor unsettling me. "It sounds like you have everything you require."

"Not quite," he murmured, his fingers distracting me, moving along my jawline. "There is the question of my mother's ring, which I suspect you slipped from my fingers."

"Say you haven't lost it." *If only he knew.* It hung even now around my neck, as I dared not lose sight of it while he was still on English soil. I deliberately mimicked his words from the first time we'd ever spoken. "Perhaps you simply loosened it, and it fell away as you ran?"

Rafe grinned, remembering as well. "I do seem to have a habit of losing it around you." He nodded. "If you care to, you may return it to Beatrice. She has more need of it than I do."

I thought of Beatrice, and her words just yesterday. *Another slight. Another indiscretion.* How many sins of her father had she redressed? What else had she done to maintain the prestige of her family? "Thank you," I said simply.

"I do regret, however, that I have only your favor to remember you by," Rafe said.

"My favor?" I asked, and he dropped his hand and fished inside his cloak. A moment later he drew out a creased and many-times folded white ruff, late of the Queen's midsummer ball.

Something broke inside my chest.

Rafe smiled and tucked the ruff away. When he lifted his hand to my face again, I felt him brush away a tear. His eyes were dark with intensity now, and his gaze leveled on mine. "I will return to keep you safe. On that you have my promise."

I felt my brows shoot up. "I've no need of your protection."

"Needed or not, I will come back to you, sweet Meg," he murmured, his fingers now firming on my chin. "There is naught in the world that would keep me away. But before I go . . . this is the boon I would ask. Our first kiss."

I blinked at him. "We have kissed before."

"We have kissed when you were stealing from me. When I was stealing from you. And we have kissed in haste and danger, never knowing when we'd have to run," he said. "For once, my beautiful Meg, I would like to simply kiss you. A perfectly ordinary kiss."

He tilted up my chin.

There are moments in my life that I believe I'll remember forever. A perfect sunset, the sight of ships coming into port, the first breath of spring.

And the moment of a perfectly ordinary kiss from Rafe Luis Medina, the Count de Martine.

It was nothing at all like I'd expected it to be. It was strong—but curiously soft at once, and Rafe exhaled a strangled breath that sent a thrill completely through me as he crushed my body to his. In that moment, his lips over mine, it seemed he poured his very soul into me, his soul and all his memories and everything he was, everything he would be. I could not get enough of him, and when he lifted his face away, I wanted him back, immediately.

"You will return?" I gasped as he trailed soft kisses over my lips and cheek, straying to my neck. This part I remembered from before, but now his touch took on a new level of magic, like tracings of fire that were now branded deep into my skin, warming me in the darkness that even now I felt drawing close.

"I will return," he vowed. "The Queen's birthday is hard upon us, and I would be a very poor courtier indeed to not show her my appreciation for her gracing the world with another year of life. And, I'm given to understand, there is to be a wedding at Windsor soon as well."

I smiled, thinking of Beatrice. "It will be an event not to be missed," I agreed.

"With a fortnight of de Quadra's diplomacy and with a handsome gift from the Spanish monarchy for the Queen's troubles, I suspect I will be a welcome guest."

"Until the wedding, then," I said, pulling back from him, but my heart seemed to shrink even at that simple parting. "It is still too far away," I sighed, hating the sound of my own weakness. "Whole lives can be changed in such a long time, and freedoms won and lost."

I spoke with conviction, for I knew it to be true. After all, it had been barely a month since he'd arrived on our shores. And how much had my life changed in that time?

"Then perhaps you should be still," Rafe murmured. "And let me kiss you again."

And so I did.

We stood there long and silent in the brilliant morning light, the great promise and danger of the world held at bay, unwilling and unready to be caught up again quite yet in our work for Crown and country. For in these stolen moments, this at least was one lesson I'd learned:

Among the ranks of the Maids of Honor, love was the most precious freedom of all.

Reading Group Guide

Further explore the world of the Maids of Honor with these questions:

1. List the most important facts that you learn about Meg in her life in the Golden Rose acting troupe from Chapters One and Two. What characters are introduced in this exposition?

2. Summarize the events that lead to Meg being captured by the crown. What will she be used for? Cite evidence from the text that reveals the Queen's purpose in her capture.

3. List the three most important aspects of Meg's new role at court. To whom must she answer? How are these characters' motivations in conflict? Whom should Meg, and therefore, the reader, believe?

4. Describe the Count de Martine and Meg's task with him as her mark. What skills does she rely on to become invisible in her quest? Find a key quote that best represents Meg's unique skill set and summarize her actions at the ball.

5. Compare the characters of Cecil and Walsingham. Which do you find more disturbing? How does the author develop their characterization? What makes an excellent villain?

6. What bargain does Meg make for her freedom? Is it a reasonable offer? Her life is far more luxurious inside the castle walls, and yet she dreams of her life with the acting troupe. Given her situation, which would you choose? Why?

7. Describe the setting of the novel. How do the descriptions and details of the palace add to the plot? How would this story be different set in another time period? Another location? How important is setting for you as a reader? Why?

8. Describe the romance between Rafe and Meg. In what ways does it serve as an interesting subplot to the mystery? What does the romantic element provide the reader?

9. Meg creates friendships with the other maids despite their differences. Which one of the maids is your favorite? Why? Is that who you would most like to be friends with or not?

10. In Chapter Twenty-Eight, when Meg incurs the wrath of the Queen, does she deserve it? Have you ever felt as ashamed and disappointed in yourself as Meg does?

11. What does Meg learn about the Queen that could compromise the Queen's position as monarch? Would you be willing to forgo romance, marriage, and children to have the power of Queen Elizabeth?

12. While Anna is naive about relationships (and men in particular), Beatrice is decidedly worldly and knows how to manipulate them. What point is the author trying to make by using these two characters as foils for each other? What do we learn about the main character through these characters?

13. Meg loses practically everything, including her freedom. Why does she end up in the dungeon after trying to save Lady Amelia? For you, what would be the worst part of Meg's time in the dungeon? How is she saved from this awful fate? What does this reveal about her friendships and the Queen?

14. In the end, where is the relationship with Meg and Rafe headed? Do you think that despite their conflicting motivations they will be able to build a relationship and romance?

15. Predict what will happen to each of the five maids over the next year and state why you believe this to be so. Use evidence from the novel to support your hypothesis, drawing key quotes as proof.

Reading Group Guide excerpted from guide written by Tracie Vaughn Zimmer, author and English teacher.

TURN THE PAGE FOR A SNEAK PEEK OF THE ROMANTIC SEQUEL, MAID OF DECEPTION.

SEPTEMBER 1559
WINDSOR CASTLE, ENGLAND

There would be no tears on my wedding day. I would not allow it.

As the music from the Queen's own orchestra filled Saint George's Chapel, a perfect blend of viol and harpsichord to complement my perfect union with Lord Percival Andrew William Cavanaugh, I clasped the clammy hands of my fellow Maid of Honor Sophia Dee and smiled into her large, worried eyes.

"Hush, Sophia. All is well," I said, giving her fine-boned fingers a light squeeze. She shivered despite the stifling heat of the chamber. "If you keep crying, you'll draw attention to yourself."

That caught the girl up short. The youngest of our group of royal spies, and the most uncertain, Sophia hated attention. Her eyes, if possible, got even bigger.

"But, Beatrice—you should b-be *happy*—"

"I *am* happy, Sophia," I assured her. And, strangely enough, I was. For all my well-rehearsed sophistication, Lord Cavanaugh represented more than just my crowning achievement at court. Yes, of course, he was one of the richest men in the kingdom. And he was from a respected family whose reputation was not at daily risk from either a drunken father or a muddle-minded mother. And his ancestral home was not overrun by brawling foundling children.

And, perhaps most important, he had no idea whatsoever how desperately I needed this marriage.

But there was more to it than that. Lord Cavanaugh was gentle, fine, and soft-spoken, with a rich, drawling voice that I thrilled to hear. He was gracious and educated, in a court filled with rakes and curs more intent on the hunt than on conversation. He was devout, respectful at service and in court. He was polite to women of every station; he appeared to genuinely care for his mother.

And he loved me.

I saw it in his eyes, in his smile. In the way he nodded his approval as he took in my gowns and hair. I saw it as he watched others watching me. Though I'd worked very hard to ensure that I was perfect for him in every possible way, I still could not believe I had succeeded so well. . . . Lord Cavanaugh *loved* me. The rest meant nothing beside that truth.

"Babies with my husband will come in time, I am sure," I said now, addressing Sophia's current cause for distress. She'd seen—somehow—that my groom and I would have no children, and the shock of her vision was quite undoing her. Sophia, it should be said, had a gift of intuition that might well become the full-fledged Sight at any moment. But Sophia's predictions were not always clear, and she was definitely wrong on this score. My marriage to Cavanaugh would be perfect. It had to be. "Today I am the most joyful woman alive." Still, the tiniest thread of fear skated along my nerves.

Sophia raised a trembling chin and gave me a smile, looking like a frail raven-haired ghost in her gorgeous white silk gown. That gown had cost five pounds if it had cost a shilling, and it was embroidered with Italian lace. It would have taken a farmer a *year* just to earn enough to pay for a dress like that, but it was only one of a dozen gowns Sophia's betrothed had gifted to her. I pondered that a moment. Had Cavanaugh given me any gifts of late? I'd been so busy with my duties to the Queen, I hadn't much noticed.

"It's almost time, Beatrice," Anna Burgher chirped from the doorway.

We'd participated in the loud and boisterous procession from the Upper Ward of Windsor Castle down to Saint George's Chapel, and then—just as I'd orchestrated it—my bridesmaids and I had slipped in here while Lord Cavanaugh had moved toward the front of the chapel, to give me a last opportunity to make sure I was completely prepared.

Now Anna was up on her toes, bouncing in her yellow satin skirts, her ginger mass of hair brutalized into a tight coil of braids. I smiled at the back of Anna's head, imagining her eyes darting this way and that. She'd record every person in attendance of this, my most triumphant public appearance yet. We would spend hours poring over the lists she made, analyzing who was most appropriate to approach, to flatter, and to watch in the weeks following the wedding. The Queen's birthday was coming up, and there would be time to cement alliances there.

Speaking of. "And Elizabeth? Has she arrived yet?"

"No! She must wish to do you proud, Beatrice," Anna said staunchly, still scanning the chapel floor. "She will grace you like the Queen of the Fairies at exactly the perfect moment."

I pursed my lips, the thread of doubt within me thickening to a coarser yarn. Elizabeth was many things, I knew from long experience. "Fairy Queen" was not among them. But she had blessed this union, taken pride in it as if it were her own. That was what mattered.

The music shifted in subtle counterpoint just then, and I straightened, casting a glance over my soft pink gown. Unlike the rumored splendor of the recent bridal ensemble worn by Mary, Queen of Scots—all white, if you can believe it—my gown's skirts flowed down in rich, pale pink panels, parted at the front to reveal a luxurious swath of cream-colored satin, delicately picked out with golden thread. The skirts were attached above to a stiffly embroidered V-pointed bodice that featured a virtual garden of pink, gold, and brilliantly red roses, all of them swirling, twirling, and fanning out along a neckline cut to showcase my blushing porcelain skin—still modest enough, but an effective display of maidenly beauty. My lace sleeves were so fine as to be nearly sheer, ending in delicate cuffs edged, once more, in pink and gold. I was a vision of English sensibilities, from head to toe.

Everything was perfect.

"God's bones, half of England is out there," Meg Fellowes observed as she ducked into the doorway, tall and straight in her simple gown of dove-grey satin. I smiled, feeling uncharacteristically charitable toward our resident thief, which I never would have believed possible at the start of the summer. I'd even loaned her the dress she was now wearing. Of course, it was two seasons out of date, but Meg didn't seem to mind. Probably didn't know, either.

And she was no rival, that much was certain. Somewhere out in that audience was Meg's special Spanish spy, Rafe de Martine. I'd watched her sneak glances at the boy since he'd entered the chapel, and now I felt something curiously empty in my chest, as though I'd gone too long since breaking my fast.

Anna, usually the smartest of our select company, was convinced that Meg was truly in love, though I couldn't quite see the point of that. Rafe de Martine was a courtier, but he was Spanish. He was fine for a turn on the dance floor, or even a stolen kiss—or a dozen—behind a darkened tapestry, but nothing more. Rafe had wanted me first, of course, but I could never have given him what he wanted. So he'd turned to Meg.

It wasn't as if he were going to tuck himself into a corner with Jane Morgan, after all. Her unkind cuts would have left him bleeding.

Still and all, the Queen would never approve a match between Meg and the Spaniard. And Meg, for her part, insisted she had no interest in marriage. This of course was utter folly, but the girl was still new to court. She would learn, I thought as I returned my attention to my gown. Marriage was not about love. I knew that, no matter how desperately glad I was that Cavanaugh loved me.

Marriage was about power.

"So who created this guest list, exactly?" Jane was the last to enter the chapel, and her flat voice interrupted my reverie. Our troupe's official ruffian generally kept her mouth shut, which is how I preferred it. Still, my attention sharpened not at Jane's wry words so much as Anna's reaction to them. Even Sophia lifted a hand to her mouth, her eyes darting first to Anna and then to Jane, and then, resolutely, not to me.

I frowned at Jane's profile as she turned to stare back out the doorway, but the girl's grin wasn't cruel or dark. Just amused. Irritation kindled along my nerves, and I steeled myself against it. I was the future Marchioness of Westmoreland, a future that would be arriving in a few short moments. I would be kind and patient. Even if it killed me.

"*I* created the guest list," I said, then offered a careless wave of my hand. "And Cecil and Walsingham reviewed and approved it, of course." As if there'd be any chance those two wouldn't want to control every aspect of such a grand court event.

Sir William Cecil and Sir Francis Walsingham were not just the Queen's most powerful advisors, after all. They were instructors to a very special group of spies within the Queen's court. The Maids of Honor comprised five young women from all stations of life. Anna and Jane, Sophia and now Meg—and, of course, me. Each of us with unique skills, selected by Queen Elizabeth herself to serve her in a very specific capacity. To be her eyes and ears—and sometimes mouth—and to ferret out secrets that no mere man could hope to uncover. I had been the first young woman chosen to head up this secret sect, a favor that had, I daresay, shocked Cecil and Walsingham. I had not been surprised, however.

The Queen and I had more history between us than Cecil and Walsingham could ever guess.

None of the other girls spoke, and I frowned into the silence. "And probably the Queen stuck her nose into the guest list, as she is ever wont to do. What of it? Who do you see?"

"The Queen?" Meg's voice had a peculiar tone to it, but I never could tell what the Rat was thinking. "Well, that would do it."

Irritation crested with a snap. "Who do you—"

"Oh, Beatrice, darling! You look lovely!" I glanced up, startled, then moved forward three quick paces to catch my mother as she stumbled into our little chamber, her breath smelling of honeyed mead and, more faintly, a light, sweet tang; a scent I'd come to know too well.

"Lady Knowles," Jane said stoutly, and suddenly she was at my side, her strong arms around my mother as if she knew exactly what to do with a woman too muddled to stand upright. My cheeks burned with mortification. Today of all days!

"Beatrice, your father is coming!" Anna squeaked. I whipped my gaze back around toward the door. No! Not now, not with my mother in one of her states.

"He can't see—he can't see her like—" I swallowed the words, remembering discretion too late. I turned to the only maid who could possibly understand. "Oh, Anna!"

"Relax. We'll take care of her," Meg cut in smoothly. "You just smile like it's your wedding day, and keep moving. Don't let him stop to look and see anything." She sounded like she was directing a play—or a battle. I'm not sure which comparison was more apt. In any event, she took up her place on the other side of my mother and nodded to Jane, two serious maids escorting the mother of the bride. "We'll be back in a moment."

"Or two," Jane muttered, eyeing the woman now listing between them.

Then the pair of them was through the door as they clutched my mother, who'd begun to burble something about "beautiful." She was the beautiful one, not me. Even with her eyes going glassy and her expression a little lost. My father had done this to her, I knew. Had killed her with a thousand cuts.

If only . . .

My jaw set. I had no time for "if only." I just needed the woman to keep herself together for another quarter hour. I boosted myself up on my toes, using Anna's shoulder as a brace, and watched Jane and Meg smoothly steer Mother into her place, even as their attention was captured by someone in the crowd. All three of them were staring, actually. Including my mother.

What in the world could have penetrated her fog?

"Beatrice! Now!" Anna breathed. I dashed back to the table to catch up my bouquet, and turned to receive Lord Bartholomew Edward Matthew Knowles with my face set into an expression of perfectly practiced ethereal joy.

My reward was swift and complete. "Beatrice, you are the most entrancing of women, and the grandest lady in all of England," my father said, bowing with a flourish.

"And you, my father, are the most depraved lord in all of Christendom."

"I own it." He grinned at me with a smile that I knew—from long and occasionally bitter experience—had made women's hearts melt for the past thirty years. "But say, Lord Cavanaugh is standing up like a strawman at the tilt. Think he'll have the stamina to make it through the ceremony?"

Anger flashed through me even as my father turned my hand into the crook of his arm. "Lord Cavanaugh is a good man, Father, and will do far more for our fortunes than—" I hastily swallowed my ill-advised words. *Control!* "Than we have any right to ask."

Father snorted, seeming not at all convinced, for someone who had heartily approved of this match. "Lord Cavanaugh will have a care around you, anyway, you can be sure of that," he said, patting my hand as we moved back through the doorway.

His fingers grazed the ring I'd decided to wear next to my betrothal ring, and he glanced down at it now. I felt his fingers tighten as he recognized the bauble I'd recently received from Rafe and Meg. Oh, he recognized the ring all right, more the shame to him.

When Rafe had first arrived on our shores these several weeks past, the Spanish spy had carried with him a ring that his mother had retained as a "souvenir" of her own visit to the English court during the reign of old King Henry. Of course, the King hadn't been old then, and neither had Rafe's mother . . . nor my father. The nature of the "friendship" between Rafe's mother and my father was not something I wanted to dwell upon, but thank heavens both Rafe and I had already been born by then. I could barely tolerate the arrogant young man as Meg's suitor; I could not have stomached him as a half brother. Still, now I had another family heirloom back, a precious treasure reclaimed. And from the guilt-ridden look on his face, Father clearly knew I had discerned yet one more of his secrets.

Vindication swept through me like a cleansing fire. *Look hard and long, you skirt-chasing ballywag.* I was the one taking care of the family.

Father blinked and stared, like a bear stumbling out of his winter slumber. "But where . . . How . . ." He bristled at me. "Where in the bloody hell did you get—"

"The music is beginning!" Anna's quick cry mobilized us, and she rushed into position behind Sophia, even as Jane and Meg hurried into place as well, both of them favoring me with knowing glances. What was going on with them? What had they seen?

There was no time, however, and we moved forward into the multicolored radiance of Saint George's Chapel, the entire hall lit up with light pouring through the stained-glass windows, as if God himself were adding his illumination to my day.

I stepped into the long aisle and held my head high. It was total perfection, and all according to a plan I'd labored to bring to light for the past ten years. Finally I would be married. Finally I would be respected. Finally I would be . . .

Safe.

We moved forward with the elegance due our rank and

station in the Queen's court, and I craned my neck this way and that, taking in the congregation that had filled Saint George's to bursting. My gaze moved along one thick knot of admirers and over to another—many of them relatives of mine or my lord's, but some who were nobles, even courtiers from other lands. There were Cecil and Walsingham, stiff in their proper garments. There was Rafe de Martine and the grinning band of Spaniards. There was even Lord Brighton, Sophia's intended, who stood a bit nervously next to a serenely lovely woman.

And all of them were looking at me.

I nodded graciously in the midst of their open stares and bright eyes. I felt beautiful, suddenly, with my pink-gold dress, my blond hair piled up in an impossibly ornate coiffure pinned with pink roses and bits of white lace, my eyes and mouth touched delicately with careful paints. Within my chest my heart swelled until it seemed almost twice its proper size, the smile on my face now completely unabashed. *I was getting married!*

The whole of the court seemed to beam back at me, sharing in my joy. I glanced past a particularly gorgeous nobleman I didn't recognize, in a blue silk doublet and a short cape. Despite myself I hesitated, favoring him with a nod even as my heart fluttered a bit in my breast at the roguish glint in his eye.

That glint seemed vaguely familiar, but surely I would have remembered *this* young man. He was tall and fierce, with the kind of arrogance that would make him a liability in any court, particularly ours. Had the Queen invited him?

Elizabeth was always looking for ways to surround herself with new men. I shook myself, realizing I was staring, but I couldn't quite tear my eyes away. Nerves, I decided.

Then the young man grinned back at me, his gaze dropping quite obviously to fix on the moderately deep V of my wedding gown as it plunged between my breasts. I knew that look. I knew that leer.

And I almost stumbled in my stride.

I wrenched my gaze away, grateful now for the near murderous grip my father had on my arm as I strode ahead, poleaxed.

This was what Meg and Jane had been grinning about, and why they'd been so eager to escort my mother into the chapel. *This* was what Anna and Sophia had known but had dared not tell me. *This!*

Alasdair MacLeod was at my wedding!

The boorish Scot had trampled into the refined English court not four weeks past, part of a grand onslaught of foreigners who'd come to pay court to the Queen. He'd seemed instantly out of place to me, for all his apparent high standing within the Scottish delegation, a bull among chickens—all brawny shoulders and roguish leers and rough manners and knowing grins. The Queen, with her usual perverse pettiness, had assigned *me* to fawn over Alasdair, of course, to see what secrets I might find out about his true intentions toward the English. As a result I'd been forced to dance with the hulking brute on far too many occasions, and he'd taken every opportunity to embarrass me, press me, hold me too close. The worst had been during a late summer wedding

I'd been forced to attend with the oaf, wherein the Clod MacLeod had put both hands around my waist and drawn in a breath so deep it seemed as if he'd sought to distill my own essence within himself. Thank God he'd never tried to kiss me.

Still, *had* he tried, it would have been entertaining for me to disable him. I had my choice of methods too, one of a half dozen favorites I'd honed during our schooling as spies. Each more painful than the previous.

There were some benefits to being a Maid of Honor, after all.

Still, whyever is he here? Weddings of commoners were open to all, true enough. But I was *not* a commoner.

And he had *not* been invited.

I stared ahead stonily, feeling the cur's eyes scorch through my gown as I walked sedately toward my future husband, Lord Cavanaugh. My future respected, respectable, and very *respectful* husband.

The young Scotsman may have been heir to some hulking rock of a castle in the middle of the northern sea, but he was nothing next to Lord Cavanaugh. And he had *no business* being here. Especially . . . especially looking the way he did now.

This Alasdair had been bathed and shaven smooth, his thick beard now gone; his wild, unruly mane now trimmed and luxuriously thick, its dark blond curls draped carelessly over his sun-warmed face and fierce blue eyes. This Alasdair must have stolen his clothes, so fine were they, the blue and gold doublet undone just enough to show a snowy white tunic beneath, and the slightest glimpse of his broad, firm, powerful chest—

"Beatrice, you're wounding me."

I blinked up at my father's words, and saw him now looking at me with genuine concern, all the anger that had lit his aristocratic features gone. We were at the front of the chapel. The minister was there and Lord Cavanaugh was there, looking handsome and perfect and holding my entire future in his hands. He was everything I wanted and needed, and as if in recognition of that fact, the chapel was finally quieting to allow the solemnity of our service to take place.

I smiled, my heart no longer bursting with joy as much as whirling in utter confusion, but I forced my expression into one of absolute bliss that I hoped would carry the day. My father seemed satisfied, and patted my hand before turning me forward.

To my right, Lord Cavanaugh eyed me with approval.

In front of me the minister lifted *The Book of Common Prayer*.

And behind me, somewhere in the knot of courtiers and noblemen, aunts and cousins, and neighbors and enemies and friends—stood Alasdair MacLeod.

I straightened my back and drew a deep breath, gratified at Lord Cavanaugh's soft exhalation. He was staring at me now, taking in every detail of my gown. Good.

Alasdair MacLeod could go hang himself.

The minister began to speak, and I heard his words as if from far away. ". . . for their mutual joy; for the help and comfort given one another in prosperity and adversity; and, when it is God's will, for the procreation of children and their nurture . . ." I frowned, instantly recalling Sophia's concerns. Would Lord Cavanaugh and I not have children? There must be a male heir, eventually. There had to be. I had only to look back at Queen Elizabeth's own long and troubled history to explain why. How many lives had been changed irreparably, in houses grand and small, all for the want of a son?

A bit of murmuring struck up in the back of the chapel, but my eyes were trained on the minister, and on the play of light shining down from the stained-glass windows, rendering him into soft reds and greens and blues. He looked like something out of a dream landscape, holy and inviolate, and I finally began to relax.

"Into this holy union Lady Beatrice Elizabeth Catherine Knowles and Lord Percival Andrew William Cavanaugh now come to be joined. . . ."

Behind me the whispering grew louder, and even the minister looked up, his face flickering with shock. I stared at him as he kept speaking, my stomach slewing sideways even as Lord Cavanaugh turned with a gasp that had nothing to do with my neckline and everything to do with what he saw coming up behind us, as relentless as a winter storm.

And still the minister pressed on, as if he could no more stop the sacred words than he could stop his own breath. "If any of you can show just cause why they may not lawfully be married," he cried out, his voice sounding almost desperate to my ears, "speak now; or else for ever hold your peace!"

A moment of deafening silence passed, and then another, and the clutch of terror in my throat was only just coming undone when the sudden sharp, imperious crash of a staff striking the floor nearly turned my knees to water.

"This wedding shall not go forward!" came the voice, as loud, proud, and mighty as the wrath of God, and every bit as damning.

It was the Queen.